New Orleans Nocturnes

COLLECTION ONE

CARRIE PULKINEN

New Orleans Nocturnes Collection One

Contact Information: www.CarriePulkinen.com

First Edition, 2021
ISBN: 978-1-7347624-9-5

LICENSE TO BITE

BOOK ONE

It's all fun and games until someone wakes up dead.

Governor's daughter Jane Anderson is used to getting what she wants. When a girls' trip to Mardi Gras thrusts her into the arms—and fangs—of New Orleans' hottest vampire, he gifts her with immortality, super strength, and a complexion to die for.

There's only one tiny problem. Jane faints at the sight of blood.

When Ethan Devereaux meets Jane, his cold, lifeless heart learns to beat again. Convinced she's his late fiancée reincarnated, he turns her, claiming her as his own. But when Jane wakes up dead in Ethan's attic, she's loud, sassy, and downright ornery. He doesn't know if he should kiss her or stake her, but one thing's for certain…

She is *so* not his long-lost love.

But Ethan turned her, so he's stuck with her. Jane has three weeks to learn the ways of the vampire and get her license, or she'll be staked. If Ethan can't help her overcome her aversion to blood, his undead life might also be on the line.

Join the supes of New Orleans Nocturnes as they lighten up the darker side of the Big Easy in this fun romantic comedy.

CHAPTER ONE

"I hate Mardi Gras," Ethan Deveraux grumbled as he stalked along the bank of the Mississippi River. It was cloudy, cold, and slightly damp, and while the weather had no effect on him physically, combined with the cacophony of drunken revelry, it made him ornerier than a werewolf with mange.

Six college-age women cackled, nearly tripping over themselves as they stumbled toward him, reeking of wine and sugary daiquiris, and he crinkled his nose. "It's impossible to find a decent meal anywhere near the French Quarter this time of year."

"Lighten up, young one." Gaston took one of the women into his arms, planting what looked like a passionate kiss on her neck, as her friends stopped to stare. The woman let out a moan, sliding her arms around him to grab his ass, unaware of the fangs sinking into her neck—and the meal she provided for the vampire—before he pushed her away.

"Can I at least get your number, sweetheart?" she drawled, rubbing her neck where Gaston had bitten her. Not even a scratch remained in the spot he'd pierced with his fangs.

"I'm not looking for a regular meal, *ma chère*. Just a snack."

Gaston winked and turned toward Ethan. "She's better than decent. I'm sure her friends are too."

Ethan shook his head. "No, thanks. Have a nice night, ladies, and be careful out there."

The woman's mouth dropped open at the rejection, but her friends linked arms with her and dragged her away.

Staring out over the muddy river, Ethan took in the peaceful scene, trying his best to ignore the vexatious festivity behind him. Artificial lights dotting the suspension bridge stretching from the east to the west banks of the river cast an orange glow on the dark water, and a bird of prey silently swooped down from the sky, snatching a rodent from its hiding place in the brush—much like his mentor had done to the unsuspecting drunk woman. Like Ethan would do to someone sober before the night ended. He shuddered.

The unmelodious noises behind him contrasted with the picturesque view of the river. Out of tune instruments blasted out something that was supposed to sound like jazz, and the shouting and laughter of dozens of inebriated partiers grated in his ears like sand between his butt cheeks.

Why had he agreed to come here this evening?

"You've got a little…" Ethan wiggled a finger at the corner of his sire's mouth, where a drop of red marred his otherwise perfect pale skin.

Gaston chuckled. "Whoops." He licked the blood from his lip as he smoothed his dark hair back, closing his eyes and swaying slightly while a vampire Ethan didn't recognize stalked toward them.

A long black trench coat flapped around the man's ankles, revealing pinstriped pants and polished black shoes. He wore a bowler hat, and wispy blond hair splayed around his ears. "Pardon me, gentlemen," he said with a British accent. "I need to see your license and identification, please."

"*My* license?" Gaston stepped toward the man, puffing out

his chest like a pissed-off peacock. "Have you no idea who I am? I've been in New Orleans as long as it's been a city."

The man swallowed hard, but he held his ground. "You bit within the city limits; therefore, it's within my jurisdiction to require proof of licensure."

"I did no such thing." Gaston flicked his wrist dismissively. "You've no proof."

"On the contrary, I have the evidence right here." He flashed his cell phone and tapped the screen, revealing a video of Gaston and the woman.

"Hell's bells and buckets of blood, I despise this new-fangled technology." Gaston crossed his arms, lifting his chin defiantly. "Who are you? You don't work for the Magistrate; you have no power here."

The man flipped open a leather wallet to reveal the golden badge of the Supernatural World Order and a plastic card identifying him as Constable Watson. "Your dominion is under audit. I'm here to make sure World laws are being enforced properly."

Satan's balls. If the SWO was in town, there'd be hell to pay for anyone who so much as sneezed on a human without the proper paperwork. Ethan slipped Gaston's wallet from his back pocket and showed it to the constable. "Here it is. He's been licensed from the beginning. Registered resident of New Orleans."

"Give me that." Gaston snatched it and shoved it back into his pocket. "I'm the oldest vampire in Orleans Parish, older than the Magistrate himself. I identify to no one." When he tipped to the left, unable to hold himself upright, Ethan grabbed his arm, steadying him.

"You might consider limiting the number of drunken tourists you consume, Mr. Bellevue." Watson gave him a disgusted once-over. "You certainly live up to your reputation."

Gaston growled, and Ethan patted his back, tugging him away from the constable. "We'll just be on our way then."

"I need to see your license and registration as well, good sir." Watson widened his stance, clasping his hands in front of him and straightening his spine.

"He's with me." Gaston loomed toward the unshaken officer, and Ethan pulled him back.

"I didn't bite anyone."

Watson raised his brow and typed something on his phone. "You're not licensed, then? That is a problem."

Ethan blew out a breath. This was exactly why he didn't come to the French Quarter during Mardi Gras. As if drunken tourists weren't bad enough, every vampire constable within a hundred miles swarmed the festivities, hoping to catch other vamps behaving badly. And now the SWO had sent in their own troops?

"I have a license." He pulled his wallet from his pocket and showed the identification to the officer. "But if I'm not biting, I don't see why it would be a problem if I didn't."

Watson squinted at the ID and typed the information into his phone. "Haven't you heard the new mandate?"

Ethan shook his head and glanced at his sire. Gaston rolled his eyes, threw his hands in the air, and stumbled toward a bench before plopping onto the seat.

"All vampires living within one hundred miles of a populated city must be licensed," Watson said. "The grace period ends tomorrow."

"And if they're not?"

"Why, they'll be staked, of course. Have a good evening, gentlemen." Watson tipped his hat and strolled away.

"Did you know that?" Ethan sank onto the bench next to his sire.

Gaston waved an arm. "It may have been mentioned at a meeting of the elders last month."

"Last month? And you didn't bother to tell me?"

"You receive the Magistrate's email newsletter, do you not?

It's his first attempt at harnessing twenty-first-century technology. Rather bold, if you ask me."

Ethan clenched his teeth. "It probably went to my spam folder." Leave it to him to miss an email from the ruler of supernatural Louisiana. He'd have to whitelist the Magistrate's address.

"Precisely why he should resume sending paper letters. The post office is much more reliable."

"It's actually not." He fisted his hands on his thighs. "You could have mentioned the new mandate. It seems like a big deal, getting staked for not having a license, even if you're not biting."

"You have a license. Trained by the best damn vampire to ever walk this continent, I might add." He leaned his head back and closed his eyes. "You haven't sired anyone, so you've no one to teach. Our bases are covered. It's of no concern." He opened one eye. "You haven't sired anyone, have you?"

Ethan let out a sardonic laugh. "I never will." He couldn't even think about cursing another human to this endless macabre lifestyle.

"No harm done, then." Gaston straightened. "I'm thirsty. Let's find a tequila bar. I'm in the mood for some Cuervo-tainted O negative."

Ethan rolled his eyes. "We'd better get you home before the sun comes up, old man. You're drunk." He reached for Gaston's arm, but the senior vampire jerked from his grasp.

"I'm not drunk! You're boring. If I'd known what a bore you would be, I never would have turned you."

Ethan's jaw ticked. "If I'd known what a drunk you were, I never would have let you." He ground his teeth, quelling the ancient memories. "You promised to end my suffering." Now, he'd have to live with the pain for all eternity.

"And I did." Gaston rose to his feet. "You were a lonely, miserable wretch when I found you. You were out of your mind, nearly killed when you stumbled into traffic, and if I hadn't been the one who'd run you over, you'd be an invalid now. Or dead."

"You should have let me die."

"But you wanted to live." He took Ethan's face in his hands. "I gave you a choice, and you chose life, my friend. It's a gift. Embrace it."

He looked into his sire's ice-blue eyes, and the memory of that fateful night twenty-five years ago came into crisp focus. Gaston was right. He didn't want to die then any more than he wanted to now. He'd only wanted the pain to stop.

Gaston patted his cheek. "I can ask the Magistrate for permission to stake you, but I've grown rather fond of you."

Ethan sighed, resigned. "I don't want to die."

"That's my boy." Gaston wrapped an arm around his shoulders and guided him down the riverbank, toward Jackson Square. "The emotional pain will heal with time. You're young, and you have your entire undead life ahead of you. Now, how about that tequila shot?"

Ethan chuckled. "One more, and then we find a meal who hasn't drunk her body weight in liquor."

"Deal. Although, I'm suddenly in the mood for Irish whiskey."

He followed Gaston's gaze toward a tall redhead tugging her reluctant friend down a side street toward an Irish bar. "Whiskey it is, then."

The place was packed, as were all the bars near Bourbon Street this time of year. The final parade of the evening had ended hours ago, giving the humans plenty of time to get shit-faced and the vampires a smorgasbord of unsuspecting victims. Mardi Gras and New Year's Eve were the only times a vampire was allowed to bite inside a bar. All other times of the year, they were required to have their meals in a secluded courtyard, an alleyway, or a bathroom stall, depending on how classy the vampire was.

"Vodka's nice too." Gaston followed a blonde onto the tiny dance floor, and Ethan leaned against the wall, crossing his arms and taking in the chaotic scene.

Patrons shouted their orders at bartenders, who rushed behind the bar, filling glasses and opening bottles, running credit cards and taking cash. An ass filled every seat in the room, but three-quarters of the patrons stood, laughing and talking with old and newfound friends.

Twenty-five years ago, Ethan might have enjoyed it. He liked to let loose every now and then, until the night he lost his fiancée, Vanessa.

He closed his eyes for a long blink, making room for the pain expanding in his chest. If he were honest with himself, he'd admit the ache had subsided over the years. But the pain was all he had left of the woman he'd loved, and he wasn't ready to let her go.

He let it resonate for another moment or two before opening his eyes and returning to the present. He'd never forgive himself for what happened to Vanessa, and he didn't deserve happiness. Not an ounce of it.

Shaking his head, he pushed from the wall and headed toward the dance floor. He'd given Gaston enough time to get his fill; it was time to go.

He maneuvered through the throng of people and made it halfway to his destination before a brunette stumbled into him. She fell backward, but he caught her by the shoulders, setting her on her feet with ease.

"Wow. Either you're really strong, or I've lost a few pounds since I last looked in the mirror." Her smile drew the air from his lungs, and though he technically didn't need to breathe, shock brought out his human instincts, making him cough.

She had long brown hair, chocolate eyes, and a sprinkling of freckles across her nose. Her voluptuous curves made his fingers twitch with the urge to run his hands along the peaks and valleys of her gorgeous body. The woman looked so much like Vanessa, his body seized. He stood motionless, staring at her as he calculated the time in his head. Could it be?

"Are you okay?" She touched his shoulder, and something inside him burned.

He composed himself, making sure his fangs hadn't extended, and smiled. "I'm fine."

"Yes, you are." Her friend, a tall blonde, handed her two shot glasses, and they both tossed them back, one after the other. The blonde smelled like warm cinnamon and cider. Like a witch. "You should do shots with us. I'll go get more."

"That's okay," he said, but she was already on her way to the bar.

"She's trying to drunk me...get me drunk." The brunette hiccupped and stumbled again.

"I'm afraid you already are." Ethan tapped a man on the shoulder and motioned with his head for him to give up his seat. The guy blinked, then got up without protest, Ethan's vampire glamour working its magic. "Have a seat. What's your name?"

"Jane." She sank onto the stool, rubbing her forehead.

"I'm Ethan."

"You're right."

He tilted his head. "I hope I know my own name."

"No, I mean I'm drunk. I don't feel very good." She held her stomach.

"Shots, shots, shots!" Her friend returned, carrying three glasses filled with bright yellow liquid. "I don't know what these are, but the bartender promised they're good."

"Sophie." Jane squinted at her through bloodshot eyes.

"I believe Jane has had enough." Ethan held up his hands, refusing to accept the drink Sophie shoved toward him.

"Fuck you." Sophie drank her shot and the one she'd bought for him. "Nobody tells Jane Anderson what to do." She handed Jane the glass. "Drink up, babe."

"Except for you, I see." Ethan crossed his arms.

Sophie gaped, and when Jane didn't drink her shot, she took the glass and set it on the bar. "Look, I don't know who you think you are with your looming presence and pecs you could bounce a quarter off of." She pressed her fingers into his chest. "Wow. Is your ass this tight?" She shook her head. "Who are you again?"

"Good evening, ladies." Gaston approached from the dance floor, and Sophie gave him a once-over, cocking a brow like she wasn't impressed.

"It's time to go home, Soph." Jane leaned her head on the bar. "I don't think I'll make it much longer."

"It would be an honor to escort you both." Gaston bowed formally, and Ethan caught a glimpse of fang as he smiled.

"Oh, no. That's not happening." Sophie crossed her arms and squeezed her eyes shut. "We can make it on our own. We can…" She swayed and opened her watery eyes. "Shit. I'm starting to feel those shots." She spun toward a trash can and spewed the alcohol and part of her dinner into the bin.

"Get them out of here." The bartender pointed to Ethan and jerked a thumb toward the door.

Jane rested peacefully on the bar, while Sophie leaned a forearm against the wall, dry-heaving into the trash can.

"I think I'm done." Sophie stepped toward Ethan and doubled over.

She was definitely *not* done. Vomit hit the floor, splashing onto his shoes, the sharp, tangy scents of alcohol and pineapple juice burning his nostrils. Jane's head slipped off the bar, and he caught her before she could fall out of her chair.

"You know how to pick them, my friend." Gaston touched Sophie's arm, and she yanked away.

"We're not going anywhere with you. C'mon, Jane." She reached toward her friend, and Jane slid off the stool, stumbling into Ethan again. They wouldn't make it to the door without help, much less all the way back to their hotel.

Gaston shook his head, making a *tsk* sound as he brushed his fingers to Sophie's temple, activating his glamour. "You will allow us to escort you to your hotel."

Sophie's expression went blank for a moment before she blinked, scrunching her forehead and turning to Jane. "Maybe we should let them take us. Our rental house is all the way on Esplanade. We can't walk that far."

"We don't need an escort," Jane said as adamantly as her current state of inebriation would allow. At least she had some of her wits intact, but how long would it last before someone took advantage of her vulnerability?

Ethan wiped his shoes with a napkin as Gaston gestured with his head toward Jane, but he hesitated to use his glamour. She, and this entire situation, reminded him so much of Vanessa, he wasn't sure his undead heart could handle being so close to her.

But he had to see these women to their hotel. If he could get them back safely, maybe he could atone for his sins. He slid his fingers into her soft, dark hair, focusing his magic to ensure her trust in him. "We'll take you to your rental house. I promise you'll be safe."

Jane's face slackened, and a pang of guilt shot through Ethan's chest. He would have preferred she trust him willingly, but with the pair of bouncers approaching from the left and the manager giving him the stink eye, he didn't have time to woo her with his charm. Not that he had any to begin with.

He pulled her to his side, lifting her slightly to feign the appearance that she could walk, and carried her out of the bar. Too many monsters lurked in the shadows of the French Quarter, most of them human, and he'd never forgive himself if anything happened to the women.

Especially since—judging by the way his body was reacting—this Jane could very well be his Vanessa reincarnated.

His body hummed at the thought, and his fangs instinctively elongated, his mouth watering with the desire to taste her. If she'd been sober, he wouldn't have been able to help himself, but he'd spend eternity rotting in hell before he'd ingest another drop of alcohol.

"Keys, Gaston." He held out his hand as they approached his sire's jet-black Maserati Quattroporte in the parking lot.

Gaston hit the key fob, unlocking the car, but he kept the keys clutched tightly as he lowered Sophie into the back seat. Ethan settled Jane in the front passenger side and buckled the seatbelt across her lap before zipping over to the driver's door and blocking Gaston's entrance.

"Step aside, young man," Gaston said.

Ethan held out his hand again. "Keys."

"You, sir, are mad as a hatter if you presume I'll allow you to drive Genevieve. She's the only bit of modern technology worthwhile in this day and age."

"And you're batshit crazy if you think I'm letting *you* drive." He snatched the keys from Gaston. "This was part of the deal. You bring Genevieve into the city, but *I* drive her home, remember?"

Gaston narrowed his eyes. "Even drunk out of my mind, my senses are a hundred times sharper than a sober human's."

"I don't care."

"You really aren't any fun at all, my friend." He touched a fang with the tip of his tongue as he eyed Sophie in the back seat.

"Don't even think about drinking from her. We promised to get them home safely."

"Boring," Gaston sang as he sank into the back seat. "I'll oblige you this one. I'm still rather full from the bar, and I'm not sure what kind of magic she possesses. If she belongs to the coven, I'd hate to break our truce." He gently shut the door, running his hand along the leather armrest, caressing his precious car. "I do miss the taste of witches."

With the slightest pressure on the gas pedal, the car zipped through the streets, cornering like it was on rails. Speed and power. It was a car fit for a vampire, much more appropriate than Ethan's sensible Ford Taurus.

Ethan's glamour had sobered Jane enough for her to give

him directions, and she sat quietly in the passenger seat, grinning at him as he rolled to a stop in front of the rental house, a white, two-story Second Empire style with green shutters and a balcony. Jane had a disarming smile, and his overwhelming need to see her to safety convinced him this was fate. He'd been given another chance, and he would not fail this time.

"Shall we rid ourselves of the baggage and return to the fun?" Gaston slid from the car and carried Sophie to the front door.

Ethan rolled his eyes and helped Jane out of the car.

"Did he just call us baggage?" she asked.

"Ignore him. He's old and ornery."

She giggled. "I like you. You're funny. Sweet too."

If that were only true. "You don't know me."

"I'm an excellent judge of character." That had to be the glamour talking. She'd completely misjudged him.

He'd seen her home safely tonight, but even through the alcohol, the scent of her blood sang. She'd be a temptation for any vampire who got near her, and the thought of another person's fangs piercing Jane's neck made his muscles crawl beneath his skin.

He couldn't let anyone else have her, so, brushing his fingers across her forehead, he marked her. The temporary magic would glow in her aura for a week, making her off-limits to any other vamps while her body replenished her blood supply. Some of the SWO regulations had their merits.

As he pulled his hand away, something in his core snapped, like a glow stick cracking and coming to life. Funny, he'd never felt that sensation before. Then again, he was supposed to drink from her *before* he marked her. It had been against the law to mark humans without consuming their blood for the past hundred years, ever since some asshat decided he wanted every woman in New Orleans for himself and went around marking them all, leaving the rest of the vamps to fight over the men.

Still, it was a minor law to break, and it wasn't like anyone would find out. He scanned the sidewalk for signs of the British constable just to be sure.

No one saw him do it, so no harm done.

By the time he walked her to the porch, Gaston had returned to the car and laid on the horn. *Impatient bastard.*

"Goodnight, sweet Jane." He kissed her hand, and the light that she'd sparked inside him glowed a little brighter.

"Thank you. You're a good man." She smiled and closed the door.

CHAPTER TWO

"I can't believe how badly my head hurts." Jane stared into her café au lait and gingerly pressed her fingers against her temples. It was two o'clock in the afternoon, and she finally felt well enough to venture out of her room. They'd waited in line half an hour to get a table under the famous green and white awning of Café Du Monde, but the nausea churning in her stomach killed her appetite for the beignets she'd been dying to try.

"It feels like I'm giving birth to a bowling ball through my nose. Are my nostrils dilated? I think it's crowning."

"I can't believe we got in a car with two strange men and let them take us to our house." Sophie bit into a beignet, and sugar rained down on the table. "They could have murdered us."

Jane pressed her thumb between her eyes to counter the pressure in her skull. "I know. What were we thinking?"

"We weren't."

She sank deeper into her chair. Her memory of the events that led up to meeting the men was a blur, but the car ride back to their rental house remained vivid in her mind. She couldn't explain why she'd let her guard down, aside from drinking way too much, but the man had been sweet, nothing but a gentleman. "At least they turned out to be nice guys. Especially the one who drove."

"We got lucky."

"Damn lucky. I wish I could remember his name."

"I'm surprised you remember anything." Sophie sipped her coffee. "You were trashed."

How could she forget a man like that? He stood half a foot taller than her, which made him at least six-foot-three, and he had the kind of wavy, dark hair a girl could run her fingers through for hours. His eyes were blue…or maybe green…and his muscular arms and broad shoulders that tapered down into a narrow waist alluded to time spent in the gym. Nice view, but probably not much going on upstairs. A man that good-looking couldn't hold up his end of a conversation if The Rock himself was his spotter.

"You looked pretty cozy with his friend in the back seat." Jane arched a brow and immediately wished she hadn't when pain sliced through her skull.

Sophie laughed and then winced, resting her fingers on her temples. "The goth-looking dude with black hair in a man bun? You know me better than that."

Jane shook her head. *Damn.* They were both smarter than that. In their defense, it had been their first night in New Orleans, *and* it was Mardi Gras. Everyone went a little crazy their first time, but still. "That was pretty stupid of us."

"*Very* stupid. They could have been vampires."

Jane scoffed. "Not this again. Ever since you found out about your grandma supposedly being a witch, you've been harping on all this magic shit."

"I found her grimoire in Pop's attic." She crossed her arms. "She *was* a witch."

"So you found a book of spells. Big deal. You can't get any of them to work."

"Because *she* was the witch. Not me. Anyway, that palm

reader said I'd find magic in New Orleans. It's just a matter of time."

"Right, well, vampires are about as real as your boobs."

Sophie's mouth formed the shape of an O as she clutched her chest. "How dare you insult my girls. They're real."

"I drove you to the surgery."

"They're *enhanced*, not fake." She grinned. "Like vampires."

Jane rolled her eyes. When she first told Sophie she was planning a month-long stay in the Big Easy, her friend had droned on and on about the secret magical societies in the city, as if witches and werewolves, and…God forbid…vampires actually existed. They hadn't been in town two hours yesterday when Sophie squealed like a stuck pig and ran inside a store that claimed to be run by witches.

The employees had been tight-lipped when she plied them with questions about shapeshifters and creatures of the night, which only made her more convinced they were real.

"You're twenty-five years old, Soph. The only monsters lurking in the darkness are of the human variety."

Sophie shrugged. "You never know. The green-eyed one kept looking at you like he wanted to eat you."

So his eyes were green. "If I'd known my head from my ass last night, I might have let him. He was hot."

Sophie wrinkled her nose. "His friend was way too slim and pale for me. I want a big, tanned, hairy guy to warm my bed. I've got to figure out where the werewolves are hiding."

"Good luck with that."

Jane's phone buzzed on the table, her brother's name lighting up the screen. "Ugh. It's Justin. They're bringing out the big guns if he's calling." Her other three older brothers had already called twice today, which she'd neglected to answer, but Justin knew better. Two years older than Jane, he was the only one who attempted to understand her. To treat her like an adult.

"You better answer it, or your dad will send the Texas Rangers out looking for you."

Jane grinned. "The baseball team or the police? I could learn to be a sports fan."

Sophie snickered. "Seriously, though. They're not going to leave you alone until you pick up."

Jane groaned and grabbed the phone, pressing it to her ear. "Hello, dear brother. What can I do for you?"

"Why didn't you tell anyone you were going to New Orleans?" He sounded resigned and not at all happy about making this call. At least he knew he was doing her wrong. No doubt their dad had badgered him until he'd agreed to do it.

"I'm fine, Justin. And how are you and Amy? Any luck in the baby department yet?"

He sighed. "C'mon, Jane. Don't make this hard."

She straightened her spine, despite the fact he couldn't see her indignance. "I'm sorry. I didn't realize I needed permission to live my life."

"It's a dangerous city. You know Dad worries about you."

"All fathers worry about their daughters. Most recognize when they become adults." She'd purposely kept quiet about the trip for this reason. Her dad would have done everything in his power to stop her from going. And as the Governor of Texas, he wasn't lacking in the power department.

"He saw your Instagram posts. Here, he wants to talk to you."

Her mouth dropped open at her brother's betrayal. "He's there with you?"

"I'm sorry, Jane."

"You traitorous bastard."

Shuffling sounded through the receiver before her dad's booming voice filled the line. "Jane, sweetheart, what are you doing in New Orleans unescorted?"

Her eye twitched at his choice of words. Resting an elbow on the table, she cradled her head in her hand. "My job, Daddy. I'm a travel blogger. It's what I do: travel and blog."

"I'm not going to argue about your so-called occupation.

We'll discuss finding you a real job later, but you and Sophie need to come home right now. It's not safe there."

If her eyes rolled any harder, she'd have seen the back of her skull. "We're fine, and we can take care of ourselves. You raised a fighter, not a victim."

"I know you can defend yourself, but there are criminals there you can't even imagine. Two women alone in a city like that is asking for trouble. Your self-defense skills are useless against…" He sighed heavily. "Come home, sweetheart. You can blog about somewhere safe, like Friendswood."

She ground her teeth, quelling the urge to go off on her father. Justin or Jared, or any of her brothers, could travel to the middle of a war zone, and the old man wouldn't bat an eye. But Jane was a woman. Fragile. Less than. "I'm staying in New Orleans."

Silence filled the line, and Jane's heart pounded as she awaited his response. "Okay. Have it your way," he said, "but I'm sending Paul to keep an eye on you. If you don't have a spare bedroom, he can sleep on the couch."

Now he'd crossed the line. She was not a child, and there was no way in hell her father was sending a babysitter to look after her. "I don't need your bodyguard following me around, and if you send him, I will never forgive you. In fact, I won't come home for Easter. Good luck getting one of the guys to wear that awful rabbit suit on the Capitol lawn."

"Jane."

"No, Daddy." Her head pounded even harder. She was way too hungover to deal with this shit. "I'm twenty-six, an adult. You have to trust me and let me live my life."

"What would your mother think about you running all over the place and never settling down?"

Oh, he wanted to play the dead mother card, did he? He must have forgotten how good Jane was at this game. "She would think you raised a strong woman who can take care of herself."

He sighed again. The man always sighed around her, like she was the biggest disappointment in his life. "All right, sweetheart. But if you get into any trouble at all, you call me. Understand? No matter what it is."

"Okay. I will."

"I love you, Janey."

"I love you too." She mashed the "end" button and shoved her phone into her purse. "I'm going to strangle Justin next time I see him. I swear my dad acts like I'm an idiot."

"Do you think he'll send the babysitter anyway?" Sophie asked.

"He better not." Her phone buzzed, and a text from Justin read *Don't worry. I won't let him send Paul. Stay safe.* She flashed the screen to Sophie.

"Maybe we should skip the shots tonight?" Sophie stretched her arms above her head, dropping them on the armrests as if they were heavy. "Keep our wits about us better."

Jane clamped her mouth shut as the phantom flavor of those syrupy drinks crept up her throat, triggering her gag reflex. Okay, maybe she was an idiot every now and then, but she wouldn't let it happen again. "Good idea. I can hardly stomach this coffee. Excuse me, ma'am." She flagged the waitress over. "Can I get a shot of morphine in this?"

The waitress gave her a sympathetic smile. "The best cure for a hangover is a Bloody Mary. Tujague's across the street makes a great one."

Jane groaned, her stomach turning. "Don't even mention blood."

Sophie snorted. "There's no actual blood in the drink. It's tomato juice and vodka."

"I know what it is, but is alcohol really the cure for too much alcohol?" She shrugged. *When in New Orleans...* "Why the hell not? I'll try anything at this point."

They paid the tab and crossed Decatur Street toward the restaurant. A few tables lined the wall across from the bar, but all the chairs were taken, and not a single bar stool offered her aching feet relief from all the walking she'd done since arriving in New Orleans.

"Where are all the chairs?" She leaned her elbows on the bar and propped one foot on the metal railing near the floor. "Can't a girl take a load off in here?"

The bartender finished pouring a thick green liquid into a fancy glass and nodded at Jane. "This is a standing bar." He ran his hand across the polished wood surface. "Oldest bar in America, in fact. That mirror is older than the country itself."

Jane followed his gaze to a massive antique mirror with intricate swirling designs etched around the edges. "Well, this is the oldest my tired bones have ever been, so we'll take two Bloody Marys to go and find a seat elsewhere, thank you."

"The restaurant is open." The bartender poured way more than a shot of vodka into each cup before filling it with a spicy tomato juice mixture and sprinkling in Worcestershire sauce and cayenne pepper.

"Ugh. No food," Jane said. "This will be breakfast."

He laughed and filled the rest of the glass with olives and pickled vegetables before passing the plastic cups to her and Sophie. "Here you go, two hangover cures."

"Is that a guarantee?" Jane paid for the drinks and took a sip. The vodka registered first, sharp and strong, before the smooth, slightly sweet tomato greeted her taste buds, followed by the slow burn of the pepper.

"Nothing in life is guaranteed." He winked before turning to the next patron.

Drink in hand—which seemed to be the standard in this city—Jane followed Sophie into the cool February air and bustle of Jackson Square. Maybe it was her imagination, but three sips of this miracle concoction, and her head already felt lighter, the throbbing easing into a dull ache.

Situated in the heart of the French Quarter, Jackson Square boasted a central park area with a grassy lawn, manicured trees, and an enormous statue of its namesake, Andrew Jackson, sitting atop a cavalry horse. A paved pedestrian mall lined the fenced-in park, where local artists and street performers enticed tourists to spend their money on souvenirs and photo ops rather than alcohol. Smarter choices than the fortune Jane spent last night that left her with nothing but a massive headache and the memory of a sweet, sexy man who could have killed her as easily as he'd taken her home.

Sophie stopped in front of a dog lying on its back in the middle of the walkway. Beer bottles lay strewn around the pooch, and it had a hurricane glass tucked under its paw. It wore a dozen strings of Mardi Gras beads around its neck, and a *Beers, Boobs, and Beads* t-shirt lay next to a puddle of fake vomit. At least, Jane hoped it was fake.

"Aw. Look at this little guy. Can I pet him?" Sophie knelt beside the dog, and its owner gestured to a cardboard sign giving information about the animal and permission to pet him.

Jane dropped a dollar into a tip jar and snapped a few photos of the scene. "This'll make a great article for my blog. How long can he stay like this?"

She gathered more information about the man and his dog, and by the time she finished the interview, she'd drained her drink. "Wow. This really was a miracle cure. I feel so much better. Ready for another one?"

"Not quite yet." Sophie threaded her arm through Jane's and led her past the St. Louis Cathedral and out of Jackson Square. "The parade starts at six, and I remember you saying something about wanting to get as far down St. Charles as we can, away from the drunks, to get the full experience. Every post you write on the trip can't be about us getting shit-faced."

"True."

"Besides, I'm supposed to be working too. If I'm going to expand my company across state lines, I need to spend a little sober time in the city. I'm a small business owner, and you, my dear, are Jane Anderson, travel blogger extraordinaire, social media influencer, daughter of the Texas Governor…"

"Party girl who blogs because she can't hold a steady job." Damn it, that phone call from her father was getting to her.

Sophie opened her mouth to protest, but Jane held up a finger and defended herself. "Blogging is a real job, no matter what my dad says. I monetized my website, and tour companies pay me to mention them on Instagram. My brothers handle the investments of my trust fund and all the boring math stuff. It's my job to have fun and share it with the world." She gestured grandly with the hand that held her cup, dumping ice onto a man's shoulder.

He spun toward her, glowering. "What the fuck?"

"Sorry about that." She cringed and brushed a piece of ice from his jacket sleeve. "I can be such a klutz sometimes." She plastered on her Governor's daughter smile and batted her lashes, thickening her Texas drawl. "No harm done, right, darlin'?"

The guy blinked, disarmed. "Yeah. No problem."

"Be a doll and toss this in the trash for me, will you?" She held the empty cup toward him, and though his brow furrowed, he took it, shaking his head as he walked away.

Sophie crossed her arms.

"What? He was headed in the general direction of a trash can, and he shouldn't have cussed at me. It's rude."

"One of these days, you're going to meet someone who's impervious to your magical man-taming powers, and he's *not* going to drop everything to be at your beck and call." She laughed. "That's the man you're going to marry."

"Psh." Jane waved off the comment. She became a travel blogger to get away from her father's and brothers' control, which obviously wasn't working out as planned. She wasn't about to invite another man into a position of power in her life. "I can't help it if I'm good at delegating."

She paused, peering up at an intriguing wooden sign

hanging above a bar entrance. The words "French Quarter Absinthe" carved into the misshapen piece of reclaimed wood appeared black against the medium brown tone of the background, almost as if they were burned in. Such a fun aesthetic. "Have you ever tried absinthe?"

Sophie grinned. "Can't say that I have."

"Look. The bartenders are dressed like pirates. It's my duty to share a place like this with the world." She turned her back to the entrance, angling the front-facing camera on her phone just right to snap a selfie with the sign. "Perfect. Let's make this our last drink of the day, and then we'll head to the parade and get some food along the way."

"Sounds like a plan."

Jane strutted inside and slid onto a stool, patting the one next to her for Sophie to sit. The place was small and dimly lit, with a giant ship's wheel hanging on the wall behind the dark wood bar. A couple sat at the opposite end, engrossed in their own conversation, and rock music played softly from a speaker hanging from a wooden post. Otherwise, the bar sat quiet. Dull.

"We need to liven this place up." Jane slapped a hand on the green marble countertop. "I'll have one of those absinthe thingies."

"Make it two," Sophie added.

The bartender, a woman in her mid-fifties with gray-blonde hair and dark eyes, handed Jane a laminated menu listing at least a dozen different brands. Jane scanned the offerings before focusing on the woman. She wore a black pirate's hat and a brown bar wench dress with a nametag that read "Sally."

"Hi, Sally. I'm Jane." She held out her hand to shake, and Sally accepted. "I have no idea what any of this is. What do you recommend?"

"This one's my favorite." She pointed to the fourth entry on the list. "It's got a mild flavor, but it still packs a punch."

"We'll take two of those then." Jane leaned toward Sophie and snapped another selfie while Sally set up the drinks.

She filled a glass urn with ice water and set a small wine glass on the counter, filling it with a bright green liquid. A concentrated beam of light shone from above the bar, illuminating the drink, and Sally set a sugar cube on a slotted metal spoon atop the glass. She turned a spigot on the urn, and chilled water dripped over the sugar, dissolving it into the drink.

"Impressive," Jane said as she accepted the glass.

Sally repeated the show for Sophie's drink before excusing herself to the back of the bar to slice lemons.

"Can't say I've ever seen so much flare go into making a drink." Sophie clinked her glass to Jane's. "Cheers."

Sadly, the show was a thousand times better than the result. "Ugh. This tastes like toothpaste." Jane bucked up and chugged the rest of the awful liquid—true southern girls never wasted alcohol—cringing as the weird, minty, licorice-flavored concoction slid down her throat.

Sophie coughed, pushing her empty glass away. "We paid twenty bucks for that?"

"Live and learn." Jane typed her thoughts about the drink into her phone to reference for her blog post later: *Great show. Disgusting drink. Do not recommend unless you like black jelly beans and mouthwash...together.*

"Ow! Shit." Sally clutched her hand, lifting it in the air and gesturing at the other bartender. "Grab me a Band-Aid from the back, will ya, Jess?"

Jane's gaze locked on Sally's hand, and she froze. A half-inch gash sliced across her thumb below the knuckle, and bright red blood oozed from the opening, trailing down her wrist. Sally grabbed a towel, wrapping it around the wound, but it was too late. Jane had seen enough.

Her head spun, the sensation of her own blood dropping from her skull to her feet making the room turn on its side. Her stomach lurched, her eyes fluttering as her vision tunneled and she tipped over, sliding off her stool.

"Whoa, Nelly. I got you." Sophie clutched her shoulders, lowering her to the ground. "Deep breaths. In and out."

Jane sat cross-legged on the floor, leaning forward and willing herself to stay awake. Sophie shot to her feet and returned with a glass of water, pressing the straw to Jane's lips. "You all right, hon?"

She sipped the water, pausing for the room to stop spinning before she replied, "Blood."

"Yeah, it's cleaned up now. Not a drop in sight. Come on." Sophie dragged her up by the arm. "Let's get you some fresh air."

Leaning into her best friend's side, Jane shuffled out of the bar. The crisp afternoon air helped to clear her head, and within minutes, she felt like herself again…a little embarrassed, but no worse for wear. "Did anyone else see that?"

"Sally did, but she thought the absinthe knocked you out." Sophie rubbed her back. "Do you think you'll ever get over your aversion to blood?"

"Doubt it. My therapist tried, but all she managed to do was dig up the suppressed memory that triggered the problem."

"That time you walked outside the cabin to find your dad field-dressing a deer?"

She shuddered. "Poor Bambi."

They strolled through the Quarter, crossing Canal Street, the six-lane dividing line between the French and American sides of the city, where Royal Street turned into St. Charles Avenue. Chain hotels with floors soaring into the double digits were interspersed with tourist shops and fast-food restaurants along the busy thoroughfares, making it feel like they walked into a completely different city when they crossed the street.

They stopped at Serio's, a restaurant with a muffuletta to die for—who knew chopped olives would taste so good on a sandwich?—and Jane chased it down with a Dr. Pepper, while Sophie munched on a meatball sub.

After way too much walking, the evening sun bled into

night, and they claimed a spot on the corner of St. Charles and Conery in an upscale, safe-looking part of the city—just to make her dad happy—to watch the parade.

The crowd was thinner this far into the Garden District, which was a good thing, but Jane's feet were barking like angry dogs by the time they stopped. She made a mental note to stick with sneakers for treks like this in the future. She'd save her knee-high stiletto boots for their less athletic excursions.

Marching bands sprinkled between the massive floats provided toe-tapping background music for the spectacle that was Jane's first Mardi Gras parade, and she caught enough plastic beads to match her body weight. With a thick mass of necklaces draped over her head, she let most of the smaller, plain throws land on the ground. A girl could only carry so many, and these krewe members weren't stingy with the good stuff. Thick strands with massive beads and plaster pendants were normal here. She didn't have to show her boobs for anything, not that she ever had, unlike the carnival back home in Galveston, where krewe members expected the spectators to put on the show if they wanted the good beads.

Jane was all about having a good time, but she wasn't about to demean herself for any type of prize. Respect was the key to success. She looked down to examine a throw shaped like a loco-motive when Sophie elbowed her in the ribs.

"Hey, aren't those the guys from last night? The ones who took us home?" Sophie pointed across the street.

Jane squinted, her heart thrumming as she searched the faces in the crowd. "Where?"

Sophie pointed again and let her arm fall to her side. "I swear they were there a minute ago." She shrugged and returned her focus to the guy who'd sidled next to her. Sophie would be busy for the night.

His buddy nodded a hello to Jane, and if she'd felt like being a good friend, she'd have played wingwoman. But the possible spotting of the mysterious man from last night sent a little flush of adrenaline through her body, and she couldn't help but continue the search. If Sophie saw him across the way, he had to be there. He'd probably just slipped behind someone taller.

She stood on her toes, trying to get a better view, when the tiny hairs on the back of her neck stood on end. Her skin turned to gooseflesh, and her blood seemed to hum in her veins.

Someone was watching her.

CHAPTER THREE

Ethan's fangs elongated, his mouth watering with the urge to taste her. Jane's long, dark hair flowed over her shoulders, hiding her neck, but he could imagine the vein pulsing just beneath her creamy skin, the soothing sensation of her warm blood sliding down his throat, her naked body pressed against his as he made love to her.

His dick hardened as he watched her from the shadows, behind her now, since her overbearing friend had spotted him when he stood across the street. Though invisible to the human eye, his mark shimmered in her aura, adding to her radiance. He hadn't been this drawn to a woman since his sweet Vanessa died, and that could only mean one thing.

Jane *had* to be her.

"She is marked." Gaston activated his glamour, sending the giggling woman he'd just bitten on her way. "Is it yours?"

"Yeah." His sire should have known what his mark looked like. He dragged his gaze away from the beautiful woman. "I didn't bite her; I just didn't want anyone else to."

Disbelief flashed in Gaston's eyes as he stepped closer and lowered his voice. "Do you have any idea what you've done? This is forbidden. It's been illegal for two hundred years, ever since Willem created that uncontrollable hybrid abomination that went on a killing spree throughout the entire parish. They both deserved the stake, if you ask me."

Ethan ignored his sire's rant and cast his gaze toward Jane. She turned her head, rubbing the back of her neck, her eyes searching as if she felt his presence.

"You can't blame this on your spam container," Gaston droned on. "I'm certain I taught you this law."

"It's spam *folder*." Ethan drifted toward her, his sluggish heart beating at as close to a sprint as his undead condition allowed. She hadn't found him yet, but as soon as their eyes met, he'd—

"Oh, no you do not." Gaston grabbed his arm and yanked him into the shadows of a building. "I am far too sober to deal with this. What the devil have you done?" He thumped his forehead, and Ethan blinked, shaking his head.

"I haven't done anything."

"Your mark. She is *sensing* you."

This was fate. She was meant to be his, so why wouldn't she? "It'll wear off. No one will know I didn't bite her."

"Ethan, my dear son, you did not simply mark her as a meal. That's a mating mark." Gaston stepped back, peering at the crowd. "Satan's balls, you're an idiot. Go." He shoved him, taking him by the arm again when he didn't move, then running down the street toward the next intersection before dragging him into a yard.

With his back against the wall and Gaston's forearm pressed into his chest, Ethan watched as Jane drifted away from the parade, down the dark street toward them.

"Hello?" Her voice was music from her lips.

"It's not a mating mark." He struggled to go to her, but Gaston refused to release his hold. "It felt a little different when I did it, but I didn't claim her that way. It's not possible."

"Oh, it's absolutely possible, my friend, and you've done it.

What in hell's name was going through that thick skull of yours?"

"Nothing. I didn't…" He didn't mean to. He'd only wanted to keep anyone else from having her. To mark her as his own. *Oh, fuck.*

"'Nothing.' Of course, because you were thinking with the wrong head. What's the modern expression I'm obliged to call you? Oh, yes. Dick for brains."

"It's 'shit for brains.'"

"Is it?" Gaston leaned into him until the pressure felt like his ribs would snap. Jane stood ten feet away. "Activate your glamour so she can't find you."

"But if she wants to—"

Gaston's pupils narrowed into slits, his fangs lengthening predatorily as a low hiss escaped his throat. "Do it now, or on my mother's grave, I will stake you myself."

Uh oh. He was serious. Funny how a little adrenaline could sober a guy up.

Ethan turned on his glamour full blast, blocking her from seeing or sensing him, and Jane stopped in her tracks, scratching her head before parking her hands on her hips. "Huh." She looked up and down the street. "I could have sworn I saw him."

She spun in a circle, then something in the distance caught her eye. Her entire face brightened, and she cast a glance toward the parade, typed something on her phone, and then turned around, heading straight for Lafayette Cemetery #1.

With Ethan's hold on Jane broken for the time being, Gaston released him. "You need to remove the mark before anyone else finds out."

He drifted toward her, no longer needing the cover of shadow with his glamour concealing him from human eyes. "I'm not even sure how I marked her. I don't think I can remove it." And why should he? Accidents like that didn't just happen. It had to be fate.

"Do you have a death wish?"

"I'm already dead."

"*Un*dead. If you don't remove that mark before the Council finds out, you'll be *really* dead. Mate-marking a human is punishable by stake. You know this."

Well, shit. "Have you ever mate-marked anyone?"

"I prefer to sow my oats in the wild, an attitude I've been trying to instill in you, my friend. Now fix this."

"It really was an accident, man. I don't..." He blew out a hard breath. Damn it, he didn't want to remove the mark. "I think she's Vanessa."

Jane pranced across the deserted street toward the cemetery gate, her posture deflating when she found it locked. She rattled the chain, tugging on the lock before attempting to slip between the bars. Ethan smiled, admiring her tenacity.

"What in Satan's domain would make you think that?" Gaston cocked his head as he watched her snap pictures through the fence.

"She looks like her, doesn't she? Her hair, something in her eyes, her smile."

"Mmmm... Not really, my friend. Not how I remember her."

"You never knew her."

"I saw pictures."

"Which you burned fifteen years ago."

Gaston held up his hands. "I did you a favor that day. You'd been mourning the woman for ten years, and her energy couldn't pass on with that shrine you'd made in your bedroom."

"I loved her."

"And it was time to let her go. Tell me you didn't feel lighter —once you got through your murderous rage."

"I didn't speak to you for six months."

"And you felt better. I know you did, my friend. We're connected, remember?"

Ethan gritted his teeth, nodding grimly. It killed him to admit it, but he did feel a sense of freedom after his sire burned every trace of Vanessa's existence. Social media didn't exist back then, so all he had left now were the memories, and even those were starting to fade.

"I'll be a callous prick like you any day now."

"That's my boy." Gaston slapped him on the back and cast Jane a curious look. "What is she doing?"

Jane crossed to their side of the street again and stood with her back toward the cemetery, smiling at her phone as she snapped photo after photo.

"They're called selfies, old man." Ethan laughed. "I know I've explained the phenomenon to you before."

Gaston grimaced. "I've been drunk since then."

Jane sighed, chewing her plump bottom lip as she flipped through the photos on her phone. Seemingly unsatisfied, she lifted the device and resumed snapping pictures, stepping backward, closer toward the cemetery gates after each shot.

A car horn blared as a Toyota zoomed past, and Jane flinched but resumed her selfie-taking.

"She's not the sharpest stake in the pile, is she?"

Ethan smiled, unable to take his gaze off her. "She's perfect."

Gaston shook his head. "Remove the mating mark, and then I'll leave you to her. Do what you want with her, as long as…"

"She's alive and well and has no clue what I am. I know the rules."

Jane took a step backward. Then another. Right into the path of a jacked-up pickup truck. Ethan's stomach lurched, the sounds of crunching bone and tearing flesh clawing through his ears as the *thump, thump* of the tires sounded like the vehicle had done nothing more than hit a speed bump. She didn't scream, and with everyone at the parade, no one witnessed the accident.

The truck stopped for a moment before peeling out and speeding away, leaving poor Jane crumpled and dying—or already dead—alone on the pavement.

"Well." Gaston shoved his hands into his pockets. "Problem solved. Let's go find dinner."

"Jane!" Ethan ran to her, lifting her flattened body into his arms. The coppery, sweet scent of her blood greeted his senses like the smell of fresh-baked cookies straight from his grandma's oven. Her breath came in short, shallow pants, and her lids fluttered, her eyes rolling back so far he saw nothing but white.

With a burst of supernatural strength, Ethan leapt over the cemetery wall, landing gracefully in a patch of grass inside the graveyard. He laid Jane on her back, folding her hands on her stomach, and stroking her hair from her forehead. "Stay with me. I can't lose you again."

Gaston drifted down in front of him and dropped her purse and phone next to her before clasping his hands behind his back. "If you're going to drain her, be sure you're done before her heart stops beating." He tilted his head. "Better make it fast, or she won't have much blood left."

A burning lump of hot coal lodged in Ethan's throat as he gazed at his long-lost love, slipping away from him again. "How do I turn her?"

"Pardon?" Gaston held a hand to his ear. "This being sober nonsense is affecting my hearing. I thought you asked how to turn her."

"How?" Ethan's voice grated in his throat. "I have to save her."

"If I recall, when I tried to teach you this lesson, you swore on your still-living-at-the-time mother's grave that you would burn in hell for all eternity before you'd curse another human to this fate."

"I never said that."

"Oh, but you did. You can be quite the dramatic monarch." Gaston picked at his nails absently.

"It's drama queen, you relic. Now, are you going to help me or not?"

Jane gasped, and blood bubbled from her throat.

"Gaston..." Ethan growled through his teeth. "She's Vanessa. I know she is, and I can't lose her again."

"And damning her to darkness is the perfect way to show the woman you love that you care. What if she's not Vanessa?"

"I marked her. She's mine. Please help me save her."

"You're making a mistake, my friend."

Ethan trailed his fingers down her cheek, wiping the blood from her lip with his thumb. "I don't care."

Gaston shrugged. "Drink from her; absorb her essence and use your magic to form a connection. When you feel the bond tighten, stop. Then she'll need to drink from you."

She wasn't even breathing. He may have already been too late.

He pulled the mass of beads over her head and sank his fangs into her neck, sucking the delicious life force from her veins. Resting a hand on her battered chest, he instilled her with his magic until a connection formed, like a cord running from her core to his.

He licked the puncture wounds—vampire spit had magical healing properties—and her head lolled to the side.

"Time is not your friend." Gaston toed her limp leg with the edge of his boot. "Get your blood into her."

Ethan bit into his wrist, hard enough to tear his skin to delay his quick healing, and squeezed his forearm, working his slow-moving blood to the surface. As a drop gathered inside the wound, he pressed it to her lips, massaging his arm to encourage the flow into her mouth. "Come on, *cher*, swallow."

Jane didn't respond. The heavy weight of despair slammed into his chest, and he hung his head, leaning down to press a goodbye kiss to her forehead. As his lips met her skin, she swallowed, latching on to his arm and sucking with the force of a top-of-the-line Dyson. Her lids flew open, her pupils constricting into pinpoints as her body's injuries began to heal.

"Don't let her drain you." Gaston placed a heavy hand on his shoulder. "You have to be functioning when she awakens."

Ethan pried his arm from her vacuum grip, and she sat up, her wide eyes blinking as she took in her surroundings. She looked at him and tilted her head. "I remember you."

His chest tightened, a strange flitting sensation forming in his stomach as he held her gaze.

Bringing her fingers to her lips, she wiped the blood from the corner of her mouth and peered at her hand. Her brow furrowed before her eyes rolled up, and she flopped onto her back, unconscious.

Ethan looked up at Gaston. "Is that...normal?"

Gaston shrugged and lifted her shirt, examining her injuries. "You were conscious a bit longer before the death sleep took over, but she's healing. She should awaken at dusk tomorrow."

Ethan yanked her shirt down, covering her torso. "What do I do now?"

Gaston chuckled. "Take her home and hope to hell she's the woman you think she is. You're stuck with her now."

CHAPTER FOUR

What on God's green Earth did Jane drink last night? Hell, what did she *do*? She squeezed her eyes shut, rolling over and willing herself to go back to sleep. Her throat felt like the Mojave Desert on an August afternoon, complete with a prickly little cactus growing at the base of her tongue. She swallowed, and another cactus cropped up just below the first one.

She moaned, the sound grating in her esophagus, and someone in the room stirred. Had she and Sophie passed out in the living room of their rental? They'd only been in New Orleans two nights, and they'd managed to get shit-faced both times. They needed to slow down.

Jane rolled onto her back and rubbed her face, still afraid to open her eyes. These sheets weren't nearly as soft as the ones on her bed, and the room had a musty scent to it, while the rental house normally smelled like peach pie.

Oh, dear Lord, she never made it home last night. The person sitting on the mattress next to her wasn't Sophie. *Think, Jane. Think. Who did you pick up?* She racked her brain for a memory of what drink could have fucked her up so badly and what man she could have followed home, but aside from the nasty absinthe she'd had that afternoon, she couldn't recall a single shot.

Well, Jane, you made this bed…and probably did a helluva lot more than lie in it. Time to make nice with the bear you poked and get the hell out of Dodge.

She pried her eyes open, expecting the morning—or possibly afternoon—sun to stab into her pupils like daggers, triggering the massive headache she was sure to have, but darkness engulfed the room. Her vision adjusted quickly, and she found herself staring up at wooden rafters not five feet from her head. *What the hell?*

A lamp switched on, bathing the room in yellow light, and the dagger effect came on full-force. She expelled a breath of air, but with her throat so parched, she sounded like a spooked house cat guarding its favorite toy.

"Hi, Jane. How do you feel?" A familiar, smooth, deep voice drifted toward her, and the tension in her chest eased. If she had to spend a wild, drunken night with a stranger, at least he was a hot stranger.

She rolled onto her side and found him fully dressed in jeans and a dark gray t-shirt. He sat on the edge of the bed, his hands folded in his lap, nervous tension rolling off him in waves. A lock of dark hair fell across his eye, and he brushed it back, his biceps flexing with the movement.

Her stomach fluttered, and a warm, fuzzy feeling flooded out from her chest to her toes. *Damn.* The last time she felt this giddy about a guy was with Aaron Dicks, freshman year of college. That man sure lived up to his name, unfortunately in more ways than one. Her asshole meter functioned at full capacity these days, though, and this guy seemed okay.

"Jane?" His eyes held concern. Concern was a good, nonassholish emotion.

"Hey." She propped herself on her elbow. Her clothes were still on too. *Weird.* "I didn't mean to hiss at you. My throat's dry."

He shrugged. "It's normal."

She laughed. "Women hissing at you when they wake up in the morning is normal?"

He pressed his lips together.

"Where are we?" She sat up, taking in her surroundings. Cobwebs clung to the corners of the rafters, and dust motes hung stagnant in the air. That explained the smell.

"We're in my attic. Jane, what do you remember about last night?"

"We must've had one helluva time to wind up sleeping in your attic. Did I do shots again? Sophie and I promised each other we wouldn't do shots this time, but I don't remember what happened after the parade. We weren't planning to drink anything."

Why was he asking her what she remembered? Could he not recall the night either? She sucked in a sharp breath. "Did someone drug us?"

"No. We weren't drugged."

"Oh, good. That makes me feel better, though I'm pissed at myself for doing shots again." Hold on, she was in this man's *attic*. Warm fuzzies or not, shouldn't she have been panicking or at least calculating a quick exit? Any woman in her right mind would be out the door the moment she found her shoes, but something about the quizzical look on this guy's face and the way his jaw ticked as his brow furrowed had her more curious than frightened. In fact, she wasn't the slightest bit scared at all. Lord knew she'd found herself in situations much weirder than this.

She slid to the edge of the bed, setting her socked feet on the plywood floor. "Be a doll and grab my boots for me, would you?" She pointed to her shoes and purse sitting in the corner.

"You didn't do shots, and your boots are within arm's reach." His face was so serious, she'd have thought he was going to tell her he gave her crabs or something.

Oh, God. There were quite a few somethings a lot worse

than crabs. She stretched an arm toward her belongings, wiggling her fingers. When he didn't take the hint, she sighed and grabbed them herself before slipping them on. "Please tell me we used protection."

He blinked, confusion clouding his eyes for a moment before his brow rose. "We didn't have sex."

A sense of relief battled with the sting of rejection. She wanted to ask *Why the hell not?*, but if she'd been as drunk as she thought last night, maybe that was a good thing. He'd had two chances to take advantage of her now, yet he hadn't touched her. The fluttering in her stomach reached up to her chest, and she warmed to him even more.

"That explains why my clothes are still on." She tugged on the hem of her shirt, and her eyes widened as she took in its condition. A crusty, dark red substance was smeared across the front, and…was that a tire mark?

"Holy fuck." She looked at the guy, but she couldn't for the life of her remember his name. "John?"

He tilted his head, looking offended.

"Paul? George? Ringo? What's your name again?"

"Ethan." He blinked once, his dark lashes fringing emerald green eyes. Was he smoldering at her?

Judging from the way the flutter in her core had settled below her navel, his smolder was about to set her ablaze. Damn, he was hot. Good-looking and a gentleman, yet somehow, he'd gotten her into his attic. This didn't add up.

"Ethan. That's right. What the hell happened last night, Ethan?" She stood and knocked her head against a rafter with a smack. A quick, sharp pain sliced through her skull and dissipated just as fast. "Seriously, dude. Why are we in your attic? Is this some weird fetish? I'm usually down for just about anything, but I need to know what I'm getting into before I agree to it."

He didn't crack a smile. "What do you remember?"

So he wanted to play this game, did he? It seemed Mr.

Serious watched a tad too many docudramas on the old TV. She had two choices: walk out the door now, look for a new vacation rental so he couldn't find her, and get on with her life...or sit down and play along.

She scanned the room for any possible murder weapons, but other than the mattress and a lamp, the room sat empty. Not that she was worried about becoming his next victim. In addition to her black belt in karate, Jane was an excellent judge of character, and not a single warning alarm had gone off in her mind since she woke up. Not to mention, the man could make her clothes fall off with a simple look, and Jane never fawned over men. There was something special about Ethan, even if he didn't have much to say.

Besides, she was dying to know how they ended up spending the night in his attic. "This is almost as weird as the time I woke up in Brock Johnson's grandma's panic room. Do you live with your parents?"

He arched a brow. "No."

"Wife? Girlfriend?"

"No."

"Okay, you win." She sank onto the edge of the mattress. "I'll play your game, but only because the curiosity is driving me bonkers. Why are you looking at me like that?"

He pursed his lips, looking thoughtful for a moment and not at all pleased. "You're not what I expected."

"Well, you don't have to look so damn disappointed. I thought you'd be a little more exciting too. You know what? Never mind." Her tolerance for bullshit had reached its limit, so she rose to her feet, hunching over to avoid slamming her head into the ceiling again. "I don't even care how we ended up here. If we didn't have sex, then no harm done. I'm out."

Clutching her purse, she made for the door, but he shot to his feet and leapt toward it, blocking her exit faster than she could say, "Holy hell raisers, you're fast!"

"Hell raisers?"

"I don't know where that came from. Move. I'm leaving."
She grabbed the knob, but he palmed the door, keeping it
closed.

"You can't leave. It's still daylight."

"I sure as hell hope it is. Move." She tugged on the knob,
but it wouldn't budge.

"I can't let you leave." His voice deepened like he actually
thought he had some kind of authority over her.

"Fuck that. I said move." She shoved him—a smidge harder
than she planned to, but the guy was trying to hold her hostage
—and he stumbled, his eyes widening in surprise before his
head smacked into a rafter. *Damn, adrenaline is something else.*

She yanked the door open, and the brightest, goddamn
blinding light she'd ever seen sliced through the opening like
hellfire exploding through a ground fissure. Her vision went
solid white, and her eyeballs burned like they were melting out
of their sockets. Her skin sizzled, and as she fell back on her ass,
she could have sworn she smelled the aroma of burning flesh.

Ethan slammed the door, engulfing the room in glorious
darkness, before he scooped her into his arms and laid her on
the mattress. "I told you not to do that." Was he scolding her?

She blinked, her vision coming back into focus, her eyes,
thankfully, still solid and in their sockets. Her face stung, and
the sand content in her throat doubled along with the cacti.
"Holy Mother of God..." The moment she uttered the word, a
coughing fit racked her body, and it felt like she'd swallowed hot
coals.

Gasping for breath, she curled into a fetal position, slowly
getting herself under control. "Jesus Christ." Another coughing
fit consumed her, and if she didn't know any better, she'd have
sworn smoke escaped from her throat. "What the fuck?"

Ethan hung his head in his hands, muttering what she
thought sounded like, "I've made a mistake."

Sitting up, she slid her feet to the floor. "*You* made a
mistake? I'm the one who opened the goddamn—" Again with

the coughing. She doubled over, nearly expelling a lung before she could breathe again.

"Rule number one: obey your sire. Your life is in his hands until you're trained."

"Obey my what?" Gripping the edge of the mattress, she chose her words carefully. "Back up a minute, Christian Grey. I don't know what kind of kink you're into, but Jane Anderson obeys no one. Got it?" *Whew.* She spoke a whole sentence without her lungs trying to make a break through her mouth.

He narrowed his eyes, and his jaw ticked, but he remained silent, almost stoic. Something outside that door had nearly killed her, yet the only emotion he seemed capable of expressing was disdain.

She took a deep breath and let it out slowly. She had to keep her cool. "What just happened? Why did I feel like I was on fire?"

Ethan sighed dramatically, as if he were the one nearly burned alive by opening a door, and dragged his hands down his face. "You were hit by a car last night, and I brought you here to save your life."

Jane opened her mouth to argue, but the memory crept back into her mind. She'd been at the parade, and something had compelled her to wander down the street. She'd found that creepy cemetery with all the aboveground tombs, but the gates were locked. It would have made a sensational article for her blog. Her stomach sank. "I was trying to get a photo." And that truck had come from nowhere.

He angled his body toward her. "Do you remember anything after that?"

"I remember…" Her jaw trembled, so she snapped it shut. It wasn't possible. This wasn't a memory; it was a hallucination. He didn't float her over the cemetery wall, and he certainly didn't… She swallowed hard. "Did you bite me?"

"I'm a vampire, Jane. And now, so are you." He said it so matter-of-factly, like it was just a…well, a matter of fact.

A nervous giggle bubbled from her throat. "What?"

"Vampire." He bared his teeth and tapped a fang.

A goddamn fang.

"Oh, come on." She scooted away. "Those are prosthetic. Vampires aren't real." They couldn't be.

"Aren't we? You didn't take too kindly to daylight just then, and that was filtered through glass. Imagine what direct sunlight would do to you." He narrowed his eyes at her, giving her that full-on smoldering effect again, making her stomach flutter, and an annoying little voice in the back of her mind whispered that she should believe him.

But she couldn't. "That was... You put something out there to keep me in. A massive heat lamp or something."

"Do you really think I'd go to that much trouble to keep you trapped inside my attic? I could have just locked the door."

"Well..." He had her there, but still. Vampires? "Tell me the truth, Ethan. This isn't funny. Did Sophie put you up to this?" Her friend had been trying to convince her vampires were real since they started planning this trip. It wouldn't surprise her.

"Your friend is a witch, yet you refuse to believe in vampires?"

So it *was* Sophie. "I knew it. I knew that little tramp set this up. What did she tell you?"

"She didn't tell me anything. She smells like a witch."

Jane scoffed. "Smells? Tell me then, what does a witch smell like?"

"Like spices. Sophie's magic smells somewhat like cinnamon. It's faint, though. Is she aware she has powers?"

"Oh, come on. Cinnamon? Really?" She threw her hands in the air. "Tell me the truth, Ethan, and cut the vampire crap."

"I wish this wasn't the truth, but it is. Do you have a mirror? Your face still hasn't healed from the light. Look at it."

"Ha. See, I knew you were lying." She dug in her purse for her compact, a smug smile curving her lips. "Vampires don't cast reflections." She flipped open the plastic container and looked at herself in the mirror. "Oh, my."

Her hair was a rat's nest, and mascara stains streaked her face, but the most disturbing sights were the bright red blisters on her cheeks and forehead. She tilted her head, staring as they shrank into nothing right before her eyes.

She caught Ethan's reflection over her shoulder, his expression unreadable. Her lips twitched, and she hesitated to open her mouth. If she had fangs too, she'd...

She smiled, and her teeth were normal.

Blowing out a breath of relief, she looked over her shoulder. "You know, you're so serious about all this, you almost had me believing you. I can see you in the mirror."

"Of course you can. Everything casts a reflection, even vampires. Unless we're using our glamour." He nodded at the mirror. "Look again."

She rolled her eyes and glanced in the mirror again. Wait a minute, that couldn't be right. She squeezed her eyes shut and opened them again, but her face was the only reflection she saw. She jerked her head toward him, but he hadn't moved from his spot on the corner of the mattress. She scooted closer, holding the mirror directly in front of his face, moving it to the side and all around him. Nothing.

"Holy shit."

"Believe me now?"

"How are you doing that?"

"Glamour. It's a type of vampire magic that allows us to go unnoticed among humans. It's why you didn't see me when you wandered down that side street last night, which wasn't the smartest thing to do in New Orleans."

"I never claimed to make the best decisions." *Damn.* Maybe she did need a babysitter after all.

She snapped the mirror shut and shoved it into her purse. Pulling her knees to her chest, she wrapped her arms around her legs and chewed her bottom lip. She didn't want to believe him.

It sounded impossible, but the more she thought about last night, the more his explanation made sense.

That truck had hit her head-on, and she was still alive when it rolled over her like a speedbump, crushing her ribcage. She didn't imagine that. And Ethan… She didn't imagine what he'd done to her either. He'd bitten her neck, but it didn't hurt. After that, she could only recall waking up here. *Holy bloodsuckers.* She was a fucking vampire.

"This glamour of yours… Is that why I'm not scared of you? Why I don't remember anything after you bit me? Did you put me under some sort of spell?"

"The death sleep pulled you under shortly after I bit you, so you could complete the transformation. That's why you have no memory of arriving here. And it's natural for you to trust me. I sired you."

"Sired?"

"I turned you into a vampire."

"Ew. Okay, let's say that then. Saying you sired me makes it sound like you're my daddy or something, and that's a kink I could *never* get into." Ethan was way too hot to think of him as a father figure. Even with all the weirdness of discovering she'd been turned into a vampire—and this definitely took the cake for her weirdest experience yet—she still felt an underlying attraction to him. "I won't call you Daddy, no matter how much you beg."

The corner of his mouth twitched, but he still didn't smile.

She narrowed her eyes, vowing to make this man smile if it killed her. Could vampires die? "Are you always this serious?"

"This is a serious matter."

"Are all vampires this broody? Or is it just you?"

His eyes tightened. "We retain our personalities from our human lives."

"Oh, so this Edward Cullen act isn't an act? This is what you've always been like?"

He closed his eyes and went utterly still, so still, she

wondered if he'd turned to stone. Could vampires do that? She had so many questions.

"Can you teach me to turn into a bat?"

He opened his eyes, and his jaw ticked again like he was annoyed. "No." What on Earth did he have to be annoyed about?

"Why did you save me?"

His eyes softened, a look of regret drawing down his brow. "I thought you were…" He clamped his mouth shut and shook his head. "You would have died. The sun has set. Let's get out of the attic."

"Thank God." Her throat closed up, and she fell into another coughing fit. "Why. Do. I. Keep. Coughing?" she asked between breaths.

Ethan squatted by the door, remaining silent until she finished nearly dying again. "I thought you'd have figured that out by now."

"Figured what out?"

He shook his head like he was disappointed. "Hundreds of years ago, after an unfortunate event involving an entire choir, the church smote our kind. We can't speak the name of a certain religious icon or his son without…" He gestured toward her. "Without *that* happening."

"You could have told me that after my first incident."

"I hoped you'd learn it on your own." He opened the attic door, and Jane shielded her eyes. No light sliced through the darkness this time.

"Is there anything else I need to know?" She followed him down a ladder into a narrow hallway.

"Plenty. You also can't go inside a church, and holy water burns." He led her into a small living room with a dark blue sofa and matching recliner. A television sat atop an oak entertainment center, and beige drapes covered the windows.

So not what she'd expected for a vampire's house. Where was his coffin, and shouldn't the upholstery be red velvet? "No holy stuff. Got it. What else?"

He stopped in front of the door and turned toward her. "You'll need to feed. We have to visit the Magistrate to get your permit, and then I'll teach you everything you need to know."

"Feed?" Her stomach sank. The shock of the situation had messed with her brain, and she hadn't stopped to consider what being a vampire actually meant. What she'd have to consume.

"You need blood to survive, but it's illegal to bite without a license." He opened the door, gesturing for her to exit. "Once you have your permit, I can teach you how to feed. Let's go."

The mere thought of biting a person...of drinking blood... had her head spinning. She swallowed the sour taste in her mouth, cringing as the cactus needles dug into her throat, and straightened her spine. She'd let him teach her how to glamour and do all the fun vampire shit, but there was no way in hell she'd be drinking blood.

CHAPTER FIVE

E than sent out one more mental distress signal to his sire and opened the front door. Unfortunately—though not unexpectedly—Gaston was nowhere to be found. He stepped onto the porch, closing his eyes and willing the sound of Jane's obnoxious voice to stop grating in his ears.

What had he done?

"Be a doll and get me a glass of water before we go, okay? I feel like I've swallowed a desert." Jane stood in the doorway, resting a hand against the jamb. Her dark hair hung in tangled knots, and smeared makeup marred her otherwise perfect complexion. Even in bloodied, torn clothes, the infuriating woman was stunningly beautiful.

Unfortunately, her superficial beauty didn't make it beneath her skin. He tilted his head, staring at her neck as she droned on about how thirsty she was. Actually, there was one beautiful thing beneath her skin. Her blood was as sweet as maraschino cherries. He'd never tasted anything like it. Beautiful on the outside, with sweet blood, but the positive traits ended there.

"Water won't quench your thirst." Her first taste of blood should be straight from the source, but he couldn't stand another minute of her whining. He stomped past her into the kitchen and took a glass from the cabinet, setting it on the countertop.

"You're right," she said. "A beer would be better. Or, hell, after what I've been through, I'll take a shot of whiskey."

He took a jug of O positive from the fridge. "You're a vampire, Jane. Only one thing will ease the burn in your throat."

"Whoa, Eddie." She held up her hands. "Is that blood?"

"Of course. What else would it be?"

She shook her head. "Don't pour it." She backed up until her butt met the counter. "Seriously, I just want water."

Without saying a word, he returned the jug to the fridge and filled the glass with tap water. If she wouldn't take his word for it, he'd let her learn the hard way. "Here you go, princess."

She snatched the glass from his hand. "Don't call me that."

"Don't call me Eddie."

"If you didn't act like such a brooding, teenage-romance vampire, I wouldn't."

"If you didn't act like such a stubborn, spoiled brat, neither would I."

Her mouth dropped open. "Jane Anderson is not spoiled."

"Riiight…" A tingle in the back of his mind alerted him to Gaston's approach. "Drink up. We've got company."

She chugged the water and slammed the glass on the counter before wiping her mouth with the back of her hand. "See? All better now. I just needed a drink."

"Uh huh." He stalked out the front door and descended the porch steps.

Gaston approached from above—in bat form, no less—his wings flapping wildly as he tilted from side to side, spiraling down before transforming into his human form. He stumbled as he hit the ground and caught himself on the porch railing.

Ethan shook his head. The sun hadn't been down a half-hour, and his sire was already lit.

Jane parked her hands on her hips and gaped. "Eddie, you fucking liar. You said I couldn't turn into a bat."

He groaned, giving Gaston the stink eye. His mentor had only done that to show off. "I said I couldn't teach you to turn into a bat. Gaston can shapeshift; I can't."

Sweeping the tails of his black duster behind him, Gaston stepped in front of Ethan and bowed at Jane. "How nice to finally see you conscious, Miss Jane. I'm sure Ethan has told you all about me."

She arched a brow, raking her gaze up and down his form. "Who are you?"

"I'm Gaston, Ethan's sire, of course." He went to lean a hand against the railing, but he missed by half a foot and stumbled into her.

Clutching his shoulders, she righted him and stepped back, looking at Ethan. "Is he drunk?"

Ethan lifted his shoulders, giving a slight nod. There weren't enough excuses in the world to make for Gaston. "He has a thing for Irish whiskey."

"It's rum tonight, my friend. A bachelorette party was drinking hurricanes."

Jane rolled her eyes. "Fantastic. It's just my luck to get turned into a vampire by an Edward Cullen wannabe who has Captain Jack Sparrow as his mentor."

Gaston held up a finger. "I resemble that remark."

"I think you mean 'resent,'" Ethan said.

Gaston smirked. "Do I?"

"When can I meet some real vampires?" She crossed her arms. "If I have to be a creature of the night, I want to learn all the tricks. Glamour, mind control, turning into a *bat*." She gave Ethan a pointed look.

"Shape-shifting magic can only be acquired by drinking copious amounts of were-blood," Gaston said. "Unfortunately, we've had a truce with the shifters for one hundred and fifty years, so I'm afraid that ability is out of reach for newly-turned vampires."

"Just...give me a minute. Gaston, can I talk to you privately?" He walked his sire out of Jane's earshot, though at this point, it wouldn't matter if she heard what he had to say. "I screwed up, man. You were right."

Gaston grinned. "What was I right about, old friend?"

"She's not Vanessa." Not even close, and the longer he looked at her, the less and less she resembled the memory of his fiancée. Hell, he couldn't even picture Vanessa's face at the moment, but he was positive she looked nothing like Jane.

"No? Are you sure? I remember Vanessa having long brown hair." Amusement danced in his ice-blue eyes.

Ethan gritted his teeth. "I'm positive." Vanessa was quiet, timid, mild-mannered. "She hasn't *shut* up since she *woke* up. What am I going to do? She talks about herself in the third person."

A deep laugh rumbled in Gaston's chest. "You're going to take care of her like I took care of you. Train her. Make her the best vampire you can, then...and only then...you will set her free."

His breath came out in a hiss. "Can't you take her on? You're a fabulous sire. The best there is. She'd do much better having you train her."

Gaston clapped his shoulder. "Flattery will get you nowhere in this case, my friend. You made her; she is yours." He walked back toward the house, and Ethan followed. "Besides, she still bears your mark. No one else can touch her."

Jane had been sitting on the porch steps, but she shot to her feet. "His mark? What are you talking about?"

"She doesn't know?" Gaston looked far too amused. "He marked you, my dear. Did you not wonder why you haven't been the slightest bit afraid of a vampire? He claimed you as his own."

"Nobody *claims* Jane Anderson. I'm my own person, so

you'd best remove that mark before you have to remove my boot from your ass." She shook her finger in Ethan's face.

He gladly would if he knew what to do, but he wasn't about to admit to this insolent woman that he had no clue how to remove it. He'd have to get Gaston to teach him in private. "When a vampire drinks from a human, he puts a temporary mark on them to let other vampires know they're low on blood. It's our system for keeping humans safe. We aren't allowed to drain anyone."

She pursed her lips, and for half a second, she almost looked disappointed. "That's all I was to you? A snack?"

For another half-second, he felt a twinge of guilt for hurting her feelings. "I didn't drink from you until I had to save your life. I marked you the night before so no one else would either, but the Magistrate doesn't need to know that."

She flinched as if she were slapped. "You didn't *want* to drink from me, but you also didn't want anyone else to? I don't understand."

He didn't understand why he felt the need to explain himself to her. Why—though her attitude drove him batshit crazy—he wanted to make her happy. It must have been the mating mark. As soon as he figured out how to remove it, these conflicting emotions would dissipate and his attraction to the woman would finally cease. "You were wasted, Jane. If I'd drunk from you, I'd have been wasted too, and someone needed to see you home safely."

A smug smile curved her lips. "Oh, Edward, you do care."

No, no, he didn't. These emotions weren't real. "The constables are out in full force lately. Let's get you registered so no one gets the stake."

"Neither of you can be in the Magistrate's presence looking like criminals." Gaston reached inside his jacket. "You both need a shower and a change of clothes before we go. Jane, dear, I took the liberty of stopping by your lovely house on my way. I think this crimson chenille sweater will suit your vampire-pale skin nicely, along with a pair of dark jeans."

He handed her the clothes. "Oh, I almost forgot the best part." He reached into his jacket again and pulled out a matching set of lingerie. The bra was black satin trimmed in lace, and the panties, what existed of them, were sheer with black lace around the waistband.

Ethan's throat thickened, his dick hardening as an image of what she'd look like wearing the lingerie—and nothing else— flashed in his mind. His fingers twitched as he imagined peeling the fabric from her body, a smile lighting on her lips as he trailed his tongue over her soft skin.

Jane snatched the clothing from Gaston's hand, her gaze locking with Ethan's for a moment before she looked away. "I was saving these for a special occasion. I suppose becoming a registered vampire will have to be good enough."

Gaston steepled his fingers, grinning like a fool. "Perhaps you can model them for us later."

"Fat chance. Where's the shower?"

"Down the hall. Second door on the left." He stared at her curvy backside as she sashayed into the house and disappeared around the corner. "She didn't have any more modest underwear?"

Gaston chuckled. "Mildly so, but I'm afraid our dear Jane is quite the firecracker. I think she's going to be good for you."

How in hell could she be good for him? They'd done nothing but bicker since she woke up. Then again, he hadn't *felt* this much in as long as he could remember. He leaned against the porch railing, trying to recall what exactly it was about Jane that had drawn him to her, made him think she was the woman he loved. He came up with nothing.

Yet, there was *something*.

"Well, well." Constable Watson appeared from around the corner, his trench coat flapping behind him as he strode up the sidewalk. "What kind of trouble are we getting into tonight, gentlemen?"

Ethan straightened his spine. "None at all, Constable."

Watson narrowed his eyes, glancing at the open front door. "Hmm."

"This one wouldn't know trouble if it bit his ass and drained him dry." Gaston stood between Watson and the entrance. "What kind are you looking for?"

"Anything, really." Watson glanced at his nails and buffed them on his lapel. "You've the highest concentration of supernatural beings on the continent in this city alone, yet I'm regretful to say I haven't found nearly as much mayhem as I'd hoped."

"Our Magistrate runs this city like a well-oiled machine," Ethan said. "What were you hoping to find?"

Watson shrugged. "Chaos. Disorder. Signs of a much-needed change in command. When this position with the SWO opened, I jumped at the chance to audit New Orleans. Alas, you're all too good at following the rules."

"All right, Eddie. Your turn." Jane strutted onto the porch, stepping around Gaston and crossing her arms, cocking her hip out as she gave Watson a once-over. "Nice hat."

Gaston was right about the red sweater flattering Jane's skin tone. It also hugged her curves, dipping just low enough to reveal a bit of cleavage and making Ethan's mouth water. Her damp hair hung past her shoulders, and her makeup-free skin had an ethereal glow.

Watson pulled his cell phone from his pocket. "May I see your license and registration, madam?"

"Madam?" Jane dropped her arms to her sides. "Do I look eighty to you?"

"She's not registered yet." Ethan positioned himself between the constable and Jane, but she stepped aside, refusing his protection.

A devilish smile curved Watson's lips. "Oh, dear. The grace

period has ended, I'm afraid. Perhaps tonight won't be as uneventful as I first thought." He pocketed his phone and rubbed his hands together. "It's been a while since I've gotten to stake anyone."

Ethan grabbed Jane's arm, shoving her behind his body and sandwiching her between him and Gaston. "You're not touching her. She's newly-turned, and we're on our way to see the Magistrate now."

"Laws are laws, and she should be registered. I'm sure you understand." Watson cracked his knuckles.

No way in the seven levels of hell was this asshole laying a finger on Jane. "She just woke up dead an hour ago. Fledglings have until the end of their first night to register."

"That is the law, an SWO law, I might add," Gaston said over Jane's shoulder. "Shall I make a call to the Magistrate and sort this out? I've known him since he was a fledgling himself."

Watson glowered, stepping back as he clasped his hands behind his back. "I'll be watching you. One mistake, and you'll be mine." He turned, jerking his coat so it waved like a cape, before disappearing around the corner.

"Now's there's a stereotypical vampire." Jane laughed, but it didn't mask the tremble in her voice. She slipped from between him and Gaston, reaching across her body to rub one arm. "Did he really want to stake me?"

"I wouldn't have let him." Ethan gripped her bicep softly, and her breath caught as he held her gaze.

She swallowed hard, cringing, though he wasn't sure if it was from the dryness in her throat or the threat to her life. "Thank you. You might be as sullen as a teenage guitar player, but you're a good man."

If she only knew.

Jane stood in the foyer of the vampire headquarters, trying to ignore the sensation of her underwear riding up her ass. That particular set of lingerie wasn't meant to be worn longer than a few minutes and never outside the bedroom. She ran her fingers through her damp hair, tousling it a bit to give it some lift. Even with all that dark, wavy, sexy hair, Mr. Broody Vampire didn't own a hairdryer. She looked in an antique mirror hanging on the wall of the nineteenth-century mansion's foyer and marveled at her complexion. She was a few shades paler than she'd been before, but otherwise, her skin was perfect. Once she got ahold of some eyeliner and mascara, she'd be smokin' hot.

This vampire gig was turning out to be a blessing. She had super strength, which she'd figured out when she pushed Ethan earlier, and when Gaston had fallen and she'd picked him up like he was light as a cotton ball. She was gorgeous, immortal, and the only things that could kill her were stakes to the heart, beheading, and sunlight, which, to be honest, already killed a lot of people anyway. *Skin cancer's a bitch.*

The only drawback to her condition was the blood-drinking issue, but Jane was resourceful. She'd figure out a way to find sustenance. That water hadn't quenched her thirst at all, but she'd never tell Ethan that. Maybe she could order her steaks rare. That might work.

She'd have to watch all her friends and family die eventually, but death was inevitable. She'd miss Sophie the most. "Oh, shit. Sophie. She must be worried sick about me." She sank onto the little couch next to Ethan.

"I used your phone to text her. She knows you're with me." He stared straight forward, his face unreadable. Only his fists clenched in his lap gave away his emotions, and she still couldn't tell if he was angry or nervous. And what was he angry or nervous about? That British twit who wanted to stake her an hour after she woke up or the whole situation of having to register a new vampire?

Her stomach fluttered again when she thought about the way he'd jumped in front of her, protecting her as if he cared.

"What did you tell her?" She pulled her phone from her purse and swiped open the messaging app. Her eyes widened as she read the exchange:

Ethan (pretending to be Jane): *Hey. I ran into that hot guy who took us home last night. I'm going to spend the night with him.*

Sophie: *You go, girl. I can't wait to hear all about him.*

She cast Ethan a sideways glance. "'That hot guy?' Seriously?"

He shrugged. "I was trying to be authentic."

She snorted. The man had nerve—and possible mind-reading abilities. She continued reading their texts.

Sophie (twelve hours later): *Wow, he must have ridden you hard and put you up sopping wet. What time are you coming back?*

Ethan: *Actually, I'm going to spend the day with him. He's amazing.*

Sophie: *K. Stay safe and use protection.*

She dropped the phone into her purse. "'Amazing?' You're full of yourself, aren't you?"

"Would she believe you'd spend the day with me if I were anything less?"

Jane narrowed her eyes. "I have to see her tonight. She definitely won't believe I'd ditch her two nights in a row. What's taking Gaston so long, anyway? He disappeared fifteen minutes ago to 'introduce' us to the Magistrate."

Ethan closed his eyes. "Vampire politics are complicated."

Jane rolled hers. "I know more about politics than you can shake your dick at."

"That's not how the saying goes."

"My dad's the governor of Texas."

He glanced at her. "That explains a lot."

"What's that supposed to mean?"

His nostrils flared as he let out a slow breath. "You expect others to do everything for you. With a father in a position of high authority, now I understand why."

"Because you think I'm spoiled." Which she *so* wasn't. She worked her ass off to earn the respect of the men in her family, and for what? Her own father still thought she needed a babysitter.

"I won't fault you for your upbringing, but I won't enable you either."

"Enable me? Oh my Go—olly gosh jeez." She crossed her arms. "See, I can learn."

His brow lifted, and the corners of his mouth twitched. Did the man ever smile? Why did she want him to so badly?

"You need to lighten up," she said. "If I'm going to be part of your clan, you'll have to learn to have fun."

"It's a coven, not a clan."

"I thought witches had covens."

He closed his eyes for another long blink. "They do. Vampires do too."

"And werewolves?"

"Packs, of course."

She chewed her bottom lip, taking in her surroundings. A thick burgundy rug covered most of the hardwood floor, and dark wood furniture gave the room a period vibe. "Are there any werewolves in New Orleans?"

"Plenty."

"Are they our natural-born enemies?"

His nostrils flared again. "That's a myth."

"Am I annoying you?"

"Very much."

Was he serious? *She* was annoying *him*? "You're the one who turned *me* into a vampire. And you never told me why you did it. Everyone dies. Why did you choose to save me?"

"Jane." He turned toward her, taking her shoulders in his hands.

His grip was firm, yet somehow gentle at the same time, and

his touch set off a chemical reaction inside her body. She shouldn't have been attracted to him. He had all the personality of a wet tissue, but there she was, staring into his emerald eyes while he smoldered back at her, warmth blooming in her nether region, threatening to soak her lace panties.

His gaze flicked to her mouth for half a second before he released her. "You haven't stopped talking since you woke up."

She brushed her hair from her forehead, composing herself. "What do you expect? I'm suddenly not human anymore, and I have questions."

"I know you do, but I didn't plan this. I… In a city that never sleeps, I value silence. I've been alone for the past twenty-five years, and I'm not used to…" He closed his eyes and took a deep breath. "Give me five minutes of peace. Please. Can you keep your mouth shut for five minutes so I can get my thoughts together?"

She narrowed her eyes, chewing the inside of her cheek. If he wanted silence, she'd give him silence…and a cold shoulder to go with it.

Rising to her feet, she stepped toward a baby grand piano sitting in the back corner of the room. She lightly ran her fingers across the cool ivory keys, stopping at middle C and giving it a tap. The note rang out, filling the room with music.

"I asked for silence," Ethan grumbled.

She raised her hands. "Okay, okay." Her boots thudded on the hardwood floor as she strolled toward the window. Behind the curtain rod, a mechanical device was mounted to the frame. She flipped the red switch on the wall next to it—because c'mon, a red switch? How could she not flip it?—and the device hummed to life, a thick black shade sliding down to cover the window.

"Jane!" Ethan didn't move from his spot on the couch, but his tone was sharp enough to slice skin.

"Sorry. Couldn't help myself." She flipped the switch in the opposite direction, and the shade rolled back up. "How come you don't have something like this at your house? Wouldn't you rather sleep in your bedroom than up in the dusty old attic?"

"They're too expensive."

"Vampires need money?"

"How else would we buy things?"

She plopped onto the couch next to him. It had been five minutes, hadn't it? Close enough. "What's it like having Captain Jack Sparrow as your mentor? Is he always so…drunk?"

"Gaston is a good sire and a good friend. He's been around more than three hundred years, so I can only imagine the things he's seen. What he's been through." He unclenched his fists and laid his palms on his thighs. "He gets this way during Mardi Gras. With so many drunk humans in the Quarter, he can't seem to help himself."

"Is that it? Or did something happen to him during a past Mardi Gras, and he's trying to numb the pain?"

Ethan looked at her as if he'd never considered the idea. "I don't know. He doesn't talk about his past much, unless it's to recount a fight. Nobody fights like Gaston."

Jane giggled. "What about cheap shots? I bet nobody takes those like Gaston either."

"He does what he has to do."

"Is he good at expectorating? *Especially* good?" She was cracking herself up.

He blinked. "What does that have to do with anything?"

"Oh, come on. Haven't you seen *Beauty and the Beast*? Gaston is the bad guy, and he has a fantastic song."

"No."

"How old are you?"

"I've been dead for twenty-five years."

She narrowed her eyes, studying him. "You look like you're in your early twenties, which means you've been around for about forty-eight years or so. Am I right?"

"He nodded."

"I know what your problem is. You're a Gen Xer"

His brow arched. "And your point is?"

"You don't give a shit about anything."

"And you're an entitled Millennial who thinks the world owes her everything."

She crossed her arms. "You don't know anything about me."

"I know enough."

The door Gaston had disappeared through finally opened, and he stepped into the room, grinning as it closed behind him. "Come, children. The Magistrate awaits."

CHAPTER SIX

J ane strutted toward the door, stopping in front of it as
Gaston whispered something to Ethan, who grimaced and
whispered something back through clenched teeth. These
boys needed a lesson in subtlety…and manners.

Ethan stepped behind her. "What are you waiting for? Let's
get this over with."

"I'm waiting for someone to open the door for me."

"You're capable of opening it yourself."

She gaped, waiting for him to take the hint and open the
damn thing like a gentleman, but he just stood there staring at
her like she was out of her mind for expecting chivalry. "Fine."
She yanked on the knob and stomped into the hallway, but
Ethan caught her by the arm, holding her back as Gaston
passed.

"There's an order to things here. The senior vampire enters
first. Do you remember everything we taught you on the way
over?"

She tugged from his grasp and straightened her sweater.
Why the hell did he make her open the door if Gaston had to
go in before her anyway? "Of course. I'm not an idiot."

He walked next to her toward a set of double doors. "They'll ask us some questions, and then you'll recite the rules you learned. You can answer everything honestly, but if you want us to make it out alive, I did not mark you until *after* I drank from you. Got it?"

"You want me to lie under oath?" She pressed a hand to her chest, feigning shock. Her dad was a politician. She learned to lie from the best.

"It's against the law to mark someone unless you've drunk from them. I could get the stake for it." His eyes were even more serious than normal.

No way in hell would she let some vampire Council kill Ethan for trying to protect her. He may have been as fun as a pap smear, but the man did save her life. Twice. She patted his cheek. "Don't worry, darlin'. I won't tell a soul." She owed him that much.

Gaston threw open the doors and strode into the room.

"Stay two steps behind me," Ethan whispered as he crossed the threshold.

She was about to protest that Jane Anderson stayed behind no man, but the sight of the Council froze her to the spot.

Four men in black robes sat atop a raised platform in gold and gem-encrusted thrones. Jane squinted, trying to determine the types of jewels and whether or not they were real. If they were, this room alone would be worth a fortune.

The men looked old as the gods themselves, with shoulder-length, scraggly hair and skin so paper-thin, she could have torn it with a fingernail—and Jane always got the "squoval" when she had a manicure. Stilettos belonged on the feet, not the hands.

"I thought vampires didn't age."

"These guys don't get out much. With little interaction in the modern world, they've lost touch with most of their human traits." Ethan grabbed her hand, tugging her into the room, and his touch sent another jolt through her body. They stopped in the middle of the room, and he released her, while Gaston joined a group of vampires along the wall.

Gas lamps enclosed in glass cases provided the only light in the room, but Jane could see just fine—another plus to this vampire business. The windows lining the right side of the room were all equipped with the same light-blocking mechanism as the sitting-room window, and the long, rectangular shape of the room made it look like it might have been a grand ballroom back in the day.

Upon closer inspection, the vampire Council didn't seem quite so elderly. More like scary…and incredibly bored. "Holy shit, Edward. You didn't tell me we were coming to meet the Volturi."

"Shh…"

A door opened behind the dais, and a man who could only be the Magistrate drifted in. He wore the same black robes as the Council members, and his movements were so fluid, he seemed to float above the floor. His long, dark hair was woven into dreads, making him look like Idris Elba in that *Thor* movie, but he had a menacing glint in his eyes and crackling power in his aura that screamed authority. With his strong jaw and piercing hazel eyes, he was sexy as all get-out, but not someone Jane wanted to piss off.

Idris sank into the center throne, and Jane waved. "Hey, guys. Nice to meet you."

Every single one of those suckers leaned toward her, hissing —literally hissing—as they bared their fangs. She parked her hands on her hips and turned to Ethan. "Is this for real? Are they hissing?"

His nostrils flared for the umpteenth time tonight as his hands curled into fists. "You don't address the Council without permission to speak."

"You could have told me that beforehand. Nobody hisses at Ja—"

Ethan bared his fangs and hissed at her too.

Her mouth fell open. "Oh. My. Go— goat cheese pizza. Not you too." She ran her tongue along her teeth. No fangs, but she refused to be out-hissed. She bared her blunt teeth and did her best angry cat impression. Then she turned to the Council and hissed at them for good measure. *Jesus Christ.* Hey, at least she could still swear in her head. She was stuck in the middle of a *What We Do in the Shadows* episode.

Ethan clapped his hand over her mouth and wrapped his other arm around her from behind. "Apologies, Magistrate. She's freshly turned and ornery as hell. I don't quite have her under control yet."

Control? Who did he think he was? She tried to protest, but he kept his hand pressed tightly against her mouth.

The Magistrate nodded. "You will apprise her of the laws and exert your control as her sire."

"Yes, sir."

The moment he released her, she whirled to face him. "Let's get one thing straight, Eddie. You don't control me. No one does. And why are there no women on this Council? Is this a patriarchy? Because I'm all about busting glass ceilings."

Ethan growled low in his throat. "Permission to stake her, Your Honor?"

She gasped. "You wouldn't dare."

"Try me."

"Enough." The Magistrate had an *I don't get paid enough for this shit* look on his face, so Jane clamped her mouth shut. She could totally feel for the guy. Her own bullshit meter didn't go very high either. "You will recite the rules to receive your permit."

Jane rattled off all the crap Ethan wanted her to memorize on their way over: She had to stay with her sire—*ew*, that word still didn't sit right with her—at all times until she was licensed; she wasn't allowed to bite anyone—not that she ever would... EVER—until she'd been properly trained, and a bunch of other nonsense about not leaving bite marks and only using her glamour responsibly.

This Council took all the fun out of being an undead creature of the night.

Ethan let out what sounded like a breath of relief when she was done…as if he'd actually been worried she'd fail the test. *Please*, Jane had never failed a test in her life. Not one she studied for, anyway.

When she was done, the Magistrate steepled his fingers and rested his elbows on the arms of his jewel-encrusted throne. "Very good. You will be tested for your biting license in three weeks." He glanced at the man next to him. "Put her on the schedule." He turned to address Ethan. "How did this pairing come about, and why has the mating mark not been reciprocated?"

Jane blinked. "Mating mark?"

Gaston snickered from his spot on the sidelines, and Ethan hung his head. "It was an accident, Your Honor." Ethan lifted his gaze to Jane's and looked away, ashamed.

"Umm…" Jane's mouth opened and closed a few times before she could form words, which was probably a good thing. She didn't want to engage in another hissing match. "Permission to speak?"

The Magistrate nodded.

She turned to Ethan. "What the hell is a mating mark? You said you marked me as a meal."

"She's unaware you've claimed her as your mate?" The Magistrate leaned forward, the boredom in his eyes morphing into curiosity. "Please explain."

Ethan cast Gaston a *help me out here* glance, but his sire just laughed, shaking his head. He looked at Jane again before focusing on the Magistrate. "I…thought she was someone else when I turned her. I made a mistake."

Jane tilted her head. "Which was the mistake? Turning me into a vampire or marking me as your mate?"

He pursed his lips, hesitating to answer. "Both."

"Well, shit." Her knees suddenly weak, she plopped onto the

floor, sitting cross-legged and holding her head in her hands. It shouldn't matter. She didn't want to be his mate, and the vampire thing…what was done was done, but…

The fact that not only did he not want her, but he didn't even want her to be a vampire, was like a knife—no, like a stake—to her heart. She shouldn't have cared, and maybe it was the shock of this whole situation wearing off and her real emotions breaking through, but pressure mounted in the back of her eyes, and a sob attempted to bubble up her throat. Thankfully, she was so parched, the sob didn't make it past her chest.

She flopped onto her back dramatically. "Go ahead and stake me. You heard the man; I'm a mistake. He doesn't want me."

"Come now, Jane. Let's not be dramatic." Gaston lifted her to her feet.

"You're one to talk, Captain Jack."

He laughed and pinched her cheek. "I like you." He motioned Ethan over and wrapped an arm around both of them. "It's true he thought you were someone else, but I distinctly remember him saying he didn't care if you weren't her right before he turned you."

She stared at Ethan until he met her gaze. "Is that true?"

He held eye contact. "Yes."

"So you don't regret turning me into a vampire?"

"Well…" he began, but he jumped when Gaston pinched him. "Honestly? No, I don't regret it. I find you…interesting."

"Interesting? Like a science experiment?"

"Intriguing."

She smiled, and the imaginary stake slipped from her chest. "I'll take intriguing."

"You wear it well," Ethan said.

The Magistrate cleared his throat. "Now that your domestic dispute has been settled, the mark must either be removed or reciprocated."

"Removed, please." Jane stepped out of Gaston's embrace. "I hardly know him."

"I'd love to remove it." Ethan's hands curled into fists. "But I don't even know how I put it on you. It just happened."

"Interesting." The Magistrate steepled his fingers again, drumming them together like he was amused. "Subconsciously applied marks are rare. Perhaps we should require it stays."

"No, please." Ethan pressed his palms together. "It was my mistake. I'll take responsibility, but please don't punish her. She deserves a choice."

Her eyebrows shot up. *Wow.* Mr. Sexy Brooding Vampire had a heart.

"Very well." The Magistrate rose to his feet and looked at Gaston. "I assume you are coherent enough to instruct him in mark removal?"

"Of course, Your Honor." Gaston bowed as the Council filed out of the room, and then he whispered something in Ethan's ear.

Ethan nodded and placed his hands on either side of Jane's head. Her skin tingled, and electricity shot through her core, gathering below her navel. His eyes turned stormy, like a sea at night, and her knees wobbled. This guy was sex on a stick.

Something seemed to snap inside her; the cord that had been tugging her toward him was severed, leaving a small, hollow space in her heart. She rubbed at the spot where she felt the discomfort, and he dropped his arms to his sides, stepping back and sweeping his gaze over her.

"It's done." Something she wanted to call regret flashed briefly in his eyes.

She wanted to call it regret because that was the only name she could find for her own emotions at the moment. Why on Earth would she feel that way? Being tied down to a man was the last thing she wanted, yet she already missed the connection to him. *You're going cuckoo, Jane. Woman up.*

"Good job, my friend." Gaston patted him on the back.

"Now, any emotions you felt for each other that were fabricated by the mark will cease."

"Thank the l—lady next door. Every time he touched me, I wanted to rip his clothes off. That'll go away now?"

Surprise widened Ethan's eyes, and a bit of a blush reddened his cheeks. How cute. Wait a minute. She wasn't supposed to be feeling attraction to him anymore.

Gaston chuckled. "Time will tell."

"Do you have a driver's license?" Ethan asked. "I need to fill out the paperwork to register you."

"I'm capable of filling it out myself."

He shook his head. "It has to be completed by the sire."

"Ew." She wrinkled her nose.

He rolled his eyes. "By the person who turned you."

"Here. It's from Texas, but it'll have to do." She tugged the license from her pocket, handing it to him, and he shuffled into the next room.

"So." She turned to Gaston. "Who did he think I was when he turned me?"

Gaston smiled sadly and shook his head. "The poor sap thought you were his dead fiancée reincarnated. I told him you were your own woman, but he wanted you to be her so badly."

Poor guy. "No wonder he's disappointed. What happened to her?"

"That's his story to tell, I'm afraid." He leaned in closer. "Honestly, I don't remember all the details. He can be quite the…what's the phrase? Drama queen."

Jane giggled and then bit her lip as she caught a glimpse of Ethan through the doorway. He leaned over a desk, filling out a form, and she swept her gaze to his backside, admiring the way his jeans hugged his muscular thighs.

"You still find yourself attracted to him, even without the mark?"

He had a broad back and strong shoulders—and that ass…

scrumptious. "He is easy on the eyes. Are these feelings going to wear off since the mark is gone?"

Gaston grinned. "Time will tell."

"You already said that."

"Miss Jane, I believe you're going to be good for our friend Ethan."

She tore her gaze away from his magnificent derriere. "Do you now?"

"He's had a stake wedge up his ass since I turned him. Hopefully, you can remove it."

Jane laughed. "I'll make it my mission."

CHAPTER SEVEN

"Good luck, my friend." Gaston slapped Ethan on the back and grinned. He even had the nerve to laugh, the bastard. "I'm just a thought away if you need me." He spun on his heel and disappeared into the crowd.

Jane strutted next to Ethan, matching his pace as he strode up Royal Street. "Oh, that's cute." She paused to look at a red vintage-style dress, reminiscent of the 1950s, in a shop window. "Too bad these stores aren't open after dark. I'll have to see if I can order this online."

He started to complain that they needed to be on their way, but she was registered and had her biting permit. Other than teaching her how to feed, they had no pressing plans. He'd just damned her to a life of darkness; he could give her a moment to look at a pretty dress. Hell, if he could afford it, he'd buy the damn thing. She'd look amazing in it.

His face pinched at the thought. He'd figured—he'd hoped —that as soon as the mating mark was removed, his attraction to her would cease. But other than the little hollow space in his chest, he didn't feel any differently about the confounding woman.

She was loud, entitled, and extremely annoying, yet every

time she smiled, his sluggish heart beat a little bit faster. And now that he knew what she was wearing beneath her form-fitting sweater and jeans, he couldn't get the image out of his mind. She wasn't the only one who felt the desire to tear off clothing every time they touched.

There was a simple solution for that. He just wouldn't touch her. He hadn't felt attraction to anyone since Vanessa died. No need to change things now.

"Hey. You okay?" She placed her hand on his arm, sending a jolt to his heart and yanking him out of the daydream he'd lost himself in.

"Yeah. Fine." He rubbed the spot where she'd touched him, trying to erase the images flashing through his mind of her rubbing *another* spot...a spot that hadn't been touched in years. He stepped back, out of arm's reach.

"What did Gaston mean by just a thought away? Can y'all put thoughts into each other's heads?"

He shoved his hands into his pockets. "We can."

Her dark eyes sparkled. "Can you teach me to do that? Can you do it to anyone?"

"I will eventually, and you can, but it takes time and intense practice to communicate with anyone other than your sir— the person who turned you." She was right. Calling him her sire did sound wrong. He wasn't into the daddy fetish either.

She smiled. "Now is as good a time as any."

"Your constant talking already grates in my ears. I don't need you inside my mind too."

"Whoa." She clutched her head. "You don't have to be so rude." Her smile returned. "I've got to learn how to do that."

"More importantly, you need to learn how to feed. Let's leave the Quarter and find dinner, shall we?"

Her nose crinkled. "Let's have dinner *in* the French Quarter."

"That's not a good idea for your first time. During Mardi

Gras, most of the people are drunk, and the alcohol in their blood will affect you. I'd hate for you to end up like Gaston."

She pressed her lips together, a disgusted expression contorting her features. "Let's have *food* for dinner. We can still eat, right?"

"Well, yes, but it provides no sustenance, and you only have three weeks to learn the proper biting techniques to get your license."

"Why do we have to be licensed anyway?" She continued strolling along the sidewalk…and talking before he could answer her question. "We're at the top of the food chain; we should be able to do whatever we want."

"Our kind has an agreement with the human government." He walked next to her, but far enough away that she couldn't touch him casually. He had to get his reactions to her under control. "We follow a set of rules, and we coexist in peace."

She stopped and faced him, her eyes widening. "The human government knows vampires exist?"

"They know about all the supernatural beings. Part of the arrangement is for them to help keep our existence a secret."

Her mouth hung open. "So my dad knows vampires are real?"

"He most likely does, but I don't recommend you tell him you are one until you're officially licensed." *Or at all.* Ethan had no idea how the Texas government felt about supes. Fear could drive people to madness.

"Unbelievable." She shook her head and chewed her bottom lip, looking thoughtful and awfully cute. "What happens if I miss the deadline? I've got plenty of money. I can pay a fine."

"Unlicensed vampires pay with their lives. The punishment is the stake."

"No one in their right mind would even think about staking the Governor's daughter." She waved a hand dismissively. "This is only my third night in the city. I have a super-long to-do list, and trying all the amazing food is a big part of it. Please? Sophie is meeting me at the rental house in two hours. That's plenty of time for us to have dinner and get to know each other."

"I don't know, Jane." A strange desire to make her happy tightened his chest, but restaurants in the French Quarter weren't cheap. He hadn't worked in weeks, and he barely had enough to pay the water bill this month.

"I may be a vampire, but I still have a job to do. My Instagram has been silent for more than twenty-four hours, and that's not a good thing in my line of work." She hooked an arm around his elbow. "C'mon. It'll be my treat. I can write it off as a business expense."

This close to her, he could smell his shampoo mixed with her own sweet scent, and damn it if it wasn't the most delicious aroma to entice his senses in ages. "Do you always get what you want?"

"Most of the time, yes."

He didn't have the energy to argue with her. Besides, it had been years since he'd had a bite of human food, and Jane still seemed healthy enough. Her body would finish processing her own human blood soon, and then she'd require a real vampire meal.

"Okay. But after you see Sophie, you need to start your lessons. I'll do the biting in the beginning, and you simply drink. There will be two puncture wounds from my fangs, directly in a vein, so you'll create suction with your lips around the wound. Hopefully your fangs will come in soon, and you can learn to do the biting yourself."

She pressed her lips into a hard line, giving her head a tiny shake. "There's got to be a way to sustain ourselves on human food."

"There isn't."

"How do you know? Have you tried?"

"We are *undead*. Our own blood has thickened to the point of sludge. Our hearts beat once every ten seconds, barely moving that sludge through our systems. We require the nutrients of fresh blood daily, or we will shrivel up and waste away."

Her eye twitched every time he said the word "blood." "Jeez Louise, Edward. Do you have to be so morbid?" She gestured across the street. "I heard that place is good. Let's grab a bite and talk about something less nauseating."

He followed her across the street and into Royal House Oyster Bar. A massive mirror hung behind a long, wood bar, and three men stood between, shucking fresh oysters and arranging them on platters for the patrons. Tables lined the walkway between the bar and the front windows before the restaurant opened up into an expansive dining area.

The hostess led them to a table near the kitchen, but Jane paused, batted her lashes, and touched the hostess on the elbow. "Would it be at all possible to get the table by the front window?" She slipped a folded bill into the woman's hand, and the hostess nodded, weaving her way toward the table Jane asked for.

Impressive. "I may not have to teach you any glamour at all. You seem to do fine without it." Ethan opened the menu and peered at her over the top.

She shrugged. "When I promise to be a good girl, Daddy lets me be seen in public with him. I've bumped elbows with plenty of people in power. I know how things are done."

"A good girl?"

She folded the menu on the table. "Two of my brothers are lawyers; one's a CPA, and the other is a doctor. You could say I'm a disappointment. In fact, you probably have said that in your mind at least once since you turned me."

Initially, yes, he did think that. But if he were honest, he'd have to admit he hadn't been this entertained in years. And for the first time in forever, he felt like his life had purpose. Even if it was simply to teach the woman to feed herself, he had something meaningful to do.

"My dad wanted me to go to law school too," she continued, "but I couldn't bring myself to work those hours. I got a degree in communications, and I blog about my adventures. Of course, now that I'm a vampire, I'll have to figure out what I'm going to do. Can we travel easily? Do we need to have coffins shipped like we're dead bodies, or can we fly like regular people?"

She droned on and on, only stopping her laundry list of questions to order her meal: a Taste of New Orleans with etoufée, gumbo, and jambalaya all on one plate.

"I'll have the roast beef po-boy." Ethan handed his menu to the waiter.

"Oh, that sounds good. I'll have one of those too. I'm starving." She looked at him. "What's the best drink to ease the burning in my throat?"

He arched a brow. "I believe you know."

She nodded. "Beer. I'll take a tall Abita Amber too, please."

He shook his head. When Gaston first turned him, he'd been somewhat averse to drinking blood, but the thirst quickly overpowered his hesitation. She'd give in eventually.

Their food arrived, and Jane devoured everything on her plate, sucking down her beer like it could save her life. Ethan ate half of his po-boy and a few fries. The savory beef with gravy and bits of debris, little pieces of meat that simmered for hours in the bottom of the pan, were as delicious as he remembered. He'd have to take a moment to enjoy a human meal every now and then in the future.

Jane leaned back in her chair and patted her stomach. "That was the best food I've ever had in my life. It's weird because I'm full, but I'm still hungry." She rubbed her throat. "I guess thirsty is a better word for it. Parched."

"You'll remain that way until you feed."

She visibly shivered. "Just let me make a few notes about this place for my blog, and then we can go. Remind me to get my charger from Sophie too. My phone's almost dead." Her laugh turned into a snort. "Almost dead...like us!"

"Well, well. Look what the cat dragged in." Sophie crossed her arms, grinning, and leaned against the door jamb as Jane tugged Ethan up the front walk. "There are thousands, if not millions of people in the French Quarter right now, and you found *him* again." She gave him a once-over with an approving nod. "What are the odds?"

You have no idea. "Hey, girl." Jane dropped Ethan's hand and pulled Sophie into a tight hug. "I have *so* much to tell you."

"I want every delectable detail."

The only delectable thing so far was dinner tonight...oh, and the fact she'd never grow old. That was a tasty little morsel she couldn't wait to share. "Ethan, you remember Sophie?"

"She puked on my shoes. How could I forget?"

Sophie cringed. "Sorry about that. Come on in." She stepped to the side and motioned for them to enter. "And in case Jane hasn't said it yet, thank you for not murdering us that night."

"Someone had to see you home safely."

"Yeah, but you could have just as easily been the thing we needed to stay safe from, so..." She shut the door and paused, cocking her head at Jane. "You look different. I mean, besides the no-makeup look, which you are totally rocking. Did you get a new moisturizer?"

Jane grinned. "I look good, don't I?"

"Fabulous. What's your secret?"

"Ethan turned me into a vampire."

Sophie laughed. "Fine. Don't tell me."

Ethan sank into a chair and crossed his arms. He wasn't keen on Jane telling Sophie what happened, but she'd convinced him the only way to keep the secret was to tell her best friend. Besides, he still insisted Sophie was a witch, so what did it matter?

"It's true. Ethan, show her your fangs."

He shook his head, looking perturbed, as usual. "I don't perform on command."

Jane rolled her eyes. "How else is she going to believe me?"

"He doesn't have fangs, and neither do you." Sophie put her hands on her hips. "Are you making fun of me because my grandma was a witch?"

"I told you she smells like a witch," Ethan said.

"I do?" Sophie lifted her arm and sniffed her pit.

"Listen," Jane said, "I don't have fangs because they haven't come in yet, but he does. Please, Ethan? Show her?"

He pressed his lips into a hard line, and when he peeled them back, revealing his pearly white fangs, a little thrill shimmied through Jane's body. Who knew she'd find teeth sexy?

"No way. Are those real?" Sophie leaned in for a closer look, and Ethan clamped his mouth shut. She went through the same stages of denial that Jane did, only Sophie didn't have to be nearly burned alive by sunlight to convince her. Instead, she perched on the arm of the sofa and smiled smugly. "I told you vampires were real."

"And you were right."

"Do you feel okay?" Her eyes widened. "Do you have to kill people now?"

"No, there are laws and junk. Ethan's supposed to teach me all of it: magic, glamour, and the boring rules. I'll live forever, never age, and I have super strength and speed."

"But you have to drink blood to survive." Sophie gave her a *how the hell are you going to pull that off?* look, and Jane glared back. That was all it took for her friend to get the message that her aversion to blood hadn't been mentioned yet. Best friends were awesome like that.

"I'm going to figure out a way to sustain myself on human food. Jambalaya, though incredibly delicious, doesn't cut it, so I'm thinking maybe rare steak."

Ethan rubbed his forehead. "We've been through this, Jane.

You require blood, and you only have three weeks to get your license."

"License?" Sophie laughed. "You need a license to drink blood?"

Jane shrugged. "It's a biting license. If I'm not biting anyone, I don't see why I need one."

"Because it's the law." Ethan pleaded with his eyes. Why did he have to look so damn cute when he did that?

"What happens if you don't get your license?"

"She'll be staked," he said.

"They'll kill you for not getting your license? That seems harsh."

"It's a new law. The Supernatural World Order is cracking down on unlicensed biting, and we've got a British constable in town forcing us to comply. She needs to learn the proper biting techniques, or she won't be around much longer."

Sophie's eyes softened. "Is that true, Jane?"

Jane scoffed. "My dad is the Governor of Texas. They wouldn't dare lay a fang on me."

"That's true. I can't imagine they'd want that kind of publicity for the state. If the Texas Governor's daughter goes missing in Louisiana, that could cause all kinds of trouble." Sophie stood next to Jane. "The government knows about the vampires, right? I'm sure there's some kind of conspiracy going on to keep magic a secret from normal people. Like in *The Originals*. Remember that show?"

Jane nodded. "I do, and it's just like that, except the vampire Council would fit better in a B movie."

Sophie snickered. "I bet that's a hoot. I'd love to meet them."

Ethan leaned his head back on the chair and let out a long, slow, dramatically loud breath.

Sophie leaned closer and whispered, "Is he always so..."

"Grumpy? Serious? Boring? Ornery?"

"Well...is he?"

"All of the above. He thinks I talk too much." He opened one eye, and she blew him a kiss. If she didn't know any better, she'd have said the corner of his mouth twitched like he was fighting a smile. She might just yank that stake out of his ass yet. "I'm going to pack my bag, darlin'. I'll only be a minute."

"Sure thing, princess."

She pursed her lips, fighting her own smile, and grabbed Sophie's arm, leading her down the hallway to her bedroom. "I hate to leave you like this, but I have to stay with him. It's *the law*, and I'll fry in the sunlight, so..." She tugged her suitcase from beneath the bed and began tossing her things inside it.

"I can't believe my BFF is a vampire. I'm going to have to check out the local witch stores and see if I can get inside their circle." She ducked into the bathroom and returned with Jane's toiletry bag. "Have you met any werewolves? That's what I really need. A big, burly man with lots of chest hair that I can run my fingers through, and we can howl at the moon together."

Jane laughed. "If I meet anyone who fits that description, I'll be sure to let you know."

"So..." Sophie crossed her arms and drummed her hot pink nails on her biceps. "You've given me details, but not the juicy ones. What's Mr. Uptight like in the sack? Is he an angel on the streets, a demon in the sheets, or what?"

She closed her suitcase and zipped it shut. "I wish I could answer that for you, but I have no idea."

Sophie's mouth dropped open. "You spent the night with the hottest man in New Orleans, and you didn't sleep with him?"

"I was nearly killed by a car, and then he turned me into a vampire. It wasn't exactly the most romantic of nights. Besides..." She lowered her gaze as her stomach soured. "For one thing, he doesn't like me very much, and for another... He thought I was his dead fiancée. That's why he turned me."

"Like reincarnated? Are you?"

"No, definitely not, but… Personality-wise, he's not my type at all. There's something about him though."

"He is hot. I'd do him."

"Girl, me too. He could just lie there dead to the world, as long his dick is hard and proportionate to the rest of him. With that body, I could have a blast on my own."

"You know I can hear you, right? Did I not mention vampires' above average hearing?"

Jane clutched her head. "Crap. He's listening. Come outside with me for a sec. I need a favor, and it's none of Edward Cullen's business." She yelled the last part just to grate on his nerves.

Sophie followed her out the back door and whispered, "That man swept you out of your Nikes before you realized they were untied. You really like him, don't you?"

"I don't know. Maybe. He did turn me into this fabulous creature." She gestured at herself. "The problem is, he's got us sleeping in his dusty old attic. I think he's poor and can't afford the light-blocking gadgets, which I know exist because I've seen them. So, I need you to go to the bank for me and take out some cash. I'm going to talk to his friend Gaston and see about having his place fixed up. It's the least I can do to show my appreciation."

"Janey's got a boyfriend," Sophie sang.

Jane shook her head. "I'd be dead now if it weren't for him."

"Actually, you kinda are."

CHAPTER EIGHT

"Oh. My. Goat cheese pizza. An ice cream shop!" Jane grabbed Ethan's sleeve and tugged him across the street. "I could use some mint chocolate chip therapy right now."

What she could have used was a pint of O positive, but his attempts to get her to feed over the past two weeks had been fruitless. She was becoming pale and weaker, sleeping fitfully during the days and sluggish to awaken at night. He'd heard of starvation being used as punishment for unruly vampires—before the Supernatural World Order decided the stake would be the cure for everything—but he'd never witnessed anyone starve themselves on purpose.

"Come on, slowpoke." She held the door open and motioned for him to enter.

Reaching above her head, he grasped the edge of the door. "After you, princess."

Her smile warmed his cold heart, which was why he'd given in to some of her whims, opening doors for her and following along as she experienced the city for the first time. He'd forgotten what an adventure New Orleans could be, taken his home for granted for far too long. Simply seeing the awe in her eyes sent a tiny thrill of life humming through his veins.

"What kind do you want?"

He stood against the wall, inhaling the scents of sweet cream and warm waffle cones, unable to remember the last time he'd had ice cream. "None for me, thank you."

She cocked one hip to the side, resting her hand on it. "If it's about money, I've got loads of it, so don't worry."

"It's not about money, though I do need to work again sometime soon if I'm going to pay the bills."

"What would I do while you worked?"

"I suppose I'd have to take you with me until you get your license." Not that he would get much done with her hanging around the office, talking constantly.

"What kind of work do you do?"

"I'm an accountant. I do temp work here and there." Just enough to get by. The rest of the time he spent alone in his home. In fact, he'd been out more in the two weeks he'd known Jane than he had in the past ten years.

She lifted her hands. "Oh, no. I'm not sitting in a stuffy office all night while you crunch numbers. Your job right now is to take care of me—which is a stupid law, and I'm only letting you because you'd probably be staked if I didn't—so I'll pay the bills."

He crossed his arms. "I don't need you to pay my bills." Nor did he want her to.

She tapped a finger against her lips, looking thoughtful and too damn cute again. "I know. My brother has been managing my accounts, but I can transfer them to you. I'll bring in the money. You manage it. We'll be a perfect team." She stepped up to the counter and ordered a cone of mint chocolate chip.

He couldn't imagine Jane Anderson wanting to be a part of anyone's team, though he had to admit the idea sounded appealing. He was starting to enjoy spending time with her. But it was enjoyment he didn't deserve. No, he and Jane could never be a team.

"What kind do you want, Ethan? Don't make me eat alone."

He sighed. "It has no nutritional value."

"It never has." She grinned and licked the blob of ice cream sitting atop her cone.

Heat pooled in his groin, and his dick hardened as the image of her tongue sliding across his skin flashed behind his eyes. How could he say no to her when she affected him this way? "Surprise me."

She placed the order and handed him a cone. "You look like a dark chocolate kind of guy. Deep and smooth, with just a little bit of a bite."

He took a lick, and creamy, sweet chocolate danced on his taste buds, making him shiver. Closing his eyes, he took another bite and savored the decadent sensation. He always drank warm blood. It had been ages since something cool had slid down his throat.

He opened his eyes to find Jane biting her lip, watching him with a fire in her eyes. Damn, he wanted her. He couldn't deny her allure, but he refused to give in. A happy life was not in the cards for him. Not after what he'd done to Vanessa.

He stiffened, stomping out of the ice cream shop and onto Decatur before he could drown in the depths of her gaze.

She hurried to catch up. "Did I say something wrong?"

"No." He stalked forward, tossing his half-eaten cone in a trash can.

"Why do you do that?"

He clenched his fists, continuing his march. "What do I do?"

"We've been together twenty-four-seven for two straight weeks. Every now and then, you start opening up...being *nice* to me, letting me know Ethan, and then, bam. The gates slam down, and Edward Cullen is back. What gives?" She jogged. "And slow down. I'm not as fast as you."

He whirled to face her. "You would be if you'd feed." If she would get her damn license he could be done with her and away from the temptation.

LICENSE TO BITE | 89

She flinched. "Yeah, well, I don't want to. And no one makes Jane Anderson do anything she doesn't want to do."

He lifted his hands, dropping them by his sides. "You're impossible."

"So are you."

A woman tripped on the curb in front of them, falling to her knees before her elbows scraped across the pavement. The coppery scent of fresh blood mixed with the warm, earthy tones of spiced rum, and despite his efforts, Ethan's fangs extended. He clamped his mouth shut and gripped Jane's arm as the woman stood and examined the blood dripping down her elbow. Surely the enticing aroma would do Jane in. Her fangs were probably fully extended as well. He had to get her away before she lunged for the woman.

Jane froze, her nose crinkling as the ice cream slipped from her grasp, splatting on the sidewalk. "Blood," she murmured before her eyes rolled back and she crumpled to the ground.

Without a second thought, he scooped her into his arms and marched her to his car parked in the lot near the river. Her eyes fluttered open as he positioned her in the passenger seat and buckled the seat belt around her.

"Oh, man. Sorry about that." She clutched her head.

He squatted beside the car. "This has gone on long enough. You need blood."

"I saw enough blood tonight, thank you."

He shook his head, frustration gnawing at his chest. "You need to consume it."

"Why am I in the car? Where are we going?"

He slammed the door and stomped around to the driver's side, yanking on the handle. "To see Sophie. Maybe she can talk some sense into you, because I am done, Jane."

Her mouth fell open. "Done? You can't be done."

"Your stubbornness is killing you and making me miserable in the process."

"I can't die, and you're already miserable." She inclined her chin.

"You're wasting away, and you *know* what the punishment will be if you don't get your license."

"Still can't get your girl to feed?" Gaston smirked as he approached.

If Ethan had been paying attention, he'd have sensed his sire's proximity, but he was so torn between his concern for Jane's health and his desire to choke her, he couldn't think of anything else. "Aside from force-feeding her, I don't know what else to do."

"Well, I bring two pieces of information. First, I want to tell Miss Jane that her request has been completed." He leaned down and looked at her in the car.

"Thank you, Gaston. You're the best." She smiled and laid her head back on the headrest, closing her eyes.

"She doesn't look well," Gaston said as he straightened.

"She's not. What was her request?"

He chuckled. "I'm not at liberty to divulge that information, my friend. Get her healthy, and then I'm sure she'll tell you."

He didn't have the strength nor the patience to argue. "What's the other thing?"

"Oh, yes. You've both been summoned by the Council. They want to see you tomorrow evening."

His heart sank. He couldn't let them see her in this condition. They'd probably stake him for being the crappiest sire in existence. "About what?" She had another week left on her permit. They didn't need to see her now.

"That I do not know, my friend, but I suggest you get some blood in her before you arrive. Neglect of your offspring is punishable by stake."

Every damn thing was punishable by stake these days. He said goodbye to Gaston, got in the driver's seat, and sped toward Esplanade Avenue to Sophie's rental house. Jane sagged into his side as he guided her up the front steps and banged on the door.

A few minutes later, Sophie's grumbling voice filtered through the wood. "I know y'all keep undead hours, but this human needs her beauty sleep." She swung open the door, and her eyes widened. "What happened to her?"

He scooped Jane into his arms and carried her into the living room, laying her on the sofa. "She passed out. A woman was bleeding, and I think this fasting is too much for her. I expected her to lunge toward the blood, but instead, she hit the ground."

Sophie darted into the kitchen and returned with a wet rag. "She hasn't told you why she won't drink blood?"

"No. Just that Jane Anderson refuses to do anything she doesn't want to do."

She tilted her head, giving him a sympathetic look. "She faints at the sight of it. Always has."

He paused, blinking a few times as her words sank in. "Please tell me you're kidding. A vampire who faints at the sight of blood?"

"I wish I were."

He dragged his hands down his face. No wonder she was so adamant about not learning to feed. Every time he'd tried to demonstrate, she'd turned her head the moment his fangs met flesh.

"We've been summoned to the Council tomorrow. I can't take her there in this condition, and, well…I'm worried about her health. Will you talk to her? She won't listen to me."

Sophie knelt beside the couch and dabbed the rag on Jane's head. "Listen, babe, you've got to drink some blood."

Jane shook her head. "Never."

"Look at you. You're a fucking *vampire* with a black belt in karate. You're a badass. An immortal. You don't want to live all eternity like this, do you? And, frankly…" She leaned closer to her ear and whispered, "You're shriveling up like a raisin. I think I see crow's feet."

"I can't do it, Soph. Will you get me some water? My throat's on fire."

Sophie sighed and stood, jerking her head toward the hallway before strutting to the back of the house.

Ethan followed. "What am I going to do? I can't stand to see her suffering like this, and if the Council finds out she refuses to feed, they'll stake us both for her incompetence."

"Okay, at first you had me believing you actually cared about her...until the incompetence line."

He rubbed his forehead. "I do care about her. More than I planned to." And wasn't that the devil's honest truth? No matter how infuriating the woman was, he was into her. *Really* into her.

"Can she hear us?" Sophie asked.

"Possibly."

"Come outside with me. I have a plan." She opened the back door and strutted onto the porch. "Can you drink blood not straight from a person? Like, can you put it in a cup?"

"Sure, but it's still blood. If she can't stomach it from the vein—"

She held up a hand. "Listen, Jane is stubborn as all get-out. She always has been, and she's used to getting what she wants."

He crossed his arms. "I hadn't noticed."

"Sometimes what Jane wants and what Jane needs aren't the same things. Then, you have to get creative."

"I'm listening."

"Can you get some blood? I don't want to know how, but can you bring some here?"

"Sure." The Blood Bank wasn't far, and he had a line of credit there. "I can get a pint or two."

"Great. However much you think she needs, put it in a Styrofoam cup with a lid and a straw. We're going to trick her."

"Do you think that will work?"

Sophie shrugged. "If she needs it that badly, she won't be able to stop once she starts, right?"

"I suppose she won't. It will instantly soothe her throat." But

Jane was smart. He couldn't see her being fooled easily. "If I bring her a random drink, she'll suspect."

"No, she won't. She trusts me. You get the blood, and I'll convince her to drink it."

He nodded. "Give me half an hour."

Jane squeezed her eyes shut against the overhead lights and nestled deeper into the sofa. If only the damn thing would open up and swallow her whole, putting her out of her misery. That ice cream didn't help her throat a bit, and now Ethan was mad at her for no apparent reason. Her head pounded, and she was so damn thirsty, she could have drunk the entire Mississippi River.

"All right." Sophie shuffled into the room. "I sent that man of yours out to get you a miracle cure. It's the only thing that will help you."

"Miracle cure?" She opened her eyes and squinted. "Can you turn off the lights?"

"Sure." Sophie flipped the switch and turned on an end table lamp instead. "Remember the drink we had that cured our hangovers?"

"Oh yeah." She'd forgotten how much better that one little drink made her feel. But that was a hangover; this was a dire need for a substance she couldn't stand to look at, much less ingest. "Do you think it will help?"

"It's worth a try."

"Okay." She pushed to sitting, folding her legs beneath her. "Is he still mad at me?"

Sophie sank onto the cushion next to her. "Why would he be mad at you?"

"I don't know. We were talking and getting along, and then he just shut down. I don't know what I did."

Sophie grinned. "He's not mad. Frustrated, but not mad."

"What are you smiling at?"

She folded her hands in her lap. "You care."

"So?"

"You normally don't give a damn if someone gets mad at you, but you care about Ethan, and he cares about you. It's so cute to watch this little relationship blooming."

Jane shook her head. "He only cares so he can get me a biting license and be done with me."

"That's not true." A knock sounded on the door. "He went all the way to the French Quarter to get your miracle cure. He likes you."

Sophie opened the door, and Ethan came in carrying a Styrofoam cup. He handed it to Sophie before sinking into a chair and fisting his hands in his lap. Always fisting.

"Here you go." Sophie passed the cup to Jane. "One miracle cure to remedy your woes."

Jane examined the cup, plain white with a dark red straw. "Did it come from the same bar? It might not work otherwise."

Sophie looked over her shoulder at Ethan. "You got it from the place we talked about, right?"

His fists clenched tighter. "I did precisely what you told me to do."

"It's exactly what you need, hon. Drink up." Sophie pushed the cup toward Jane's face.

"Okay, okay. Here goes nothing." She touched the straw to her lips and took a giant sip, hoping the first gulp would be enough to extinguish the fire in her throat. She cringed at the metallic taste—like someone had dropped an entire roll of pennies in her drink—but as soon as the liquid slid down her throat, the inferno in her esophagus cooled like a glacier sliding over the flames.

She knew this was blood. It couldn't be anything but. And her mind wanted her to choke, to throw the cup across the room and curse them both for tricking her. But her body took over, instinct forcing her to chug the entire contents of the container.

"Whoa. Slow down and breathe." Sophie put a hand on her shoulder.

"She technically doesn't need to," Ethan said.

Sophie's eyes held concern as Jane sat up straight and set the cup on the coffee table. "How do you feel?"

Jane looked at Ethan. Apprehension etched lines into his forehead, and his fists were clenched so tight, his pale skin had gone completely white around his knuckles.

She rolled her neck, running a hand over her throat because she couldn't believe how instantly it had healed. But the most miraculous thing? She'd just ingested sixteen ounces of human blood, and she didn't feel the slightest bit lightheaded.

Scooting to the edge of the couch, she slowly stood, expecting her normal reaction to overcome her any second and send her crumbling to the floor. It didn't happen. She felt fine. Better than fine—she felt amazing.

"You both think you're real smart for tricking me like that, don't you? I know that was blood in that cup." She fisted her hands on her hips, fighting her smile and glaring at them both.

Ethan's hands relaxed on his knees, his entire demeanor shifting as his posture softened. One corner of his mouth tugged into an almost-grin—the closest thing she'd seen to a smile on the man since the day he turned her—and he rose to his feet. "Technically, Sophie did the tricking. I merely acquired the provisions."

Sophie laughed. "'Acquired the provisions.' He's funny."

"He's definitely something." She smiled at Ethan, and when he looked back at her, she got the overwhelming urge to throw herself into his arms and show him just how much she appreciated his efforts to keep her functioning. Instead, she hugged Sophie. "Thanks for everything."

"He's good for you," she whispered back.

"I know." She shuffled to the door. "Well, I guess this settles the license issue. I can drink blood from a straw, so I'll never have to bite anyone."

Ethan's almost-smile faded. "I have no issues with buying you blood. I keep a supply in my fridge anyway, but the law states everyone within one hundred miles of a city must have a license…whether you're biting or not. The Council has every right to stake you if you don't."

Jane took his hand. "Let me worry about the Council. Right now, we need to get home. I've got something to show you."

CHAPTER NINE

Relief flooded Ethan's body, the sensation making him lightheaded as he drove up Dauphine toward his home in Bywater. Small Creole cottages in pastel shades lined the narrow street, and his Ford lurched as he hit two potholes in a row.

Jane bubbled with excitement in the seat next to him. What she could possibly want to show him that had her this worked up, he couldn't fathom, but seeing her happy…and healthy again…sent a zing through his chest, sparking life in his undead heart.

If it weren't for that stupid law, and especially that damn British constable, Jane might actually stand a chance of survival. She may have had the upper hand with people in human politics, but she was clueless when it came to the inner workings of the supernatural world.

"I have an idea," he said as he made a right on Gallier. "Gourds."

Jane gave him a quizzical look. "You mean, like pumpkins? What about them?"

"Yes. Yellow squash would probably be a good place to start, though. Or zucchini."

She laughed. "What on Earth are you talking about?"

"To practice biting. The consistency is similar. The flesh of the gourd would have a similar give, and you could—"

"I don't need to learn biting techniques. I can buy my meals from the bank. Or, rather, I can give you the money, and you can buy them. I doubt I could step foot inside the place. Do they have the blood on display? Like bags hanging from hooks in a refrigerated case? Or is it kept in a tank?" She shivered. "Never mind. Don't answer that."

He reached for her hand across the console. "I know you think you can convince the Council to bend the law for you, but…"

She placed her free hand on top of his. "I *know* I can."

He bit back a growl of frustration. "Okay, but even if you do convince them, will you humor me? Let me teach you the technique just in case the situation ever arises where you might be forced to?"

She fake-smiled and tapped her canine tooth. "I don't have fangs."

"You can still learn." He squeezed her hand and slipped from her grasp as he rolled to a stop and turned off the engine.

Jane twisted in her seat to face him. "Would it make you happy if I did?"

"Very."

"Okay. Gourds it is, but let's start with zucchini. I don't like yellow squash unless it's fried." She opened the car door. "Now, come on. I can't wait for you to see this."

He followed as she pranced up the walk, bouncing on her toes as she waited for him to let her inside. Damn, she was cute when she was excited.

"What are you so worked up about?"

"You'll see. Open the door." She pushed it open the moment the lock disengaged and zipped inside at vampire speed—finally. Whoever donated the pint she consumed must've been a heavy coffee drinker. He stepped through the threshold and closed the door.

"Are you ready?" If she got any more excited, she'd explode.

"As I'll ever be."

She giggled and flipped a switch on the wall…a switch he was certain had never been there before. Machinery hummed to life, and blackout screens lowered over all the windows, locking into place in unison as a metal barrier rose up from the floor, blocking the door. She'd equipped his home with the most state-of-the-art vampire protection system on the market. The simple systems cost a fortune, but this…

He stepped toward a window and ran his finger along the rubber seal. This system was built for fortresses. For royalty. For…

"Well?" She clasped her hands together in front of her chest and looked at him with wide, wondrous eyes. "What do you think?"

"I…" His jaw trembled, so he snapped his mouth shut. It was too much. How could he accept such an extravagant gift when all he'd done for her was damn her to darkness?

"It's great, isn't it? Now we don't have to sleep in the attic."

"I can't accept this, Jane."

Her smile faded. "Why not? It's the least I could do to show my appreciation."

He raked a hand through his hair. "Your appreciation for what? I damned you."

"You saved my life."

"By turning you into a monster."

She crossed her arms. "We are not monsters, Edward. Now take a hike and bring Ethan back. I like him a lot better."

"How much did all of this cost?"

"It doesn't matter, and anyway…it's not just for you. Jane Anderson does not belong in a dusty old attic."

"That's true. You don't." Leave it to Jane to turn his pity

party around and defuse all his arguments by making it about her.

"So…what do you really think?"

"I…" This woman never ceased to amaze him. "I love it. Thank you."

"There's more," she sang as she took his hand and led him down the hall to the master bedroom. "Your twenty-five-year-old mattress was full of dust, so I bought you a new one. The sheets were toast too, so I got a new set. Emerald to match your eyes. If you don't like it, I can have Sophie return it tomorrow."

"It's perfect." It seemed his initial impression of Jane had been all wrong. She wasn't the selfish, entitled princess he'd originally pegged her for. She was thoughtful, and while she still talked way too much, he'd grown fond of the sound of her voice and the little blast of electricity he felt every time she touched him.

"Oh. My. Goat cheese." She parked her hands on her hips and cocked her head. "You're smiling."

"I am not." He tried to flatten his lips into a neutral expression, but it was no use. The woman had gotten to him.

"Yes, you are." Her grin could have burned the entire coven to ash. "Does this mean brooding Edward is gone for good, and Ethan is here to stay?"

He chuckled. "I'm not making any promises."

"I hope you'll find reasons to smile more often. It looks good on you." She looked into his eyes, and he looked into hers, and that hollow spot in his chest that had been there since he removed the mating mark started to ache.

"Oh, I almost forgot." She grabbed his hand and tugged him to the next room. "I know I get on your nerves, and since you're not allowed to get rid of me during waking hours…" She pushed open the door to reveal a queen-sized bed with a deep purple duvet. "I figured I'd give you a little space at bedtime at least."

"But that's the only time you're tolerable." He winked.

She flipped her hair behind her shoulders. "I'm growing on you. Admit it."

"Maybe a little." Or a lot. He was getting used to having her around, that was for sure. There hadn't been a dull moment since he turned her.

Her face went serious. "So, this meeting with the Council tomorrow. Are we in trouble?"

"I honestly have no idea, but it's probably best if you let me do the talking." She opened her mouth to protest, but he lifted a finger to quiet her...and it actually worked. "Stay silent in the beginning, until we see what the issue is. Once they've said their piece, then you can turn on your charm, okay?"

She nodded. "Deal. Well, I can feel that the sun will be up soon. We better get some rest."

He stilled, opening his senses to the atmosphere. Sunrise wasn't for another half-hour, but young vampires could barely keep their eyes open during early daylight hours. She'd be dragged down into the death sleep shortly after morning broke.

Moving toward her, he opened his arms, and she stepped into them as if she belonged in his embrace. "Thank you, Jane."

She hugged him tightly and stepped away, a look of uncertainty clouding her eyes. "You're welcome. See you tomorrow." Slipping inside the bedroom, she closed the door, leaving him alone in the hall.

Alone. It was all he'd wanted since the night she woke up as a vampire, but now that his treasured silence had returned, it was deafening.

He shuffled to his bedroom and stripped down to his boxer briefs, something he hadn't been able to do since he met Jane. Lifting the blanket, he slid beneath the sheets and stared at the ceiling fan hanging stagnant above him.

Ten minutes later, a soft knock sounded, and Jane hesitated in his doorway. She wore pale pink flannel boxer shorts and a cream-colored tank top nearly the same color as her skin.

He rose onto his elbows. "Something wrong, princess?"

She bit her bottom lip and padded to the foot of the bed. "This whole being *dead to the world* thing is scary alone. I've never done it without you."

The vulnerability in her eyes nearly tore him in two. So Jane Anderson wasn't invincible after all. He pulled the sheets down. "Want to join me?"

"Do you mind?"

He shrugged. "I've gotten used to falling asleep with you too. Though I better warn you, I'm only wearing my underwear."

A tiny smile tilted her lips. "I promise to behave myself." She hopped into bed and snuggled under the covers, turning on her side to face him. "Can I ask you a personal question?"

He rolled over to face her. "Ask me anything."

"How did Vanessa die?"

He closed his eyes and chewed the inside of his cheek. Why did she have to bring up his past when he was just starting to enjoy the present? He tried to roll onto his back, but she caught his hand, clutching it tightly in hers.

"Don't shut down on me. Please, I want to know you."

With a long exhale, he opened his eyes and met her pleading gaze. "It was my fault. I killed her."

Her mouth dropped open, horrified. "Did you drain her?"

"No. It happened before I was turned. We got in an argument, and..." He shook his head. She didn't really want to hear this.

She took his other hand, lacing their fingers together. "What happened? What was the argument about?"

"It was Halloween. She wanted me to go to this costume party with her dressed as a Thing One and Thing Two. Blue wigs and all. It was a couple's costume, but I refused to wear it. It was ridiculous, and I don't do costumes to begin with, but I... I should have. I should have just worn the damn thing."

She scooted closer until their arms touched from hands to

elbows. "You don't strike me as a costume-wearing kind of man."

"I told her the only way I'd go to the party was without the costume. She agreed, but we argued the whole time. We started doing shots, trying to outdrink each other." His jaw clenched. "It was so stupid. I don't know what we were thinking. What *I* was thinking."

"Did you have to Uber home?"

"Uber didn't exist back then. When it was time to leave, she insisted on driving. I should have taken the keys, called a taxi, or... My tolerance was so much higher than hers, but I was so sick of fighting, I let her get behind the wheel." His gaze lost focus, and he stared blankly at their entwined hands. "We ran off the road and hit a tree. I survived. She didn't."

"I'm so sorry."

"If I'd made her let me drive. Hell, if I'd worn the stupid costume, it wouldn't have happened. She would still be alive."

"Maybe. Or maybe if *you'd* driven, you'd both be dead now. You don't know."

"Death would be better than the past twenty-five years of my life," he mumbled.

"Don't say that. You don't mean that." She tightened her grip on his hands. "Alcohol messes with your head, believe me. You both made bad decisions, but you couldn't have known what would happen. You can't keep beating yourself up for a past you can't change."

"I know. Believe me, I've thought about it for twenty-five years, but it's easier to hate myself for it. I haven't let myself really live since she died." He met her gaze. "Until now."

"It's been long enough, don't you think? Don't you want to move on? Let it go?"

"I do. I am trying. I just haven't had anything to live for until now."

She pressed her lips together, lowering her gaze, not taking the hint, not hearing what he wasn't able to say. "I know you wanted me to be Vanessa. I'm sorry I'm not her."

"I'm not." He lifted her chin with a finger. "Sometimes, the things we want aren't the same as what we need. I'm glad you're you, Jane Anderson. You are exactly what I need."

"Aren't you sweet?" She leaned toward him and pressed a kiss to his cheek.

His heart thumped, and she lingered there, slowly pulling back, her nose gliding along his skin until her lips were a scant half-inch from his mouth. Her gaze flicked to his, and she swallowed hard, hesitating as if asking his permission.

He tilted his head, brushing his bottom lip against her top, and that was all the invitation she needed. Reaching a hand to his face, she crushed her mouth to his. It had been so long since he'd kissed a woman, he was afraid he'd forget what to do, but the moment Jane's tongue slipped between his lips, it all came back to him.

His fangs extended, a normal reaction to sexual attraction— or so Gaston had assured him—and his dick hardened like a steel rod. Jane moaned, gripping the back of his head to tug him closer, but then she pulled away, gasping as if she'd lost her breath.

"It's morning." She touched her lips with trembling fingers. "I can't stay awake."

"Then go to sleep, princess. I'll be here."

She smiled, and, brushing one more gentle kiss to his lips, she rolled over, snuggling her back against his front, his rock-hard dick pressing against her ass. "Oh, my. I'm sorry I'm going to miss out on that."

He chuckled. "You're not the only one. Sweet dreams, sweet Jane."

She yawned. "See ya later, alligator." Then she went still as a corpse, the death sleep overtaking her.

CHAPTER TEN

E than sat on the sofa, staring at the blank TV screen while last night's kiss played on a loop in his mind. He'd been awake for nearly an hour before Jane began to stir, but he'd only allowed himself to remain by her side for ten minutes before he rose and dressed for the evening.

He'd caught a glimpse of her scurrying down the hall to the shower, but she hadn't emerged from her bedroom since she entered it half an hour ago.

Her Styrofoam cup, filled with blood, sat on the coffee table, and as footsteps sounded from the hallway, Ethan rose to his feet.

She appeared in the living room wearing black leggings and a long, burgundy sweater with a deep V-neck that revealed the delicate curve of her neck and the sweet swell of her breasts. She looked good enough to eat.

"Good morning...er...evening, I guess." She tousled her dark hair and smiled softly. "Sleep well?"

"Like the dead." He offered her the cup. "Breakfast?"

"Thanks." She shuffled into the living room and took the cup from his hand. Pausing, she grimaced and stared at the straw. "I know I need this, but my mind won't let me."

He knew the feeling. "Pretend it's vodka and tomato juice. Your miracle cure."

She chuckled and lifted the cup in a toast. "Breakfast of champions." Pressing the straw to her lips, she took a quick sip, which turned into a huge gulp, and within seconds, she'd downed the entire contents. "Damn, that's good."

His tongue slipped out to moisten his lips against his will, and her gaze flicked to his mouth.

"Listen…about last night." She set the cup on the table. "I'm sorry?"

He cocked his head. "Why did you say it like a question?"

She shrugged. "I guess because I'm really not. But it seemed like the thing to say in a situation like this."

"What situation?"

"I don't know." She flung her arms in the air and dropped them at her sides. "Why are you making this hard on me? We kissed last night, and now we have to talk about it, right? That's how these things go."

He fought a grin. She was adorable when she was flustered. "So, you're not sorry you kissed me?"

She crossed her arms, cocking a brow. "That depends on how you feel about it."

"I enjoyed it, personally. Quite a lot, actually."

She giggled and glanced at his pants. "I remember. Vlad wanted to come out and play."

He opened his mouth to respond, but as her words sank in, he paused. "Did you just name my dick Vlad?"

"It's fitting. If the death sleep hadn't pulled me under, I might have let him impale me."

He shook his head, a deep chuckle vibrating in his chest. "Oh, Jane. What am I going to do with you?"

"I can think of a few things." She bit her lip and gazed at him for a moment. "We're still cool then? Things aren't going to get awkward now?"

"I really hope not."

"Then why do you still look worried?" She pointed at his face. "Your brow is pinched, and you keep clenching and unclenching your fists."

He shoved his hands in his pockets. Damn, this woman was perceptive.

"Are you worried about the Council?"

"I am. The only reason I can think that they would call us back would be about your biter's license. We haven't done anything illegal…that I'm aware of."

She raised her hands. "Don't look at me like that. I haven't left your side since I died." She chewed her bottom lip, her face scrunching the way it always did when she was deep in thought. "Do you trust me, Ethan?"

"Of course." His answer came without hesitation, taking him by surprise. He did trust Jane. With every fiber of his being.

She smiled. "I trust you too. So get the Council warmed up, get them to give me *permission* to speak." She stuck her finger in her mouth, making a gagging motion. "Then I'll handle it from there. My ability to schmooze will amaze you."

"If you try to use even a smidge of glamour on them, they'll sense it. Using glamour against the Council is punishable by stake."

She rolled her eyes. "Cheese and crackers, everything is *punishable by stake* with you guys. You need a woman on the Council. That's what you need. How do you get elected? I'll make a run for it, and being a vampire will be fun again."

He chuckled. "You have to be at least fifty years dead to even be considered."

"Damn. Well, it's never too early to start campaigning."

———

Ethan rolled his neck, attempting to stretch the tension from his shoulders, but as soon as he stopped, they crept back toward his ears. He sat on the sofa in the sitting-room of the coven's headquarters, holding on to Jane's hand as if she were his lifeline. If he'd done something to get her into trouble, he'd never forgive himself.

"Relax." She put her free hand on top of his. "We've got this."

"You underestimate the power and temperament of the Council."

"You underestimate the power and temperament of Jane Anderson. We're going to be fine."

"I hope you're right."

"I got you to smile yesterday. That in itself is a feat worthy of recognition."

The door creaked open, and Jeffrey, a squat man with blond hair and a bushy mustache, stepped through. "You may enter."

Ethan's heart crept into his throat. His entire death, he'd kept his head down, stayed out of politics, and minded his own business. He rarely socialized with anyone, including other vampires, and he'd managed to stay out of trouble because of it. Until Jane, he'd only been summoned to the Council twice—once to get his biter's permit, and then again for his license.

He'd heard stories of vampires who'd been randomly called before the Council, and holy Satan's balls, he hoped they were only stories.

With Jane's hand clutched tightly in his, they crept down the hallway and entered the Council's chamber. All five members donned their robes and sat perched atop their thrones. Off to the side, Watson, the British constable, sat in his own ornate chair, like a little kid's version of a throne. Who did this guy think he was?

"What's with the man-child?" Jane's voice echoed in his head.

"I think he wants the Magistrate's job. How did you send me your thoughts? I haven't taught you to do that."

Her eyes sparkled. *"I'm full of surprises."*

"That you are."

"There's that smile, again. It really does look good on you."

They stopped in the center of the room, and Ethan lowered his head in a bow, squeezing Jane's hand to remind her to do the same. Thankfully, she followed his lead. The Magistrate shuffled through a stack of papers as if he'd lost the one he needed.

"They don't have their files digitized?" Jane's voice drifted through his mind.

"I told you they're old school here. Now stop thought-talking before you get us both staked."

She laughed softly. *"I can't wait to shake things up in this place."*

"Ethan Devereaux," the Magistrate's voice boomed.

He swallowed, willing his heart to dislodge from his throat and settle in his chest where it belonged. "Yes, Your Honor?"

"It has come to my attention that your recently-turned subject belongs to the Governor of Texas."

Jane opened her mouth, sucking in a breath to protest the Magistrate's use of the word "belong," Ethan assumed. He squeezed her hand and sent her a mental message: *"Let it go, Elsa."* She pursed her lips.

"She is the Governor's daughter, Your Honor. A fact I was unaware of at the time." His heart willingly fell from his throat, plopping into his stomach. That's what this summoning was about? That Ethan turned someone of high importance, so now *he* was in trouble?

Constable Watson wiggled in his chair like an overly excited puppy. The bastard probably carried pickets inside his trench coat just in case he got the chance to stake someone.

"Turning people in her position of power is…" The Magistrate glanced at Watson. "It's frowned upon."

The constable shot to his feet. "The Supernatural World Order has decreed it can't be done without filing the proper paperwork first. You've committed a crime, Mr. Devereaux. It's time to pay the price." He brushed back his jacket, and sure enough, a set of stakes were attached to the underside.

"Now hold on a second." Jane slipped from his grasp and

strutted forward. "He saved my life; how can that be considered a crime? Don't y'all have some kind of Good Samaritan law or something?" She glared at Watson.

"Calm down, or we'll both be staked."

She glanced at Ethan. *"Neither one of us is getting staked on my watch."*

The Magistrate scanned Jane's registration papers. "She has a good point." He passed them down the line of Council members. "She'd been struck by a car and would have died otherwise."

The men murmured amongst themselves, and Ethan wished it mattered that he held his breath. The pain in his chest would have been a nice distraction from his impending death.

"Honestly, gentlemen, Ethan did us all a favor," Jane said. "The state of Louisiana wouldn't want to have the blood of the Texas Governor's daughter on its hands. Imagine the drama that would have caused. The humans owe you one now, if you ask me."

"Go on." The Magistrate leaned forward.

"You've got a bargaining chip now, one you can use with both Louisiana and Texas. I absolutely love being a vampire, so the next time one of ours gets into a tiff with the humans, you can remind them that you saved my life, and I'm thankful for it. I know my father. He'd rather have me around as a vampire than buried six feet under."

"Are you sure about that?" Ethan asked in Jane's mind.

"Absolutely, and I'll tell him everything when the time is right. You'll see."

Ethan watched in awe as Jane schmoozed the men in the room—all but Watson, of course—convincing them Ethan's turning her hadn't broken a law he wasn't even aware existed. By the time she finished her speech, they were all nodding in agreement.

The Magistrate rapped his gavel on the table in front of him. "Ethan Devereaux, you are acquitted of all charges and are to be commended for your efforts to save this woman's life."

The constable shot to his feet. "Preposterous! What's next? Will you allow someone to turn the President? I cannot let this go unpunished."

"You have no authority here." The Magistrate's pupils narrowed to slits, his irises glowing red. "You're nothing but a messenger for the Emperor of the SWO, who allows his Magistrates to interpret the laws and hand out punishment as they see fit."

Watson sank into his baby throne. "She should at least be sent back to Texas where she belongs. This coven doesn't need to stir up any more issues with the humans."

"You want me here, Magistrate." Jane turned on the charm. "Think of it. The Governor's daughter, a vampire, willingly living in Louisiana. I could be a liaison...a bridge between the states as well as the human and vampire governments." She flipped her hair behind her shoulder. "I'm the best thing that's ever happened to supernatural New Orleans."

Ethan tensed, waiting for the Magistrate to unleash his wrath at her statement, but the man simply nodded, his lips curving as he considered her words.

"You may be right, young lady." The old man winked— actually winked—at Ethan. "I like her."

"You have good reason to, sir." He clasped his hands behind his back and let Jane continue her magic.

"I have a few ideas I'd like to run by you while I have your ear, sir." She leaned forward and lowered her voice. "But I'd rather not discuss it in front of outsiders." She nodded toward the constable.

"Give us the room, Watson," the Magistrate said.

"But—"

"I said leave." He hissed as Watson cinched his coat closed and scurried out the door. "Good call getting rid of the weasel, Ms. Anderson. He was getting on my nerves."

Her smile could have lit an entire city block. She went on to propose an idea for a nightclub where patrons paid a cover charge to be bitten by vampires. "Everyone knows there are vampires in New Orleans, but most people—myself included, until I met Ethan—think they're just humans with a few screws loose who like to play pretend and drink real blood."

She shuddered. "Of course, our vampires will be the real deal, and they can use their glamour to make it a pleasant… possibly erotic…experience for the donors. I haven't worked out all the details, but people will be lined up around the block to experience a bit of the darker side of the Big Easy."

The idea made sense, but when had she thought all this up? It was the first Ethan had heard of it.

"I'm happy to oversee the operations…behind the scenes. I know how to throw a party. Think of all the revenue it would bring in. You'd have more bargaining power with the humans and…whoever else you bargain with."

"It's a fabulous idea." The Magistrate clapped his hands. "Your new subject is proving herself indispensable, Mr. Devereaux. Good choice."

"Thank you, sir. She is pretty amazing."

"Wonderful. Oh, Ms. Anderson, since you're here, would you like to test for your biter's license and save yourself a trip? It's the least I can offer for your advantageous ideas."

She pressed her lips together and looked at Ethan. He lifted his brow and spoke in her mind: *"Turn the charm back on, princess. They've been staking people for this for weeks already."*

Straightening her spine, she lifted her chin and explained her issue with blood. "I'm sure if Ethan had known, he wouldn't have turned me, but he didn't, so here we are. I have plenty of income to buy what I need from your bank, so I'll be contributing to society monetarily. But there's simply no way I could bite a person, Your Honor. Not anytime soon. Would you be so kind as to give me an extension on my permit?"

The Magistrate steepled his fingers, glancing about the room as if making sure Watson didn't sneak back inside. "Three weeks, just to spite that little shit, and you mention this to no one. If word gets out that I've gone soft on you, that weasel will report me to the SWO and have me removed."

"Thank you, sir. I won't utter a word of it. New Orleans is lucky to have you as a leader, and I would never do anything to jeopardize your position." She glanced over her shoulder at Ethan and winked.

The Magistrate nodded. "This city has thrived under my rule for the last hundred years. Then that weasel Watson shows up with his Supernatural World Order mandates, and all hell breaks loose. He's staked four of my people already."

She gasped, placing a hand on her chest. "A tragedy."

"Indeed."

Wow. This two-week-dead vampire was talking with the Magistrate like they were old friends. *The Magistrate.* The man who struck fear into the hearts of every vampire in the city... except for maybe Gaston. He was too drunk to be afraid. Never in Ethan's twenty-five years as a vampire had he seen someone take command with her superiors like this.

She was fierce, intelligent, incredibly savvy, and insanely beautiful on top of it all. Vlad had stood up and taken notice. It was time Ethan did too.

The Magistrate dismissed them, and as they exited the coven headquarters, thunder clapped from above. A static charge built in the air, and ominous dark clouds gathered in the night sky.

His elation at their—at Jane's—accomplishment quickly tumbled into darkness, his mood growing grimmer than the brothers themselves. They had to get home, out of the storm.

CHAPTER ELEVEN

Jane followed Ethan up the front steps and waited as he unlocked the door. He'd been quiet on the way home, nervously glancing at the sky as if he were afraid it would open up and swallow him whole. No doubt, he was in shock at the way she'd handled the Council tonight. He'd doubted her, but Jane had grown up in politics; she knew how to stroke egos. Vampires were no different than men in that arena.

He fumbled with the key, dropping it on the porch and cursing before picking it up and jabbing it into the lock.

"Are you okay?" She put her hand on his arm, and he tensed.

"Yeah. Just want to get inside before the rain starts."

She laughed. "Don't tell me we'll melt. That's just witches, right?"

Lightning flashed in the distance, and thunder boomed as he threw the door open and marched inside. "No one melts in the rain, Jane."

She ignored his irritated tone and followed him into the living room as rain fell from the sky. "We were brilliant in there tonight. What did you think about my idea for the vampire bar? I came up with it on the fly, but I think it could really work. I won't be able to travel for my blog much, so I'll need to supplement my income. I could totally run a night club, as long as I don't have to watch anyone actually biting people. I'd call the evening a success, wouldn't you?"

His hands curled into fists like they always did when he wasn't happy—which was often. "You only got a three-week extension on your permit. You still have to get over your aversion to blood."

"Oh, pish." She waved her hand dismissively. "I'll get it extended indefinitely. I didn't want to push too far tonight. Don't worry."

"Whatever you say." He flipped the switch to close the light-blocking blinds and plopped onto the sofa, his expression going from grim to confused and back again.

She turned the switch back up, raising the blinds. "Sunrise isn't for another three hours. Let's enjoy the storm."

"I do not enjoy storms." He shot to his feet and hit the switch again, sending the blinds back down.

"What's not to love about them? The energy in the air alone is fantastic, and I adore the sound of rain falling on the roof, rapping against the windows. It's so relaxing." She waited for him to step away from the switch before she hit it again.

"This is my house, and I want them closed," he growled before tapping the switch and covering it with his hand.

"Oh, wow." Jane raised her hands. "I see how it is. It's your house, and you want the blinds *that I had installed* closed. The blinds you wouldn't even have if it weren't for me."

His eyes softened. "Look, Jane, it's been a long and tedious night. Can we not do this right now?"

She crossed her arms. "Not do what? Talk about the fact that I saved your ass tonight, and you won't even let me listen to the rain?"

"I just need some peace and quiet."

What the hell was his problem? "Oh, I'll give you peace and quiet. If you want to live your death like your stuffy, dusty, boring old attic, you go right ahead…but I don't want any part of it." She flung open the door.

He sighed, resigned. "Where are you going, Jane?"

"To dance in the rain." She marched outside and slammed the door behind her.

Peace. That man wouldn't know peace if it bit him on his cold, hard, very enticing, undead ass. And to think she'd actually allowed herself to fall for him, to *like* his uptight personality. *You've gone insane, Jane. That's all there is to it. Becoming a vampire has corrupted your mind.*

No more. She strutted onto the sidewalk, letting the downpour soak her to the bone. Tilting her head toward the sky, she closed her eyes and just *felt*. The fat droplets splattered on her cheeks and rolled down the contours of her face before sliding onto her neck, washing away her worries, as her mother liked to say.

The thought warmed her soul. Her fondest memory of her mom was dancing in the rain when she was five years old, splashing in the puddles and not having a care in the world. Mr. Broody McBroody Pants wasn't the only one who'd lost a loved one. Even after her mother passed, Jane still enjoyed a good thunderstorm, because it reminded her of simpler times. Of love and laughter.

Something she'd never get from Ethan Devereaux. She'd have to inform Gaston that the stake wedged up Ethan's ass had become a permanent fixture. She'd managed to wiggle it loose, but he seemed to like it right where it was. Another meeting with the Magistrate was in order. If she could get them to extend her biter's permit indefinitely, maybe she could get them to free her from Edward Cullen too. This vampire gig was easy peasy. She didn't *need* a mentor.

The front door opened, and Ethan appeared in the doorway. He hesitated there, looking up at the sky, shaking his head slightly. Jane ignored him and held her arms out to her sides, spinning in a circle before kicking her boot through a puddle, sending muddy water splashing across the walk in a wave.

He leaned against the door jamb, silently watching her until the weight of his gaze became too much to bear. She stopped her dance, parking her hands on her hips and returning the stare. He didn't budge, didn't open his mouth to speak, but if he wanted a standoff, he'd better have his big boy britches on. Jane was the queen of the silent treatment, believe it or not.

She moistened her lips and cocked a brow as his gaze fell to her mouth. His lips twitched before he pressed them together hard and looked into her eyes.

"It was storming the night Vanessa died. Rain has put me in a bad mood ever since." His eyes held pain and guilt, and her heart softened into mush.

"It's been twenty-five years. It's time to stop beating yourself up over it."

"I know. I'm sorry." He uncrossed his arms and let his hands dangle at his sides. No fists. "I'm ready to move on."

"Prove it. Come dance with me."

"Jane…"

"I'm a master of words, Ethan, and they go a long way. But real emotional connections between people happen because of actions. You can't change the past, but you can decide, right now, to change your future."

"It's forty degrees outside. If you were human, you'd be freezing."

"Well, it's a good thing someone turned me into a vampire." She held out her arms. "Dance with me."

His lips curved into a half-smile, and he stepped off the porch into the rain. "There's no music."

Thunder clapped in the distance, and she took his left hand in her right, resting her other hand on his shoulder. "Nature is its own symphony."

They swayed softly, and she inched closer as he slid his arm tighter around her waist. "Tip your head back," she said, and he obeyed. "Let the rain wash away your guilt, your pain. Make the decision to let it all go and be in the moment. To live your undead life in the best way a vampire can. To—"

"Hey, Jane?" He opened his eyes and locked his gaze with hers.

"Yes?"

"Shut up and kiss me."

"Now that's what I'm talking about." She crushed her mouth to his.

His lips were cold...because he was dead...but not in an icky corpse kind of way. Probably because she was dead too, and they were the same temperature. Despite the lack of warmth, they were soft, and as he coaxed hers apart with his tongue, she went all in, pressing her soft curves against his rock-hard... *Wow. And I thought his muscles were big.*

She couldn't help herself; she had to feel it. Working her hand between their sopping wet bodies, she grabbed a handful of cock, and sweet Satan's balls, it was *way* more than a handful.

He sucked in a sharp breath as a deep, sexy growl rumbled in his chest. "Ready to be impaled?"

"Fuck, yes."

He scooped her into his arms and carried her into the bedroom, tossing her on the bed like she weighed no more than a bean bag. She wiggled out of her shirt and threw her bra aside as he peeled off his clothes. The button on her jeans unfastened easily, but wet denim was like shrink wrap on a curvy woman, and she flopped on the mattress, lifting her hips and trying desperately to get the damn things off...to no avail.

Ethan stood there in his boxer briefs, Vlad straining against the fabric, and he smiled. Cheese-and-crackers, that man had a gorgeous smile. If her clothes had been dry, they'd have fallen off on their own. "Need me to help?"

"If you want access to the goods, you're gonna have to." She lay back and lifted her hips while he worked the fabric down her legs.

"Fuck, Jane, you're gorgeous." His eyes devoured her. He hadn't even touched her yet, but she felt like he'd caressed every inch with a simple sweep of his gaze.

"I like to think I can rock these curves."

"They're delicious." He licked his lips, and her center went slick. Good goat cheese, the man might make her come before he laid a finger on her.

Sitting up, she yanked his underwear down, freeing his dick, and man, oh man, had she hit the jackpot. She gave him a lick from base to tip…all nine inches of him…and sucked him into her mouth. He groaned and gripped her shoulders, letting her get in a good three or four strokes of her tongue before he pushed her onto her back and dove for her sweet spot.

Sweet baby Hades the man knew how to lick, but Jane hadn't gotten enough of his dick. She wiggled free from his grasp, using her vampire strength to toss him onto his backside so she could go back for more.

He was having none of it, lifting her and putting her right where he wanted her, but Jane knew a thing or two about wrestling. They rolled about, grappling—in an oh so sexy way—for dominance, until she got him on his back where her mouth could reach him and his mouth could reach her, and devil have mercy, that man had a way with his tongue.

He worked her into a frenzy while she sucked him, and as the most powerful orgasm she'd ever experienced exploded inside her, she was overcome with the urge to bite. His dick was in her mouth, so she released him and leaned over, taking in a mouthful of duvet and biting hard as she screamed.

With that need satiated, she sat up, removing herself from his face, and flopped onto her back. "Quick question. Do we have to worry about pregnancy or diseases?"

He chuckled. "We're dead. What do you think?"

"I think you need to give me everything you've got."

"Are you sure you can handle this much man?" He winked.

"Try me."

He climbed on top of her, filling her with one swift thrust, and stars danced before her eyes.

"Holy fuck."

He groaned. "It does feel a bit like a religious experience, doesn't it?"

"Take me to church, baby. Yes!"

He pumped his hips, and it didn't take long before another orgasm coiled in her core, ready to unleash like a river bursting through a dam. His rhythm increased, and as he shuddered inside her, her entire world flipped upside down and turned inside out. This man had a magic cock.

They lay still for a few moments—not catching their breath, since neither of them was breathing—but holding each other as Jane tried to figure out what the hell just happened to her heart. Sex had always been just sex, completely separate from love.

But what she and Ethan did was so much more than that...for her.

"Vampire sex is amazing," she whispered against his ear.

"Sex with *you* is amazing." He rolled off her, and she moved to her side, propping her head on her hand. Her lips tugged into a smile she couldn't have fought if her undead life depended on it. Ethan smiled too, melting her heart even more, and his gaze flicked down to her mouth.

His eyes widened, and he reached for her, running his thumb along her teeth. "Your fangs are coming in."

"Really?" She felt her mouth, and her canines extended into two tiny points. She sat up and looked in the mirror on the dresser, baring her teeth and furrowing her brow. "They're so much smaller than yours."

"They're not fully grown in, but it's a start." He folded his hands behind his head. "They look good on you. Very sexy."

Her stomach fluttered. "You think so?"

"I do."

"When we were going at it, the first time you made me come, I had this incredible urge to bite you."

Mischief sparked in his eyes. "Why didn't you?"

"Well, for one, your dick was in my mouth at the time."

He cringed.

"I didn't figure you'd want me biting that."

"Good call."

"Is that normal? To want to bite the man I…" She almost said love, but she *so* wasn't ready to go there. "The man I'm screwing?"

He chuckled. "I wanted to bite you too."

"Why didn't you?"

"I didn't want you passing out on me. You wouldn't have bled—vampires rarely bleed—but I was afraid even the act of biting would trigger you."

She lay beside him. "So, if I sank my baby fangs into your shoulder, even if I broke the skin, you wouldn't bleed?" Her mouth watered at the idea, which was beyond weird, but hey, she was a vampire. Who knew what was normal anymore?

"Do you want to try it?"

"You'd be okay with that?"

He gestured to his dick, which was hard already. "Just talking about it has gotten Vlad's attention, so yeah. I'd be more than okay with that."

She leaned down, softly grazing her teeth over his skin before nipping just hard enough to get a reaction out of him… and he reacted by moaning, tossing her onto her back and commencing a festival of biting and sexing that lasted until the death sleep pulled her under.

Two and a half weeks had passed since their first foray between the sheets, and Ethan couldn't get enough of Jane. Who knew vampire sex would be so hot? He hadn't allowed himself any form of pleasure while his guilt ate him from the inside out, but Jane… Jane had changed him. She'd changed everything.

He'd finally let go of his past and embraced his eternal death, and it was all because of the undead angel wrapped in his arms. He craved her with a ravenousness so much stronger than anything he'd ever felt. He needed her more than he needed blood.

She'd agreed to let him train her, and he'd bought the supermarket out of zucchini on more than one occasion, trying to help her learn the proper biting techniques. But her fangs hadn't extended past the tiny pricks that formed the first time they made love, so every time she bit into a squash, she tore the flesh with her incisors. She'd cause way too much pain for her donor, and though vampire saliva had medicinal properties, the gash she'd leave on someone's neck would require stitches to heal.

If she could just get over her aversion to blood, her fangs might fully extend. Her mind was holding her back, but he had no clue how to help her overcome it. Sophie had suggested Jane watch him feed, thinking since they enjoyed biting in the bedroom, she may enjoy watching him bite someone else.

Frankly, that made no sense at all. He also enjoyed impaling her, but hell would freeze over before he'd watch another man touch her. But he was out of options, so he tried feeding in front of her. Again, the moment his fangs met flesh, Jane either turned away, or if she witnessed the puncture, she fainted.

Feeding from a human and biting a lover during sex were in no way related. And Jane was no closer to passing her test to receive her biter's license than she was a month ago.

Still, he couldn't fault her. As she lay next to him, her dark hair spilling over the pillow, he ran his fingers through the silky strands and pressed a kiss to her forehead. She was perfect. Exactly who he needed.

She smiled and stroked his cheek with the back of her hand. "I'm getting thirsty."

"Me too."

"Do we have any miracle cure left in the fridge? If so, we can stay in tonight, see if Vlad wants to come out and play."

"Mmm… As wonderful as that sounds, I'm afraid we're out. I'll need to at least make a run to the bank to restock."

A pounding on the door echoed through the house a second before Gaston's voice sliced through Ethan's mind. *"Get up, both of you. We have a problem."*

"Oh, for fuck's sake." He rolled out of bed and pulled on his jeans.

"That eye roll used to be reserved for me." She sat up and scooted to the edge of the mattress. "Gaston must be up to his shenanigans again."

Ethan slipped his shirt over his head and ran a hand through his hair. *"The devil himself better be here to claim our souls, or I swear to Satan, Gaston…"*

"He may be, my friend. Constable Watson's shown up with a directive from the Supernatural World Order. Every vampire must be licensed by tonight or die."

CHAPTER TWELVE

"I'll handle this. Don't worry." Jane patted Ethan's hand, and while he appreciated her attempts to calm him, he'd have preferred to hightail it out of Louisiana and never come back.

"I can talk circles around that weaselly constable. By the time I'm done with him, he won't know his fangs from his fingers. We've got this."

Gaston tipped back his flask of alcohol-laced blood, draining it dry before shoving it in his jacket pocket. "I'm truly sorry I missed your previous session. I hear you were quite impressive."

Jane straightened her shoulders. "I was on fire."

"This, I'm afraid, is a different matter," Gaston said. "A directive from the Supernatural World Order is binding. Even the Magistrate has extremely limited options."

"But he does have options."

Gaston sighed and looked at Ethan. "She's insufferable, isn't she?"

"She used to be." He kissed her on the cheek, and the door swung open. Jeffrey escorted them to the Council's chamber and closed the door, the lock sliding into place sounding like a nail in a coffin.

"Did he just lock us in?" Panic flashed in Jane's eyes.

Now it was his turn to calm her, though his own fear was evident in the crack of his voice. "It's...normal, right, Gaston?"

Gaston opened his mouth and touched his tongue to a fully extended fang. "Completely."

Constable Watson had dragged his baby throne from the side of the room to sit in line with the Council, and his beady eyes gleamed as he flashed a shit-eating grin. The Council members sat utterly still, their black robes engulfing their frames, and Ethan could finally see why Jane found them so amusing the first time she came in. The whole lot of them looked as if they'd stepped off an eighties B horror movie set.

His lips betrayed him, curving into an amused smile as they stopped in the center of the room to address the Council. Watson narrowed his eyes, obviously annoyed at the fear he failed to strike, and rose to his feet.

He unrolled a scroll—a fucking scroll...who still used those? —and read in a haughty voice. "The World Order of Supernatural Relations hereby decrees that all vampires within a one-hundred-mile radius of any populated city must be licensed to bite by seven p.m. this evening, or they will face the stake." He pulled a watch from his breast pocket. "Oh, look at the time. It's seven-thirty."

"What? No!" Jane stepped forward, addressing the Magistrate. "Sir, I have three days left. You gave me an extension. He can't do this. *You're* in charge here."

"Laws are laws, and this comes from the SWO." Watson rolled up the scroll and set it in his chair. "The Magistrate has no power in this case."

"Of course he does. He rules Louisiana," Jane said. "You're just a grunt. A messenger for the Order."

"Surely there's something you can do, Your Honor." Ethan stepped beside Jane. "She's a valuable asset." *"Precious,"* he added in Jane's mind, and she took his hand.

The Magistrate straightened, emboldened by their ego

stroking, and turned to Watson. "I've read the directive, and I am well aware of my rights and jurisdiction." He turned to Jane. "Unfortunately, Ms. Anderson, my rights are very limited in this instance. I can grant you a one-hour extension. Find a donor, properly glamour them and bring them here for your biting test. Pass it, and you will be licensed and legal."

Jane's mouth hung open, and Ethan's posture deflated along with his hope. The glamour she might be able to pull off, but her tiny fangs would never get her through the biting test, even if she could manage to stay conscious through the ordeal.

She would never pass that test, and he couldn't live a single day without her. "Stake me instead."

"Are you crazy?" She whirled to face him. "You're not taking the punishment for my limitations."

He pulled from her grasp and stepped toward the Council. "Sir, if you keep her under your care as one of your own, surely the license won't be an issue. It's not her fault I turned her against her will. She shouldn't suffer for my sins."

"Keep me as one of his own? Like a slave? Oh, hell no. That's not happening."

The Magistrate steepled his fingers. "It is within my right to take a servant, whom I can do with as I please."

Jane paled.

The Magistrate continued, "Of course, Ms. Anderson, I have no interest in women sexually, but you'd make a fine business associate." He frowned at Ethan. "I rather liked you, Mr. Devereaux, but we do need to send a message that things like this won't go unpunished."

He swallowed hard. "I understand, sir."

Gaston, standing off to the side, hung his head.

"No, no, no. Nobody's getting staked." Jane held up her hands. "When does my hour start?"

"Jane." Ethan reached toward her but let his hand fall to his side. "You can't pass that test."

She straightened her spine and shook a finger at him. "I love you, Ethan Devereaux, but don't you *ever* tell me what I can't do."

His heart swelled, feeling as if it burst in his chest. "You love me?"

"Well, duh."

Jane strutted up Esplanade Avenue, a woman on a mission, her five-inch stiletto boots clicking on the concrete with each determined step.

No way. No *fucking* way was she letting that weaselly bastard lay a claw on her man. If she had to eat a human's still-beating heart, she'd do whatever it took to keep Ethan safe. She paused, the mere thought of the bloody organ making her head spin.

She could do this. She didn't have a choice. Straightening her spine, she turned in a circle. "I know you're following me, Gaston. You can turn off your glamour."

His form shimmered in front of her before coming into focus. "You're getting good if you could sense me."

"I'm already good." Really, she hadn't sensed him, but she knew they wouldn't send an unlicensed, fledgling vampire out into the night unescorted.

"What is your plan, Miss Jane?"

"I don't have one yet. Right now, I'm winging it, and for that I need a wingman...wingwoman. I have to talk to Sophie." They'd been in plenty of pickles together, and they always managed to talk themselves out of the mess. Aside from both her and Ethan's lives being on the line, this was no different. *Think, Jane. You can't stand to look at blood, so what can you do?* She marched up the front steps and threw open the door.

Sophie sat on the couch with a dark-haired man with brown eyes and buff shoulders. He was twirling a lock of her hair around his finger, but he jerked his hand away when Jane stomped into the room.

"Sophie, I need your help. You." She pointed at the man and thumbed toward the door. "Out. She'll call you later. This is an emergency."

"Yeah, I've got your number. I'll totally call you." Sophie stood and stepped around the coffee table. "Bye, John."

"It's James, but…" He screwed up his mouth on one side, glaring at Jane until Gaston stepped into the room. One look at the ancient vampire, and John-James scurried out the door.

"Well, hello, tall, pale, and gothic. What can a human girl do to help out a couple creatures of the night?" She paused and glanced over Gaston's shoulder. "Where's Ethan?"

"He's about to be staked if I can't get my act together and bite someone." She told her what went down in the Council chamber.

"That son of a bitch." Sophie crossed her arms. "If I ever get my hands on the little prick, I'll kick him all the way to Alaska in the summertime. A little midnight sun will take care of him." She wrapped an arm around Jane's shoulders. "Tell me what I need to do."

That was the problem. Jane worked best under pressure, but this was more than her undead mind could handle. Ethan's life…err, death…was on the line.

She chewed the inside of her cheek as an idea formed in her head. "You're good at faking it, right?"

Sophie grinned. "Darling, I'm the master." Her smile slipped. "Which is actually kinda sad, come to think of it."

"If we get through this, I'll find you the biggest, burliest werewolf in New Orleans, and you'll never have to fake it again. I promise."

She narrowed her eyes. "Are werewolves any good in the sack?"

"How should I know?"

Gaston cleared his throat. "I have heard they exhibit quite a prowess in the bedroom. Nothing compared to vampires, I assure you." He smoldered at Sophie, but his smolder didn't hold a candle to Ethan's sexy stare. Besides, Gaston was *so* not her type.

Sophie gave him a once-over, as if considering his offer— *man, it must've been a while for her*—and then turned to Jane. "Okay, but I'm not doing it doggie style every time."

"I'm sure he'll do you any style you want, babe. Now, about my dilemma…?"

"Right. What am I faking?"

"I will try my best to glamour you, but if it doesn't work, I need you to pretend like you're hypnotized. Just stare straight ahead. Don't fall over yourself or anything, but…basically act like me before I've had my morning coffee."

Sophie went still, a blank stare filling her eyes as she dropped her arms to her sides.

"That's perfect." Four years in the high school drama club had served her friend well.

"Ah, yes…" Gaston cupped his chin in his hand as he examined her. "But at the moment of the bite…or pretend bite…you must react; they always do. An erotic moan won't work, as you're best friends. Try a quick inhale as you might do at the moment of *another* type of penetration." The poor guy was still trying to smolder at Sophie. He could have easily used his own glamour to make her want him, but then Jane would have had to kick his ass. Good thing he knew better.

Sophie sucked in a breath and even gave her body a little shudder, tilting her head slightly.

"Damn, that's sexy. You really are good at this." Jane grabbed her shoulder, giving her a shake to see if she could hold character. "We've got to find you a good man."

Sophie blinked, coming back to herself. "Tell me about it."

"I'm going to have to put my mouth on your neck, but I won't bite hard. You don't want to see the damage I've done to all the squash in New Orleans. Then I'll have to lick your neck to pretend like I'm closing the punctures. Stay hypnotized until we leave the building. I doubt they want humans knowing where their coven headquarters is."

"Jane…" Sophie took her hand, squeezing it tight. "If you have to bite me for real, do it. I'm down for whatever it takes to keep you and Ethan safe."

How the hell did Jane get so damn lucky? Aside from her current predicament, of course. She had the absolute best friend in the world, a vampire sex god for a boyfriend, and she'd stay young forever.

She pulled Sophie into a tight hug. "It won't come to that."

"Let's hope it doesn't." Gaston opened the door. "If you're not glamoured properly, the pain will be excruciating."

"Cheese and crackers, Debbie Downer, that was the least helpful thing you could say." She hooked her arm through Sophie's and strutted outside, glaring at Gaston as she passed. "No more negativity, Nancy, or I'll ban you from my club when it opens."

"Please accept my apologies, Miss Sophie. If you need someone to kiss it and make it better when she's done, I'm happy to oblige."

Sophie patted his cheek. "Thanks, Gaston, but I'll take a big hairy wolf over a cadaver any day. No offense, Jane."

She laughed. "None taken. Now, let's go get my man."

CHAPTER THIRTEEN

Jane stopped a block away from the coven headquarters and took Sophie's face in her hands. "Remember, if this glamour doesn't work, you're me first thing in the morning."

"Zombie girl. Got it."

"But not too zombie." Jane stared into her eyes, calling on her magic and focusing on wiping Sophie's mind.

Sophie froze, her eyes widening for a moment before she stared blankly in front of her, her lips parting slightly. Jane snapped her fingers in front of Sophie's face, and she didn't flinch. Either her friend's acting skills were top notch or Jane had gotten better at glamour. She didn't have time to worry about it, though. Her extension ended in ten minutes.

She guided Sophie into the Council's chamber, and her heart wrenched when she found Ethan chained to the wall, his arms out to his sides, exposing his chest. "Motherfucker." She started toward him, but Gaston's heavy hand on her shoulder reminded her of her mission. If she could get that damn license, all of this would be over.

"I put in a call to the Supernatural World Order," Watson

sneered. "If you fail, you'll both be staked. Insolence will not be tolerated."

Jane fisted her hands to keep them from shaking—maybe that was why Ethan did it so much—and looked at the Magistrate.

He shook his head, his eyes apologetic. "The order comes from the Emperor himself. I've done all I can."

She straightened her spine, feigning confidence. "It's okay, boo. We got this." She winked and flashed a smile at Ethan. The sadness in his eyes nearly tore her in two. *You've got this, Jane. Fake it 'til you make it,* she said to herself.

Mr. Weasel Watson stood and brushed his trench coat back, giving Jane a glimpse of the stakes secured inside. What kind of a sadistic fuck carried around weapons, flashing them at people to exert his dominance? *A fuck with a tiny dick, that's who.*

"Proceed, *woman.*" Watson said woman like it was a bad thing to be one.

Misogynistic, sadistic, tiny-dicked fuck. Jane positioned herself in front of Sophie, looking into her blank eyes and searching for any sign of awareness. Sophie didn't even blink. She leaned toward her neck.

"You can do it, Jane. I believe in you." Ethan strained against his chains. "Just pretend it's tomato juice. You're sucking it right from the fruit."

She paused and looked at him. "Tomatoes are vegetables."

"They're actually fruit."

"You wouldn't put them in a fruit salad."

"And that's the difference between knowledge and wisdom," Gaston growled. "You have two minutes, Miss Jane."

"Right." She looked at the curve of Sophie's neck and instinctively knew exactly where the vein lay beneath her skin. Her head spun, and she closed her eyes, placing her open mouth over the target.

The bitter taste of Sophie's jasmine body lotion battled with the sweet fragrance, and Jane focused on the disjointed sensation waging between her senses of smell and taste. She swallowed, but before she could pull away, the weasel shot to his feet and marched toward her.

"I'll inspect the puncture wounds before you seal them."

"Uhh…" Jane's voice was muffled against Sophie's neck. "There's no need for that."

"Oh, but there is." What was it with this guy's diabolical-sounding voice? You'd think the fate of the world hinged on Jane passing this test.

She licked Sophie's neck and straightened. "Oops. Already sealed. Sorry not sorry." She shrugged.

Watson glided his nose along Sophie's neck, inhaling deeply before glaring at Jane. "Lies! There's no trace of blood. No linger of vampire magic. This woman has never been bitten." He yanked a stake from his coat and lunged. Jane jumped out of his path, so he headed for Ethan.

"No!" Jane hissed, and her fangs extended fully, not because she craved blood, but because she would fight to the death for the man she loved. Sadly, fighting wouldn't help her in this instance. "I'll do it. I'll do it. Don't hurt him!"

The Magistrate lifted a hand, freezing Watson to the spot, and he rose, descending from his throne and approaching Jane. "You have thirty seconds, my dear, before I'll be forced to release him."

"Wow. I've got to learn that little trick." No wonder he was the man in charge.

"Twenty-five seconds."

Jane squared her shoulders, clutched Sophie by the arms and opened her mouth. Then she closed it again. The entire room spun, and her head felt so light, it might float away.

"Fifteen seconds." The Magistrate lifted his hand, ready to release his magical hold.

Oh, fuck it all. She sank her fangs into her best friend's neck.

Blood pooled from the wounds, and she created a seal around the punctures with her lips, sucking like her life depended on it—which, it did.

Really lightheaded now, she pulled away and looked at what she'd done to her friend. No ripped flesh. Sophie had barely reacted. Only two small holes marred her skin, and thick, red blood oozed from them, sliding down her neck.

Jane didn't pass out. In fact, she felt energized, and the blood dripping from her friend's neck had her mouth watering for more.

The Magistrate nodded. "Seal the wounds."

Jane licked Sophie's neck, and the sweet, coppery taste danced on her tongue one last time as the punctures sealed, leaving no trace of their existence behind.

"Mark her," the Magistrate said.

Jane held Sophie's head and claimed her as a meal, which felt odd as all get-out, but whatever. She'd done it. She'd drunk a human's blood, and it actually wasn't bad. "Did I pass?"

The Magistrate steepled his fingers, a small smile curving his lips. "Indeed, you did, my dear. Well done." He bowed his head slightly and returned to his throne.

Gaston released Ethan from the chains, pulling him and Sophie aside as the Magistrate unlocked Watson. Jane laughed as the weasel stumbled, his stake sticking into the wall where Ethan had stood.

Watson hissed, baring his fangs as his pupils narrowed to slits. "I will not be made a mockery by a woman."

He unwedged his stake from the wall and lunged at Jane. The fucker was actually trying to stake her. *Bastard.* She feinted left, grabbing his arm and using his momentum to send him flying across the room.

As his feet hit the ground, he came for her again—*did this guy not know when to give up?*—and she spun around, delivering a back kick straight to his chest. Her stiletto pierced his ribcage, puncturing his heart, and he exploded into a pile of ash before her foot hit the floor. *Oops.*

"Holy shit! Remind me never to get on your bad side." Ethan took her hand and gaped at the mess she'd made of the weasel.

Jane looked up to find the entire Council and every member of the coven in attendance staring at her with wide eyes. The room went so deathly silent, you could have heard a mosquito fart.

As Ethan noticed the silence, he straightened and addressed the Magistrate. "She acted in self-defense, Your Honor. There's no crime in fighting for your life."

No one spoke. No one *moved* for a good thirty seconds, and Jane was just about to kiss her undead life goodbye when the Magistrate did his signature finger steeple and nodded.

"Indeed, she did, Mr. Devereaux." He looked at Jane. "The little bastard has been after my job since the moment he arrived. You've done us all a favor tonight, my dear. Jeffrey." He waved a hand, and Jeffery approached, presenting her with a credit-card-sized piece of plastic. "Congratulations, Ms. Anderson. You are now licensed to bite."

She looked at Ethan and wiggled the card. "I told you I had this."

He smiled and wrapped his arms around her. "I'll never doubt you again. Good job, princess."

She laughed. "Jane Anderson, Princess of Darkness. It has a ring to it."

"It certainly does."

"I'm going to need a prince, though. Are you interested in the job?" She slid her hands up his shoulders to cup his face.

He returned the gesture. "If it means spending every night of the rest of my death with you, sign me up."

She kissed him, using her magic to mark him, to claim him as her own forever and ever. He did the same to her, and the small hole she'd felt in her heart filled in.

He tucked a strand of hair behind her ear. "I love you, Jane."

"Words I never thought I'd hear from your mouth." She grinned and grabbed his ass, pulling him toward her. "I love you too."

EPILOGUE

Seven Months Later

E than adjusted his black silk tie in the mirror and smiled at Jane's reflection behind him. She wore a deep red strapless ball gown with a full skirt and tight bodice that accented her delicious curves. She'd swept her long hair up in a twist with a few silky strands spiraling down around her face to accent her crimson lips. He'd never seen a more lovely sight.

Jane rested her hands on his shoulders. "Ready to go, Edward?"

He pressed his lips into a line, glaring at her.

"You're right. You're way too hot to be Edward. Louie? Lestat?" She tapped a finger against her lips before snapping. "I've got it. You're Elijah Mikaelson."

He turned to face her, taking her in his arms. "I'm simply a vampire."

"And I'm simply your victim."

"There's nothing simple about you, princess."

"Damn straight." She gave him a quick kiss before turning and tugging him out the door.

They'd worked together over the past seven months to organize and open New Orleans' first vampire bar, and the premise had been a hit from day one. Jane's social skills were unrivaled, and patrons lined up down the sidewalk and around the building for a chance to experience Nocturnal New Orleans at its finest.

Ethan kept the books, working five nights a week alongside his bride, living his death to the fullest with the most wondrous woman in the world. With her aversion to blood cured, Jane fed like a natural, and when she flashed her sexy fangs as they approached the club, Vlad sprang to attention.

He pulled her close. "We could skip the club and have a party of our own."

She bit his bottom lip, and his knees nearly buckled. "Let's save it for the after party. I promise it'll be worth the wait."

"You're killing me, woman."

"You're already dead." She nipped his earlobe before taking his hand and strutting through the entrance.

Sophie sashayed toward them wearing a black witch costume, complete with a pointy hat and broomstick, owning her ancestry though she didn't possess an ounce of magic to speak of. Gaston's meal mark glowed in her aura. "There you two are. I was getting worried." She waved her broomstick at them. "It's Halloween, not a formal ball. Where are your costumes?"

Ethan bared his fangs, and Jane turned her head, revealing two fake puncture wounds with synthetic blood dripping down her neck.

Sophie rolled her eyes. "A vampire and his victim? How original."

Jane snickered. "I'd like to know why you're wearing Gaston's mark so early in the evening. Is there something you want to tell me?"

"Yeah. You said there'd be werewolves here, and you promised to introduce me to one." She crossed her arms. "I was nervous. I can't tell which guys are checking me out because I'm hot and which ones are looking for a drink, so Gaston took a sip and marked me as a favor."

"How nice of him." Jane winked at Ethan.

———

Sophie glared at both of them. They could think whatever they wanted about Sophie's relationship with Gaston, but it would never go the way Jane would love to see it go. Gaston was a nice guy, and he and Sophie had become friends over the past few months, but despite his repeated offering of certain benefits, she couldn't imagine climbing into bed with a man who was as cold as a corpse.

"I can't tell who's human and who's a supe, so if any were-wolves show up, you're going to have to point them out to me."

"Most everyone here is a supe. This is an invitation-only party, and just a few humans were invited." Jane linked her arm through Sophie's, turning her to scan the crowd. "Let's see. I'm not great at reading magic in auras yet, but I can tell you that good-looking guy over there is one hundred percent human." She turned some more. "What do you think about him? He's got a magical shimmer around him."

Sophie eyed the man. He was tall with broad shoulders, which she liked, but going on looks alone, he was blond. She preferred dark hair. "Hmm. The initial spark of attraction isn't there, but if he's a werewolf and a nice guy, he might grow on me."

Ethan leaned his head between theirs. "He's fae. Werewolves have an orange glow in their auras."

Sophie sighed. "Damn. I need a beer."

Jane joined her at the bar, though she had a glass of the

"house red," which was really blood, and Ethan sidled next to his wife, sliding his arm across the back of Jane's seat.

"What do you know about werewolves?" he asked.

"Nothing. While you've been integrating your wife into the supernatural world, I went back to Texas to get that branch of my business running under new management, and I've been so busy since I moved here, between getting the new office set up and trying to activate whatever magic I may have inherited from my grandma, I haven't had much time to research."

"Why are you so interested in dating one?" Why did he care?

"Because they're part animal. They're wild and untamed." And Sophie had never met an animal that didn't like her. She had a way with them that astounded most people, and it was why her dog walking business had taken off so well. "I might even let him bite me if he has magical healing spit like y'all do."

Ethan shook his head. "Werewolves aren't allowed to bite other supes. It's part of the truce."

"It's a good thing I'm not a supe then. Sometimes I like it a little rough."

Jane snorted, and blood dribbled down her chin. "It's true. She's told me stories."

Ethan ignored their banter. "If a werewolf bites you, you'd better hope the only magic you got from your grandma is your scent. Otherwise, his magic will mix with yours, triggering the were mutation, and you'll turn into a wolf too."

"Oh. Ew. Okay, I'll do all the biting then." She definitely did *not* want to turn into an animal herself. "Honestly, guys, I don't know. There's something about a man who can turn into a predatory animal at will that's sexy as all get-out. You vampires are cool...too cool for my liking, and witches are bitches, so I've learned. I just really want to meet a werewolf."

"Oh. My. Goat cheese pizza." Jane gripped her arm. "The Magistrate is here." She slid from her seat. "I have to go welcome him. If any werewolves show up, Ethan and I both promise to introduce you, right, Ethan?"

"Sure." He stood and followed Jane as she sashayed toward New Orleans' most powerful vampire.

Sophie had another beer alone at the bar. Between having no magical signature in her aura and Gaston's meal mark making her off limits to the vamps, no one paid her any mind, except for her bladder, which, after her third beer of the night, demanded attention.

She slipped out of her seat, tipping the chair forward to lean the back against the bar, the universal signal for *this seat is taken,* and began the trek to the restroom. Two steps into the journey, her bladder decided she wasn't moving fast enough and threatened to soak her panties in a not-fun way. She practically did the pee-pee dance the next fifteen feet toward the door until a broad chest and thick, auburn beard caught her gaze, making her forget all about her problems down under.

Now here was a man she'd happily take home, whether he was a werewolf or not. His golden-brown eyes gleamed the color of dark honey, and thick, wavy auburn hair matched his beard perfectly. His tanned skin said he worked outside, and that cop outfit. *Damn.* Whether it was a costume or he was an actual cop didn't matter. It would look amazing on her bedroom floor either way.

Her bladder protested as she altered her course, but it could wait a few more minutes. She'd never forgive herself if she didn't say hello to a man who could melt her panties off with a simple smile.

His devilish grin widened as she approached, and she licked her lips, taking in all six-feet, three inches of him. "Hi. You're a cop." She'd meant for it to be a question, but something about being near the man made her brain go haywire.

He chuckled. "And you're a witch."

She adjusted her hat. "Guilty. I'm Sophie, by the way." She

bit her bottom lip, willing the sudden urgency of her bladder to ease so she could talk to the man.

"Are you okay?" Amusement danced in his eyes. "You look like you might be in pain." He gestured to her crossed legs, and she looked down, horrified to find herself standing in the classic little kid *I've got to pee* pose.

"I, uh…was on my way to the bathroom." Heat flushed her cheeks as she jerked her thumb toward the ladies' room.

"Do you need an escort?"

"I can make it on my own." She turned but paused, refusing to let her embarrassment get the best of her. "Will you be here when I get back?"

One corner of his mouth lifted into the sexiest crooked grin she'd ever laid eyes on. "If you're lucky."

"I always am. If you play your cards right, you might get lucky too." Before he could respond, she tossed her hair over her shoulder and turned, using every ounce of control she could muster to stop herself from sprinting to the toilet.

With her ill-timed potty break complete, she adjusted her bra in the mirror, tugging her witch dress down just a bit to show a little cleavage. There was nothing wrong with tempting the man. If his personality was as nice as his looks, she'd be a sure thing. It had been months since she had a man in her bed.

Her excitement faded as she exited the restroom. The handsome cop was nowhere to be found. She scanned the club, skirting the edges of the dance floor and searching for a sexy man in uniform, but he'd disappeared. *Well, what did you expect, Sophie? The pee-pee dance isn't exactly a mating dance.*

She started toward her lonely seat at the bar, but movement in the courtyard caught her attention. Had her sexy cop stepped outside so they could talk in private? She could only hope. The door stood ajar, but as Sophie slipped through it, she found the enclosed park area empty. *Damn.*

As she turned to head inside, the bushes rustled in the back corner, and a whine emanated from the darkness.

"Who's there?" She glanced toward the door, but no one had followed, so she tiptoed deeper into the courtyard toward the movement. As she approached, the bushes rustled hard, and something in the corner growled.

She crouched down, peering into the dark shrubs, and found a pair of yellow eyes staring back at her. She couldn't make out exactly to whom they belonged, but the silhouette looked like a medium-sized dog. "Hey, buddy. Are you okay?"

Her voice should have soothed the beast instantly. She reached for the dog, but instead of coming toward her like most animals did when she spoke to them, it inched back.

"Come on, sweetie. It's okay. I won't hurt you." She scooted closer, her hand just a few inches from its furry muzzle.

The dog growled. Then it snarled. Then it lunged, snapping its jaws around her arm. Sophie yelped, falling back on her ass and clutching her arm as the creature bounded out of its hiding place and leapt over the fence.

"Goddammit, that son of a bitch bit me!" Blood dripped from the gashes, sharp pain stinging down to the bone as a strange tingling sensation shimmied up to her shoulder.

Jane ran to her side and dropped to her knees. "Are you okay? Let me see." She clutched Sophie's arm and examined the wound as if her previous issues with blood never existed. "Come inside so we can clean this up." She tugged her friend to her feet.

Sophie's shock turned to anger. "I own a fucking dog walking business, and I've never been bitten. Never. This is bullshit." She turned her arm, peering at the mark before looking at Ethan. "Did you see what kind of dog it was? I think it was a German Shepherd. We should call animal control."

"That was no dog." Ethan shook his head, his expression grim, though that wasn't unusual. Shoving his hands in his pockets, he glanced at Jane before focusing on Sophie, pity softening his gaze. "I hate to say this, but you've been bitten by a werewolf."

SHIFT HAPPENS

BOOK TWO

She wants to bang a werewolf, not become one.

Sophie Burroughs is determined to be a witch. Her grandmother was a witch. All the other supes say she smells like a witch, but she can't cast a spell to save her life.

Sprouting fur is *so* not on her to-do list.

But when a smokin' hot werewolf bites her and then accuses her of crimes against his pack, she has until the next full moon to prove him wrong and stop his magic from transforming her into a wolf.

A romp in the sack would be a nice bonus, too.

Trace Thibodeaux didn't mean to bite Sophie. The red wolves have been cursed, she's the prime suspect, and if he wants to keep his rank in the pack, he has to end her magic by any means necessary.

But that doesn't include sheathing his sword in a witch's scabbard.

He's gotten into bed with the enemy before, and that's a mistake he'll never make again.

Or will he?

CHAPTER ONE

"If doing this buck naked doesn't work, I don't know what will." Sophie Burroughs dropped her blue silk robe onto the back of a chair and smoothed a soiled shirt on the kitchen table. She ran her finger over her grandmother's handwritten incantation in the grimoire, tapping the line beneath the title. "It says, 'A simple spell to remove stains from clothing.' Simplicity must be the key, and you can't get any simpler than being buck naked."

"I think the preferred term is 'skyclad.'" Jane, her vampire best friend, leaned against the wall, peering at Sophie's ancestral book. "And I don't think being naked is going to make it any easier to cast a spell."

"Hey, being naked makes a lot of things easier. Sex. Shaving. You don't have to do laundry." She ticked the list off on her fingers. "Anyway, I read about this online. Some witches perform their spells naked because it intensifies their magic. Maybe my grandma was one of them."

Jane scrunched her nose. "Ew. Now I'm picturing a wrinkly old lady with sagging boobs dancing naked around a bonfire. Thanks."

"She was twenty-five when she died, and she was gorgeous. I've seen pictures."

"I still don't think it's going to help."

"You never know until you try." Sophie scanned the short incantation one more time, though she'd already memorized it during the first seven times she tried to cast the damn spell.

Jane grabbed her boobs through her red cashmere sweater, pushing them together and up before narrowing her eyes at Sophie's. "I should have gotten implants while I was alive. Yours are fabulous."

"Oh, please." She waved a hand dismissively. "Yours will stay perky for all eternity, while I've got about twenty years tops before gravity comes a-callin'. Besides, the hottest vampire in New Orleans thinks you're utterly perfect, so I don't want to hear it." Sophie jerked her head toward the exit. "Either get naked or get out. I don't want anything contaminating this spell. It has to work this time."

Jane lifted her hands, a look of pity softening her eyes. "I'll be in the living room." She flipped her long, dark hair over her shoulder and strutted out of the kitchen.

Sophie closed her eyes, taking a deep breath and trying her damnedest to sense some kind of magic sparking inside her. Nothing happened, as usual, but she ignored the empty sensation like she ignored her best friend's looks of sympathy every time one of her grandma's spells refused to be cast. Which was literally *every* time.

If she could just get one to work—any spell, it didn't matter which at this point—she could prove she belonged in the coven and finally get those secretive bitches—err...witches—to accept her. It was her destiny. A palm reader told her so.

Focusing on the stain, she recited the spell three times, each repetition growing louder, intensifying along with her frustration. As she ended the final chant, she swiped her hand across the fabric, exactly like the directions told her to do, and waited, willing the damn spot to disappear. Nothing happened.

"Fuck me with a wooden dildo. I give up." She jabbed her arms into the robe sleeves, cinching the belt around her waist before dropping into a chair.

"The Sophie I know never gives up." Jane appeared in the doorway faster than Sophie could blink and sank into the chair next to her. Damn vampires and their super-speed. They could also wipe a person's mind and make them dumber than a turkey lining up for Thanksgiving dinner—at least for a short period of time. It was so unfair.

"Meet the new Sophie, quitter extraordinaire." She crossed her arms, and as her bottom lip poked out in a pout, she left it there. Even badass bitches deserved a little pity party every now and then.

Jane shook her head, leaning an elbow on the table and flashing that look of pity again. "You're not a quitter. You moved five hundred miles away from home to expand your business on the advice of a fortune teller, and you're doing great. This magic stuff is weird. A lot of it boils down to fate and meant-to-be crap that I never believed in before, but listen..." She grasped Sophie's hand. "You can't force it. If you're meant to have powers, they'll come when it's time. Good goat cheese, do you hear me? I'm starting to sound like Ethan."

"Great. And in the meantime, I'll just stay the awkward weirdo who gets along better with animals than she does people." She touched the scabbed-over bite marks on her forearm. "Most animals."

Jane rolled her eyes. "I'm married to a drama queen. I don't need this shit from my best friend too. You and I both know you're not a weirdo; lots of people are good with animals, and that's a werewolf bite. It doesn't count."

She pulled her sleeve down, covering the wound. "Whoever it was, they were in animal form when they bit me. Has Gaston had any luck figuring out who did it?"

"None. Apparently, it's illegal for werewolves to bite witches without permission, and since you smell like a witch and had a witch grandmother, the entire supernatural community is being tight-lipped about it."

She leaned an elbow on the table, resting her chin in her hand. "Fabulous." The one time they acted like Sophie was actually a witch, she didn't want them to.

"How's it healing? Do you need me to lick it again?"

"It's fine." Sophie laughed. Vampire spit had healing properties, but she would never get used to hearing Jane talk about this stuff like it was the most normal thing in the world. "My best friend just offered to lick my wounds. Maybe I'm not the weirdo in this pair after all."

"You're definitely not."

Sophie sighed and flipped the grimoire shut. The leather spine creaked as the cover closed over the thousand-plus pages of secrets Sophie apparently wasn't meant to be privy to. "I think I've found a witch who might be willing to help me. She lives upstairs and runs the coffee shop on the first floor."

"Are you sure she's a witch? Have you asked her?"

"Not yet. She's kinda my last hope, so I'm giving it time, getting to know her before I start bombarding her with questions."

Jane nodded, tapping a finger to her temple. "Smart."

"I just can't believe I did this, you know?"

"Did what?"

She toyed with the belt on her robe. "Moved here on the advice of a psychic."

Jane patted her hand. "You also moved here to be with your BFF."

"I know, but I got so caught up in the apparent magic of the situation, I couldn't see it for what it really was. A coincidence."

"You've always been a believer, and that psychic did come highly recommended. I read the reviews after you saw her."

Sophie had seen a palm reader on a whim one night when

she was out with a few of her employees. After a flourish of ringing bells and chanting in a language Sophie didn't understand, the psychic told her that her business would prosper in New Orleans and if she went there, she'd find magic and a man who'd make her innermost dreams come true.

The very next day, Jane had told her she was planning a trip to the French Quarter for Mardi Gras, and Sophie pounced at the chance to make the palm reader's premonition come true.

Now, her dog walking business was doing well, and she'd found magic alright. Her best friend was turned into a vampire the second night they were there, but the witches in the tourist shops wouldn't give Sophie a hot minute, much less the time of day.

New Orleans was full of supernatural beings, but they blended in with the humans, leaving Sophie dancing around the edges of a magical world she wanted so badly to join. And the man who would make her innermost dreams come true? Yeah, right. Aside from the hunk she'd encountered briefly—and quickly lost—at the party last night, she hadn't met a single man remotely capable of making her orgasm, much less making her dreams come true.

That palm reader must have had her wires crossed, because the prophecy didn't come true for Sophie, it happened for her best friend.

"Ugh." Sophie angled her head toward the sky. "God, Grandma Burroughs. Why did you have to die before you could teach me how to be a witch?" Her jaw clenched shut, and she shoved the grimoire away from her. The book slid across the smooth wood tabletop, teetering on the edge before falling to the floor with a thunk. Damn, that little hissy fit felt good.

"Careful. That's an old book." Jane slipped out of her chair and crouched on the floor to retrieve it. "Hey, Soph? Have you read the whole thing?"

"It's more than a thousand pages. I haven't made it past the basic stuff." And it seemed she never would. It was time to face the facts. Sophie just wasn't a witch.

Jane rose onto her knees, peering at her friend over the kitchen table. "A year ago, I wouldn't have thought anything of this, but I think you need to come see the page it fell open to."

"Why? Is it a spell to create the perfect man, because I think I found that in my cookbook. Gingerbread men. They're quiet, sweet, and if they get on your nerves, you can bite their heads off." She plopped cross-legged on the floor next to Jane.

"Look at the date on this." Jane pointed to the script in the top right corner. "Wasn't your dad born in 1963?"

Sophie nodded. "She wrote this spell a week after his birthday."

Four lines of elegant cursive writing were positioned in the center of the otherwise blank, yellowing page.

My heir will land where the Spanish reigned.
When man turns beast, her path will be forged.
What is done will be undone.
All must be lost to find everything.

"What the hell is that supposed to mean? I thought spells had to rhyme." Sophie scanned the text again. "'My heir will land where the Spanish reigned?' That doesn't sound like an incantation."

Jane picked up the grimoire, gently placing it on the table. "I think it's a prophecy." She turned the page. Finding it blank, she turned the next one, and then another. "The book is empty after this."

"Because she died shortly after my dad was born." Sophie flipped the page back to the supposed prophecy. "Do you think it's about my dad? He's her heir, right? Her son?"

"Could be." Jane leaned over the grimoire, running her tongue over her teeth.

"Oh, hon, your fangs are out." Sophie wiggled a finger at Jane's fully extended canines. "Do you need to go?"

Jane didn't take her eyes off the book. "I'm supposed to meet Ethan at eleven for a meal, but this is too fascinating to interrupt. Do you still have my stash in your fridge?"

"There's a bottle of O positive on the bottom shelf. Last one."

Jane's lip curled as she sent a text to her husband. "I prefer O neg these days, but it'll do. I asked Ethan to pick some up on his way home."

"He doesn't mind you standing him up?" Sophie opened the fridge and took out the bottle of blood—another thing she would never get used to. The mere sight of blood made Jane faint not too long ago. She popped it in the microwave to heat it as close to 98.6 degrees as she could get it and poured herself a glass of chardonnay.

"He's with Gaston. As long as I'm home for playtime before dawn, he won't mind."

"You're so lucky." Sophie set the warmed bottle and a wine glass in front of Jane before sinking into the chair. "I'm on my third set of batteries this month."

"You know all you'd have to do is bat your lashes, and you could have any man you wanted in your bed."

This was true. Sophie had never had any trouble landing a man. It was holding on to one she hadn't mastered yet. That, and finding one who actually knew his way around a woman's body was next to impossible. If not for her trusty vibrator, she'd be wound tighter than her Spanx after an all-you-can-eat buffet. "I'm tired of casual sex. I want more. I want what you have with Ethan."

"You'll find it when the time is right. I know you will."

She could have argued, but what was the point? She'd either find Mr. Right, or she wouldn't. No use crying over milk that couldn't be spilled because it didn't even exist. "So, 'land where the Spanish reigned.' Do you think she meant Mexico? We went to Cancun once for summer vacation when I was a teenager."

Jane chewed the inside of her cheek, her brow furrowing as she stared at the book. "I don't think this is about your dad. Read the second line."

"'When man turns beast, her path will be forged.'" Sophie gasped. "'*Her* path.' But, my dad is an only child. My grandma didn't have any female heirs."

"She has you."

"Me?" Her mouth dropped open. "How can it be about me? I wasn't even a glimmer in my dad's eye when she wrote it. He was just a baby himself."

"It's a prophecy, duh. It's about the future. Look." Jane pointed to the third line. "'When man turns beast, her path will be forged.' Soph, a werewolf bit you last night. That's the very definition of a man turned beast."

This was crazy. Sophie's dead grandmother did not write a prophecy about her thirty years before she was born. "Okay, maybe that fits, but what about the first line? 'The land where the Spanish reigned.' We're in the *French* quarter. All the cute little sayings here are in French: *lagniappe, laissez les bons temps*, and all that jazz. Ethan calls you *cher*, not *mi amour*."

"You haven't been on any of the walking tours since you moved here, have you?"

"I walk fifteen dogs a day. I'm not about to pay money to walk more."

Jane laughed. "The Spanish were in control of New Orleans at the end of the seventeen hundreds. Most of the architecture in the French Quarter is actually Spanish."

"Oh." Her eyes widened, and she straightened her spine. "Oh my God. We flew here the first time, so I did technically *land* where the Spanish reigned." A flurry of adrenaline rolled through her veins, making her heart pound. "A man did turn into a beast, and then the sucker bit me. But what's my path?"

She clutched Jane's shoulders, her voice coming out in a whisper. "What's my path, Jane?"

"I don't know. Maybe you're really going to turn into a werewolf?"

Gaston, their three-hundred-year-old vampire friend, informed Sophie there was a 99% chance the bite would heal, and Sophie could get on with her life. But since her ancestor was a witch, she might have had a little dormant magic inside her that could activate the werewolf mutation and make her sprout fur at the next full moon.

Wouldn't that be her luck? She wanted to sleep with a werewolf, not become one herself. "I obviously don't have any magic, or I'd be able to get one of these spells to work."

"Read the next line." Jane pointed to the book. "'What's done will be undone.' What do you think that means?"

"It'll be undone. The bite will heal, and I won't turn into a werewolf." That had to be what it meant. Sophie was intent on becoming a witch, not a werewolf. She loved animals more than she loved people, but hair only belonged on her head and between her legs. She refused to sprout fur. It wasn't ladylike.

Jane poured the blood into the glass and swirled it like a fine wine. "That sounds feasible. It makes sense if you think about it."

"It does. Definitely."

"So, all that's left is the last line. 'All must be lost to find everything.'" Jane took a swig of O positive and grimaced. "That doesn't sound promising."

"Okay, but everything else has been vague. I mean, 'when man becomes beast.' If we'd read this a year ago, that wouldn't have made a lick of sense either. None of it would have. Maybe I'm going to lose my purse, and when someone returns it, I'll buy a lottery ticket because I'll be feeling so lucky. Then I'll win."

Jane arched a brow. "That's a stretch."

"It could happen."

"I guess."

"Anyway, the important thing right now is that I'm *not* going to turn into a werewolf. It says so right here." She jabbed her finger at the third line of the prophecy. "And the path that has been forged is my way to becoming a witch. I was ready to give up, but now I have a renewed drive. 'All must be lost' is so vague, it could have already happened. Hell, maybe it happened tonight. I'd lost my will to continue, and now I've found a reason to go on. That's it!"

Sophie closed the book and stood, parking her hands on her hips. "I figured it out. I'm going to become a witch, and the only werewolf I'll ever have in me is the massive dick of the one who's going to make my innermost dreams come true."

Jane laughed. "You go, girl. Grab your destiny by the cock...I mean horns."

"Who's Destiny?" Sophie grinned. "Oh, that's right. She's my bitch."

CHAPTER TWO

S he smelled like a witch. Five male dogs, at least three of them alphas, strolled along in a semicircle around her without so much as a raised hackle or growl of warning, and that feat in itself would require mad magical powers. That many males never got along so peacefully, especially tethered together like they were.

She had to be a witch—an unregistered one, the most dangerous kind. And he was the dumbass who bit her.

Trace Thibodeaux crouched behind a trash can on St. Philip Street, looking like a lunatic as he observed the woman walking the dogs. Sophie Burroughs. Her warm cinnamon and cider witch scent drifted on the breeze, igniting a fire inside him the way it did the night he met her. But now, a slight woodsy hint tainted the fragrance, an indication that his magic was mixing with hers, possibly turning her into a werewolf by the next full moon.

If she was the one responsible for the hell that had broken loose within his pack—and he was 99.9% positive she was—he could've used any means necessary to force her to lift the spell and turn over his missing friend.

Could have. Until, in a flash of confusion he still didn't understand, he'd bitten her, transferring his magic and possibly turning her into one of the most powerful weres alive. Sure, she'd lose the ability to cast spells if she made the shift from woman to beast, but her inborn power would remain. Anyone who had that kind of control over alphas was a threat to his kind. He'd screwed up royally, and now he had to do something about it.

That was what he got for mixing business with pleasure.

She turned the corner with her pack of leashed dogs, and Trace straightened, shoving his hands in his pockets and strolling toward the intersection. He peered around the corner and paused, admiring the swing of her hips and the way her thick blonde hair bounced with each confident stride. It was just his luck the woman he'd been sent to investigate was the most gorgeous creature he'd ever seen.

During their brief encounter at the Halloween party a few nights ago, her stunning smile and contagious laugh had almost reeled him in. He would have gladly spent the night with her—but thank the gods he didn't—using their mutual attraction as a way into her house to investigate her crimes. *Would have.* Until she'd excused herself to the "restroom" and the weirdness had begun.

He followed her a few more blocks, pausing as she bent down to pet one of the dogs, scratching it behind the ears and flashing that breathtaking smile. *Damn.* The things he'd like to do with that woman...

But he was on a mission, damn it. He had to find his missing packmate and the witch who cursed his kind, and this exquisite blonde was the prime suspect. The only suspect. The head on his shoulders needed to have a come-to-Jesus meeting with the one in his pants, because he was *not* getting in bed with the enemy. Not again.

The evening sun began its descent behind the nineteenth-century French Quarter buildings, painting the sky in shades of deep purple and orange, casting long shadows across the pavement still damp from the afternoon rain. A violinist played a classical tune on the corner of Royal Street, drawing a crowd, and Trace almost lost sight of the beautiful vixen.

His heart began to sprint, but as he rounded the corner, he found her on the front steps of a Creole townhouse, unleashing a boxer and patting it on its flank before it bolted inside. She wound up the leash, clipping it to a ring near the wrist strap of her dog-walking apparatus, and continued on her way.

Trace blew out a relieved breath and followed as she delivered the rest of the animals to their homes. He was pushing it staying this long in the Quarter. Hell, spending five minutes within a two-mile radius of the place was dangerous for a red wolf shifter these days.

Someone, and he was looking at the probable culprit, had cursed his pack, forcing them to shift at random times. Whatever form they happened to be in when the spell struck, their bodies seized, their vision tunneling as the magic forced them to shift.

A wild boar had nearly impaled Andy when he chased it too close to the city and was force-shifted mid-fight. He came to seconds before the tusk pierced his neck and then had to run home naked as a newborn.

Whatever magic she was using, it was sticky, and it took a good half hour for it to wear off so they'd have control of their forms again.

Poor Becky was in bed with a human when the spell struck her. Imagine her date's surprise when the woman he was doing doggie style turned into an actual doggie. She'd had to enlist the help of a vampire to glamour the guy and make him forget he'd gotten lucky that night. Of course, he *was* lucky Becky didn't bite off his willy when she came to and found herself nose to nose with a shotgun. She'd made it out an open window before he had the chance to shoot, but that situation could have gone downhill fast.

The witch had to be stopped, and Trace was the werewolf to do it.

He followed her two more blocks, waiting on the sidewalk as she disappeared inside a coffee shop. Through the front window, he kept an eye on her as she chatted with the barista. She laughed, tossing her thick golden hair behind her shoulder, and as she turned, he caught a glimpse of the most radiant smile he'd ever seen.

His heart rate kicked up again, and he fisted his hands at his sides. He had to shake these unwelcome emotions stirring up his hormones. If the shit hit the fan between the red wolves and the witches, he did not want to get caught sheathing his sword in the enemy's scabbard.

Sophie rubbed the chill from the back of her neck as she waited for Crimson, her upstairs neighbor and owner of Evangeline's coffee shop, to finish mixing a weird concoction in a copper bowl. She'd had the strangest feeling that someone was watching her all afternoon, but every time she looked over her shoulder, no one seemed to be paying her any mind.

She'd been paranoid the past three days, ever since that damn werewolf bit her on Halloween and then took off without so much as an apology. Gaston still hadn't had any luck finding the bastard, but he assured her that if any of the wolfman's—or wolfwoman's—magic transferred to Sophie, they'd come looking for her to make sure she wasn't going to become one of them.

Her mind drifted to the delicious man she'd met that night before everything went to shit. Big and buff, with a full beard and thick, wavy hair, the guy was as close to a werewolf as she could imagine, and he looked like the perfect candidate to fulfill the palm reader's prophecy. Even if he couldn't have made her innermost dreams come true, she would've had a blast watching him try.

But her bladder had other plans for her that night, damn the bitch, and she'd lost him. She'd looked all over the club, but he'd vanished like the last homemade brownie at a church picnic. Disappointed that her awkwardness had once again lost her a potential date, she'd wandered into the courtyard and found what she'd thought was a dog cowering in the bushes.

It *so* wasn't a dog. She should have figured that out when it didn't calm down and take to her immediately. All animals loved her. All except werewolves, it seemed. She'd glimpsed yellow eyes and massive teeth as it snapped at her arm, and then it shot out of sight before she could get a good look at it.

So, she'd finally met a werewolf, but she still didn't know what one looked like. If this bite wound healed, she may never know. Hell, with the way things were going, it seemed she'd stay just as clueless about supes as the day Jane told her she'd become a vampire.

Sophie still couldn't get the witches in the tourist shops to give her a lick of information about their coven. Even when she showed them her grandma's grimoire, proving she was a descendant of a witch, they turned up their noses and directed her to the bookshelf if she wanted to learn about magic.

She watched the barista sprinkle a white powder into her bowl. Crimson was a witch. Sophie was sure of it, but she'd learned her lesson. They were becoming friends, and she wasn't mentioning magic until her neighbor brought it up.

Crimson's dark spiral curls bounced as she giggled and jumped, apparently pleased with whatever she'd been mixing. "Sorry about that."

She poured the mixture into a small glass bottle—a potion bottle for sure—and wiped her hands on a dishcloth. Her deep purple nails matched her satin shirt, a color that looked amazing against her dark brown skin tone. She wore skinny jeans with black ankle boots, and a gold rope belt accented her hoop earrings. The woman knew how to dress.

"Agrimony leaves have to be mixed when they're fresh, or

they lose potency." She locked eyes with Sophie, suppressing a smile.

"What were you making?"

"It's an herbal remedy for a friend who isn't feeling like himself lately." The corners of her mouth twitched like she wanted to say more, and Sophie raised a brow, urging her to continue. Instead, Crimson inhaled deeply, two lines forming between her eyes as she cocked her head. "You smell different."

"I do?" Sophie sniffed her shoulder and then lifted her arm to smell her pit. She'd remembered to put on deodorant, so at least her friend wasn't reacting to BO.

"Yeah." Crimson leaned forward over the counter, inhaling again. "You've got a hint of a rustic, outdoorsy scent to you."

"I've been out walking dogs. Maybe that's what you smell?"

Crimson crossed her arms, drumming her fingers on her biceps. "Maybe. What do I smell like to you?"

Now there was a weird question. Well, weird for a human, which added more proof to Sophie's theory that the barista was a witch. "All I can smell is coffee."

"Really?" Crimson looked disappointed. If she was human, maybe she got a new perfume, and no one had noticed. Seriously, though, how could they over the rich, decadent scent of the best coffee in the South?

A black cat hopped onto the counter and let out a deep meow before rubbing against Sophie's arm.

"Hey there, handsome." Sophie ran a hand down the animal's back. "I didn't know you had a cat."

"Shoo, Jax. I told you to wait." Crimson chased the cat from the counter, and it sulked into the back room. "I've had him for a week or so. It's temporary. Like fostering, actually. He doesn't usually venture into the front like that. I'm not sure what's gotten into him."

"I have a way with animals." Sophie pushed up her sleeves. "Always have. Sometimes I could swear they understand me when I talk to them. Crazy, I know."

Crimson reached for a mug but paused. "That doesn't sound crazy. More like a gift."

"I've been thinking about getting a dog of my own. Taking care of other people's animals is fun, but it would be nice to have someone warm and loyal to come home to at the end of the day." She'd put off getting a pet in her younger years, when she was going out a lot and bringing random men home. Now that Jane was married, and Sophie's life had calmed down, she was itching for some stability. For somewhere to belong.

"Pets are a helluva lot easier than men, that's for sure." Crimson laughed then sucked in a quick breath, touching her fingers to her lips. "What happened to your arm?"

"Oh. A w…weird dog bit me. It's nothing." She jerked her sleeve down, clamping her mouth shut to keep the word "werewolf" from slipping out. Supes weren't too keen on their secrets getting around, and if whoever bit her did come looking for her, she didn't need them knowing she'd blabbed, even if it was to a probable witch.

Crimson glanced toward the doorway the cat disappeared through before leaning her forearms on the counter. "What did it look like?"

"I don't know. It was dark, and it ran off before I got a good look at it. A German shepherd, maybe?"

"Are you sure it was a dog?" Her dark eyes were intense, and Sophie almost gave in and told her what she knew. She wanted in with the witches of New Orleans so badly she could taste it, and Crimson was her ticket. She could feel it in her bones.

Instead, she simply shrugged. "Yeah. It's a little sore, but it'll heal. It hurt my pride more than anything. I started my dog walking business in college, and this is the first time I've ever been bitten."

"I thought you were new in town? You just moved in below me a few months ago."

"I started the company in Texas. I've got a manager running the business over there now, while I'm operating the new branch in New Orleans. I moved here to be with my bestie, but she works nights, so I don't get to see her as much as I'd like." Her bottom lip started to poke out, so she bit it. It wasn't Jane's fault she was dead to the world during daylight hours and would fry in the sunlight. The perks of being a vampire far outweighed the drawbacks, according to her best friend.

Crimson smiled. "Well, if you're ever in need of a friend to paint the town with, you know where I live."

"Thanks. I might take you up on that."

"I hope you do. Now, what can I get you?"

"The usual. A nonfat decaf vanilla latte."

"One *what's the point?* latte coming right up!" Crimson turned to the espresso machine, and Sophie laughed, tossing her hair behind her shoulder and glancing out the front window.

A man stared back at her, his dark honey eyes and auburn hair adding warmth to his tanned skin tone. He had a thick, well-groomed beard and a broad, muscular chest, and my, oh my, he looked like something she needed in her life. In fact, though it was hard to tell from the glare in the window, he looked an awful lot like the scrumptious man she lost in the club on Halloween.

"Hey, Crimson, hold off on the coffee. I may have found something else to warm me up tonight."

As her gaze locked with his, he jerked his head down and strode away, like he didn't mean for her to notice him. But honestly, how could she not? He was exactly the type of big, burly, alpha-looking man she'd been searching for.

The witch's smile slipped as her gaze locked with his through the glass, and her lips parted slightly. *Crap.* Trace ducked his head and paced up the sidewalk, the hairs on the back of his neck standing on end as he sensed her exiting the coffee shop.

Two more steps would have taken him to the corner, where

he could disappear from her view, but the magic slammed into him like a frying pan to the face, knocking him mindless and sending him careening into a pothole the size of Lake Pontchartrain. Muddy water splashed around him as he shifted against his will, and he barely had time to shimmy out of his shirt before the entire world went dark.

"Oh, you poor little guy." The sweet voice danced in his ears, bringing him back to coherence.

He blinked his eyes open and found the blonde he'd been tailing hunched over him, biting her bottom lip and glancing up and down the street before returning her gaze to him. How long had he been out?

She offered him her hand, palm-down, holding it near his muzzle as if she expected him to sniff it. "Are you okay?"

Of course he wasn't okay. The witch had just forced him to shift in the middle of the street, and now his clothes lay beneath him, covered in mud, and he had to play the role of a house pet to avoid attracting any attention. Lucky for him, she'd made sure no witnesses were around, but damn she was bold performing magic in the open like that. He didn't know whether to admire her tenacity or bite her again.

He sniffed her hand, going along with the charade, a little whine emanating from his throat so she'd think he was scared.

Her smile brightened her sky-blue eyes. "That's a good boy. I thought I was losing my touch."

As she scratched his head, her sleeve slipped up to reveal the bandage on her forearm. A little pang of guilt shot through his chest before he reminded himself who she was and what she'd done to his pack. Her magic must have been animal-related, because his beast had been tamed at the first sound of her voice. Luckily, the man in him remained in control.

The sound of tires rolling on the pavement came from behind him, and Sophie looked up before rising to her feet. "Let's get you out of the road, okay, buddy? Can you stand?"

She scratched under his chin, urging him to rise, and damn it if he didn't obey her command.

With her hand on the scruff of his neck, she guided him to the sidewalk as the car splashed through the pothole, ruining any chance he had at retrieving his clothes.

The witch knelt in front of him, taking his head in her hands, still pretending like she had nothing to do with his canine condition. "You're a mess, big guy. Do you have an owner around here anywhere?"

He blew out a hard breath through his nose. Was this woman serious? A witch knew better than to treat a werewolf like a house pet. Unless she thought her spell bound the man altogether... He might be able to use this to his advantage.

Her brow furrowed as she looked him over, running her hands along his neck and shoulders. "What are you? Some kind of German shepherd mix? You look a little bit like a coyote, but you're way too tame to be a wild animal."

Oh, he'd show her wild. As soon as he found his missing friend, this witch would be wishing she never messed with the red wolf pack.

She glanced around the empty sidewalk and leaned toward his ear. "You're not a werewolf, are you? One of those bit me a few nights ago, and my arm's been throbbing ever since."

As if she didn't know. What game was this woman playing?

"You didn't happen to see a big guy with a sexy beard walk by a few minutes ago, did you?" She pursed her lips, shaking her head. "I should be so lucky." Rising to her feet, she rested her hands on her hips and gave him a curious look. "I'm probably going to regret this, but I think I'll take you home with me. We can get you cleaned up and then look online to see if anyone's missing you. What do you think?"

This could be his chance. If she took him into her home in wolf form, with his heightened senses, he'd be able to sniff out his missing packmate. Then, with Jackson's help, they could subdue her, powerful magic or not, and get her to lift the spell before his pack broke the truce with the witches and started a war.

He followed her back toward the coffee shop and into a side entrance of the building, where she stopped at the foot of a staircase.

She glanced up the steps and down at him, her eyes calculating. "What do you weigh, boy? About sixty or seventy pounds? I can't have you tracking mud through the place."

He backed up. Was she seriously considering carrying him?

Squatting, she scooped him into her arms and rose to her feet, letting out a little grunt on the way up. "It's a good thing I work out," she said, her voice strained.

She struggled up the stairs, and Trace did his best to remain still, ignoring the humiliation of being carried. He wasn't about to ruin his chance at getting inside the enemy's lair.

She set him on the landing to tug a key from her pocket and open the door before scooping him up again and carrying him inside.

She marched through the living room, and he noted a door leading to a balcony as well as an archway that probably led to the kitchen. As they entered her bedroom, she made a sharp left straight into the bathroom, depositing him in the tub. A closet door stood closed against the far wall, but he didn't get a good enough look at the bedroom to determine any other openings that could lead to his friend.

He sat on his haunches, watching as she regarded her soiled shirt in the mirror. She frowned and sighed, and he started to feel a little bad for ruining her clothes. Evil witch or not, he couldn't deny the effect she had on him. His wolf wanted to please her. Hell, she'd have the beast rolling over and eating from her hand if the man didn't hold on to control.

She had a calming effect, which was why she was able to wrangle so many alphas on leashes earlier today. The man in him found her drop-dead gorgeous, which set off warning sirens in his mind. If he wasn't careful, she'd have both man and beast entranced with her magic, and he'd never accomplish his mission.

Turning on the water, she dropped to her knees beside the tub and grabbed a large plastic cup from a shelf. Holding her good wrist under the stream, she heated the water and then filled the cup, dumping the contents over his fur until he was sopping wet.

She squirted some flowery-smelling shampoo onto his back, and while he wanted to protest the girly scent, when her fingers dug into his coat, massaging him, he may as well have been a pile of putty on the floor. He didn't sense her using her powers, but her hands felt like magic.

He shouldn't have enjoyed it so much, but technically, he was doing his job. He'd penetrated the enemy's stronghold, but as she leaned into the tub to wash the mud from his paws, he caught a glimpse of flesh and satin down her shirt, and his mind immediately went to another form of penetration.

Damn, this woman was gorgeous. And the rustic scent of his magic mixing with the warm cinnamon fragrance of hers created an intoxicating aroma he wanted to wrap himself up in.

Focus, Trace. He shook his body, hoping to shake the intruding thoughts from his mind, and water flew everywhere, coating the blonde in suds and wetness.

"Hey, now. That was rude, mister," she scolded him, but an amused smile curved her lips as she spoke. "Let's get you rinsed so I can have a turn, okay?" She dumped cups of water over him, and the bubbles spiraled down the drain before she grabbed a fluffy towel and dried his fur. A man could get used to this kind of attention.

"A beautiful dog like you needs a name. Do you have one?" She held his face and stared into his eyes. "It's not Rover, is it? You'd be surprised how many people still call their dogs that."

He huffed to let her know his name was definitely not Rover, and she laughed. Staring into her blue eyes, he focused his thoughts, pushing his name toward her mind. If she really was a witch with animal-controlling powers, she should pick up on the message. It would explain how the dogs she walked knew exactly where she wanted them to be.

She narrowed her eyes, pursing her lips. "I suppose I can give you a name."

He focused again, sending her his thoughts.

Her eyes widened. "For some weird reason, I want to call you Trace. It's not really a dog name, but it fits. What do you think?"

He licked her nose. Suspicion confirmed.

"Okay, okay. Come on." She gestured for him to get out of the tub, and his wolf obeyed before the man could even think about her request.

Picking up a hairdryer, she held it toward him. "This is going to make some noise, but it'll be warm, and it'll help you dry faster. Is it okay if I use this on you?"

He sniffed it like a good boy and was rewarded with another sweet smile. How could someone this kind and gentle with animals be responsible for the turmoil in his pack? It didn't make sense.

With his coat dry and fluffy, and shinier than it had ever been, she released him from the bathroom. He darted from room to room, sniffing the floor and furniture, using his snout to open doors and check out all the closets. Jackson wasn't here. In fact, even with his heightened sense of smell, he didn't detect a trace of magic. She must have performed her spells somewhere else.

Her gaze weighed on his shoulders, and he stopped, cocking his head at her as she stood in the doorway, leaning against the jamb with her arms crossed. "Are you done?"

He inched toward her and sat, trying his best to act like a domesticated dog.

She laughed and scratched behind his ears. "Don't mark your territory while I'm in the shower, okay?"

No worries about that. As soon as he accomplished his

mission, he'd be getting as far away from this entrancing witch as he could. He jumped onto her bed, expecting her to protest, but she simply smiled again. After turning in a circle, he plopped onto the mattress and rested his head on his paws, his gaze trained on the bathroom door as she closed it behind her.

CHAPTER THREE

Sophie cinched the towel around her chest and tousled her damp hair. Wiping the fog from the mirror, she stared at her reflection and sighed. A dog that sweet probably had an owner, and even if he didn't, he was too big to keep in an apartment.

Then again, if he got along with her clients, she could walk him three or four times a day. That should be enough exercise, shouldn't it? Lord knew she could use the companionship. Making friends proved difficult when she had one foot in the supernatural world and one in the human. She couldn't talk about Jane or Ethan, or even Gaston with humans, but she didn't fit in with the supes either. It was like high school all over again.

She ran her fingers over the bite mark on her arm, and the wound tingled. Thanks to her BFF's magical spit, it was healing nicely, but as much as she was averse to sprouting fur, she almost wished she'd turn into a werewolf so she'd belong somewhere. She'd prefer a coven, but being part of a pack might be nice.

In the meantime, she could make her own pack. As long as Trace didn't have an owner out there looking for him, the dog would stay.

She grabbed her lavender-scented deodorant from the shelf, and her vision tunneled. Her head spun, and she squeezed her eyes shut, steadying herself with a hand on the edge of the sink. "Whoa. I shouldn't have skipped lunch."

As she shook her head, the fogginess dissipated, the light-headed sensation ceasing as quickly as it had begun. She lifted her arm to apply her deodorant, and instead of finding her smooth, freshly-shaven pit, a patch of tan hair occupied the space under her arm.

"What the hell?" She examined it in the mirror, running her finger over the soft strands. *Holy shit.* That wasn't hair. It was fur. A freaking tuft of fur had sprouted in her pit like one of those carpet sample squares on display at Home Depot. She lifted the other arm, and that pit was furry too.

"Oh, no," she whispered to her reflection. "I said I *almost* wished I'd turn into a werewolf. I don't really want to." Snatching the razor from its hook in the shower, she shaved the patches of fur, collecting the strands in the sink before wrapping them in a piece of toilet paper.

Maybe it was a side effect of the bite. Maybe once it healed, this problem would go away. *Please let it go away.* She stuffed the fur wrapped in toilet paper into the medicine cabinet and closed the mirrored door. Jane would be there soon, and she'd know what to do. Her BFF always had a plan. In less than a year of being undead, Jane had managed to befriend the vampire Magistrate, the highest-ranking blood-sucker in the state. Surely she could find out what the hell was happening with Sophie's body and how to stop it. Supes were supes, and while they didn't share their secrets, they all knew each other. Jane could get her in contact with someone who could help.

Biting her lip, she hesitated to lift her arms again. If the fur had already grown back, she'd have to splurge on laser hair removal at the local medspa.

Oh no. What if, since she was only part witch, this werewolf gig was only going to affect her underarms? Would lasers even work to remove magic-induced fur?

Squeezing her eyes shut, she raised her arms above her head and held her breath. She opened one eye, then the other, and a gush of air made her cheeks puff as she exhaled her relief. For the time being, at least, she was fur-free.

As she opened the bathroom door, a cloud of steam wafted into the bedroom. She stepped from the tile to the carpet and froze. As if her armpit ordeal wasn't enough, there, lying on his side, his knees pulled to his chest, was not the fluffy, rust-colored dog she'd brought home. It was a tall, muscular, totally naked man.

"Ah!" She dove for the pepper spray in her nightstand drawer. Holding it in her right hand as threateningly as possible, she rocked from foot to foot, her mind scrambling to catch up with what was happening. "Who are you? What have you done with my dog?"

"Huh?" The man blinked his eyes open and glanced around, disoriented. He held his hands in front of his face and groaned. "Oh, shit." He slid off the mattress, putting the bed between them, and rose to his feet, his hands lifted in surrender.

"Who are you?" She waved her weapon, trying to hold a fierce expression as recognition dawned in her mind. She knew exactly who this guy was. "How did you get in here? Where's my dog?"

She tried to hold eye contact, but her gaze kept dropping against her will. He had a broad chest with a sprinkling of auburn hair that trailed down the middle of chiseled abs, leading right to his... *Oh my.* Even flaccid, the man was hung.

"My eyes are up here, sweetheart." He had a deep, rumbly voice that melted as smooth as Velveeta in her ears.

"You..." She looked into the deep honey-brown of his irises, but her gaze dipped below his waist again, her eyeballs completely ignoring the command from her brain.

He chuckled and held a pillow in front of himself. "Better?"

"No, now your dick is on my pillow. I lay my head there at night, you know." She waved her weapon again, and he laughed.

"Would you rather I put my dick somewhere else?" Mischief danced in his eyes, and she tried to ignore the flutter in her belly.

"Are you hitting on me? First you disappear on me at the club, then you stalk me at the coffee shop. You break into my house, climb into my bed buck naked while I'm in the shower, and *now* you're hitting on me?"

"You're the one waving a dildo around. Who's hitting on whom?"

Her eyes widened as she realized she did, in fact, have the vibrator she'd affectionately named Big Blue in her hand. "Dammit." She snatched the actual can of pepper spray from the drawer and held it toward him. "Don't come near me. What did you do with Trace?"

"I *am* Trace."

"Don't try to be funny, mister. If you hurt that dog, I'll…"

He arched a brow. "You know exactly what I am, so stop pretending. Where's Jackson?"

"Pretending? You're the delusional one, breaking into my apartment, rubbing your man bits all over my bed like a…" Her mouth fell open as the voice in the back of her head began shouting. "Like a dog." She lowered the vibrator and the pepper spray, but kept them clutched tightly just in case. "You're a werewolf?"

"As if you didn't know."

"But…you're so small."

He frowned and held the pillow tighter against his groin. "It's cold in here, and you're threatening to beat me with pepper spray and a dildo. What do you expect?"

She dropped the vibrator into the drawer. Big Blue was a lover, not a fighter. "I meant your wolf. I thought you were some kind of German shepherd mix. Aren't werewolves supposed to be gigantic? They are in *Twilight*."

He grunted. "Don't even mention that movie. Anyway, I'm a red wolf. We're smaller than our gray cousins, but we're no less fierce."

The pillow slipped down so she could see the tuft of hair right above his dick, and her tongue involuntarily slipped out to moisten her lips. Damn her body and its inappropriate reactions to finding a strange man in her bed. "Where are your clothes?"

He pulled up the pillow. "Probably still in the muddy pothole where you forced me to shift."

"What on earth are you talking about? Here." She ducked into the bathroom and grabbed a towel from a shelf, tossing it to him. "Put that on at least."

He dropped the pillow on the bed, completely unashamed —honestly, the man had absolutely nothing to be ashamed about—and wrapped the towel around his waist.

Sophie swallowed hard, willing her brain to catch up. "What do you mean I forced you to shift? I didn't even know you were a man." With his bottom half covered, she finally focused on his face. "Why were you following me?"

"You're the witch who kidnapped my friend and cursed my pack." He crossed his arms.

"I did no such thing, and I'm not a witch."

"I can smell the magic on you."

"Oh, really?" She mirrored his posture, still clutching the pepper spray. "What does it smell like?"

"Cinnamon and cider. Warm." He inhaled deeply. "Delicious." His eyes flashed as if he hadn't meant to say the last part.

That's exactly what the vampires said she smelled like, but she still didn't have any powers. The bite mark throbbed from clutching her arms so tightly, so she dropped them to her sides.

He looked at the wound and winced. "Have you started exhibiting any canine attributes? Growing fur in strange places or craving raw meat?"

"Ew. No." Raw meat? She would never. "You're the one who bit me, aren't you? Gaston said you'd come looking for me.

What? You can't find a mate on your own, so you thought you'd turn a human?" Okay, maybe that was a little harsh, but the man had been stalking her.

His jaw clenched. "If I wanted you as my mate, you'd come to me willingly, sweetheart."

"Oh, you're sure of yourself, aren't you? How do you know I'm even interested in men?"

He chuckled, shaking his head. "Your pupils are dilated, for one thing, and you can't keep your eyes off my dick."

She gasped, trying to act offended, but the guy had a point. She may have turned into a bumbling idiot every time she tried to flirt, but she couldn't deny the attraction.

"And your hormones make your scent stronger. The whole room smells like wassail and gingerbread cookies, and I can only imagine it's because you like what you see." He swept a heated gaze down her body. "The view's nice from my end too, by the way."

Her mouth opened and closed a few times as she tried to gather her thoughts. This naked werewolf was making some pretty heavy accusations—kidnapping, cursing—yet all she could think about was yanking that towel from around his waist and seeing what his package looked like fully extended. *Get a grip, Soph.*

"So why did you bite me? It was pretty shitty of you to run off, too. You could have at least apologized."

He started to answer, but the doorbell rang, and she held up a finger. *Finally.* "That'll be Jane. She'll be able to sort this mess out. Wait here."

Sophie padded to the living room and opened the door. "Hey, girl. You're just in time."

Jane's dark eyes took in Sophie's state of undress before she peered over her shoulder. "Just in time for what? I'm not having a three-way." She leaned closer and whispered, "When were you going to tell me you finally found your werewolf? He's cute. Do you want me to come back tomorrow?"

"Trace!" Sophie whirled to face him. "I told you to stay in the bedroom."

He crossed his arms over his chest, his biceps bunching as they contracted, looking sexy as hell and doing it on purpose. "You may be able to control animals with your mind, but the *man* is in control of this werewolf."

"Why's he talking about controlling animals?" Jane strutted in and perched on the arm of the sofa.

"He's accusing me of kidnapping his friend and putting a curse on his pack. Something about forcing them to shift. I don't know." Sophie threw her arms in the air. "Will you watch him while I get dressed?"

"Shouldn't you both put on some clothes?" Jane swept her gaze over Trace, nodding her approval. "Or not."

"He came here naked."

Jane's eyes widened.

"I was in wolf form when she supposedly mistook me for a dog and brought me inside. My clothes are in a muddy pothole on Royal Street." He turned to Sophie. "This doesn't have to be difficult. Just tell me where Jackson is, lift the curse, and we'll be on our way. I won't tell the witches what you did; my pack won't start a war, no harm done."

Sophie looked at Jane with pleading eyes. Luckily, that was all it took for her BFF to take action.

"Go get dressed." Jane tugged her phone from her pocket. "I'll call Ethan and get him and Gaston to come. This is way over my head." She looked at Trace. "What are you? About a 34/36?"

He nodded. "How'd you know?"

"I worked retail for a little while."

Sophie marched into her bedroom and tossed her pepper spray in the drawer. Trace didn't seem like a threat, and even if he were, he'd be no match for a bunch of vampires. She threw on some skinny jeans and a lowcut sweater. Even if the guy was accusing her of crimes she couldn't possibly commit, he was hot as sin. No harm in flaunting her physical gifts, including the rack she spent four grand on.

She returned to the living room to find Jane chatting with the intruder like they were old friends. "Did you know Trace is a police officer? A werewolf and a man in uniform. You hit the jackpot."

"I'm taking a leave of absence from my job until the culprit is apprehended," he said.

So his outfit at the Halloween party wasn't a costume. He was a real cop. His ranking on the sexy scale just tipped over the edge. "Too bad he thinks I'm the culprit." Sophie sank into the recliner and crossed her legs, grinning as Trace's gaze landed on her chest. Her pupils weren't the only ones dilating. *Take that, Mr. Sexy Wolfman.*

"Can y'all explain this from the beginning?" Jane asked. "These bits and pieces you're throwing at me aren't making any sense."

"He pretended to be a dog so I'd bring him inside my apartment. While I was in the shower, he turned back human and started throwing accusations like spaghetti, seeing what he could make stick."

"I wasn't pretending anything. You forced me to shift."

"Hold on, both of you." Jane held up her hands. "Back it up all the way. Trace, I think you have details we're missing."

He narrowed his eyes at Sophie for a moment before focusing on Jane. "A little over a week ago, Jackson Altuve went missing from the pack. I talked to him that afternoon, and he told me he was hooking up with a witch. No one has seen him since."

"Okay," Jane said. "Now we're getting somewhere. Soph, did you go out with Jackson?"

She scoffed. "No! Whose side are you on?"

"I'm just trying to get all the facts. Trace, why do you think Sophie is responsible for Jackson's disappearance?"

"Because our Alpha met with the coven's high priestess. She

questioned every registered witch in the French Quarter, under oath. They all denied it."

"Well, someone obviously lied," Sophie said.

"And risk having her magic bound for life?" Trace shook his head. "No witch in her right mind would take that chance. The coven values honesty and truth. They don't take lightly to liars."

Another knock sounded on the door, and Ethan and Gaston strolled in. Ethan's face was serious, like always, and he said something to Jane in her mind because she smiled and nodded, taking the clothes he offered her and handing them to Trace.

Must be nice to have all those special powers. All Sophie had was a yummy scent only supes could smell and furry armpits.

She introduced the vampires to the werewolf...*will this ever feel normal?*...and Trace disappeared into the bedroom to finally put some clothes on as she and Jane updated the guys on his story.

Gaston laughed. "He thinks you're responsible for cursing his pack?"

"She's the only unregistered witch in the Quarter whose magic hasn't been tested. She has to be responsible." Trace stood at the living room entrance wearing faded jeans and a gray t-shirt that hugged his muscular chest. *Woof.*

"I can assure you, wolf, that Miss Sophie had nothing to do with a curse on your pack." Gaston rested his elbows on the arms of the chair. "She has no magical powers. You can see that in her aura."

"She's hiding them. I can smell the magic on her." He sauntered into the room and offered his hand to Ethan. "Thank you for the clothes. I'll pay you back when I find my wallet."

"No problem." Ethan rested a hand on Jane's knee. "Tell us about the curse. Someone is forcing you to shift?"

"It started on Halloween night. I was at your party, keeping tabs on Sophie, when her magic slammed into me like a baseball bat to my skull. I managed to stumble into the courtyard before

I shifted and blacked out. When I woke up, I hid my uniform in the brush because I couldn't shift back."

"So you bit me because you thought I made you shift?" *Unbelievable.* It figured her first werewolf would be the *bite first, ask questions later* type.

"I hid in the bushes when you came out, and when you found me, your magic subdued my wolf. He wanted to roll over and let you scratch his belly, but I held him back. I was trying to run, but you kept reaching for me. My wolf wanted to go to you; I wanted to bolt. The signals got crossed, and I accidentally bit. I didn't mean to, and I'm sorry for that."

"Well." She crossed her arms, lifting her chin defiantly. "Thank you for finally apologizing, but I did not make you shift, and I don't know your friend. You're the first werewolf I've ever met, and like Gaston said, I don't have any powers. My grandmother was a witch, and that's what you smell. Believe me, the witches don't want me in their coven. I've tried. Now." She stood and dusted imaginary lint from her jeans. This was all too much to process, and with her hormones battling for control of her brain, it was best if Trace was far, far away. "I'd like you to leave. I've had about all I can take tonight."

Trace glanced at the vampires as if weighing his options, but honestly, what more could he do? He couldn't prove Sophie had anything to do with his friend or his pack problems, because she didn't. It was his word against hers, and she had three badass vampires backing her up.

With a heavy sigh, he stood and shuffled toward the door. "Do you have a pen and paper, so I can leave you my number?" He gestured to her arm. "If anything happens with the bite, we'll need to take care of you."

Take care of her how? By nurturing her or by taking her out? "Nothing's going to happen with it. It's healing just fine."

"Please? For my peace of mind."

"Fine." Anything to get him out the door. It wasn't like she actually had to call the man. She marched to the kitchen and grabbed a pen and a Post-It note.

He scribbled his name and two phone numbers on the yellow sheet. "The second one is my landline, just in case something happens before I get a new phone. I'm sure my old one is toast."

"I'd say I'm sorry, but I'm not the one who made you shift. And if you hadn't been stalking me, you wouldn't have been in the street to begin with."

With a sardonic chuckle, he straightened his spine and opened the door. "I'm sorry we didn't meet under different circumstances, Sophie. Your bed is comfortable." He winked and slipped out the door.

She clenched her teeth, angry, not at him, but at herself for the stupid flutter in her belly his comment caused. She should have been offended. Hell, a normal woman would have at least been a little scared of a big, burly, dominant guy like Trace, but all Sophie could think about was the shape of his body, the cut of his muscles, and all the things she'd like to do with his dick.

"This is an interesting event turning." Gaston rose to his feet, his eyes glinting with his devilish smile. "I told you you'd be better off with a vampire."

"It's *turn of events*, and I've told you cold and dead is not my type."

"Undead." Gaston smirked. "There's quite a difference, *ma chère*." He winked, and Sophie wanted to laugh, but the gravity of the situation weighed her down.

"Can you guys excuse us for a second? I need to talk to Jane privately."

Gaston bowed. "We'll be right outside the door."

Jane looked at Ethan. "Take him down the street. This is girl stuff."

"Got it." Ethan escorted Gaston out of the apartment, and Sophie motioned for Jane to follow her to the bathroom.

"Promise you won't tell anyone what I'm about to show

you?" Sophie held up her hand, and Jane linked her pinky finger with hers.

"On my life."

Sophie tilted her head.

Jane sighed. "On my *undead* life. What's going on? You're on the pill, aren't you? Did he hurt you? Does he have a disease?"

"No, he didn't touch me, and yes, of course I'm on the pill. Look at this." She pulled the toilet paper bundle from the medicine cabinet and unwrapped the contents.

Jane peered at her hand. "What is that?"

"It's fur, Jane. Fucking fur."

CHAPTER FOUR

"You were in her house, and you found nothing?" Teresa shook her head, unbelieving.

"Not a thing." Trace glanced into the Alpha's eyes before lowering his gaze, showing respect to the woman in charge of his pack. "No trace of Jackson and not even a splash of magic."

His back ramrod straight, he clasped his hands in his lap and glanced at the portraits on the wall. Three Alphas, all men, stared back, their judgmental gazes boring into him, making him sweat. Teresa was the first female Alpha in the history of his pack, sworn in fifty years ago after a war with the neighboring gray wolves cut the red wolf population in half.

The office, an expansive room in the Alpha's two-story cabin in the woods, boasted rustic hardwood floors and brick-lined walls. A massive oak desk took up a quarter of the space, and Trace sat in the center of a line of seven wooden chairs facing it.

Teresa wore her dark brown hair pulled back in a tight bun, and she crossed her arms, the vinyl office chair squeaking as she leaned back and narrowed her eyes skeptically. "Did you look, or were you too busy dipping your pen in the enemy's inkwell?"

He blinked once, refusing to flinch at the verbal slap in the face. "No, ma'am. I didn't lay a finger on the witch. I went in with the mission, and only the mission, in mind." Maybe that was stretching the truth a little, but his attraction to Sophie didn't matter as long as his actions reflected the pack's interest in her and not his own.

The witch was beautiful, kind, caring, great with animals. And she wasn't the slightest bit embarrassed when he called her out for trying to defend herself with a vibrator, which hinted at how adventurous she might be in the sack. His lips attempted to curve into a smile, but he fought the urge, keeping his expression neutral. If the Alpha knew his real feelings for Sophie, he'd be off this case quicker than a vampire could down a pint of blood.

"This is your chance to redeem yourself," she said. "To prove you still deserve to be my First Lieutenant."

"I know." He clenched his teeth, trying to keep his mind out of Sophie's bedroom.

"Jackson is your best friend."

"Yes, ma'am. I won't screw it up."

Ever since that wood nymph who'd hidden all the prey animals from his pack seduced him, he'd been busting his ass to prove he still deserved to be the Alpha's second. In his defense, she had put him under a spell. He didn't know his snout from his tail when he was around the nymph, and Teresa herself had come in to save him and chase the creature away.

The minute the nymph left New Orleans, the spell was broken, and Trace could think straight again, but he'd been wary of anyone with magical powers ever since.

He should have been wary of the witch. He was until he woke up naked in her bed. Her stunned reaction wasn't fake, and he couldn't fathom a reason why she'd force-shift him back to human in the first place. Her magic centered around animals, so she wouldn't have given up control. Something didn't add up.

"Do you want me to make another appointment with the high priestess?" he asked. "Maybe they missed a witch during the questioning."

"Don't you dare. Our relations with the coven are already on edge. They held up their end of the truce by questioning everyone under oath. The culprit is unregistered, untested, and there's only one untested witch in the French Quarter."

"I don't think Sophie is responsible. She doesn't seem capable—"

"Like that nymph didn't seem capable of setting up a magical barrier to keep all the prey out of our hunting grounds?"

"That was different," he grumbled, sounding more like a pouting child than a grown-ass man. *Get yourself together. You're acting like a scolded pup.*

"Was it different?" She rose to her feet and paced behind her desk. "She has *vampires* vouching for her. Why not witches? The coven is convinced she's not a threat, but I'm not. She's hiding something, and you need to find out what."

"How would you like me to proceed?"

"I need someone to get close to her. Befriend her and her vampire allies. Can I trust you with the job, or should I send in one of the new recruits?"

His hackles rose. Trace was the pack's First Lieutenant. It was his job to handle situations like this, not some fledgling working his way up the ranks. "You can count on me, Alpha. I learn from my mistakes."

"Good. The French Quarter is still under quarantine, so spend as little time there as possible. I expect a report in three days, if not sooner."

"Yes, ma'am. I won't let you down." He turned to leave.

"Trace." She fixed him with a serious gaze. "She's not part of the coven, so the truce doesn't apply. Once you find Jackson, you're authorized to use any means necessary to end her magic."

Pressing his lips into a hard line, he nodded once and stepped out the door. As soon as it clicked shut, he leaned against the wall and closed his eyes. Teresa's *any means necessary* line was a silent order, one he'd be obliged to obey under different circumstances. But the Alpha didn't know he'd already screwed up this mission by biting Sophie. She could be one of them by the end of the month, and then what? Taking out their own kind was illegal.

Red wolves had dwindled in numbers nearly to the point of extinction. Their non-shifting cousins hadn't been spotted in Louisiana in years, and Trace's pack, though strong, was one of the smallest in the country. If Sophie did become a shifter, and she mated within the pack…

He ground his teeth. The witch was the enemy. No matter how hot a fire she lit in his core, he had to remember his mission, and his mission did *not* include getting Sophie into bed and especially not claiming her as his mate. His attraction to her was clouding his judgment, and that ended now.

Straightening his spine, he marched out of the Alpha's cabin and into the forest. He'd have to take care of this before the next full moon. There was no way around it.

"You were such a good boy today, Ruger." Sophie sat on a concrete block outside the entrance to Louis Armstrong Park to rest her aching feet and scratched the Boston terrier behind the ears. "I'll have to let your dad know to give you some extra treats tonight."

She peered across Rampart, the divided street on the outskirts of the French Quarter, and smiled as a little girl waved from the window of a passing streetcar. Ruger's home, an orange two-story Creole cottage, stood across the intersection, with a divided shotgun home on one side and an expansive three-story brick hotel on the other.

A man with a fluffy chocolate Pomeranian walked by, making Ruger's ears perk up. Sophie rested a hand on the Boston terrier's back, and he sat still as the Pom trotted toward them, sniffing Sophie's ankles.

She tried to say hello to the man, but her brain couldn't decide whether *hi* or *good morning* was appropriate, so it came out as, "Hide 'orning."

"Hello." The man tilted his head, flashing a hesitant smile before tugging his dog down the street.

Sophie sighed, and as she straightened her spine, rotating her ankles to loosen the tension, a wave of dizziness washed over her. The edges of her vision darkened, her entire body shuddering—no, shaking—like a wet dog trying to dry its coat.

She gasped, and, glancing up and down the street to be sure she hadn't attracted any attention, she slipped her hand through the neck of her shirt to feel her armpit. *Whew. Fur-free.* That full-body shudder was the werewolf magic leaving her system. *Yeah, that's what it was.*

Ruger made a whining sound in his throat, and as she reached down to comfort him, the dog latched onto her leg and started going to town on her shin like it was his personal plaything.

"Ew! Ruger, no. Bad dog." She pried the terrier from her leg, but the moment she set him on the concrete, he went at it again, moving his little hips like he was the Energizer Bunny with a fresh set of batteries.

"Ugh!" She stood, yanking her leg from Ruger's love grip as she tightened his leash, holding him at arm's length and marching across the intersection. "What's gotten into you?" He pranced and bounced, excited as all get-out, until she shoved him through his front door and locked him in his house.

With her morning round complete, she plopped onto Ruger's front steps and checked her phone. Three new inquiries for dog walking had come in overnight. Add those to the six on the waiting list, and it was time she hired some help. She might even look into renting an office space if this branch was going to get as big as her Austin home base.

Business was finally starting to take off, and Sophie was looking at possibly turning into a dog herself. *Fan-friggin-tastic.*

She shoved her phone in her pocket and rose to her feet. If all the dogs started acting like this little guy just did, she'd be in a mess of trouble.

Of course, that big, sexy wolfman she found in her bed yesterday evening could probably help her figure out what the hell was going on, but then she'd have to admit she needed his assistance. After the way he snuck in, let her *bathe* him—she gave the man a friggin' bath for Christ's sake—and then accused her of all that crap, she wasn't about to ask him for help. He could go hump a light pole for all she cared.

She was *not* going to turn into a werewolf anyway. There simply wasn't enough magic running through her veins for it to happen, and she would keep telling herself that until the next full moon came and went, leaving her the same old awkward, boring human she'd always been.

Pushing the thoughts out of her mind, she focused on the current dilemma. Coffee or lunch? She'd hardly slept last night. Images of Trace in all his glorious nakedness danced behind her eyes every time she closed them. She'd had so many sexy dreams about the man, she had to break out Big Blue this morning just to cool herself off.

And there she was, getting all hot and bothered again. She shook her head. Coffee. Crimson's shop stood a block away, so she'd stop in for a double-shot latté and then grab some lunch.

Crimson leaned in the doorway of Evangeline's, chatting with a tall, slim guy in his early twenties. With short black hair and dark brown eyes, he was cute, but still a little lanky for Sophie's taste. Put another ten years on him, when his shoulders had filled out and a little stubble peppered his jaw, and he might have been hot. Not that it mattered what the man looked like. Sophie was just desperate for a distraction. Anything to get her mind off werewolves.

Aside from the too-young-to-be-hot man, several dozen paintings occupied the sidewalk in front of the café. Done in deep, vibrant hues, the canvases depicted cartoonish renderings of houses and famous landmarks throughout the French Quarter. A twenty by thirty-inch swamp landscape stood on an easel by the door, and Sophie stopped to admire the vivid artistry.

"I'll make you a deal on that one, since we're friends." Crimson strutted toward her. She wore knee-high boots with three-inch heels, easily putting her at six feet tall. "Three hundred, and it's yours."

"Are you nuts?" the man asked. "That one's worth at least five hundred."

"Sophie." Crimson draped an arm around her shoulders. "I'd like you to meet my baby brother, Josh."

"Hi." Sophie shook his hand and glanced at Crimson. "Your brother?"

She nodded. "When Josh isn't trying to make people pay too much for paintings once a month at my café, he's studying art history in grad school."

"Five hundred is reasonable for an original painting that size," he said. "I won't take less."

"An artist knows the value of his work better than anyone," Sophie said, leaning closer and admiring the exquisite detail of the piece. "If I had a wall big enough to put it on, I'd buy it."

Crossing her arms, Crimson smirked at her brother. "And she'd pay three hundred because the artist knows the value of *her* work better than anyone."

Sophie's eyes widened. "You painted all these?"

"I sure did. I have dozens more in my apartment too. You'll have to come up and see them sometime." She motioned for her to follow and disappeared through the café door.

"It was nice to meet you, Josh." Sophie nodded and followed Crimson inside the empty shop.

"You want the usual?" Crimson stepped behind the counter and tied an apron around her waist.

"Full caffeine. Make it a double shot. I didn't sleep much last night." She slid onto a stool at the counter.

Crimson arched a brow. "Because you were having too much fun, I hope?"

"I wish." She leaned her forearms on the counter, drumming her chipped lavender nails against the Formica. She was way overdue for a manicure. "Your paintings are beautiful. Why do you run a coffee shop instead of focusing on your art?"

"Art doesn't provide a steady income. Anyway, my mom used to own this place. I'm keeping it open in her honor."

"That's nice. How long ago did she pass?"

Crimson's laugh mixed with the sound of milk being steamed. "Oh, honey, she's not dead. My parents retired to Florida five years ago. Evangeline's is a mainstay in the French Quarter, so I promised to keep it running. Josh is supposed to be helping, but he decided he needed to go to grad school instead." She set the mug of vanilla latté in front of Sophie.

"Have you lived here all your life?"

"Since my parents adopted me when I was seven. What about you? Born and raised in Texas?"

Sophie sipped the coffee, closing her eyes for a moment to savor the rich vanilla flavor. "I'm an Army brat. We lived all over the world until my dad got a medical discharge when I was sixteen. That's when we moved to Texas, but even then, we went from Houston to Dallas to Austin in a year and a half. I haven't really belonged anywhere my entire life."

Crimson cocked her head, smiling warmly. "Well, welcome home."

The cat darted into the kitchen from a back room and leapt onto the countertop. Lifting its nose in the air, it sniffed twice before slinking toward Sophie and rubbing its head against her forearm. A deep purr rumbled in the cat's chest, and it stood on its back legs, resting its front paws on Sophie's shoulder, rubbing its head against her chin.

Sophie laughed, her heart melting. "Hey there, handsome. It's good to see you too." She really needed to get a pet of her own.

"Jeez." Crimson glared at the cat. "I know what we have is temporary, but could you at least *try* not to flirt with other women in front of me? Shoo. Go on in the back." She waved an arm, and the cat sulked toward the back room.

"He's fine. I don't mind the attention," Sophie said.

Crimson gave her a skeptical look. "Did he say anything to you?"

"He said you're feeding him too much salmon. He prefers beef." Crimson's eyes widened, and Sophie laughed. "I'm kidding. I don't understand animal speak."

"Hmm..." She pressed her lips together as if stopping herself from saying more. Because she *knew* more. Sophie was sure of it.

It was time she did a little gentle prying with her witch friend. Tracing her finger along the cool countertop, she chewed her bottom lip and chose her words carefully. "Yesterday, when you mentioned my fondness for animals being a gift, what did you mean by that?"

Crimson paused, searching her eyes and resting her hands on her hips. "You really don't know, do you?"

"Know what?"

She clasped her hand on Sophie's arm, closing her eyes and taking two deep breaths. Her lids fluttered open, and she shook her head, unbelieving. "All this time I thought you were hiding your powers, but they've never been unbound."

"Could you be a little less cryptic? I have no idea what you're talking about."

A slow smile curved Crimson's lips, and she glanced about the empty café, checking over her shoulder toward the door the cat disappeared through. "You have an ancestor who was a witch." She whispered the last word. "Do you know who it was? Mom? Grandma?"

A thrill shot up Sophie's spine as she straightened and leaned toward her. "My grandmother was. She died when my dad was little."

"That makes sense." Crimson nodded. "And your mom?"

Sophie shrugged. "She was as surprised as the rest of us when we found Gram's grimoire in the attic after Pop died."

"You have her grimoire?" Excitement buzzed around Crimson, her dark eyes gleaming. "Do you have it here, in New Orleans?"

"I do, but it doesn't work. I've tried a few of her spells, but nothing ever happens."

"Because your powers were never unbound." Resting her hands on the counter, she leaned toward her. "Sophie, you're a witch."

Sophie snorted. "Yeah, right. I've tried talking to every witch in the city about their coven, but they all just shut me down and point me to the bookshelf."

Crimson waved a hand dismissively. "You can't get into the coven unless you're sponsored by another witch. I guarantee the high priestess has checked you out and determined you were harmless with bound powers. Most people this happens to go their entire lives thinking they're human."

"Hold on. Slow down." This was too much to process. In less than a year's time, her BFF became a vampire, married a vampire, and opened a vampire night club. The hottest man in New Orleans wound up in her bed as a werewolf, and now... "You're telling me I'm a witch? Like a full-blown magical being? Spells and incantations and sparkles and shit?"

"Well, you're not going to shoot glitter out your ass, but you are a witch." Crimson took off her apron and sashayed around the counter, parking on a stool next to Sophie. "Witches are born with their powers bound. It's up to the magical being who passed on those powers to unlock them when they're ready to begin training. If your grandma died when your dad was young, she took all that knowledge with her, and you've been living as a human ever since."

"Wow." She blinked.

"I know, right? My guess is your ability to talk to animals is your inborn gift. All witches can cast spells, but some of us are born with special psychic abilities: premonitions, talking to the dead, psychometry."

"Of all the cool powers I could have inherited, all I can do is talk to animals. That sounds about right."

"Maybe if your powers weren't bound, they could talk to you. I think you're a fauna witch." Her eyes gleamed, her smile brightening her entire face.

"Is there any way to unbind my powers?" Then again, maybe the binding was the only thing keeping her from sprouting fur and howling at the moon. Would she still be a witch if she turned into a werewolf? Did were/witch hybrids even exist?

Crimson's face turned serious. "I think we might be able to help each other." She yanked a strand of hair from Sophie's head.

"Ow! I'm not even sure I want to have magical powers, though. I need some time to think about all this." Did those words really just leave her lips? Being a witch had consumed her thoughts ever since she found her grandma's grimoire, and now she was second-guessing herself?

"I may need a little more." Crimson yanked on another strand of hair.

"What do you need my hair for?" She rubbed her sore scalp.

"Divination." She wrapped the strands in a napkin and shoved them into her pocket before prancing around the counter. "Come by my apartment tonight around eight, and we'll talk. Bring the grimoire with you."

"You're not going to do anything to me before then?" Sophie gathered her hair into her hands, sweeping it over her shoulder, away from Crimson. "I don't want to be walking down the street and have magical sparkles explode out of my pores…or my ass."

The door chimed behind her, and a group of tourists entered the shop. "Hi, y'all. Welcome." Crimson waved a hand at the customers before leaning toward Sophie and lowering her voice. "I'm just going to read your energy. Now, shoo. No more witch talk around the humans." She gave her a conspiratorial wink before grabbing a tray of pastry samples and sashaying toward the customers.

Sophie grinned, excitement bubbling in her chest like champagne as she strode out the door. Sure, the fact she might have magical powers that could be unlocked was cool, but that wink from Crimson meant so much more. It meant there was a chance, however slim, that she could join the coven. That she might *belong*.

CHAPTER FIVE

Find Jackson. Stop the witch. They would have been simple enough orders if the witch in question hadn't been on his mind since the moment he saw her wrapped in a towel, waving a dildo around like a sword.

A slow smile curved Trace's lips. He could show her a sword. She'd never need that puny contraption again if he warmed her bed every night. *Damn it.* He clenched his fists as he stalked up Royal Street, following her scent. *Focus on the plan.*

He passed two- and three-story structures in shades of burgundy, yellow, and mauve as Sophie's entrancing, magical fragrance grew stronger. Vibrant ferns and colorful flowers adorned the galleries trimmed in decorative wrought iron, and American, Spanish, French, and Rainbow flags flapped in the cool November breeze.

Trace stuck close to the buildings, scanning the structures for the gates blocking the alley entrances. The magic had struck him enough times now that he could sense the force-shift before it happened. He should have time to scale a gate and hide somewhere secluded if he felt it coming on.

So far, so good.

With his gaze locked on a dark green wooden gate across the

street, he made a sharp right onto St. Philip, and a body smacked into him. She bounced off his chest, and he caught a whiff of her intoxicating cinnamon and cider scent before she landed on her ass in front of him.

Sophie wore black leggings that hugged her curves and a deep blue sweater with strands of silver woven through the fabric that caught the sunlight in sparkles, almost making her shimmer. Her golden hair had fallen across her face, and as she swept it behind her shoulders, her sky-blue eyes locked with his, making his heart go *thump...thump-thump-thump.*

"Wow. You're not even going to offer me a hand up? If this is what all werewolves are like, I take back what I said about wanting one of my own."

She wanted a werewolf of her own, did she? As a pet—or as a lover? That statement could be taken several different ways, but the scoop neck of her sweater revealing her delicate collarbone had his mind permanently parked on Lover's Lane. As she started to get up, he dragged his mind out of its lust-drunken stupor and took her arm, easing her to her feet. "Sorry about that. You caught me off guard."

"I suppose that's my fault too?" She dusted off her pants and straightened her sweater. "You like to accuse me of things."

"No, that was my fault. I wasn't watching where I was walking, and I'm sorry I bumped into you." Well, he was sorry he knocked her down. Bumping into her had been part of his plan, minus the physical aspect.

"Oh." Her brow lifted. "Well, I'm sorry too." She held his gaze, her soft pink lips moving slightly, trying to form words her mind wouldn't allow her to speak.

"Are you okay?"

"I'm fine." She crossed her arms, jutting her hip to the side, composing herself. "You'll be happy to learn that whatever magical powers I might have, they've never been unbound, so I couldn't possibly have cursed your pack." Her face pinched in an adorable way, and he fought his smile. "Or maybe you won't be happy, since now you have no idea where your friend is. I don't know. I'm not good with people."

She lifted her hands in the air before dropping them at her sides. "It was easier to talk to you when you were a wolf."

"Why do you think that is?" He was fully clothed in jeans and a t-shirt, so she couldn't have been distracted by his body this time. Though he had to admit, she was cute when she was flustered.

She inhaled deeply, letting out a heavy sigh. "It's this witch business. Apparently, I'm supposed to be a fauna witch, but no one ever released my powers. I don't even know why I'm telling you this. It's not like you're deserving of my trust." She bit her bottom lip, searching his eyes.

"Maybe it's because I'm part animal?" It made sense. If her power was with animals, the beast inside him might've been what drew her to him, the reason she'd even speak to him after he accused her of crimes against his pack.

"Maybe. Or maybe it's because my bestie is dead to the world until sundown, and I'm bursting at the seams to talk to her about all this."

"You could talk to me." He opened his arms, trying to look as inviting as possible. With his height and build, his presence was intimidating to most, but Sophie didn't seem fazed.

"Psh. After you accused me of kidnapping and possible murder? No thanks." Her words said no, but she didn't make a move to leave. In fact, she held his gaze, practically begging him to ply her with questions.

"I'm sorry about that too." He shoved his hands into his pockets. "My pack determined you were to blame, and…"

She crossed her arms. "They sent you to gather evidence."

"I was doing my job, but I didn't find a thing. Jackson is still missing…and this curse…" He shook his head.

"I didn't do it."

"I'm starting to believe you." He reached toward her,

touching her arm and stepping to the side, shielding her from the homeless man riding a wobbly bicycle down the sidewalk.

As he whizzed past, her nose scrunched, and she waved a hand in front of her face. "Ugh. Now there's a man who could use a bath. Maybe I should open a bathing business instead. It would help with all the smells out here."

He moved closer to her to replace the aromas of BO and weed with Sophie's delicious scent. The idea of her hands on another man's body didn't sit well with him, and though he knew she was joking, he couldn't ignore the jealousy rolling through his core. *Not good, Trace.* "You being here improves the scent of the French Quarter. Your magic smells amazing. The rest of you does too."

A nervous giggle escaped her throat as she stepped back. "So people tell me. I guess I'm nose blind to it."

"Supes generally can't smell their own magic."

"There is so much I need to learn. So many questions. I can't wait to talk to Jane."

She wasn't the only one with questions. Had her magic been bound so long, she didn't even remember having powers? None of this made sense. He had to keep her talking. "How long has your friend been a vampire? Not long, right?"

"About nine months."

"I've been a werewolf my entire life. I'm sure I can answer your questions."

"I don't know. Jane and I are a team. We do everything together, so I know she can help."

What was this strange dependency on her vampire friend about? Was it because they were both apparently new to the supernatural world, or did it run deeper? And why did he feel the need to explore every nook, cranny, and hidden corner of her mind? "If you're not busy, I'd love to take you to lunch. If your powers really are bound, that's going to change my entire investigation of you."

"I'd think it would end it. No powers, no curse."

If the Alpha called right now and told him Jackson was home and the case was closed, he'd still insist on taking Sophie to lunch. This was a massive red flag flapping in the wind, but he closed his eyes to it, just like he'd closed them to the warning signs with the damn nymph two years ago.

This time was different. He wasn't under a spell, and he could handle himself around Sophie. Hell, he needed to if only to prove to himself he deserved his rank in the pack and a pretty face with a gorgeous body couldn't get in the way of his job. His nostrils flared as he let out a slow breath. After his last conversation with the Alpha, he needed to prove it to her too.

"I'm not ready to end things with you."

"Oh, you're not? Hmm..." Mischief danced in her eyes. "I have exactly ninety-three minutes until I pick up my first client for the afternoon round. That's all I can offer right now."

"I'll take it. We're going to have to head out of the Quarter, though. Can't risk turning into a wolf in the middle of a restaurant, and if you're not the one doing it, I'm still in danger."

"I'm not, so I guess you are. My car is a block away. I'll drive."

Trace gave Sophie directions to Honoré's, his favorite place on Magazine Street. Located in a blue and white, nineteenth-century Victorian mansion, it boasted an expansive front porch dotted with pink and yellow wrought-iron tables and chairs. Inside, his shoes thudded on the original wood floors as they made their way to a corner table in a quiet back room.

Mismatched furniture in shades from dark to light wood to distressed white paint gave the entire restaurant an eclectic vibe, and Trace pulled out a mahogany chair, tucking it under Sophie as she accepted the gesture.

He was doing his job. The Alpha had ordered him to befriend her, so taking her out to lunch was part of the plan. It didn't matter that his pulse sprinted every time he looked into her eyes. So what if her laugh sounded sweeter than jazz music dancing in his ears?

"What?" She smiled, glancing at him over her menu.

"What?" He folded his hands on the table.

"Why are you staring at me like that?"

Damn it. He was staring at her, wasn't he? She responded well to flirtation. Might as well keep it up. "How am I staring?" He arched a brow, and her smile widened, making a fizzy sensation run through his veins.

"If you were in wolf form, I'd assume you wanted a belly rub."

"What if that's exactly what I want?"

She folded her menu on the table, resting her forearms on the surface, mirroring his posture. Leaning forward, she licked her lips and lowered her voice. "Then I hope you'll be in human form and that you'll want more than your belly rubbed."

Hot damn. Was it getting warm in here or was this woman on fire? He straightened, dropping his hands in his lap and gripping his thighs to stop himself from reaching for her. Forget lunch. He could make a four-course meal out of Sophie Burroughs. "How much *more* are we talking about?"

Heat sparked in her gaze. "How dirty do you want to be?"

He reached across the table, taking her hand like he'd wanted to a minute ago. "Sex isn't dirty unless you're rolling in the mud."

"Now there's something I haven't tried…yet."

What the ever-loving fuck had he gotten himself into? He was supposed to be questioning her. Sure, she didn't seem to know a thing about his pack's problems, but she could have been an excellent liar. If he admitted Sophie as a lead had gone cold, then he'd have to admit the real reason he was sitting across from her about to share a meal, and he was *so* not ready to go there. *Focus, dickhead. Think with your brain.*

"Tracey, my man." Mike, the restaurant owner and Trace's good friend, sauntered in and shook his hand. His curly, dark brown hair was sheared short on the sides, and his dark eyes sparked red as he swept his gaze over Sophie. "Long time, no see, but I guess this pretty little witch has been keeping you busy. How do you do, ma'am?"

Mike took Sophie's hand, pressing his lips to her skin and inhaling deeply. "She smells divine."

She flashed Trace a quizzical look, and he cleared his throat, hoping to quell the jealousy burning in his chest. Jealousy was not good. Any territorial emotions meant his wolf was jumping on the *let's bang Sophie* train, and if his wolf was on board, they'd be headed for a lot more than banging.

"Mike, this is my friend, Sophie, and we're ready to order." He'd planned on getting his favorite, the fried oyster po-boy, but ingesting a quarter pound of aphrodisiacs when his motor was already humming might lead to disaster. He settled for catfish instead.

Sophie ordered fried shrimp and turned to him as Mike left the room. "Trace is short for Tracey?" Her lips twitched like she was trying not to smile.

He knew exactly where this was going. "It is, and you find it funny. Go ahead and laugh. Get it out of your system."

She let her smile come on full-force, and he forgot to breathe for a moment. "It's weird to see a big, buff guy like you with a girl's name."

He crossed his arms. "It's gender-neutral."

"Is it?" She laughed. "I'm sorry. It shouldn't be funny. See, this is why I'm better with animals."

"Stop apologizing. You're not the first person to make fun of my name, and you won't be the last. Mike called me that on purpose. He's probably right around the corner listening." He raised his voice on the last word, and sure enough, heavy footsteps receded toward the kitchen shortly after.

"Is Mike a werewolf too?"

He narrowed his eyes, studying hers, searching for a hint of dishonesty. She should have smelled the sulfur emanating from his skin like any other supe would. She didn't even flinch when his eyes flashed red, which meant she'd either dealt with plenty of demons or, more likely, she didn't see it happen. "Your powers really are bound, aren't they?"

"Uh, yeah. We've been through this already."

"Mike is a demon."

Her mouth dropped open, her eyes going wide as if this was her first time learning demons existed on Earth. Trace inhaled deeply, searching her scent for signs of deceit, but aside from the remnants of arousal left over from their earlier conversation, she smelled exactly the same.

"You're friends with a demon?" She shook her head. "More importantly, demons are real?"

"Mike's a great guy, as long as you don't make any deals with him. And yes, there are plenty of demons in New Orleans. I'm sure you've met a few."

"If I have, I had no idea. Aren't they...you know...evil? Are we safe eating here?" Her gaze darted about the room like she was on high alert.

"Don't worry. He left hell for a reason, and an angel owns the bakery next door. She keeps him in check."

She sat back in her chair, her voice rising in disbelief. "Get. Out." A woman at a table in the next room leaned over to glare at her, and Sophie covered her mouth, whispering, "Are you serious? Angels and demons walk among us?"

He couldn't fight his smile. She really was clueless about magic. "Absolutely. They've got some balance between good and evil thing going on that the rest of us try to stay out of."

"Wow. Next you're going to tell me fairies are real too."

"They are."

She giggled. "Unicorns?"

"Only in Montana. They need a lot of room to roam."

"Nymphs?"

He missed a beat in his reply, and his eyes tightened. "They're real too." He straightened, trying to brush off his reaction. Hopefully she didn't notice his change in tone at the mention of the woman who'd nearly cost him his position in the pack. "We're all real, and really good at hiding."

She pursed her lips, eyeing him skeptically. "You have experience with a nymph, don't you?"

Damn it. He was not getting into his past mishaps with her. "I've met a few."

She leaned an elbow on the table, resting her chin in her hand. "Tell me about her."

"No." He had defended that woman to the end. Hell, if he'd been under her spell any longer, he might have assisted with her plan to drive the red wolves out of Orleans Parish, and his life would have been over.

His stomach soured as the similarity of his current situation sank in. This time was different though. He felt it. His wolf felt it.

"Okay. We'll put a pin in that one. Maybe I do need my magic unlocked, so I'll be able to tell who's who. Witches have your fancy magic-detecting olfactory sense, right? That's how you can tell?"

He nodded. "And the visible magic in auras, though that can be hidden. Which is what my pack thought you were doing, since your scent is so strong."

There was no way in hell this sweet, innocent woman had anything to do with the pack curse or his missing friend. Of course, hell also didn't offer him any ways to convince his Alpha of her innocence, and that was a problem. Teresa would send in someone else to do the job if Trace didn't pull through, and he couldn't allow that to happen.

He needed a new plan and fast. "Tell me more about your magic being bound. How did you discover this information?"

She told him a story about being shunned by the witches in the Quarter, finally meeting one willing to talk to her, and learning that witches were born with their powers bound, something he never knew. A real witch would never divulge such sensitive information.

Their food arrived, and between bites, she told him everything she knew about her grandmother, how her best friend came to be a vampire, and her tentative entrance into the supernatural world.

"Is the witch who told you all this in the coven?"

"I think so." She finished the last bite of her shrimp and washed it down with a swig of sweet tea. "She talked like she was."

"It's probably best if you don't tell anyone else about this. You've just let me in on some pretty juicy secrets the coven doesn't want anyone to know." Secrets that could upset the balance of their truce.

"Oops." She covered her mouth with the tips of her fingers.

He flashed her a reassuring smile. "I promise not to tell."

"What about your pack? Don't you have to tell them everything you learned about me, so they'll know I'm innocent?"

He bit the inside of his cheek, his gaze dancing around her face as he tried to formulate a plan. "My pack, and especially my Alpha, are convinced of your guilt. They won't believe me if I tell them otherwise."

"Why won't they believe you?"

"It's a long story."

"It has to do with the nymph, doesn't it?"

He stiffened. For someone who claimed to be bad with people, she could read him like a large print e-book with an audio companion. "How did you know?"

She shrugged. "Your wolf talks to me."

He cocked his head. "Go on."

"I mean, not with words. He just…I don't know. I can sense things from the animal side of you. I know it sounds crazy, but I feel like we have a connection." She dropped her face into her hands for a moment as she shook her head. "Listen to me, I must be crazy thinking I have a connection with a man I've known all of three or four days."

"That doesn't sound crazy at all. I feel it too."

She smiled. "You or your wolf?"

"Both." Though how much of these feelings came from which side, he wasn't yet sure. The man in him found her insanely gorgeous and fun to talk to. His wolf could've felt the connection for one of three reasons. It was either her magic drawing him to her, his mating instincts kicking in, or his magic from the bite running through her veins.

He took her hand across the table and gently ran his finger over the spot where he'd hurt her. "Have you shown any signs that my magic might be taking hold in you?"

"Umm." She tugged from his grasp, folding her hands in her lap and staring at the table.

"You need to tell me if you do, because it's going to throw another wrench into our situation."

She glanced up at him, a questioning look in her gaze.

"My pack doesn't know I bit you, and if they think you cursed us, and you're becoming one of us, they'll want you dead before you shift. I need to know so I can protect you."

"No." She shook her head adamantly. "I'm definitely not sprouting fur or anything like that. This morning, one of my clients started humping my leg, which doesn't usually happen, but other than that, no." She clamped her mouth shut.

"By client, you mean…"

"A dog."

He nodded. "Right. For some reason, I was picturing a man."

She laughed. "That would be something. Oh, now I'm picturing it. Thanks."

"My pleasure." He held her gaze for a moment, and the connection between them seemed to strengthen, tugging him toward her.

Her smile faded. "Your pack wants me dead?"

"My orders were to find Jackson and end your magic by any means necessary, but I believe you, Sophie. After the time we've spent together, after everything you've told me, there's no way you could be involved in this mess."

A look of bewilderment danced in her eyes. "You were planning to kill me?"

"No. Absolutely not." How could he? From the moment he laid eyes on her at the party, he knew she was special. His wolf wouldn't have let him lay a finger on her in a harmful way.

She leaned away from him, wary. "But the thought crossed your mind."

"I was given an order, but I never intended to obey it. Sophie, if you know anything at all about Jackson or the curse, I need you to tell me. I'm already going to be in deep shit for biting you, and if I go against pack orders and protect you, they might want to take us both out."

"I don't know anything. I swear. If I knew where to find your friend, I would tell you." She paused, chewing her bottom lip and looking thoughtful. "Let me talk to Jane. She runs the club where we first met, so she knows people. She can help."

"I can't get another group of supes involved. This is between the red wolves and the witches."

"She'll be discreet. Trust me, she knows how to handle situations like this, and anyway, *you're* not getting her involved. I am. I have a right to defend myself, so let me help you find Jackson. Then we can prove I had nothing to do with it, and neither one of us will be in trouble."

Wow. After everything he'd put her through—sneaking into her house, accusing her, stalking her—she was offering him her help. That said so much about her character. His chest warmed at her generosity, and he couldn't stop the words tumbling from his lips. "Go on a date with me."

She gestured at the table. "I thought that's what this was."

He shook his head. "This was more of an interrogation. Let me take you out on a date. I want to get to know you."

"Aren't you supposed to be hunting for your friend?"

"I am. Every second of my day is spent trying to figure out

what happened to him, but I've got to keep up the charade that I'm investigating you."

"Oh." Her posture deflated. "And here I thought you wanted a real date."

Damn it. That wasn't how he meant for that to sound. "I do. It'll serve double duty. Let me show you how I would have treated you had we met on better terms." How he could still treat her once this mystery was solved.

She narrowed her eyes, calculating a response. "Saturday night, and in the meantime, I'll help you find your friend any way I can."

"Okay. Saturday night it is. I'm looking forward to it."

She grinned. "Me too."

CHAPTER SIX

Holy chihuahua. What the hell just happened? Sophie's hand trembled as she pulled her phone from her pocket and dialed Jane's number. The call went straight to voicemail, of course, because it was two in the afternoon. "Jane, it's Sophie. I know you're dead right now, but I need you to call me the moment you open your eyes. I've got a problem. A big one." And his name was Trace Thibodeaux.

She shoved the phone into her bag and pulled out her leash as she trotted up the steps to her first client's home. "Hey, Captain." She scratched the shelter dog behind the ears and guided him out the door, a calmness washing over her as the part-lab, part-husky, part-who-knew-what-else nuzzled her hand. "We can figure this out, can't we, boy?"

Captain woofed his agreement, and they walked side by side to the next client's house. She focused, trying to sense the dog's thoughts, to see if she could hear something the way Trace had put his name into her head when he was in wolf form last night. Pausing, she squatted in front of Captain and held his head in her hands, staring into his eyes and willing him to speak in her mind. "Talk to me, boy. I might be one of you by the end of the month."

A slobbery tongue swiping across her cheek was the only response she received. She stood and continued down the sidewalk. Maybe she should have told Trace the truth about the fur that sprouted on her yesterday. Heat flushed her cheeks as she imagined lifting her arms to show him her furry pits. No, she definitely should not have told him. She wasn't even sure if she could trust him yet.

When Sophie had first come to New Orleans, she'd wanted nothing more than to meet all the magical beings who called the Big Easy home. She'd created a fantasy world in her mind, but she'd neglected to consider the dangers that might come with a realm inhabited by creatures with otherworldly powers. That the things going bump in the night weren't always headboards and uglies.

All her life, she'd known she was different. Beyond her affinity for animals and the teasing she'd endured because of it, she'd never felt like she quite fit in anywhere. The fact she never lived in one place more than two years at a time growing up added to it, but deep down, she'd never known anyone she really clicked with besides Jane.

Discovering her grandmother's grimoire gave her hope that she could meet others like herself, and New Orleans was—so she thought—the perfect place to find them. Meeting Crimson, she finally felt like she was on her way in.

Then, she'd met a werewolf like she wanted, one with a seductive grin and hot enough to melt her panties off, and now his pack wanted her dead. Talk about bad luck.

At least she was getting a date out of it. She'd been fully prepared to stay mad at Trace for what he'd done, but all he had to do was look at her with concern in his dark honey eyes, and her will crumbled. He was kind, sweet, funny, and hotter than molten lava. She didn't want *a* werewolf. She wanted Trace.

It was possible—God, how she wanted it to be true—that he was the man from the palm reader's prediction, the one who would make her innermost dreams come true. He obviously fit into her grandmother's prophecy, so why not? Even when she'd consciously tried to be mad at him, their flirtatious banter always drew her in, and she found herself enjoying his company, even when he thought she was a criminal.

Once she talked to Jane, it would all get worked out. They'd find Trace's missing friend and figure out what was going on with the curse. Hell, while they were at it, Crimson would help Sophie unlock her powers, and she'd become a real witch. A member of the coven. She'd find her place in the supernatural world and have a hot werewolf by her side while she did it. Talk about her innermost dream coming true.

She finished her afternoon round and delivered all the clients back to their homes. With thirty minutes to spare before her final round of the day, she plopped onto a bench in Louis Armstrong Park and gazed out over the pond as she rotated her ankles, working the soreness out of her calves. It was time she invested in a new pair of walking shoes.

Her phone buzzed, and she dug it from her bag to find Crimson's name lighting up the screen. She pressed the device to her ear. "Hey Crim, are we still on for tonight? I have a gajillion questions for you."

"I need your help." The sound of drawers opening and closing followed her voice.

"Sure. What do you need?"

"My mom fell and broke her collarbone. I need to fly out to Florida to help my dad with her." More shuffling noises sounded through the receiver.

"Oh, no. Is she going to be okay?"

"Probably, but...can you watch the cat while I'm gone? I hate to put this burden on you, but you're the only one I trust to do it."

"Of course. No problem. Do you want me to stop by and feed him twice a day?"

"Actually, can you take him to your apartment? I don't trust him in my place alone. He's been through a lot."

"Sure. Yeah, I can take him home with me."

"Great. I'm leaving a key under the doormat." A suitcase zipped shut, and footsteps on a wooden floor echoed through the line.

"That's not a safe place to leave a key."

"You're the only one who will be able to find it. I enchanted it."

"Oh, wow." Her shoulders slumped. Just when she thought she was finally going to get some answers, her only hope had to go to Florida. "How long do you think you'll be gone?"

"A few days, tops. And we're still going to talk when I get back, but...this cat is different. He's a familiar, so he's much, *much* smarter than your average feline."

She mentally added getting information about familiars to her laundry list of questions. "Okay. Is there anything else I need to know? Does he have any magical powers of his own? Is that why you don't want to leave him alone?"

"No, he won't cast spells or anything, but don't try to feed him cat food. He only eats regular people food, so just make a plate for him when you're eating."

"Interesting. Where should I keep his litter box?"

"He uses the toilet."

She laughed. Sure he did. "Does he flush too?"

"Of course. If you turn the water on, he'll wash his paws."

Sophie paused, expecting her friend to laugh, but she sounded as serious as could be. "You're kidding."

"When I get back, we're going to talk, and this will all make sense. I promise."

"I was going to argue that it wouldn't, but with the amount of weird I've seen the past few months, it'll probably make perfect sense. I hope it will, anyway."

"It will. And it's important that the cat stays inside at all times. He can't come into contact with any supes outside your apartment, okay?"

"Got it. I'll keep him indoors and away from people.

Anything else?"

"I've been analyzing your magic from the hair you gave me."

Sophie rubbed her head to chase away the phantom stinging sensation. "You mean the hair you yanked from my scalp?"

"If you want to be dramatic, sure."

She laughed. "Drama is my middle name. So, what did you find out? Am I really the chosen one who's supposed to be ruler of all witches?"

"Now, that would be something," Crimson said. "I discovered that your inborn gift is animal communication, like I suspected, so if the cat says anything to you—"

Sophie scoffed. "Animals don't talk to me."

"This isn't an ordinary animal."

"Right. A familiar. You're going to have to explain exactly what that means."

"When I get back. I'm heading out the door now, and I'll call you later to check in. Thank you so much for doing this. I owe you one."

Sophie ended the call and made her way toward her first canine client's home, a little thrill of excitement washing away the disappointment of not getting her questions answered tonight. She was going to cat-sit a witch's familiar, and if that wasn't the coolest thing ever, she didn't know what was.

Not only that, but Crimson said Sophie was the only one she trusted to do it. Surely she had other friends she could have called, but she'd chosen her. Sophie was one step closer to securing a spot in the coven, finding a place where she belonged.

She finished her final round of dog-walking and hurried up the stairs, past her own apartment, to the third floor. Lifting the mat, she found the key where Crimson said it would be. Nothing seemed out of the ordinary. No sparkles exploded from the rug when she moved it. The key didn't glow or feel any temperature other than what a normal key that had been sitting under a doormat for hours would feel. *Bummer.*

With a shrug, she unlocked the door and slipped inside her

friend's apartment. Flipping on the lights, she gasped as the overhead lamps illuminated a studio filled with canvases painted in rich hues. Most were landscapes and local landmarks, but a few portraits sat among the array. An easel near the window held an unfinished painting of a man with light brown skin, dark hair, and intense chocolate eyes. He was striking, and the details were so lifelike, it could have been mistaken for a photograph if it were finished.

When Sophie stepped toward the canvas to get a closer look, the cat leapt down from a windowsill, landing in front of the painting and pinning her with an intense yellow-eyed gaze. He meowed, regarding her as if sizing her up, determining whether or not she was a threat.

"Hey, handsome. Remember me? My name's Sophie." She dropped to her knees and held out a hand. "Crimson asked me to look after you while she's away."

The cat slinked toward her, sniffing her hand before darting under the couch.

"Oh, jeez. You probably smell all those dogs, don't you? Let me wash my hands." She glanced at a clock as she stepped into the kitchen. Jane would be waking up soon. With her hands cleaned, she dried them on a dishtowel and returned to the loft area. The cat peered at her from beneath the sofa.

Lying on her stomach, she reached toward him. "You're going to stay with me for a few days. Come on out, little guy."

He swatted a paw at her hand, his claws scraping across her skin.

"Ouch." She jerked her hand away and rose to her feet, flustered. Sure, the cat was a familiar, but he was still an animal, right? "Listen, buddy. You're coming home with me, and we can do it the easy way or the hard way. Don't make me flip this couch over."

Her phone buzzed with a call from Jane. "Hey, girl." Jane yawned. "I haven't even had my morning O neg. What's the problem?"

She reached for the cat again, and it scrambled deeper beneath the couch. "Ugh, this stupid cat won't come when I call it."

Jane laughed. "A beast you can't tame? Are you sure it's really a cat?"

"It's a familiar. I'm not sure what that means, but it's smarter than a normal cat." She dropped onto the sofa and rubbed her forehead. "Anyway, can you come over? So much happened today, I don't even know where to begin. I saw Trace this afternoon. I think he finally believes I didn't hurt his friend, but now there's a problem with his pack. I just... Can you come over?"

"I'll be there in twenty."

"Thanks, Jane. You're the best." As she pressed end, the cat jumped onto the cushion next to her, cocking its head and looking at her quizzically.

Sophie sighed. "I've got a lot on my plate right now, including a hotter-than-Hades werewolf I can't get off my mind, whose pack might want to kill me for something I'm not even capable of doing. For the love of all that is supernatural in this world, will you please come home with me?"

She held out her arms, and the cat slinked toward her, allowing her to scoop him up and carry him out the door. *Hallelujah.*

She took him to her apartment and set him on the floor. He immediately darted to the kitchen and pawed at the fridge door.

"I'll heat something up for dinner later. Do you want a snack in the meantime?" She opened the refrigerator, and the cat touched the deli drawer with a paw. "All I've got is some ham that's about to expire. Will that work?" She put what was left of the lunchmeat on a paper plate and laid it on the floor.

The cat jumped into a chair, resting his front paws on the table and blinking at her.

"Oh, you like to eat at the table, do you?" She shook her head and put the plate in front of him. "You use the toilet. You eat human food at the table. If you're really a cat shifter, you can turn into a man and stop playing games. I've got enough to deal with right now."

The cat paused from eating, briefly narrowing his eyes at her before returning to the food.

Ten minutes later, Jane arrived, looking fabulous as always. Her vampire complexion, though pale, was as perfect as porcelain, and her shiny brown hair flowed over her shoulders like it belonged on a supermodel.

In the early months after Jane was turned, Sophie had considered asking her friend to bring her into the world of the undead, but drinking blood and sleeping all day wasn't the slightest bit appealing. Plus, the whole being mostly dead thing made their skin clammy like a corpse. She couldn't imagine climbing into bed with a cadaver, much less getting naked with one. She shuddered.

"Are you okay?" Jane touched a frigid hand to her arm, not improving her thoughts.

"I honestly don't know. I—"

The cat crept into the room, freezing as it spotted Jane and arching its back to let out a wicked hiss. Jane smirked, tilting her head in amusement before hissing right back at the cat. With a whiney meow, he jumped onto Sophie's shoulder, digging his claws through her shirt and into her skin as he began a stare down with a vampire.

"It's okay. This is Jane. She's my friend." Sophie pried the cat from her shoulder and set him on the couch. "You're getting good at hissing," she said to Jane. "You sounded just like him."

"Thanks. I've been practicing. It's incredibly satisfying to let one rip when someone's annoying me."

"I can imagine." Sophie turned to the cat and let out a puny human-sounding hiss. He responded by curling into a ball and tucking his paws beneath him.

"Best to leave the hissing to the professionals." Jane sank into a recliner. "So, spill. What's the problem, and how can I help?"

"Remember Crimson, the woman who owns the coffee shop downstairs?"

"The one you think might be a witch? We ought to go up and knock on her door, so I can confirm that theory for you."

"No need. I talked to her about it this morning, and she is a witch." She leaned back on the sofa. "Turns out, I'm one too."

Jane's mouth dropped open. "Seriously? But the spells don't work. What the...? How...?"

"It's a long story, and that's not the biggest issue. The problem is Trace."

"Your sexy werewolf." She wiggled her eyebrows.

Sophie nodded. "I think I've convinced him I'm innocent, but his pack wants me dead." She explained everything she learned today. "So the only way to make them believe I didn't do it is to either find Jackson or find the witch who cursed them. Do you think you can help me?"

The cat crawled into Sophie's lap, placing its front paws on her chest. "Oh, now you want to be my friend? I suppose you feel sorry for me?" She stroked his soft fur, and he purred.

"Wow." Jane crossed her legs, lacing her fingers together on her knee. "The pack doesn't know about your sprouting fur issue? Has that happened again?"

"No, thank goodness. It only happened once. They don't even know Trace bit me. If they knew, I'd be dead by now. He's keeping it a secret to protect me. He's going against pack orders to keep me safe." The cat sat on his haunches, flicking his tail as he watched her intently.

Jane grinned. "Well, isn't that the most romantic thing I've ever heard? You've got the hottest werewolf in New Orleans risking his status in the pack, maybe even risking his life for you. What's his plan if you do turn? Will you run away together? If you do, you can't go too far. I'd miss the hell out of you."

She stared at her hands folded in her lap. "I haven't told Trace about the fur either."

"Why not?"

Heat flushed her cheeks. "It's embarrassing."

"Maybe to you, but I bet it's not to him. His entire body sprouts fur. You having a couple of patches isn't going to faze him."

She lifted her gaze to Jane's. "What am I going to do?"

"You're going to celebrate. I'll work my vampire magic and find the missing werewolf." She held up a hand as Sophie started to protest. "Seriously, don't doubt me. I will be discreet, and I will find out what happened to him. In the meantime, you're going to go on that date, fuck his brains out, and then show him you are everything he's ever wanted in a woman."

She shook her head. "Jane…"

"Think about it. You've met a witch who's willing to help you. You have actual magic inside you that I bet she can help you unlock, and you've caught the eye of one helluva sexy werewolf who's willing to put his life on the line for you. All your dreams are coming true."

"Assuming his pack doesn't kill me."

Jane waved her hand dismissively. "They won't, and if they try, they'll have to get through me, Ethan, and Gaston to get to you. I've got another forty-nine years before I can be on the vampire council, but I've got the Magistrate's ear. Nothing is going to happen to you. You're going to be a badass witch with a werewolf boyfriend by the end of the week."

The cat curled onto her lap, closing his eyes contentedly. Her BFF said exactly the words Sophie wanted to hear, and it was easy to get swept away by her optimism. If everything worked out that way, her dreams would come true, but now that she'd had all evening to think about it…

"I have a feeling it's not going to be that easy."

"You've got this. I know you do." Jane's smile was reassuring, and as her words sank in, Sophie's chest warmed.

There was nothing wrong with optimism. "Thanks, babe. This is why you're my BFF."

"I know. Now, I've got to get out and find dinner before I shrivel up and die again. Are you going to be okay here alone?"

"I'm not alone. I've got Crimson's familiar."

After Jane left, Sophie showered and then found the cat curled up in her bed. There went her idea of breaking out Big Blue while she finished the fantasy she'd just had about Trace. "I guess you won't take up too much room." She picked him up, and, moving him to the side, she climbed under the covers.

Her phone buzzed on the nightstand, and her heart kicked into a sprint when she saw Trace's name lighting up the screen. Clearing her throat, she took a deep breath, trying not to sound too excited. "Hello?"

"Hey, Sophie. I hope it's not too late to call." His deep, velvety voice flowed through her ears like honey.

"It's okay. I was just thinking about you." Dripping wet in the hot shower, he was all she'd thought of.

"You, uh... You were?" Why did the man sound surprised? He was an Earth-bound sex god.

She bit her lip. *Shit.* He apparently didn't call because he was thinking about her. "Yeah. I talked to Jane, and she's going to help find out what happened to your friend."

"Oh." Was that disappointment she detected in his tone? "Great. Are you still willing to help? I thought of something you could do."

"You'd be amazed at all the things I can do." She pressed her lips into a line. Could she not have one conversation with this man without sounding like a nymphomaniac?

His deep chuckle resonated in her soul. "We're still on for Saturday night, right? I'm looking forward to being amazed."

A shiver shimmied up her spine. "Absolutely."

Silence hung between them as she closed her eyes, imagining the fire in his gaze as he trailed his fingers down her cheek, his thumb brushing across her lips before he...

He cleared his throat. "But about finding Jackson. Here's what I need you to do."

CHAPTER SEVEN

Trace stood between two buildings on Burgundy Street, a boutique hotel with a slate gray façade and white wrought iron gallery, and a brown, three-story structure that housed the witch's perfume and secret potion shop on the bottom floor. The gate leading to the alley between stood unlocked, so it was a perfect spot to wait in case the force-shift came on. But every time the goddamn door opened, the overpowering scents of fifty different oils and potions wafted out, singeing his nostrils and making him want to puke.

His heightened canine sense of smell made entering the shop area of the building nearly impossible for a werewolf. The store wasn't enchanted, as far as he knew. The witches relied on the overwhelming aroma to keep other supes from nosing around in their business. Aside from being able to detect magical signatures with their noses, a witch's sense of smell was no better than a human's.

That's where Sophie would come in. It had been years since the red wolves had swiped a copy of the witches' registration manifest, and it was time they updated their records. Sophie would make a perfect distraction while he sneaked in and stole the information.

Truth be told, he'd racked his brain all evening to figure out a way she could help him search for Jackson, not because he actually needed her help, but because he couldn't wait until Saturday to see her again.

He spotted her strutting toward him on the sidewalk, and he tensed, a strange urge to run to her, sweep her into his arms, and carry her away from all this mess making his weight shift to his toes. If his friend hadn't been missing for the past week, he might have done just that.

"Hey." Her smile warmed his soul, and as she stopped two feet in front of him, he fought another urge to lean in and find out if her lips tasted as good as they did in his dreams. She glanced at the perfume shop, her brow furrowing. "I was thinking last night…"

"So was I." He swept his gaze down her body, and a pink flush spread across her cheeks. "You were incredible, too."

She grinned. "It's awfully forward of you to say things like that when we haven't even been on a date yet."

"I can smell your desire, remember?"

He glimpsed a flash of tongue as she moistened her lips, and his knees nearly buckled. She let her gaze meander over him, one brow arching as she seemed to approve of the view. "Can you now?"

"You want me as much as I want you." Okay, maybe he was being too forward, but it was the truth. Every time he flirted with her, her scent warmed like spiced cider. He couldn't help himself.

She laughed and shook her head. "Are you sure you aren't getting my desire mixed up with that awful smell coming from the perfume shop?" She wrinkled her nose. "Someone must have ordered a horrific combination of scents. I walk by this place every day, and I've never been able to smell it from the sidewalk."

Interesting. She shouldn't have been able to smell it at all. His gaze drifted to her arm, where his teeth marks still marred her skin, and hope bloomed in his chest. It shouldn't have. She never asked to be turned into a werewolf, and if she wanted to press charges against him, he'd be so deep in shit, he'd drown. But if she did complete the transformation, and she felt even half of the feelings he felt for her…

"Anyway, I've got another group of dogs to walk in half an hour, so let's get this mission started. All I have to do is distract the women behind the counter?"

"Right. I'll slip in the back and find the manifest, photograph it, and then I'll text you when I'm out."

She crossed her arms. "How do you know it's even in there? Wouldn't they keep something like that in their coven headquarters? Or, more likely, on a computer?"

"You'd be surprised how backward supes can be, and they don't keep it at the coven house because that would be the first place people would look for it." He stepped toward her, resting his hand on the small of her back, his touch making her scent flare again. *Delicious.* "Being a cop in the NOPD pays the bills, but I'm also the head of security for the pack. If a supe orgasms within a ten-mile radius of New Orleans, my men know."

She pressed her lips together, suppressing a smile. "I love it when you talk dirty. Tell me more."

A shudder ran through his body, and he dropped his arm. As much as he enjoyed the flirtatious banter with this incredible woman, they had a job to do. "The manifest contains the names of every registered witch in Orleans Parish. When my men sniffed you out, the coven already knew about you. They said you were unregistered and that you were a dud. We assumed you were the only one, but now I'm thinking there may be more people like you. People who possess magic but don't know it or can't access it."

"I know I have magic." She lifted her chin.

"But you didn't until yesterday. If magic has to be unlocked, there's a chance someone on that list figured out how to unbind her powers, under the coven's radar, and she's the one responsible for the curse on my pack."

"How do you even know I'm on the list? There could be dozens of people like me roaming the city. The only difference with me is that I went looking for it."

He shook his head. "We aren't the only ones with informants. Supes of every variety work for a common goal: to identify everyone in the city who possesses magic. I promise you the first day you were here, probably within the first few hours, you'd been identified and added to the manifest. Your scent but lack of signature in your aura suggested you were trying to hide your magic, but the witches must have known your powers were bound...something the werewolves never would have figured out."

"So if I could unbind my powers and hide my aura, the coven would never know I had magic?"

"And you'd be a threat to us all. Our truces keep everything in balance, which is why the curse on my pack could be detrimental to the entire city."

"Isn't sneaking in and photographing their private documents against the truce?"

He grinned. "Only if we get caught."

Holy fur and fangs, Sophie was working with a supe, doing sneaky supe things, dangerous things. What would happen to them if they got caught? Would the war start between the werewolves and the witches? If it did, which side would she be on?

She sucked in a deep breath and blew it out hard. These were questions she should have thought to ask before Trace bounded down the alley toward the back entrance, but her rational mind went into hiding every time she was near the man.

Suck it up, buttercup. You're in this now. She'd offered to help, and he was depending on her. Maybe he'd reward her later…

Focus, Soph. She gripped the cool metal door handle and tugged it open, pausing as a blast of fragrances assaulted her senses like a forcefield over the entrance. How did these women work in here all day?

She swallowed the sour sensation creeping up her throat and forced her way through the stench and into the shop. Two witches stood behind the counter, a petite one with dark eyes and jet-black hair styled in an asymmetrical pixie cut, and one about the same height as Sophie, with striking blue eyes and long brown hair. Of course, the only reason Sophie knew they were witches was because Trace told her they were, but they must have sensed her witchy scent.

Both their heads snapped up at the same time, and the brunette narrowed her eyes at Sophie briefly before plastering on a smile. "Hey there. How can we help you?"

"Umm." Sophie glanced around at the shop. Rows of wooden shelves containing small glass bottles with cork stoppers covered two of the walls, and an archway the width of two normal doors led into a back room. Trace peeked from behind the wall and gave her a thumbs-up before disappearing again.

She cleared her throat and faced the witches. "I'm looking for a special perfume to make a man want me."

"Oh, honey, you've come to the right place." The pixie cut sashayed around the counter and offered Sophie a postcard and pen. "I'm Jade, and this is Audrey. Why don't you fill out this card so we can mix something up for you?"

"Sure." Sophie took the pen and wrote her real name on the top of the page. As she got to the "S" in "Burroughs," she froze, pressing the tip into the paper harder and harder until blue ink pooled around it. What kind of supernatural spy gave the enemy her real name?

Shit. She tightened her grip on the pen, finishing the S and forcing herself to breathe. It wasn't like she could scratch it out and write Pussy Galore instead.

"Is everything okay?" Jade linked her fingers, staring at Sophie intently.

"Yeah. Just a little headache." She finished the form with a fake address and phone number. "I don't know how you ladies make it through the day with all these wonderful scents."

"You get used to it." Jade took the card and strode toward the archway. Toward Trace.

Crap. "Why are you taking that to the back room?" She nearly shouted to warn him. Hopefully the witches didn't notice the panic in her voice.

Jade paused, turning to face her. "I'm just going to enter this in our customer database. Audrey will take care of you."

Sophie glimpsed Trace darting from one side of the arch to the other. Damn, he was fast. Not as fast as a vampire, but the man could move.

"Tell me a little about your tastes, Sophie." Audrey smiled, her gaze flicking to Jade before she focused on Sophie again. "Do you like floral scents or something warmer?"

Sophie glanced to the backroom as Jade pulled out an ancient-looking binder and flipped through the pages, running her finger from top to bottom as if reading a list. It must have been the manifest Trace was looking for. "Floral. No, I think the man I'm after prefers warmer scents."

Audrey nodded. "If men only knew what we go through to impress them."

"She's fine." Jade strutted into the shop area, mouthing something to the other witch that Sophie couldn't decipher.

If Sophie was going to be a spy, she'd need to work on her lipreading skills. Judging by the softening of both their demeanors, Jade had found Sophie's name already on the list, and they knew she was harmless. Correction: they *thought* she was harmless. She stifled a giggle. This spy stuff was fun.

"Let's mix you up something magical," Jade said. "What's this guy like?"

Sophie turned, angling herself so she faced the archway straight on and forcing Jade and Audrey to put their backs toward Trace, who pulled out his phone to snap pictures of the manifest Jade had left on the desk. These witches were so confident, they were careless.

"Oh, he's tall and built, with auburn hair and a full beard. The man oozes masculinity. He's a cop too. Sexy as hell. My panties want to drop to the floor on their own every time I'm near him, if you know what I mean." She grinned as Trace stifled his chuckle, and she forced herself to hold eye contact with the women.

"Sounds scrumptious," Jade said.

"You have no idea."

"You said you wanted something to make the man want you." Audrey ran her fingers along a row of bottles, stopping on a brown one with a white label. "What kind of *want* are we talking about? Is this purely sexual, or are you looking for more?"

Trace stopped, standing in the door with a brow arched as if he were seriously interested in the answer to her question.

Sophie locked eyes with him for half a second before casting her gaze to the row of bottles, lest she give him away. "I'm not sure how he feels, but I think I want more. I mean, the initial attraction was pure lust, but now that I'm getting to know him…"

Audrey's smile urged her to continue, though she didn't dare look to see if Trace still stood exposed. "I feel a connection with him. Like maybe he could be…" She almost said *the one*, but she bit her tongue to stop the words from escaping. That would be a sure-fire way to send him running with his tail between his legs. "He could be someone I'd like to date more than once, you know?"

"Girl, I know." Audrey took another bottle from the shelf as Sophie's phone buzzed in her pocket.

She checked the screen and found a text from Trace: *All done, gorgeous. You were amazing.* Her stomach fluttered.

"Oh, crap. I have to go." She shoved the phone into her pocket. "Just, umm…hold off on the perfume. I'll be back. Maybe." She scurried out the door, adrenaline making it feel as though her feet didn't touch the floor.

Glancing at her watch, she cursed under her breath and powerwalked toward her first client's home. She had three minutes to pick the dog up if she was going to be on time for this walk.

Her phone buzzed again with a text from Trace: *Where did you go?*

She replied: *I have to work. Talk later.*

Her heart beating like a racehorse's hooves, she made it to her destination right on time. Her excited energy rubbed off on the dogs, and she nearly had to jog to keep up with them as they made their afternoon round. Even with the extra boost of adrenaline, the male dogs kept their private parts to themselves, and Sophie's legs remained safe from their wanton advances.

Her smile didn't fade all day. The entire mission—how exciting was it to call what they'd done a mission?—had lasted no more than twenty minutes, but Sophie couldn't remember the last time she'd had that much fun. Catching glimpses of Trace as he gathered evidence for his pack had been a major turn-on too. The man was lucky she had to work, or she might have torn his clothes off right there on the sidewalk when it was done.

Then again, depending on how much of her conversation with the witches he heard, maybe *she* was the lucky one. What if Saturday night's date was nothing more than his attempt to get into her pants? Or worse, what if everything…the flirting, the heated gazes…what if it was all part of his spy persona, and he still thought she was to blame? What if the Trace she was starting to fall for wasn't the real Trace at all?

Oh, get over yourself. He'd already scoured her apartment and found nothing. At the very least, she could get a good lay out of the situation, and at best... Who knew? She might as well enjoy the rush while it lasted.

She finished her evening round and picked up some Chinese takeout with an extra serving of chicken fried rice for the cat. He meowed his appreciation and ate at the table next to her—*so weird*—before she took a quick shower and collapsed into bed. The cat crawled onto her stomach, curling up and rubbing the top of its head against the bottom of her boob.

She laughed and stroked its fur. "That's the most action I've gotten in months, but things might be changing soon. If Crimson isn't back by Saturday night, you'll need to make yourself scarce. Understand?"

The cat blinked at her, and her phone rang from the nightstand, Trace's name lighting up the screen. She pushed the cat aside to answer. "Hey there, hot stuff."

"Hello, beautiful. How was your day?" How could his voice be deep and rumbly, yet smooth as satin at the same time?

"Adventurous, actually. I had my first foray into the supernatural spy world, and it was quite thrilling."

He chuckled. "You were amazing in there. I could use you on my team."

Her lips parted on a quick inhale, excitement buzzing through her veins. "Really?"

"Yeah. If you become a werewolf, I'll hire you at the next full moon."

"Oh." Her chest deflated with her sigh. "I don't think that's going to happen." Nor did she want it to. Becoming a full-fledged witch was her number one priority. She could imagine the looks on Jade's and Audrey's faces when she strolled into the perfume shop, magic sparkling in her aura. *See if they underestimate me again.*

"Well, either way, I appreciate your help. I found three new names added to the roster since we last swiped a copy: you plus two others. I checked out one of them this afternoon, but I didn't find a trace of Jackson. I plan to drop in on the other one tomorrow."

Her chest tightened as she pictured the way he'd *dropped in* on her. Was that jealousy stirring in her belly? Surely not. "I hope you're not crawling into their beds naked like you did mine." Her teeth clicked as she clamped her mouth shut. They weren't a couple. It was none of her business how he conducted his.

A deep belly laugh resonated through the receiver. "Would it bother you if I did?"

"Yes, as a matter of fact, it would. You're starting to grow on me, wolfman."

He inhaled deeply, the sound tickling her ear. "I grow every time I'm near you, *cher.*"

She couldn't help but giggle. "Do you now?"

"Yes, ma'am. You tend to have that effect on me."

"I'd like to see for myself." She fisted her hand and bit her finger to contain her excitement.

"I can show you Saturday night."

"Is that a promise?" She dropped her head back on the pillow, grinning at the ceiling.

"It most certainly is."

CHAPTER EIGHT

Trace jogged up the steps to Sophie's apartment and blew against his palm, attempting to check his breath for the third time since he'd gotten out of his truck. Like the first two times, he couldn't smell a damn thing, but he popped a mint into his mouth just in case.

He'd been a bundle of nerves all day, the anticipation of seeing Sophie in a nonwork, non-accusing capacity winding him up tighter than a gator's ass in a hurricane. Inhaling deeply, he straightened his spine, composing himself. He was the Alpha's right-hand man and First Lieutenant in his pack. He didn't show his nerves to anyone, especially not the woman he was trying to claim...err...seduce. The woman he was trying to *seduce.*

He shook his head and lifted a hand to knock, but before his knuckles met wood, the door swung open. Sophie beamed a smile, and his gaze swept the length of her feminine form, taking in the short red dress and matching heels that made her legs look ten miles long. She rested her hand against the door jamb, and he glimpsed polished red nails that matched her outfit perfectly.

Her long blonde hair was swept up in a twist with a few soft strands framing her face, and she held a tiny gold purse attached to her wrist by a thin strap.

She was stunning. Beautiful. Magnificent. The most gorgeous woman he'd ever seen, but the signal from his brain to his mouth was fried, and the only word he managed to utter was, "Damn."

"That is exactly the response I was hoping for. Who needs designer perfume?"

"Definitely not you."

She peered over her shoulder and pulled the door shut, joining him on the landing. "I guess we better get you out of the French Quarter in case the evil witch works her magic again."

"Hold on. I need to do something first." Something he'd been wanting to do since the moment he met her. An urge he'd been struggling with for as long as he'd known her, and damn it, he was tired of fighting.

Cupping her cheek in his hand, he leaned in and pressed his mouth to hers. He only meant for it to be a quick brush of the lips, but when "*mmm*" vibrated from her throat and she threw her arms around his neck, he went for it, tongue and all.

She leaned into him, pressing her soft curves into his chest, parting her lips and drinking him in like she was dying of thirst. He didn't realize how parched he'd been until her velvet tongue brushed against his, sending a tidal wave of emotion rolling through his body. It crashed into his core, and his inner wolf howled in delight.

"You're not wasting any time, are you?" She rested her forehead against his.

"I couldn't help myself. You look good enough to eat."

She laughed and pulled away, smoothing her dress down her stomach. "While I'm tempted to drag you inside right now and let you make a meal out of me, I'm starving. I want dinner before I put out."

"I like a woman who knows what she wants."

Resting a hand on her hip, she trailed her gaze down his form, lingering below his belt. "I know exactly what I want."

"I can't wait to give it to you."

"Dinner first." Rising onto her toes, she swiveled around and strutted toward the staircase, the quick movement wafting her delicious cinnamon fragrance to his senses.

Oh, he'd take her to dinner. Then *she* would be dessert. "Hold on."

She spun to face him. "Yes?"

He focused on the sexy red high heels, silently cursing himself for what he was about to suggest. "I was thinking we'd go for a stroll in City Park after dinner. As much as I love those shoes on you…"

She looked down at her feet, twisting one inward in a way that made his mouth water. "Good call. Stilettoes aren't made for long walks. Give me a sec." She strutted inside her apartment and returned two minutes later in a pair of silver ballet flats. "Thanks for the warning. You'd have ended up carrying me if I'd tried to wear those heels all night."

"If you want to put them back on later, I won't mind."

She laughed. "I bet."

He took her to Marie's, a small mom and pop Creole joint a few miles north of the Quarter. Quiet and unassuming, Marie's had the best crawfish bisque and court bouillon in town. Sophie asked him questions about his life, and she did a damn good job feigning interest as he droned on about pack life and his boring upbringing. He grew up in one house near the river, and he barely moved two miles away from his parents when he left the nest, which was typical for red wolves. They stuck together.

Sophie told him fascinating stories about traveling the world when her dad was in the military, experiencing a new place every couple of years. Trace didn't even have a passport.

She finished the last bite of her shrimp Creole and traced

her finger around the rim of her wine glass. "I can't even imagine what a life like yours would be like."

He chuckled. "Boring. Routine."

She tilted her head. "With stability. Always knowing where you belong. Fitting in. I never had that growing up. I still feel like I don't."

"Why do you think that is?"

"I'm a witch with no powers who's better at talking to animals than people, for one thing."

"You're great with people." He reached for her hand across the table. "You've got me hooked."

"We'll see how long you stick around."

Forever. He clenched his teeth. The word had nearly slipped from his lips, and that would have been the end of his blossoming relationship with Sophie right then and there. He had to play it cool, but he needed her to know he was after more than her body.

Lacing his fingers through hers, he looked into her eyes. "I'm not going anywhere any time soon."

She held his gaze for what felt like an eternity before a sly smile curved her lips and she winked. "Great. I've landed myself a clingy one."

"Just call me Saran Wrap." He laughed, and she laughed, the tension between them dissolving like sugar in hot coffee. "You can't be that bad with people."

"Don't underestimate me."

"What's the most embarrassing thing you've done lately?"

She straightened her spine, smoothing her napkin in her lap as her eyes tightened. "The night Jane met Ethan, I puked on his shoes."

Trace blinked, trying to keep a neutral expression, but damn... "Okay, that is bad. What happened?"

"It was our first night in New Orleans, and it was Mardi Gras." She shrugged, and an adorable blush tinted her cheeks.

He nodded. "Gotcha. No need to say more. We've all been there."

"What about you?"

"Oh, I'm pretty calm and collected. You have to be in my line of work."

"Uh-uh. I'm not buying it for a minute, and you're not getting out of this." She crossed her arms. "I shared. Now it's your turn."

He couldn't have told her no if he tried. The problem was, aside from the incident with the nymph, which he wasn't about to bring up, he hadn't done much to screw up. Cupping his chin in his hand, he rubbed his beard and searched his memory for something embarrassing. "I found myself naked in the bed of the most beautiful woman I've ever met, and instead of asking her to join me, I accused her of crimes against my pack. I'm still working on earning her forgiveness."

"Wow. Sucks to be her. I can't imagine what I'd do if a hot, naked werewolf wound up in my bed. If he accused me of crimes against his pack, I might threaten to beat him with a vibrator." She grinned. "I forgive you."

He chuckled. "Good."

"Still no luck finding your friend?"

"I feel like I'm chasing my tail. Every time I get a lead, it comes up dry, and I keep running in circles."

"Did you ever stop to think that maybe he doesn't want to be found? That maybe he and the witch ran away together, and they're sipping margaritas on a beach in Mexico?"

He looked at the woman sitting across from him, with her sky-blue eyes and electric smile. He'd had the same thoughts about her recently, whisking her away from danger, taking her somewhere no one could hurt her, especially his pack. If it came down to it, and Sophie were in real danger, he'd do just that. "I suppose it's a possibility, though I like to think he'd at least let me know he was okay."

And it still didn't answer the riddle of why someone was

force-shifting the members of his pack. He glanced at a clock. "Oh, we've got to get going, or we'll miss our appointment."

"Our appointment for what?"

"You'll see." He stood, taking her hand again and tugging her to her feet. He'd mull over the idea that his best friend might have ditched him on purpose later. Right now, his focus was on his own beautiful witch.

They made the short drive to City Park and strolled up the trail toward Big Lake, where the gondola he'd booked for the hour awaited them. When he stepped up to the ticket booth and gave the attendant his name, a brown tabby jumped onto the counter, arching his back and hissing.

"Sylvester, what's wrong with you?" The attendant scooped up the cat, dropping him on the floor, and passed Trace a waiver to sign. "I'm sorry. He's a friendly cat. I don't know what's gotten into him." A deep mewling sound emanated from the cat's throat as it glared at Trace.

"It's okay. I'm not really a cat person." He signed the form and took the tickets from the attendant.

"You don't like cats, or they don't like you?" Sophie slipped her hand into his as they walked out on the pier toward the gondola.

"Both. Werewolves and cat shifters are natural-born enemies. We've never gotten along as far as I know."

Her eyes widened. "That was a shifter?"

He laughed. "That was a domesticated house cat, but animals can sense the wolf in me. Of course, we werewolves think we're better than cats. I'm sure the cats feel superior to us too."

"Cats feel superior to everyone." She stopped, slipping from his grasp, her brow furrowing. "I'm cat-sitting for my neighbor. He's a familiar. Is that going to be a problem later?"

"A familiar? I thought you weren't friends with any witches?" He gestured toward the boat, where a short man in a black and white striped shirt waited with his arm outstretched.

"Just the one who told me the secrets I spilled to you." Sophie took the man's hand and stepped into the gondola. "She lives upstairs, but she texted me earlier. She'll be home tomorrow morning."

"I don't have much experience with familiars, but a cat's a cat." He joined her in the boat, sinking into the seat and wrapping an arm around her shoulders.

"I'd say maybe we should go to your place after this, but I don't want to leave him alone all night. If he gives us any trouble, I'll put him in the bathroom."

"That's a good place for a feline."

The gondolier played soft Italian music on a speaker as he paddled the boat around the lake, and Sophie leaned into Trace's side, a contented sigh escaping her lips as she rested a hand on his thigh.

A walking trail surrounded the water, dotted with massive oaks to provide plenty of shade in the daytime, and the New Orleans Museum of Art stood in the distance, it's white stucco façade and Grecian columns illuminated against the darkness.

Everything about this felt right. The clear night sky twinkled with stars, and the moon, three-quarters full, shone bright, casting a silvery glow on the lake. Sophie fit next to him like she was made to be there, and for a moment, despite the turmoil in his pack, all felt right in the world.

"Why did you decide to become a cop?" She angled her face toward him and crossed her legs, hooking her ankle over his.

His chest tightened at the intimate gesture. "It's in my blood. My dad's a cop too, and it helps the pack, and all supes, to have people on the inside."

Her gaze flicked back to the gondolier, and she tensed.

"He's a water sprite," he whispered.

She turned to look at him, narrowing her gaze as if trying to see his magic. He waved, and she waved back before settling into Trace's side again. "Do any of the human police know what you are?"

"Just the chief, and he's sworn to secrecy like the mayor and the governor."

"Jane's dad is the governor of Texas. Imagine how shocked she was to learn that he knew about y'all all along and never told her." She laughed. "She was pissed."

"I can imagine. What about you? I'm surprised with your animal abilities, you didn't become a vet."

She let out a slow breath. "My animal abilities caused me so much trouble when I was young, I wanted nothing to do with them. Walking to school, stray dogs would follow me. We had a swarm of cats hanging around outside our house no matter where we lived, and I got teased because of it. I got called 'Dog Girl,' 'Crazy Cat Girl,' 'Dr. Dolittle Junior.'"

"Jeez. Such original names."

"I know, right? By the time I got into high school, I didn't have any friends. When I would start getting close to someone, it never failed. We either moved away, or I'd forget most people don't talk to animals as if they actually understand them, and they'd decide I was a weirdo. Then came Jane." A wistful look crossed her face.

"You two seem really close."

"She saved me. She took me in, and she wasn't the slightest bit put off by my quirks. At school, she was the epitome of popularity: rich, her dad was in politics, she had four hot older brothers. Everyone wanted to be her friend, but she dealt with a lot of fake people. She liked me because I was real. Her mom died when she was young, and she came to my house a lot. My mom was a mother figure for her, and we were like sisters." She looked at him, and he nodded, silently urging her to continue.

"Anyway, we were roommates in college, and I majored in business. I walked dogs on the side to earn money—I wasn't born into wealth like Jane—and the business did so well, I couldn't see myself working in a cubicle in an entry-level job when I was making a good living already. So I focused on the business and expanded, and now I'm working on a branch here in New Orleans."

"What made you decide to branch out here?"

"I moved here to be with Jane. Well, that and…" She shrugged.

"And what?" His curiosity piqued, he angled his body toward her to see her face.

"It's silly." She cast her gaze downward and drew circles on his thigh with her finger. "I saw a fortune teller in Austin. She told me my business would prosper here, and I'd find magic and a man to make my innermost dreams come true. God, saying it out loud makes it sound crazy."

"That's not silly at all. Or crazy. I've met plenty of fortune tellers who know what they're talking about." He tugged her closer and kissed the top of her head. "Was she right?"

She shrugged. "Business is starting to pick up. I've discovered plenty of magic."

"And the man?"

She lifted her head from his shoulder and searched his eyes. "I'll let you know."

He could be that man. He *wanted* to be that man.

As the boat ride ended, he tipped the sprite and tucked Sophie under his arm, guiding her down a path into the deeply wooded area of the park. Massive oak trees, some as old as eight hundred years, towered above them, their canopies reaching out to touch the branches of their neighbors, creating a natural archway along the gravel path. Spanish moss draped from the boughs like curtains, and tiny new oaks sprouted around the roots.

The sharp scent of ginger and vinegar reached his senses, and he froze, tightening his grip on Sophie. He'd recognize the smell of that magic anywhere, and date or not, it was his job to deal with it. Something rustled in the bushes to the right, and he tugged Sophie off the path, undoing the first two buttons of his shirt before slipping it over his head and handing it to her.

Sophie gave him a quizzical look. "I fully intended on putting out tonight, Trace, but here in the park? Aren't you even going to kiss me first?"

"Wait here." He kicked off his shoes and jogged into the brush before shifting into his wolf form and shimmying out of the rest of his clothes.

CHAPTER NINE

Wait here? Did he seriously just tell her to *wait here?* Who did this guy think he was? She did not spend the past two and a half hours pouring her heart out to him, letting herself fall for the guy, only for him to turn into some testosterone-laden alphahole who thought women were helpless little creatures who needed to be protected and should *wait here*. If danger lurked in them there woods, she wasn't about to let him face it alone.

Clutching his shirt in her hand, she took a moment to press it to her nose and bask in his delicious scent. Hey, he was the hottest guy in New Orleans. She couldn't help herself. Warm and woodsy, with a hint of pine, it was a smell that made her insides melt every time she got near him. *Yum.*

With the obligatory shirt sniff out of the way, she fisted it in her hand—because she was supposed to be mad at him for his caveman act—and marched into the woods where Trace had disappeared.

Branches scratched at her bare legs, and her feet sank into the soft soil as if she were walking on a sponge. Thank goodness she'd changed into flats, though even they would probably be ruined after this trek through the brush.

She stopped at the edge of a clearing and found Trace in his wolf form, a ridge of copper fur standing on end along his back. He bared his teeth in a snarl, and Sophie wondered how she'd thought him a domesticated animal at all before. He looked absolutely wild.

Standing across from him, with its back arched and a paw with razor-sharp claws lifted—in defense or offense, she couldn't tell—was the biggest brown kitty she'd ever seen. Denser than a house cat, it had muscular shoulders and thick legs, and a ring of fur accented its face, like a smaller version of a lion's mane. This mini lion sported spots like a jaguar, but it couldn't have weighed more than twenty pounds. Compared to Trace's sixty or seventy pounds of pure canine muscle, the fight hardly seemed fair.

"Is that a bobcat?" They were the only kind of wild cats she knew of in Louisiana. It was way too small to be a cougar. "Are you a shifter or a regular cat?"

She didn't expect an answer from either of them, but Trace's voice faintly echoed in her head. *She's a bobcat shifter, and she's in our territory looking for a fight. I've dealt with her and her sisters before. Give me five minutes.*

"She?" Sophie crossed her arms, a stab of jealousy slicing through her chest. She had no right or reason to be jealous, but there the emotion was, clawing its way into her heart. Exactly how had he *dealt* with her before? Damn it, she liked this guy way too much.

The cat woman hissed and swatted her paw at Trace, who growled in return.

"Oh, no. This is not happening." Sophie moved closer to them and shook a finger at the cat. "First of all, both of you are really messing with my fantasy that shifters turn into ginormous beasts that can rip your head off with a snap of their jaws. I feel like a giant watching the two of you."

Trace's lip curled as he gave her the side-eye, and the cat woman mewled deep in her throat.

"And second, how the hell did you just put thoughts in my mind? I *heard* you, Trace." She'd heard the actual words as he spoke them. When he told her his name before, it had felt like the thought came from her own mind.

"It's part of your magic." She clutched her head as he spoke again.

"Okay, that's something we're going to have to discuss later, because wow. That's cool." She focused on the cat. "Listen. I'm on a date with this man, and I do not want him getting into a fight when he's supposed to be getting into my pants. Whatever beef you have with him and his pack, you need to get over it and move along. This isn't happening right now." She wagged her finger between the two of them to indicate the possible fight she was trying to defuse.

"Both of you need to chill out. Take a deep breath with me." She inhaled, and a slight vinegary scent mixed with the woody outdoor smells. Whether or not Trace and the cat lady followed along, she couldn't tell, but the cat's back began to de-arch, and Trace's ridge of upright fur smoothed.

"Okay. Now we're getting somewhere. I understand this is a territory dispute, so I want you to leave, ma'am. If you have issues with the truce or pact or whatever it is you have with the wolves, you can take it up with the Alpha in a civilized manner. Now go. Scoot." She waved an arm at the cat woman, who turned and bounded away.

Trace sat on his haunches and cocked his head at Sophie.

"You need to turn back into a human and get dressed before someone sees you. If you're coming back to my place, I want you as a man this time." She spun around and stomped toward his discarded clothes. "And don't you ever tell me to *wait here* again, mister. Just because I'm a woman, it doesn't mean I'm defenseless."

"It has nothing to do with you being a woman."

Sophie bent down to pick up Trace's pants. When she turned around, she found him in human form—naked human form—looking at her with an expression of awe. Of course, her gaze didn't linger on his face long. The moonlight filtering through the trees illuminated his figure, giving him an ethereal glow. All that muscle. The trail of auburn hair leading down to his...

Yep. He was hung like a horse, just as she remembered. She swallowed hard.

"Can I have my clothes, please?"

When she didn't respond, a cocky smile tilted his mouth as he took the fabric from her hands. "I assume I should take you being speechless as a compliment?"

She blinked, watching his muscles bunch and extend as he dressed. "You're hot, Trace, and I think you know it."

He chuckled. "Still like hearing it, especially from you."

"What was that about? Was the cat woman your ex-girlfriend or something? Is that why you didn't want me to follow you?"

A disgusted look contorted his features. "Cats and wolves are *not* compatible in any way. Especially in the bedroom. I didn't want you to follow me because I've dealt with her before. I was afraid if she sensed my feelings for you, she'd attack you to hurt me."

"Why would attacking me hurt you?"

He looked at her as if she'd gone insane. "Because I care about you."

"Oh." She clamped her mouth shut. Reciprocation would have been the nice thing to do. She did care for the man, after all. But his sudden confession took her aback, and her brain and her mouth seemed to be operating on different channels.

He buttoned his shirt and rolled the sleeves up to his elbows. "How did you calm us down like that?"

"What do you mean?"

"My wolf was ready to attack, and I know she was too. Then you came along and told us to calm down, and my wolf obeyed. Even the cat listened. Cats never listen."

"I don't know, I just talked to y'all. I guess because you were in your animal form, I was more persuasive." She shrugged.

"You're amazing. Have I told you that yet?"

Her stomach fluttered. He cared about her, and he thought she was amazing. It seemed she wasn't the only one interested in more than sex from this pairing. "I don't think you have." She grinned and batted her lashes.

"You're incredible." Grasping her hips, he tugged her to his body and wrapped his arms around her waist. "Magnificent."

"Tell me more."

"How about I show you?" He brushed his lips to hers, the coarse hairs of his beard tickling her skin as he coaxed her mouth open with his tongue. He tasted like a peppermint breath mint, and the warmth of his strong arms enveloping her was enough to make her knees buckle.

She leaned into him, running her hands across his strong back and down his muscular arms. The man was hard all over, especially the steel rod pressing into her hip, making her think naughty thoughts. She'd seen this man naked twice now, and she'd yet to touch him. It was time that changed.

Pulling away, she sucked her swollen bottom lip into her mouth, and he gazed at her with hooded eyes, a passion-drunk smile crooking his mouth. "Take me home." She nipped his earlobe before slipping her hand into his.

"That's an excellent idea." His voice was husky. "We've probably had enough excitement for the night."

"Oh, honey. The excitement hasn't even begun." She grinned and strolled to the path leading to the parking lot, tugging Trace along behind her. "Why are you hesitating?"

He gazed at her ass. "The view is nice from back here."

She laughed. "It's even better from the front. I'll show you when we get home."

"I'm not sure I'll make it that long."

They climbed into Trace's truck, and he texted his Alpha to warn her about the intruding bobcat shifter before driving back to Sophie's apartment. As she opened the front door, she glimpsed the backside of Crimson's cat as he dove under the couch, out of sight. Hopefully he'd stay there.

Trace paused in the entry, lifting his nose as if sniffing the air. "I smell magic."

"Crimson's familiar is here. Maybe that's what you smell?" She closed the door and tugged him into the living room.

"Maybe. It's muddled. I've never smelled anything quite like it." He stepped past the couch the cat hid beneath and stroked the backs of his fingers down Sophie's cheek. "What do you want to do now?"

A shiver ran down her spine, making heat bloom below her navel. She'd wanted this man from the moment they met. There was no sense in playing hard to get now. "You, Trace. I want to do you in every way imaginable...and believe me, I've imagined plenty."

"Have you?" Mischief sparkled in his eyes as he moved toward her, pinning her to the wall with a hand on either side of her head. "With your legs wrapped around my waist, using the wall for leverage?" He swept his gaze down her body before returning to her eyes.

Jesus Christ, the man hadn't laid a finger on her, and her panties were already wet. "That's one way to do it." She touched his face, gliding her fingers across his forehead and cupping his cheek in her hand.

He closed his eyes, nuzzling into her palm as if he relished the affection. "Bent over the couch with me taking you from behind?"

"Mm-hmm." She undid the buttons on his shirt, running her hands across his pecs and down his abs. He inhaled deeply, his lids falling shut again as she explored his body. "And over the table. The bathroom counter was fun too, with the mirror and all."

"You have a vivid imagination." He shrugged off his shirt, dropping it on the floor.

She ran a finger along the waistband of his jeans, and his stomach tightened with her touch. "I'm a daydreamer."

He closed the distance between them, gliding his lips along her neck before tugging down the zipper on the back of her dress. "Let me make your dreams come true."

Oh, hell yes. She shimmied out of her dress, letting it pool around her feet, and Trace stepped back, drinking her in with his gaze.

An appreciative grunt sounded in his chest as he shook his head slowly, and a crooked smile tilted his lips. "My imagination's got nothing on reality. You are even more gorgeous than I envisioned."

Her cheeks warmed at his words. She'd had her share of casual sex and heard plenty of shallow compliments aimed at getting between her legs, but something about the way Trace said it, the way he looked at her, she believed he meant every word.

"Well, let's finish unwrapping, and I'll gift you with the best sex of your life." She popped open her bra and tossed it aside.

Trace's pupils dilated, and he licked his lips as he dropped his jeans to the floor. "Confident and sassy. I like it."

"Then come and get it."

Grinning, he reached for her, and she dodged his advance. He tried again, and she giggled, jumping just out of his grasp. He chuckled. "You get me nearly naked, and *then* you play hard to get?"

"I can't make it easy on you."

"Oh, you're definitely making it hard." He slipped his boxer briefs down his legs, and his dick sprang out at full attention. Yep, she'd made it hard alright. *Wowzers.*

Her eyes widened, and her mouth watered. "Are, uh… Are all werewolves as endowed as you?"

"It's a common trait."

"I knew it!" Jane had laughed when Sophie insisted werewolves would be better in bed than vampires. Trace's massive dick was proof of that. Now to find out if he knew how to use it.

She slinked toward him, took him in her hand, and gave him two firm strokes. His lids fluttered, and a deep, rumbly "*mmm*" emanated from his throat. With one hand on his shoulder, she leaned toward him, giving his earlobe a lick before whispering, "Hey, wolfman. Catch me if you can."

She darted toward the bedroom, but she didn't make it past the threshold before he caught her around the waist and tossed her onto his shoulder. He slapped her ass, and she gasped as he dropped her on the mattress, covering her body with his and pinning her arms above her head.

His heated gaze softened, and he gently kissed the pale pink scars where his teeth had pierced her skin. "I am so sorry I hurt you."

"Now's your chance to make it up to me."

"I plan to, *cher*. And I'm going to enjoy every second of it." He trailed his lips down her bicep toward her armpit, and her heart nearly stopped beating. A quick glance revealed smooth skin, and she let out a relieved breath. She should have checked herself for random fur patches *before* she got naked in front of him.

His beard tickled as he glided his mouth across her collarbone and down to a nipple. Keeping her wrists bound tightly in one hand, he cupped her other breast, teasing her sensitive flesh, hardening her nipples into pearls.

"Damn, you're good with your tongue." Her voice sounded breathy.

His chuckle vibrated across her chest. "You ain't seen nothing yet, sweetheart."

He worked his way down her body, not releasing her hands until he had to in order to reach her sweet spot, and Lord have mercy, he wasn't kidding. The man knew how to lick. At this rate, it wouldn't take him long to get to the center of her Tootsie Pop.

His warm velvet tongue stroked her clit, building enough pressure in her core to crumble a levee. As he slipped a finger inside her, she lost it. The orgasm crashed into her, tearing her world apart and putting it back together with magical superglue that would never break its hold.

She gripped his shoulders, digging her nails into his skin as she rode the tidal wave to its finish. "Oh, God."

He rose onto his elbows, grinning. "You can call me Trace."

She panted, trying to get her breathing under control. "Jesus."

"Really, Trace will do." He climbed on top of her, pressing kisses to her stomach and between her breasts along the way. "Are you on birth control?"

"Of course." She reached between them, taking his rock-hard dick in her hand. She couldn't wait to have this thing inside her. He put Big Blue to shame.

"Werewolves are immune to disease, but I've got a condom in my pants pocket if you want to use one."

Oh, hell no. If they waited any longer she might explode. Wrapping her legs around his waist, she guided him to her center. "It sounds like we're good to go."

His gaze grew so heated, he could have set the bed on fire, and as he pushed inside her, lightning zipped through her body, electrifying her heart. He started out slowly, taking his time to slide all the way out until only his tip remained, before taking her again, his moans saying he relished every delicious inch.

But it wasn't long before his passion overtook him. His thrusts became shorter and faster, and as he tilted his hips, he hit the bullseye...over and over until she screamed his name along with every expletive in her vocabulary.

He spasmed inside her and collapsed with the sexiest male groan she'd ever heard. Sliding his arms beneath her, he hugged her tight, nuzzling into her neck, his breath warm on her skin. His lips grazed her jaw before he nipped her earlobe, sending warm shivers cascading down her spine and through her limbs.

She untangled her legs from around his waist and released her death grip from his shoulders, but he didn't roll off her. Instead, he hugged her even tighter, pressing himself into her as a low growl rumbled in his chest.

Sophie didn't know a lot about werewolves, but the way he held her, the possessive noises emanating from his body, she imagined this might be what it would feel like if he claimed her. She bit her lip to fight her smile as a thousand butterflies flitted from her stomach to her chest. A girl could hope.

"You were good in my dreams, but my imagination did not do you justice."

He lifted his head to look at her, a satisfied grin curving his lips. "Oh, yeah?"

"The real thing is *so* much better. I could do this every night."

His expression smoldered. "Nothing would make me happier than to end my days with you wrapped in my arms. Preferably naked." He moved slightly, resting his hip on the mattress but keeping his leg draped over her, pulling her tight against his body.

Staking his claim. Her stomach fluttered again.

Closing her eyes, she lost herself to the warmth and strength of Trace's embrace and drifted to sleep. Sometime later, the feeling of tiny paws prancing across the mattress stirred her from her dreams. She opened her eyes to find Crimson's familiar staring into Trace's face.

"Shoo, Jax. Leave him alone." She waved her hand in the cat's direction, but he responded by swatting at Trace's nose.

With a deep, sexy, sleepy inhale, Trace woke, blinking his eyes rapidly at the cat before shooting up in bed. "Jackson? Holy shit. Is that you?"

CHAPTER TEN

Trace wiped the sleep from his eyes and stared into the feline's face. He thought a trivial amount of werewolf magic floated in the air in Sophie's apartment last night, but he'd grown so used to the way his own magic tainting her blood added a slight earthy tone to the warm aroma that he'd dismissed it as coming from her bite.

Now, looking into the intelligent yellow eyes of this supposed familiar, he recognized the faint, muddled scent. He focused his thoughts, sending them to his friend's mind. *"What happened? Did Sophie do this to you?"*

Sophie. He glanced at the beautiful blonde sitting next to him in bed. Her hair, mussed on one side from sleep, flowed over her bare shoulders, and as her blue eyes darted from him to the cat, his heart ached. Trace had fallen for her, hook, line, and sinker, trusting her when she proclaimed her innocence.

It appeared he'd bedded the enemy yet again. This time, no spells were involved though. He'd wedged himself into this fiasco all on his own.

Jackson's muffled voice registered in his mind. *"Communication. Hard. Stuck."*

"You've got to be kidding me." How could he have been so

stupid? She was an unregistered witch. He knew better. *Damn it.* He knew better, but he let his dick take the lead anyway. Then his heart followed, and...

"Wait. The cat is your friend?" Sophie slid out of bed and put on a blue silk robe, cinching it at her waist. "I'm confused."

"You've had him all along." He fisted the sheets in his hands, his emotions waging a war in his chest. He didn't want to believe it. That his sweet Sophie could be conniving enough to seduce him while she had Jackson in her clutches the whole time.

"That's Crimson's familiar. I told you I'm cat-sitting." An incredulous look lifted her brow. "It's a cat. It's not..." Her lips parted on a quick inhale. "Jax is short for Jackson. Trace, you have to know I had nothing to do with this."

Didn't she, though?

No, he wouldn't believe it. He couldn't. He knew Sophie, and she was the nicest, most loving person he'd ever met. *Shit.* But the evidence was right in front of him, staring him in the face. And the curse... He'd been in the French Quarter way more than he should lately, always with Sophie, and the force-shift hadn't hit him once. How could it, when the witch responsible for the spell was right beside him?

"The evidence is pretty damn incriminating." Tossing the sheets aside, he slid out of bed and stomped into the living room to retrieve his clothes.

"Are you seriously accusing me of turning your friend into a cat?" Sophie followed on his heels. "After everything we've been through... I helped you steal information from the witches. I poured my heart out to you, letting you know everything about me, and Trace, you *do* know everything. I didn't lie."

He shoved his legs into his jeans and snatched his shirt from the floor. "Really? Okay, let's say you didn't lie. Your friend named her *familiar* Jax, and you didn't make the connection?"

"Why on Earth would I think a cat was your *werewolf* friend?" Sophie crossed her arms and tapped her foot. "I'm sorry for being clueless about how magic works, but you're being clueless about how relationships work. You accused me once, and I let it slide because you didn't know me. Now you do, so I want you to think long and hard before you utter another word, mister. And, no, I am not talking about your dick."

Trace ground his teeth as Jackson jumped onto the back of the couch and rubbed his head against Sophie's leg. She was right. He *did* know her, and the Sophie he was falling head over tail for would never do something like this. Even if she would, she didn't know how.

Scooping Jax into her arms, she nuzzled him, holding him against her chest as she stroked his fur. If the bastard could have smirked, he would have. Instead, he looked at Trace, let out a garbled meow that sounded way too much like a laugh, and rubbed his face between her breasts. *Asshole.*

"You do realize his natural form is a man. He's about six feet tall, dark hair, muscles. And he's practically motorboating you."

Sophie gasped and dropped him on the couch. "Gross. I've been peeing with the door open."

Trace laughed as Jackson's voice sounded in his mind, *"Not Sophie."*

"Thanks, buddy. I figured that out, though you could have saved me the groveling I'm about to do by telling me from the get-go."

"Is he talking to you?" Sophie asked.

"Same way I talked to you last night. I guess he didn't realize you could hear us, or he might have tried." He looked at Jackson, who shook his head. "Sophie, I'm sorry. My brain jumped to a conclusion that my heart tried to fight tooth and claw. I know you wouldn't do something like this, and I don't know why I accused you. Can you ever forgive me?"

She pursed her lips, narrowing her eyes as she drummed her fingers against her biceps. "Damn, you're good at apologies. Fine, I forgive you."

He opened his arms, and she stepped right into his embrace like she belonged there. Hell, they belonged *together*.

"Crimson doesn't seem like a wicked witch." Her breath tickled his neck as she spoke. "I really thought we were becoming friends."

"Accident. Not wicked," Jackson thought-spoke into Trace's mind.

"She might not be bad. We need to confront her and find out exactly what's going on."

"She should be home within the hour. We can meet her upstairs." She glanced at Jax. "He must have recognized you when you came in last night. I wonder why he didn't say anything then?"

"Didn't want. Mess up. Game."

Trace chuckled. *"This woman isn't a game. She's the real deal."* He kissed Sophie's cheek. "He didn't want to interrupt us."

"How thoughtful of him. I'll get dressed, and we can go up and wait for Crimson." Sophie pulled from his embrace, and Jax darted into the bedroom.

He pawed at the bathroom door, pulling it open before jumping onto the counter and letting out a low meow.

Trace followed as Sophie stopped at her dresser for some clothes. "I'm not good with cat-speak, man. Can you send me your thoughts?"

Rising onto his back paws, Jackson swiped at the medicine cabinet, trying to pull it open.

"You need something from in there?" He tugged on the corner of the mirror, and it swung open. Jackson grabbed a wad of toilet paper in his mouth and set it on the counter, nosing it toward Trace.

"Are you hiding something in here?" he called through the doorway to Sophie. "Something wrapped up in toilet paper has Jax's attention."

He unrolled the paper as Sophie shouted, "No!" She darted

through the door, but it was too late. He'd already seen the contents.

"This is fur." His mind scrambled to understand what he was looking at. "Where did you...? Did this come from...? What the hell, Sophie?"

Chewing her bottom lip, she glanced from Jackson to Trace. "Yes, it's fur. It came from me." She lowered her gaze, and the tips of her ears reddened.

"You? But you said you didn't—"

"I lied, okay? It only happened once, so after a while, I didn't think anything of it. I forgot it was even in there. I don't know why I kept it."

The corners of his mouth twitched, and hope bloomed in his chest. "So, you are showing signs of the mutation. There's a chance you might become a werewolf at the next full moon."

She shrugged. "Yeah. I mean, I guess so. Why are you smiling?"

"I would love for you to become a werewolf. That's not why I bit you, of course, but Sophie, I'm falling for you hard. Werewolves are allowed to mate with any species, but there are so many benefits to mating with another were. Especially another red wolf."

Her mouth opened, the words seeming to get stuck in her throat. *Shit.* He spent one night with the woman, and he was already talking about becoming mates. He was seriously off his game. "I'm sorry. I shouldn't have mentioned the mating bit. It's way too soon for that."

"No. It's..." She shook her head, a smile lighting on her lips. "I'm glad to know you feel that way. I'm falling for you too."

His breath came out in a gush of relief, and he stepped toward her, opening his arms.

She held up her hands and stepped back. "But you have to understand that I am not going to become a werewolf. The fur thing has only happened once, and I'm not showing any other signs. I'm a witch, Trace, and if Crimson can't unlock my magic, I'll find someone else who can. It's my destiny."

He dropped his arms to his sides. Maybe her heightened sense of smell and her above-average hearing had nothing to do with his magic running through her veins. If she really thought this one instance of fur was the only sign she'd shown, maybe she wasn't going to become a werewolf after all.

"I understand." She didn't want to be like him.

"Do you still want me, even if I never become a wolf?" For the first time, uncertainty flashed in her eyes.

"Of course." The question was, would she still want him when she became a full witch?

Sophie clutched her grandmother's grimoire to her chest and led the way up the stairs to Crimson's apartment. Her instinct had been to carry Jax, but Trace's reminder that there was a full-grown man inside that little kitty body meant the so-called familiar could walk it.

What was it with shifters pretending to be house pets around her? Between giving Trace a bath and letting Jax curl up on her chest, she was about ready to be done with animals altogether. Or at least until she could spot magic with her own nose and eyes.

"Now, before you go accusing her of nefarious acts, let her explain, okay?" She unlocked the door, and Jax darted between her legs into the apartment.

Trace huffed. "She turned my best friend into a cat; she lied under oath to her coven. She's got a lot of explaining to do."

They stepped into the loft area and found Jax sitting beneath the giant portrait of a man. "That's Jackson." Trace stepped toward the painting, rubbing his beard as he admired Crimson's work. "Did she paint this?"

Sophie started to answer, but he was looking at the cat.

Instead, she sank onto the couch and opened the grimoire to her grandmother's prophecy.

"Why didn't you come to the pack for help? Or to me?" Trace followed Jax into the seating area and sat on the sofa next to Sophie.

"What did he say?" she asked.

"Whatever spell he's under is making it hard for him to communicate. All I got was 'embarrassed.'"

"Hmm. I can see why he'd be embarrassed with the way you talk about cats. I wouldn't want you to know if it happened to me."

"Like you didn't want me to know about the fur incident?"

"I told you that happened shortly after you bit me. I didn't trust you yet."

"But you trust me now?"

She placed a hand on his thigh and squeezed. Damn, this man was muscular. "I do."

"Will you tell me if anything else like that happens? I want to be prepared. If we can't get this mess sorted out, I'll either need to protect you or run away with you somewhere safe."

"I'm not running away." She moved the book in her lap to rest against his leg. "Look, I want to show you something. This is a prophecy my grandmother wrote about me shortly after my dad was born."

She ran her finger over the four lines of text as Trace read the words. "Jane helped me figure it out, and it makes so much sense. The land where the Spanish reigned is obviously New Orleans. Man turning beast is you, and what's done will be undone means I'm not going to turn into a werewolf."

He made a noncommittal sound in his throat and tapped the page. "I don't like that last line, 'All must be lost to find everything.' It doesn't sound good."

"I think it's already happened. I was about ready to pack it up and go back to Texas before I found this. It gave me hope, and I'm still here, finding magic." She took his hand. "And a man to make my dreams come true."

"Sophie, I—" He cocked his head. "Footsteps on the stairs. She's home." He shot to his feet and strode toward the door.

"What are you going to do? Ambush her?" She closed the book and set it on the coffee table.

"If she sees me sitting on the couch when she opens the door, she's likely to tuck tail and run. There's a reason she doesn't want anyone to know what she did to Jackson." He leaned his back against the wall, and as the door swung open, it concealed him from Crimson's view.

Crimson stopped in the entry and set her suitcase on the floor. "Hey, Sophie. You didn't have to bring Jax home. I would've come down and gotten him."

Sophie cringed. "We need to talk."

"We *all* need to talk." Trace kicked the door shut and stood in front of it, crossing his arms and flexing his muscles in an oh so masculine way. If he wasn't trying to be threatening to her friend, Sophie's mouth might have watered at his sex appeal.

Okay, her mouth watered anyway.

"Umm…" Crimson froze, her gaze darting from Sophie to Jax to Trace and back to Sophie. "See, this is why I told you not to let him around any other supes. With the pack involved, it's going to screw up everything."

"The pack isn't involved yet." Sophie scooted to the edge of the couch and patted a cushion. "I convinced Trace to listen to your explanation before he reports you."

"How very kind of you." Crimson gave Trace a once-over before strutting to the sofa and perching on the edge like she was ready to bolt.

Sophie couldn't blame her. Trace exuded enough testosterone to make Chuck Norris tremble.

"Oh, good. You brought your grimoire." Crimson ran a hand over the cover of the book. "We can fix this together. If my mom hadn't fallen, we'd have already fixed it. I'm a master at channeling magic."

"How is your mom?" Sophie mentally smacked herself upside the head. Even in a crisis, she could show some manners.

"She's good. Has my dad waiting on her hand and foot. Now that the worst of the pain has subsided, I think they're both enjoying it a little."

Trace cleared his throat as he dropped into a chair across from them. "Can we focus, ladies? What did you do to Jackson?"

"I turned him into a familiar, obviously." Crimson rolled her eyes and smirked at Sophie.

Biting her bottom lip, Sophie shook her head. She and Trace could talk in circles before getting to the point of a conversation, but she could tell his patience had worn as thin as a sheet of single-ply toilet paper.

"It was an accident." Crimson cast her gaze to Jackson, who sat on the arm of an accent chair, flicking his tail. "If Jax could talk, he'd tell you himself."

"He did." Sophie patted her hand. "He told Trace a little with their thought-talking magic, but he's having a hard time communicating. We need you to fill in the blanks."

Crimson nodded and glanced at Trace. "Do you swear you haven't reported it? My magic is at stake."

"I know," he said. "You lied to your high priestess under oath. They'll bind your magic permanently for that offense."

"They'll bind my powers regardless if I can't fix this. I'm on my last strike." Crimson's shoulders slumped, her mask of confidence slipping off, raw vulnerability replacing it. "I was hoping to talk to Sophie about this alone. It's rather embarrassing for us both, isn't it, Jax?"

A deep mewl sounded from Jax's throat, and he hopped onto the sofa next to Crimson, placing a paw on her leg in comfort.

"I'm sorry, Jax." She rested her hand on his back. "It was a role-playing thing we were doing. I screwed up a sex game."

Trace's eyebrows shot up, and Sophie bit the inside of her cheek.

Crimson let out a dry laugh. "It was a fantasy, you know? The wicked witch turns her familiar human and has her way with him." She paused, cutting her gaze between the two of them. "Oh, like neither of you has ever done anything kinky in the bedroom. Don't judge."

Sophie held up her hands. "I'm not judging."

"Anyway, I had to turn him into a familiar first, before I turned him into human form again. Making him a cat was easy. Undoing the spell turned out to be a problem."

Sophie scrunched her brow. "Why didn't you let him shift into wolf form and just pretend you turned him back?"

"No witch has a wolf as a familiar. Cats, ferrets, Guinea pigs, those are all possible. The closest to a wolf would be a fox, and those are extremely rare." She shrugged. "We were trying to be realistic."

Trace rubbed his beard. "And you agreed to this, Jax?" He nodded, an incredulous look widening his eyes. "He says he did, but why didn't you come to the pack for help? We could have kept it quiet."

"Look at him," Crimson said. "He's a *cat*. If his packmates saw him in this state, they'd never let him live it down. I'm sure he wasn't thrilled for you to find out either."

Trace crossed his arms. "We all make mistakes. Your secret's safe with me."

"I've tried turning him back many, many times, but it's not working. I must've done something wrong in the original spell to turn him into a cat, and now I can't undo it on my own. I need the help of a fauna witch." She looked at Sophie.

"Surely there are other fauna witches in the coven, right?"

"There's one, but I can't go to the coven for help. This really is my last strike. I've screwed up too many spells, and the high priestess told me, point blank, if I screwed up again, my magic would be bound for life. She's going to turn me human."

"Oh, no. We can't have that." Sophie had only known about the existence of magic for less than a year, and she couldn't imagine having it all taken away from her now. Crimson had been a witch her whole life. She couldn't let her friend lose her powers. "How can I help?"

"If I can channel your magic, I'm sure I can do it. Right now, *something* happens with every transformation spell I try, but it doesn't affect Jax. My magic is strong, but it's wild. I can't seem to focus it into him in the right place."

Trace straightened his spine. "How many times have you tried to change him back?"

Crimson counted on her fingers. "Half a dozen at least."

His jaw ticked as his hands curled into fists in his lap. "And how long have you been out of town?"

She shrugged. "A few days."

He looked at Sophie, and the realization hit her square between the eyes. "The force-shifts," they said in unison.

"Every time you cast a spell to change him back," Trace said, "you send out a wave of magic that forces any red wolf within a two-mile radius of you to shift against their will. My pack has been banned from entering the French Quarter while I investigate."

Crimson's jaw fell slack. "I... Damn."

"Damn indeed." Trace stood and paced the length of the coffee table. "We were about to start a war."

"Oh, no. We need to fix this," Crimson said.

"I need to report this to my Alpha." Trace pulled his phone from his pocket, and Jackson hissed before darting toward him and swiping a paw at his leg.

"No, Trace. Please." Sophie padded to him and grasped his forearm before he could dial the number. "She'll lose her powers."

"That's not my problem."

"What if it were you? What if you could never shift again? How would that make you feel? We can help her. I know we can."

His dark honey eyes held hers, and she could almost feel his resolution dissolving. The tension in his muscles eased as he lowered his phone to his pocket and laughed dryly. "The power you have over me is witchcraft."

"I promise I'm not doing a thing to force you."

"She tames your beast." Crimson stood and strutted toward them. "Your primal fight or flight instinct is tempered when she's near, forcing you to think rationally before acting." She winked at Sophie. "In other words, she's good for you."

"Don't I know it." His gaze heated as he swept it over Sophie, lighting her nerves on fire without even the slightest touch. He was good for her too.

He looked at Crimson. "I assume you have a plan then?"

"May I?" She gestured to the grimoire.

"Of course." Sophie followed her to the sofa and sank down next to her as she flipped through the pages, nodding and making *mmm* and *ahh* noises as she understood a hundred times more than Sophie did when she tried to decipher it.

Trace sat next to Sophie, his thigh pressing into hers, and he took her hand. His touch reassured her, sending the message that he intended to go along with whatever plan Crimson cooked up.

"Your grandmother was a fauna witch as well, though that's not surprising." She closed the book and smiled. "She was powerful too, which means you will be as well…once we unlock your magic."

Sophie's quick intake of air made her cough, and as she tried to speak, the coughing worsened until her eyes watered.

"Are you okay?" Trace rubbed her back as she gasped for air.

"Fine." Two more coughs, and she could breathe again. "Just choking on my own spit. I'm talented like that." She rested a hand on Trace's thigh and turned to Crimson. "You can unlock my powers? You can make me a real witch?" Excitement bubbled in her chest, making her giddy. This was it. Her dreams were finally going to come true.

Crimson pressed her lips together and shook her head. "I can't release your magic. It's sealed with a lock only your grandmother can undo."

And there went all the excitement, fizzing out like a can of soda that was shaken before it was opened. An exhilarating explosion followed by an empty container. She slumped into Trace's side. "My grandmother is dead."

A mischievous smile curved Crimson's lips. "Then we'll just have to bring her back to life."

CHAPTER ELEVEN

S ophie's hand was cold and damp in Trace's palm as he guided her down the corridor. His boots thudded on the tiles, echoing off the plain white walls, while the swarm of vampires behind them barely made a sound.

Maybe it wasn't a swarm per se, but Sophie had insisted on bringing every supe she knew along on this excursion to resurrect a sixty-years-dead witch from beyond the grave. Crimson brought up the rear of the group with Jax tucked inside the backpack slung over her right shoulder. Weren't they a motley crew?

Trace got it, though. These people were Sophie's pack. She may have thought she never belonged anywhere, but he could almost feel the concern emanating from her vampire friends as they followed her down the hall. She'd found her home, if only she could recognize it.

"Do we have to do this in a morgue?" Sophie's hushed voice trembled as he opened the door and motioned for her to go through.

"She's a necromancer. This is where she works." He led the way to the third door on the left and knocked.

"Hi, Trace." Jasmine smiled as she opened the door. Her

long, black hair was tied back in a twist, and she wore a white lab coat over tan slacks and a navy shirt. "You must be Sophie. I'm Jasmine Lee, resident necromancer and research assistant to the coroner."

"Hi." Sophie shook her hand and glanced into the office. A metal desk and computer occupied most of the space, and an old school filing cabinet sat in the back corner, collecting dust. "Are you going to summon my grandma in there? Don't you need candles and crystal balls and stuff?"

Jasmine flashed him a quizzical look. "I thought you said she was a witch?"

"Her grandmother was." He rested a hand on the small of Sophie's back. "Her powers were never unlocked, so this is all new to her."

"Gotcha." She pulled the door shut behind her as she stepped into the hall, and her lip curled. "Oh, you brought vampires. Joy."

Jane fisted her hands on her hips. "What do you have against vampires?"

Jasmine looked her up and down, clearly unimpressed, and Trace held in a chuckle. "You're dead bodies I can't use."

Jane's mouth fell open, and she looked like she was about to argue, but Ethan touched her arm, shaking his head ever so slightly.

"Our bodies are more useful than you can imagine, *ma chère*." Gaston puffed out his chest and gestured toward his hips. "Perhaps you would like to take one for an example excursion? I feel you would reevaluate your opinion if you did."

Ethan cleared his throat. "I think you mean test drive."

Gaston smiled, showing fang. "She knows what I mean."

Trace fought his eye roll, but Jasmine let hers loose and then looked at Sophie. "No, I don't need candles or crystals, but what I do need is a corpse. Follow me to the meat locker."

"A corpse?" Sophie froze, tightening her grip on Trace's hand. "Why do you need a corpse? Can't you just call to her and tell me what she says, or channel her or something like the psychics do on TV?"

Jasmine laughed and motioned for them to follow her. "You have me mistaken for a medium. I can't put a soul into a body that already has one. We need a corpse if you want to talk to your grandma, and unfortunately, your undead friends won't do."

"No. Trace, this isn't right." Sophie pleaded with her eyes. "She can't put my grandma's soul into another person's body. That's gross, and you didn't tell me we were making a zombie. I've seen *The Walking Dead*. I know what zombies do."

"She can," he assured her. "She's not making a zombie, and she does this all the time. Her main job here is to resurrect murder victims to find out who their killers were."

Jasmine held up a finger. "That's my off-the-books job that only the higher-ups know about. Officially, I'm a research assistant."

"Okay, but surely we could use a medium, right? Corpses are icky." She flashed an apologetic look at Jane. "No offense, hon. I'm still getting used to how cold you feel."

"None taken. You're sleeping with an animal. Let's call it even." Jane winked.

"Does your grandma's spirit haunt you?" the necromancer asked.

"Well, no. I don't think so." Sophie shivered, and Trace pulled her to his side. He'd been a bit disgusted the first time he watched Jasmine do her thing for a case he was working. He might have puked in the trash can, but there was no evidence of that. He'd made sure of it.

"Does she haunt your dad?" Jasmine used her ID badge to unlock the door, and it swung open automatically. "Has anyone in your family ever mentioned hearing from her ghost?"

"No."

"Then, chances are, she moved on to the place souls go to rest a long time ago, 'crossed the bridge,' so to speak. Mediums can reach out to spirits who are still hanging around the in-between, that space between the living world and the land of the dead. If you want to pull someone back to this side of the bridge after they've already crossed it, you need a necromancer." She disappeared through the doorway.

"She's right." Crimson adjusted the backpack on her shoulder. "And we need your grandma to work magic while she's here to unlock your powers. She'll need a body for that. Ghosts can't cast spells."

"It'll be okay." Trace clutched her shoulders, looking into her eyes and giving her all the reassurance he could with his gaze. "I'll be here the whole time. You've got Crimson, Jane, Ethan, Gaston. We're all here for you."

She held his gaze for a moment before looking at each of her friends in turn. Then, with a deep inhale—and thank goodness her sense of smell hadn't reached full werewolf strength because the stench of death and antiseptic was enough to make him puke all over again—she straightened her spine and nodded. "Let's do this."

Turning on her heel, Sophie followed the necromancer into the room she called "the meat locker." Two steel tables stood side by side in the center of the room, with massive lighting contraptions hanging above each. Rows of metal doors stacked three high lined two of the walls, and Sophie cringed as she imagined what each one might contain. "It's more like a meat library, don't you think? With everyone filed away in drawers."

Jasmine nodded thoughtfully. "I like it. It's not quite the Dewey Decimal system, but we are pretty organized."

Trace held his fist against his nose, and Sophie could only imagine how pungent the sickly-sweet smells of death and decay mixed with chemicals must have been for him.

"Are you okay?" She put her hand on his elbow. "You look a little green."

"It stinks to high heaven in here." He dropped his arm to his side and swallowed hard.

"There's the trash can, if you need it." Jasmine smirked, and Trace glared in return. Sophie made a mental note to find out what that was about later.

Jax let out a deep whine as Crimson unzipped the backpack, and he jumped onto one of the exam tables before licking his paw.

"We have got to get him turned back into a werewolf," Trace said. "Watching him actually behave like a cat is unnerving."

"That's why we're here." Sophie rubbed Trace's shoulder, and he covered her hand with his.

The door clicked shut behind Gaston, and he turned around, peering through the narrow vertical window. "As much as I love a good corpse raising, I'll volunteer to be lookout. I can glamour anyone who gets too close."

"That probably won't be necessary. This place is dead at night." Jasmine snorted and covered her mouth, laughing at her joke.

Sophie bit her lip. When the others didn't join in the laughter either, Jasmine lifted her hands and dropped them at her sides. "Lighten up. It's just a little morgue humor."

"It was funny," Sophie said. "But my friend's magic is on the line, and this guy might be stuck a cat forever if this doesn't work."

"Gotcha. Serious business. I did tell you to bring something that belonged to the person we're trying to contact, right?" Jasmine asked.

"No, you didn't." Trace crossed his arms.

"Well, shit. I've been working for the police so long, I forget most people don't know how this works. I need something she owned so I can connect with her."

"We have her grimoire. Crimson?" Sophie gestured to the

backpack, and Crimson unzipped another pocket. Sophie retrieved the book and offered it to Jasmine. "Will this work?"

"Perfect." Jasmine pulled a dry erase marker from her coat pocket and scribbled a design on the empty table. "This is a vévé. It's a symbol that represents Baron Samedi, the Voodoo spirit of death."

"I didn't know you were a Voodoo practitioner," Trace said.

"I'm not, but I have friends who've taught me a thing or two. I can call a spirit without the Baron's help, but having his blessing makes the process a helluva lot easier." She finished the picture, a decorative cross with two coffins behind it, and placed the grimoire next to it.

Jane moved next to Sophie. "I always pictured stuff like this being done in a cemetery on a foggy night. You're ruining necromancy for me."

"Oh, we could do this in a cemetery," Jasmine said. "But the bodies here are fresh. If you think what we're about to do is gross, imagine doing it with a corpse that's been rotting for who knows how long."

Sophie shuddered. "Here is good."

"There's also the issue of the way New Orleanians bury their dead. Those aboveground tombs essentially cook the remains, turning them to ash over time. Unless you find one that was recently buried, chances are there isn't going to be enough left of the corpse for a spirit to do anything with."

"Well, damn." Jane crossed her arms. "That's no fun."

"I raised you from the dead in a cemetery," Ethan said with a twinkle in his eyes from across the room.

Jane cast a loving gaze toward him as he guarded the door with Gaston. "Yes, you did, my sexy, blood-drinking man candy. You're the best thing that's ever happened to me, and I'll be sure to show Vlad my appreciation as soon as this is done."

"Vlad?" Crimson arched a brow at Sophie.

"She named his dick Vlad because he impales her with it."

Crimson laughed. "Clever. I like her."

"The three of us will have to grab a drink sometime," Jane said.

"I'd love that." Sophie grinned at her friends.

"Ladies, can we focus?" Trace's jaw ticked. "Jax has been a cat for long enough."

Jane leaned over and whispered in her ear, "Have you named his yet?"

Sophie snickered. "I haven't had time to think of one."

Trace cleared his throat.

Jasmine laughed. "Humor is how we handle all this death." She patted Trace on the shoulder. "I couldn't work here without it. What do you think of this one?" She opened a locker and slid a body out on a platform. "It's the freshest one we've got." She peeled back the sheet to reveal a man in his late fifties.

"Oh, no." Crimson shook her head adamantly. "That's a man."

"Spirit is spirit." Jasmine shrugged. "It doesn't matter the sex of the body."

"What's that on his neck?" Sophie asked.

"Crap. I forgot he had a tracheotomy. That'll make it hard for the ghost to speak through him." Jasmine slid the man back into the drawer and tapped a finger against her lips. "Oh! I know just the one." She opened another locker and revealed an eighty-something-year-old woman with silver hair and pale, paper-thin skin.

Sophie's stomach turned. "That's someone's grandma."

"She's about to be *your* grandma," Jasmine said. "Wait. Is this your first time seeing a dead body?"

Sophie pressed her lips together and nodded.

"A virgin. No wonder." Jasmine laughed and gestured to Trace. "He whined like a little pup the first time he watched me do this."

Trace bristled. "Watch who you call a pup. There's nothing little about me."

"It's true," Sophie said. "He's buried his bone in me. It's massive."

Jasmine blinked. "Have you heard of the expression TMI?" Shaking her head, she turned and placed one hand on the grimoire, the other on the dead woman's forehead, and began chanting in a language Sophie didn't understand.

The energy in the air thickened, and Sophie's arm hairs stood on end as Jasmine quieted. Utter silence filled the room for a good twenty seconds before Jasmine pressed her palms together and bowed at the design she'd drawn on the table.

"Voila." She gestured toward the corpse, and its eyes blinked open.

Jane clutched Sophie's hand. "Holy mother of goat cheese pizza! It worked."

The corpse's brow furrowed as it glanced around the room. Lifting its arms in front of its face, it flipped its hands over and back before slowly rising to a sitting position. "Wha—" The corpse cleared its throat. "What in the name of the goddess happened to my body?"

Sophie gasped, her head spinning as Trace gripped her arm and held her upright.

"It's not your body, ma'am," Jasmine said. "You're just borrowing it for a bit. Can you tell me your name?"

The woman tilted her head, cracking her neck. "It's Maggie Burroughs. You know that. You're the one who called me." Her gaze landed on the book. "Oh! Is that my grimoire?" She eased herself off the table, and the sheet that was covering her pooled on the floor as she waddled toward the book. Her boobs sagged down almost to her waist, and her skin had so many wrinkles, it looked like crepe paper.

Sophie sighed. She was not looking forward to old age.

Trace cleared his throat, and Jasmine grabbed the sheet, wrapping it around the woman's body and tying it at her back. With the corpse properly covered, Sophie spoke to the woman. "Grandma?"

"Who are you calling grandma? The last age I remember being was twenty-five." She wiggled her fingers. "These are not the hands of a twenty-five-year-old. I'm not the soul who belongs in this body."

"I know." Sophie touched her frigid, lifeless hand, and jerked away. Nope, she'd never get used to the feeling of cold flesh. "You're my dad's mother."

Maggie tilted her head, holding Sophie's gaze. "My baby, Mark? He had a daughter?"

"Yes, ma'am."

Maggie looked around the room at all the people staring at her. "Vampires. A witch. A werewolf. Oh, you must be a fauna witch like me," she said to Sophie. "We have a weakness for shifters, and you found yourself a sexy one." She wiggled her old lady eyebrows at Trace, and he tensed.

Sophie couldn't help but laugh. "Wait. Was Grandpa…?"

"I had a weakness for shifters, but I fell in love with a human." She reached a hand to Sophie's face, but she pulled away. Maggie looked at her fingers. "This body is a little wrinkly, isn't it? Cold too. Why am I wearing this horrid outfit again?"

"I need your help. Since you died before I was born, my powers were never unlocked. I need you to release them."

She shook her head sadly. "Oh, honey, I would, but I can't train you. I can already feel my attachment to this body slipping, and an untrained witch is a dangerous witch."

"I'll train her." Crimson stood next to Sophie. "We're neighbors and good friends. I'll teach her everything she needs to know."

"That's an awful big undertaking."

"Please." Crimson clasped her hands together. "If you can't unbind her powers, can you at least help me change him back?" She picked up Jax and held him toward Maggie.

"Oh, my. Is that a werewolf?" She placed a hand on Jax's head, and he froze. "What did you do to him, child?"

"I messed up." Crimson explained the entire ordeal. "If I

can't change him back, I'll lose my powers. The red wolves will start a war with the witches. The supernatural balance in New Orleans will fall apart, and it will be all my fault. I'm a bad witch."

"I see." Maggie looked at Sophie and then at Jax. "I can't change him back. That will require spell work I simply don't have time to conjure, and I'm afraid only a fauna witch can reverse this spell."

"What about me then?" Sophie pleaded. "If you unbind my magic, Crimson can channel it. We can save Jax together."

"You can channel?" She reached for Crimson's face. "Pardon my cold skin, but I need to touch you to properly read your magic." Cupping Crimson's cheek, she closed her eyes and nodded. "It seems that's the only way to save your friend. When is the next full moon?"

"In two days," Trace said.

"That doesn't give you much time. Sophie, my dear, sweet heir." She gasped. "My heir." Gripping the grimoire, she opened it to the prophecy and read the lines. "What's done will be undone. Goddess, could I be any more cryptic when I wrote that? It should be 'What's bound will be unbound.' I believe I was talking about your powers, dear. Come." She motioned for Sophie to come closer.

Sophie swallowed hard, willing herself to approach her grandmother wrapped in a corpse, and as the old woman reached for her face, she held her breath. The cold, dead hands cupped her cheeks, and she swallowed the sour taste from her mouth.

"Oh, dear. Now I see. I wasn't sure when I wrote this, but..." She dropped her arms to her sides. "You've been bitten, and the only thing stopping you from transforming into a were-wolf at the next full moon is the fact that your powers are bound. If I unbind them now, you'll have the magic of a witch for two days. At midnight on the night of the full moon, all but your inborn power will dissolve as you transform."

"I'll lose my magic?" Sophie's lower lip trembled, so she bit it.

"I'm afraid so," Maggie said.

"But I... It's my destiny. I'm supposed to be a witch." A spark of anger ignited in her chest. It was irrational. She knew that, but there she was, getting mad at Trace for an accident. He didn't mean to bite her, and if she thought about it, the bite was just as much her fault as it was his. She should have known not to put her hand in an unknown animal's face, especially at a supernatural night club.

"I'm so sorry, Sophie." As Trace reached for her, he let his hand fall to his side.

She swallowed the thickness from her throat and fought the tears collecting on her lower lids. "What if we wait until after the full moon? Can we call you back here in a couple of days and do it then?"

"That'll cost extra." Jasmine leaned a hip against the table.

"I'll cover the fee," Jane said. "Might as well make myself *useful*." She glared at the necromancer.

Maggie shook her head. "I'm afraid if you want to save your werewolf friend, that won't be possible. The spell Crimson used to change him will become permanent at the full moon."

"He'll be a cat forever?" Sophie asked.

"That's what permanent means, dear."

"Crimson!" Sophie scolded her friend, backhanding her on the arm. "What were you thinking?"

Crimson raised her hands. "I know I screwed up. Like I said, I'm a bad witch."

"No." Sophie shook her head. "I can't do that to Jax. If I have to lose my powers to fix this, so be it."

"Sophie," Trace mumbled, but what more could he say? If she didn't do this, his best friend would be a cat forever. A war would break out. Talk about never fitting in anywhere again. She'd never forgive herself if supernatural New Orleans went to shit when she had the power to save it.

She looked at her grandmother. "I'll do it. Please unbind my magic."

"Isn't there anything else we can do?" Jane asked. "Would biting her help? Maybe some vampire blood or our magical healing saliva? I licked her wound right after Trace bit her. Maybe I need to lick her again?"

Gaston lifted a hand. "I volunteer to lick her from head to toe."

Trace stiffened, and Sophie put a hand on his chest to calm him. "Thank you, Gaston, but that won't be necessary."

He shrugged. "Anything to help you keep your magic, dear friend."

Jane rolled her eyes. "And I thought chivalry was dead."

"You have good friends." Maggie attempted a smile, but only one side of the corpse's face lifted. "There is something you could do, though it will be expensive."

"Name your price," Jane said. "Money is no object when it comes to my BFF and her happiness."

"It's not my price, dear," Maggie said. "You'll need a spell that only a special high priestess can cast. It requires the power of three, so she'll need the help of her two strongest witches. It's called a *hechizo anular*, but with only two days to cast, I'm not sure they could create the potion in time." She looked at Crimson. "I know of two witches in existence who have the power to create the potion. I was one of them. You can ask your priestess if she knows of another nearby."

Crimson swallowed hard and lowered her gaze to the floor.

"We can't ask the priestess," Sophie said. "This whole ordeal is under the coven's radar, lest we start a war."

"Who is the other priestess who can do it?" Jane asked.

"Her name is Kathleen Simmons," Maggie replied. "Last I knew, she ran the Austin, Texas, coven. She was the high priestess over the entire state."

Crimson nodded. "She's still there. I recognize the name."

"Texas?" Jane pulled Sophie into a tight hug. "I got this. Get your magic unlocked, and I'll see you again in two days." She released Sophie and hugged Trace. "Take care of her while I'm gone."

"Always," Trace said.

"Gaston, how fast can your Maserati get us to Texas? It's time to put my Governor's daughter status to good use."

Gaston smiled. "The Fast and Feverous have nothing on me."

"It's *The Fast and the Furious*," Ethan said. "It's... Never mind. Let's go."

Ethan and Gaston stepped through the door, and Maggie tugged the sheet, letting it fall to the floor. Trace stared at his shoes, and Jane paused in the doorway. "Skyclad?" she asked.

"It's the best way to work this kind of magic."

"You're just like I imagined." Jane giggled as she slipped through the door.

Maggie borrowed a pen from Jasmine and wrote her final spell on the next blank page of the grimoire. "This potion takes two days to make, so you'll need to start it tonight. Then, the incantation must be cast on the night of the full moon for full potency, as close to midnight as possible, but it must be before the clock strikes twelve, or our friend's condition will be permanent."

Crimson scanned the spell and nodded. "Got it. We can do this."

"Once the spell on Jax has been reversed, then you must drink the potion Jane brings you before midnight as well. If you don't, you will transform into a werewolf and lose your magic forever. Are you ready?"

Sophie nodded.

"Wait. You don't have to do this." Trace touched Sophie's arm and looked at Jax. "Jackson says he doesn't want to be the reason you lose your magic. We can figure something else out."

"No. I have to do this." She patted his hand and turned to her grandmother. "I'm ready."

Placing her hands on either side of Sophie's head, Maggie whispered a spell. Her cold touch was replaced with a warm, tingling sensation that spread through Sophie's body from the top of her head to the tips of her toes. As her grandmother released her hold, the feeling subsided, and something in Sophie's core popped.

A fiery sensation rolled up from her stomach to her throat, singeing her esophagus before the heat spread across her chest and dissipated. She'd expected getting her magic unlocked to feel, well…magical. Instead, it felt like a bad case of heartburn. "That's it? I'm a witch now?"

Maggie nodded. "Indeed you are, my dear. I'm sorry I wasn't there to bring you up in magic, but I'm happy I got to meet you now."

"Me too." Sophie fought the urge to hug the corpse containing her grandmother's spirit.

"Now, where's the necromancer?" Maggie spun around and stumbled, catching herself on the edge of the table.

"Here." Jasmine padded toward her.

"Please get me out of this awful skin before I die all over again. I much prefer the freedom of being made of pure energy."

"Bye, Grandma." Sophie waved as Jasmine guided Maggie back to the shelf.

"This part can get a little icky, what with the seizures and all." Jasmine waved toward the door. "I'll send you a bill."

"Let's go get your magic on." Crimson grinned and stuffed Jax into the backpack.

Trace pressed his lips into a hard line and nodded before following them out the door.

CHAPTER TWELVE

Trace sat in a white microfiber chair in Crimson's loft and watched Sophie in the kitchen with the witch, learning how to cast spells. Correction: they were both witches now, at least until midnight tonight.

Sophie had swept her long, blonde hair into a high ponytail, and the excitement in her eyes made Trace's chest ache. Crimson handed her an apron with *Life's a Witch* embroidered on the front, and Sophie caught his gaze before spinning in a circle and gesturing to the cloth. "What do you think?"

"Witchcraft looks good on you." Hell, anything looked good on her, and despite his selfish desire for Jane *not* to get the potion to neutralize his magic in Sophie, her happiness was the most important thing. Never mind the fact that they'd both stop aging if she became a werewolf and they mated. Their strength would double, they'd live several hundred years, and they could help to repopulate the pack with full-blooded red wolves.

Those things didn't matter because he never should have bitten her in the first place. If Jane didn't obtain the potion in time, Trace would get his selfish wish, but at the cost of Sophie's happiness.

"Any word from Jane?" he asked.

Sophie glanced at the clock. "Not since you asked me two hours ago. It's daylight. She's dead right now."

Damn vampires and their stupid weakness. He should have sent someone from his pack to get the potion. Someone who could function any time of day.

Sophie repeated a rhyming spell and sprinkled dark red powder into a copper bowl. The concoction she was mixing sparked, and steam rose from the container, making her jump and then giggle. "Did it work?"

Crimson poured the liquid into a small glass bottle. "It did. You're a natural."

"You hear that, babe?" She took off the apron and laid it on the counter. "I'm a natural."

"I heard."

"All right," Crimson said. "We've got the potion, and darkness falls in two hours. You two head home and give me some time to get in the zone. I'll meet you in the designated spot at ten. Jax, are you going with them or staying?"

Jackson slinked into the kitchen and jumped onto the counter next to Crimson. He'd either forgiven the witch, or he could sense Trace's mood and wanted to give him some alone time with Sophie.

"Sounds good." Sophie took his hand and led him downstairs to her apartment.

They settled on the couch, and he gazed at the beautiful witch he'd fallen in love with. Magic now glowed in her aura, and her intoxicating cinnamon scent grew deeper, stronger. She laced her fingers through his, her grin lighting up her entire face.

"Have I told you how beautiful your smile is?" he asked.

"Maybe once or twice." She pressed her lips to his cheek, lingering near his skin as she inhaled deeply. "*Mmm…* You've always had an amazing scent, but now that I can smell your magic, it's hard to keep my hands off you." She climbed into his lap, straddling him.

"Who says you have to keep them off?"

She sat back, resting her hands on his chest, the warmth of her fingers through his shirt making him wish there was no fabric between them at all. Her eyes searched his, and she tilted her head. "I'm happy, Trace. I know this spell is going to fix Jackson, and I've suddenly found myself with everything I've ever wanted within my grasp."

"What if Jane doesn't make it back with the potion in time? What if midnight comes and goes, and you turn into a were-wolf?" She could lose it all because of him.

"She'll make it. Jane always pulls through."

"But what if she doesn't?"

"She will." She slipped her hands beneath his shirt, the skin on skin contact tightening his stomach. "And after all this is done, we're going to come back here and celebrate. A witch and her werewolf, together…" Her teeth grazed her bottom lip.

He took her face in his hands, stroking his thumbs across her cheeks. "Forever?"

She lowered her gaze before blinking up at him. "I hope so."

"No matter what happens? Even if…?"

"No ifs. It's all going to work out. You'll see."

He did see. Her refusal to even entertain the idea that she might be a werewolf by midnight sat heavy in his stomach like a brick of his grandmother's week-old meatloaf. Arguing with her now wouldn't do any good, though. Whatever was going to happen would happen, so he might as well enjoy the moment.

He winked. "Just promise you'll never try to turn me into a cat?"

"Why on Earth would I do that when I can have all this?" She roamed her hands over his chest and down his stomach, popping the button on his jeans. "We have a few hours before we have to meet Crimson and Jax. How about a little pre-cele-bration?"

"I suppose I'm up for a party."

She slid down his zipper and reached into his pants, smiling wickedly. "You certainly are."

The feel of her soft fingers wrapped around his rock-hard dick made his eyelids flutter, and as she rose to her feet, undressing before him, he marveled at her beauty. She pulled out her ponytail, and her golden hair flowed over her shoulders, swinging forward as she bent to tug off his jeans.

He stripped his shirt over his head, and as Sophie took his pants from his ankles, she knelt in front of him, licking her lips as her gaze locked on his cock. *Holy fuck,* she was sexy.

Taking him in her hand, she lowered her head, wrapping her lips around him and sucking him. The warm, wet sensation shot electricity straight to his heart, tightening his balls as she stroked him with her mouth. He wouldn't last long like this.

He tried to speak, but his voice came out as a grunt. She released him, running her tongue from base to tip before grinning up at him. "Did you want to say something?"

"Get your ass up here and ride me like a broomstick, witch."

"Ooh. I really do love it when you talk dirty." She climbed into his lap and lowered herself onto his dick, giving him the ride of his life.

He pressed his thumb to her clit as she moved, and as she screamed his name, he lost control. They climaxed together, and she leaned into him, panting, the warmth of her breath raising goose bumps on his skin. God, he wanted this woman to be his.

"Do witches really ride broomsticks?" She sat up, resting her hands on his shoulders.

"Not that I'm aware of."

She nodded. "Good. You've ruined me for all other broomsticks, I'm afraid. Even Big Blue isn't going to cut it anymore."

"Big Blue?"

She slid off his lap and retrieved their discarded clothes, tossing him his pants. "My vibrator. The one I threatened you with a while back?"

"Ah." He chuckled and stood, stepping into his underwear.

"Well, I hope to ensure you never need a toy like that again, unless we're playing with it together."

"I can't imagine wanting it…unless you and Beast are out of town." She ran her finger over his dick and wiggled her eyebrows.

"You settled on a name." He pulled on his jeans and fastened the button.

"I did. What do you think?"

"I think…" His gaze locked on a patch of tan fur growing on her shoulder.

"What?" She looked down and gasped as she covered the fur with her hand. "How long has that been there?"

"I just noticed it when you stood up. It's completely normal for a witch who's been bitten to have random patches of fur before her first full moon."

"But this'll stop once I drink the potion Jane's bringing, right? The spell will cure it?"

He tried to ignore the disappointment churning in his gut. "Yeah, I believe it will."

"I'm going to shave this before we leave."

"Wait." As he gripped her hand, his phone buzzed in his back pocket, and while he was tempted to ignore it, too much was at stake to miss a possibly important call. "Hold that thought."

He dug his phone from his pocket, and as his Alpha's number lit up the screen, he groaned inwardly. His infrequent texts of *working on it* and *might have found a lead* apparently weren't good enough for her. He'd hoped to have Jackson back to normal before reporting in, to save his friend the humiliation. "Hey, Teresa."

"We need to prepare for war."

"What? No, I found Jax." He slipped on his shoes and paced the living room. "That lead I told you about panned out. He's safe, and he doesn't hold it against the coven."

Teresa paused, and Sophie shuffled toward him, placing her

hand on his arm. "You should have notified me immediately," Teresa said.

"Yes, ma'am. It's a complicated situation, but if you'll meet us at ten tonight, we can explain everything. Jackson can tell you himself."

A low growl emanated from the receiver, and Trace stiffened. His Alpha wasn't happy, which meant no one would be happy for the foreseeable future.

"This complicates matters even more. One of our pack pups, Caitlyn, was playing in her wolf form with a coven member's daughter. The witch fell into the swamp, and Caitlyn pulled her out with her teeth. She saved the little girl's life, but she broke skin."

"Shit."

"The witchling is already showing signs of the mutation, and the full moon is tonight. They're claiming we arranged it in retaliation for Jackson and the curse. The high priestess is out of town, but the moment she returns, war is imminent. The pack is on edge, ready to strike first."

"Don't let them. Meet us at the gathering point at ten. Come alone, though. This isn't something the entire pack needs to see."

CHAPTER THIRTEEN

Sophie stood in the forest, clutching Trace's hand as they waited for his Alpha to arrive. Jax sat in a pile of leaves in the center of the clearing, licking his paw and wiping it on his ear in a most cat-like way. Trace shook his head, grumbling under his breath, and Sophie rubbed his arm.

"He'll be okay. We'll fix this." She tried to reassure him with her eyes, but he must've sensed her unease. Yes, she was a fauna witch, and if she had even a quarter of her grandma's power, with proper training she could have fixed Jax hog-tied with her eyes closed. But therein lay the problem. Sophie wasn't trained.

They were relying on a self-proclaimed bad witch, someone who had botched more spells than she could count, to focus Sophie's magic and send it into Jax. And now Trace's Alpha was on her way.

With a deep inhale, he straightened his spine and nodded. "You're right. If anyone can fix this, it's you. You're going to be a phenomenal witch."

If she stayed a witch. Jane had texted at sundown that they were on their way, but Austin was five hundred miles away. Even if Gaston drove like he was racing a Grand Prix, they still might not make it before midnight.

"Maybe we should do the spell now, before Teresa gets here." Sophie squeezed his hand and released it. "I'm nervous enough without an audience."

"Don't be." Crimson took the potion bottle from her pocket and shook it. "I can channel magic all day long. It's only my own spells that I screw up."

Not the slightest bit reassuring. A nervous giggle bubbled from Sophie's throat. "Wasn't the whole point of this to keep the pack and the coven from finding out what happened?"

"Teresa needs to see this with her own eyes, to understand it was an accident, so she can calm the pack down. If they attack before the leaders sit down to discuss it, we're doomed."

"'Doomed.'" Sophie shuddered. "Now there's a dramatic word. Can't you say 'screwed' or 'fucked'? It would sound less ominous."

A woman with dark brown hair and hazel eyes approached from the swamp. "I'm afraid everything about this situation is ominous." She wore Army-green cargo pants and a tight black t-shirt with combat boots.

A whimper escaped from Sophie's throat, and she could only assume it was the developing wolf inside her reacting to the Alpha's presence. The sadness in Trace's eyes as he held her hand confirmed it.

"Teresa, this is Sophie and Crimson." Trace gestured to each of them. "And that's Jackson." He pointed to the cat.

Teresa's eyes widened as she knelt in front of him. "Jax, is that really you?"

The cat meowed in response, and Teresa shot to her feet before stomping toward Sophie. "So the witch you tried to defend was the culprit after all."

Sophie had the sudden urge to lie on her back and show her belly to the woman, as if that would help the situation, but she squared her shoulders and faced the Alpha. "I didn't do it." The moment the woman's eyes met hers, Sophie was tempted to cower. Instead, she moved next to Trace, seeking comfort in his support.

He wrapped an arm around her shoulders, holding her close to his side. "Apart from being in the wrong place at the wrong time, Sophie had nothing to do with it."

"In bed with the enemy again? Are we having a repeat of the nymph incident?" Teresa narrowed her eyes. "What spell did you put on him?"

Again? The nymph incident? "So that's why you didn't want to elaborate on that story."

Trace huffed. "This isn't about me."

"I did it." Crimson stepped forward. "I accidentally turned Jax into a cat." She explained the sex game and the resulting so-called curse she inadvertently put on the pack. "I had no idea it was affecting all of you."

Teresa glared at Trace. "Why was this not reported the moment you found out?"

"Look at the guy. He's humiliated." Trace paused, expecting her to admonish him for his tone. When she didn't, he continued, "How do you think the rest of the pack will treat him if they find out he voluntarily let a witch turn him into a cat? He'll lose their respect, lose his rank."

She crossed her arms. "I see your point. How are you going to remedy it?"

"The witches have a spell. Let them work their magic, and then you can take Jackson back to the pack. Tell them he had amnesia. Let them see him alive and well, and they'll have nothing to go to war over."

"Nothing but the fact that one of ours bit one of theirs."

"The truce has been in place for a hundred years. I'm sure you can work it out with the coven. If the parents are calm, the high priestess won't go to war over it."

"Maybe, but tempers are already running high." Teresa bowed her head at Sophie. "My apologies for accusing you. If you can return him to his natural form, the pack will be in your debt."

Crimson tossed Sophie the potion bottle and rubbed her hands together. "Let's do this."

Sophie sprinkled the potion on Jax, who answered with an offended hiss. "Do you want to be a cat forever?" Sophie scolded. "Chill."

Crimson handed Sophie her grandmother's handwritten incantation, and Sophie tried not to picture the corpse she'd used to write it. It was an image she couldn't unsee. With Crimson's hands sandwiching her head, Sophie scanned the words on the page, then read them aloud.

"A simple mistake made difficult to break.
With this potion, I set in motion
a spell to reverse your current hell."

Something in her core popped and fizzed, like a can of soda that had been shaken before it was opened. The fizziness had to be the magic, but it flowed up to her shoulders and down to her hips, threatening to spread out to her limbs. She tried to gather it up, to focus it into Jax, but the magic foam slipped through her metaphorical fingers, and panic began to flush it out.

"Hold on, honey. I got it." Crimson did something. Whatever it was, it pulled the fizzy magic back into a ball inside Sophie's chest. Crimson lifted Sophie's arm, and the foam rolled down, past her elbow and out her fingertips, slapping Jax and knocking him over as if he'd been struck by a car.

Crimson released her, and Sophie gasped, slumping into Trace's side as nausea threatened to give her dinner a reappearance. "Nobody told me spell-casting hurts." She rubbed her burning chest, letting Trace carry most of her weight.

"The big ones always do," Crimson said. "You get used to it."

Get used to pain? No thanks.

Jackson lifted his kitty head, blinking his feline eyes, and Sophie's heart sank. "It didn't work."

"Give it a minute," Crimson said.

A fog gathered around Jackson's form, and golden flecks danced in a swirling pattern above him before swooping down like a tornado and enveloping him in sparkling magic. As the storm dissipated, a man stood in the leaf pile. He had dark brown hair and brown eyes…the same man from the unfinished painting in Crimson's loft.

He was muscular like Trace, though not as big and not quite as hairy. Sophie's gaze traveled down over chiseled abs, and *oh my word*. "Well, that answers my question. All werewolves are hung like horses. Damn. Did anyone think to bring him some clothes?"

Trace took off his jacket and offered it to Jackson. "It's good to have you back, buddy."

Jax refused the clothing. "It's good to be back. Teresa." He glanced at the Alpha before lowering his gaze. "Everything they told you was true. My own embarrassment stopped me from seeking help from the pack, and I realize now that was a mistake. I will accept whatever punishment you deem fit for my crimes."

Teresa nodded. "Right now, you need to head home, get some clothes, and meet me at the den. We've got a pack to settle down."

"Yes, ma'am. Thanks for your help, guys. Crimson…I'll uh. I'll call you." He shifted into his wolf form and bounded away.

Crimson shook her head. "That boy's never going to call me again."

Sophie laughed. "Can you blame him?"

"Not really."

"Sophie!" Jane appeared in the clearing and ran toward her, but she only made it three steps before her heels sank into the soft earth and her ankle twisted. She stumbled, stepping out of her shoes and continuing the trek barefoot. "You could have told me we were meeting you in the middle of the swamp. I'd have dressed for the occasion."

"I thought you knew werewolves were the outdoorsy type." Sophie forced a smile, her apprehension stopping it from being genuine.

"You know them better than I do. Now, who's your favorite vampire in the whole wide world?" Jane held up a corked glass bottle. "I had to ask my father for help obtaining this, and you *know* how I feel about asking him for help."

Trace gave Sophie's shoulder a squeeze before he released her and paced to the edge of the clearing with his Alpha. They talked in hushed voices, and if she tried, Sophie might have been able to make out what they said. She didn't need to hear their words to understand Trace's disappointment.

Jane had come through with time to spare, which, deep down, Sophie knew she would. If she drank it now, it would stop the werewolf mutation, and she'd remain a witch for the rest of her life. She glanced at Trace, catching his gaze, but he didn't smile.

Sophie took the potion from Jane. "Thanks, babe. I owe you one."

"If you knew what I went through to get that, you'd think it's worth at least twenty, but we'll call it even. Consider it an engagement present. All your dreams are coming true."

"You're right. They are." Sophie peered at the pale blue potion in her hand, a feeling of resolve washing over her. "I finally understand the last line of my grandmother's prophecy."

"What does it mean?"

She looked at Jane. "I've found everything, and I have to lose it all. I have to lose my magic."

"What?" Jane looked at her like she was crazy, and maybe she was. But Sophie knew what she had to do.

Turning on her heel, she marched toward Trace, her long strides quickening into a jog as she neared him. Teresa grimaced at her phone, and Trace's expression was solemn.

"The witch's parents are starting to freak," he said. "It's an hour until midnight, and she's starting to grow fur."

"Here." Sophie handed the bottle to Teresa.

"What's this?"

"It's a potion that will stop the mutation. Get it to the girl and have her drink it before midnight."

Teresa stared at the potion, a look of awe in her eyes. "Where did you get this? My entire life, I've only heard of two witches capable of creating such a spell."

"One of them was my grandmother. Consider it a peace offering. If I'm going to join your pack, I want everyone to know there are no hard feelings."

"Sophie." Trace shook his head.

"Go." Sophie gripped Teresa's shoulder. "You're running out of time."

"Thank you." Teresa bowed her head and then sprinted into the trees.

Trace swallowed hard, his lips twitching as an array of emotions crossed his face. Taking her shoulders in his hands, he let his gaze roam around her face, his feelings seeming to seep into her body through his eyes and his touch. "You gave up your chance to have all your dreams come true to save a little girl and keep the peace in my pack. You never cease to amaze me."

"Becoming a witch was *a* dream, but it wasn't *all* of them. It definitely wasn't my innermost dream." She tapped a finger to his chest. "The one you're supposed to make come true."

He raised his eyebrows, silently urging her to continue.

"I thought I wanted to become a witch and have magical powers and all that jazz, but what it really boils down to is…my innermost dream has been right in front of me all along. All I've wanted all my life is to belong somewhere. To have a group of people I can count on and a place that feels like home. I already have that here with you. I don't need to be able to cast spells. Besides, magic kinda hurts."

He shook his head, still unbelieving. "You're going to turn into a werewolf."

"I know. Will your pack accept me?"

"Of course they will. You'll be one of us, and…" He pressed his lips together.

"And?"

"And you'll be with me. I love you, Sophie."

She stepped into his arms and wrapped hers around his waist as she glimpsed Jane and Crimson standing off to the side. Crimson gave her two thumbs up, and Jane clutched her hands over her chest, making heart eyes at them.

"You mentioned some perks to werewolves mating within their species." She brushed a kiss to his lips. "What are they?"

"Our strength doubles."

"Mmm… Stamina too? Not that you're lacking." She laced her fingers behind his neck.

He chuckled. "I guess we'll have to find out."

"Anything else?"

"Mated werewolves stop aging. Not completely, but it slows tremendously. Teresa is a hundred and fifty."

Sophie gaped. "She doesn't look a day over thirty!"

Jane snickered. "You should have told her that from the get-go. It would've saved you both a lot of trouble."

"Go ahead and laugh." Sophie pulled a face over her shoulder at her friend. "This just means I'll be around to taunt you forever and ever."

"I'm looking forward to every minute of it." Jane hugged them both. "You've got ten minutes before you sprout fur and howl at the moon with your man. Call me later and let me know how it goes." She turned to Crimson. "How about that drink we talked about?"

Crimson smiled. "I'm down. See you later, Sophie."

As her friends left the clearing, Sophie looked into Trace's dark honey eyes and grinned. "I'm going to be a werewolf."

"A wolf I'd like to *wear* all night."

She laughed. "Are you *aware* of the pun you just made, wolf?"

His face turned serious. "Are you aware that I want to spend the rest of my life with you, which will be a really, *really* long time if you agree."

"I am."

"Will you be my mate?"

"I will."

He grinned wickedly. "Good, now take off your clothes so we can howl at the moon."

EPILOGUE

Turning into a wolf wasn't as weird as Sophie imagined it would be. Once the fur sprouted over her entire body, it wasn't the slightest bit embarrassing. In fact, from the look in Trace's eyes, she must have been the hottest wolf in the forest.

Hunting wasn't as icky as she expected either. Trace took her through the woods, searching for prey, and once she figured out how to let go and let the wolf part of her take the lead, she caught her dinner and satiated the canine hunger like she was made to be a wolf.

After the hunt, they ran. And ran and ran. No wonder Trace was solid, sexy muscle. Sophie hadn't exercised this hard since she tried losing five pounds the week before her high school prom. Of course, then she'd overdone it, pulled a muscle and limped her way through the school dance. Tonight, she was a beast. Literally.

They ran for hours, never tiring, and only stopping for a drink from a nearby stream. As they circled back around, Trace poured on the speed, pouncing on her, and they tumbled through the grass until a small cabin came into view. It had a wrap-around porch and brown shuttered windows, and Sophie knew without even having to ask him with her thoughts, it was Trace's home.

She looked at him, and he sent his thoughts to her mind. *"If you're ready to stand upright again, we can go inside and test your stamina theory."*

Sophie gazed at the full moon, shining brightly above the cabin, and a calmness washed over her. Here, in the forest with Trace, was exactly where she belonged. Giddy happiness bubbled in her core and came out in a beautiful howl.

Trace howled along with her, until the faint sound of other wolves howling in the distance drifted on the air. Everything about this moment felt right. There was no reason to end it by going inside. Instead, she focused, and though she'd never been taught how to shift, she just did it, as if it were ingrained in her soul.

Trace's canine eyebrows shot up as he took in her form lying naked in the grass, and he shifted quickly before covering her body with his and making love to her beneath the moon.

Sophie was fully accepted and integrated into the pack. She split her nights between Trace's house on the outskirts of town and her apartment in the French Quarter, and her new duties in the pack, along with her dog-walking business, kept her so busy, she couldn't tell her head from her tail.

Two weeks after her first shift, she finally had a moment to breathe, so she did what any newly-turned werewolf woman would do and had a girls night out with a witch and a vampire. She met Jane at Evangeline's Coffee Shop ten minutes before closing and sat on a barstool next to her BFF while Crimson closed up.

"I had my first peace-keeping assignment yesterday." She straightened a stack of napkins on the counter.

"And how did it go?" Jane asked.

Crimson slid onto the stool next to her. "Oh, yeah. Tell us all about it."

Sophie shrugged. "It was rather uneventful. There's a group of bobcat shifter sisters who like to get into it with the wolves every now and then. Trace says the meetings usually involve lots of shouting, and sometimes they meet up after and fight."

Jane's eyes widened. "Don't tell me you had to fight a bobcat."

"Oh, goodness, no. You know me better than that. All I had to do was remind them to chill out every now and then, and they actually came to an agreement over territory. First time in thirty years, so I hear."

"Wow." Crimson smiled. "Look at you, already an asset to your pack."

"She makes a great werewolf, doesn't she?" Jane asked.

"Definitely." Crimson stood. "Are you ladies ready to go?"

As Sophie and Jane followed Crimson toward the front door, a short, heavy-set woman strutted through. She wore black leggings and a deep burgundy tunic, and her dark hair hung in long braids around her shoulders.

Crimson froze, gripping Sophie's arm until her nails dug into her skin. "Fuck me," she whispered under her breath. "That's the high priestess."

The woman stopped in front of Crimson and shoved a white card toward her. "You're summoned to be judged by the council of elders."

Crimson took the card. "Judged for what?"

"Misuse of magic, lying under oath, conspiracy with the werewolves…" She ticked the items off on her fingers. "You're lucky I'm listening to my advisors, or I'd have bound your magic already."

"What misuse of magic?" Jane crossed her arms. "She hasn't done anything wrong."

"Tell that to the werewolf she turned into a cat."

Sophie's mouth dropped open. "How did you know that? The pack swore to secrecy."

The priestess raked her gaze over Sophie and lifted one shoulder in a dismissive shrug. "Her ex-lover has a thirteen-year-old sister. Teens love to talk. Word got back to the coven." She turned to Crimson. "Lying under oath is reason enough to bind your powers on its own."

"I didn't lie." Crimson straightened her spine. "You specifically asked if I'd kidnapped or killed a werewolf or put a curse on their pack. Jackson stayed with me willingly after the accident, and I had no idea my attempts to undo the spell were affecting the others."

"That's true." Sophie nodded. "She didn't know."

"You will appear before the council for judgment tomorrow. If you fail to show, we will consider it an admission of guilt." She leaned closer and lowered her voice. "And I can't wait to find you guilty." She turned on her heel and marched out the door.

Sophie and Jane scanned the accusations listed on the card in Crimson's trembling hand, and Sophie rubbed her back. "It'll be okay. We'll get you through this."

Crimson pressed her lips into a thin line and shook her head. "I'm screwed."

LIFE'S A WITCH

BOOK THREE

Crimson Oliver is a bad witch.

She's not wicked, but every spell she tries to cast goes awry in one way or another. After her last screw-up, the high priestess has threatened to bind her powers and turn her human for good.

Crimson's solution? Challenge the priestess to a battle of magic she can't possibly win.

Not without a miracle, anyway.

Enter hotter-than-hellfire demon Mike Cortez. He's a devil's advocate who can make anyone's dreams come true...for a price. He's had his eye on the seductive witch for a while, and Satan is in the market for a new assistant.

But Mike wants to date her, not damn her.

When he accidentally makes a deal condemning Crimson to an eternity of satanic servitude, they'll have to go to hell and back to outsmart the devil and save the witch's soul.

Ride along on a journey from the Big Easy to the underworld and back again in this fast, steamy romantic comedy!

CHAPTER ONE

Crimson Oliver was a bad witch. Not bad as in wicked. She wasn't green—most witches weren't—and she didn't run around cackling at little girls, telling them she'd get them and their little dogs too.

She didn't ride a broom, and though she'd inquired about an army of flying monkeys, her request was ignored. No, Crimson didn't have a wicked bone in her body, but she was bad.

"Bad" as in nearly every spell she tried to cast went awry in some way or another, and that self-proclaimed "badness" was what had landed her in the hot seat in front of the entire Council of Elders in the New Orleans Coven of Witches.

Crimson sat in a straight-backed wooden chair, facing a long, rectangular table that occupied a two-foot-tall platform in the great room of a nineteenth-century mansion. Four elders flanked the high priestess perched in a burgundy velvet armchair at the center of the table. At five-foot-four with a stocky build, the priestess Rosemary wore her dark brown hair woven into long braids that cascaded down to her waist, and her eyes held contempt as she waited for the rest of the high-ranking witches in the coven to file into the room.

Tugging at the neck of her sweater, Crimson tried to alleviate the warmth her nerves were producing. It didn't help that the thermostat was set to eighty-five degrees.

She knew this trick. Every witch who'd ever screwed up knew Rosemary liked to turn up the heat—literally—just to watch the accused sweat.

What Crimson didn't know was why. Rosemary was the most powerful witch in the coven. Sure, her moral compass could have used some fine-tuning, but her position of high priestess granted her powers no other witch could achieve, no matter how much they practiced. Powers like the ability to bind another witch's magic, rendering her nothing more than human. She had everything a witch could want, so why did she take pleasure in tormenting her people?

Because she's a witch with a capital B. That's why.

As the last person entered the chamber, the door thudded shut, and Willow, a lanky blonde with icy blue eyes who sat to the left of the priestess, lifted her head. "Crimson Oliver, please stand."

Crimson turned her head slowly to the right and then the left before pressing her hand to her chest and mouthing the word *me?* She sat alone in the center of the room, for goddess' sake. It wasn't as if no one could tell who was being accused. The only reason they wanted her to stand was to increase the pressure, hoping she'd crack under the weighted gazes of all those high-ranking witches.

But Crimson was the queen of pressure. Her misfiring magic had landed her in enough sticky situations that she picked up everything but money and men. Pressure. *Ha!* She was like an Instant Pot on steroids when it came to pressure. She'd found herself in plenty of trouble more times than she could count, but she always found her way out of it. Well, almost always.

Willow blew out a hard breath through her nose. "Please stand so you may hear the charges brought against you."

"How will standing improve my hearing?"

The blonde witch's mouth fell open as she looked at the

priestess, and Crimson rose to her feet. That was enough pushing back for now. She rested one hand on her hip and scanned the faces of her jury. Agatha's green eyes held concern, but Fern, the red-headed fauna witch, took resting bitch face to a whole new level.

Laila, the coven's second-in-command and advisor to the priestess, rose to her feet. Her curly black hair spilled over her shoulders, and sympathy filled her gaze as she locked eyes with Crimson. "Your charges are as follows: one, lying under oath when questioned about the disappearance of werewolf Jackson Altuve; two, reckless and intentionally harmful use of magic when you cast a spell you were unable to break; three, conspiring with the werewolves to cover up your misdeeds."

Laila pressed her lips together and shook her head. "If found guilty, the high priestess recommends the binding of your powers indefinitely. How do you plead?"

Crimson swallowed hard, lifting her chin in defiance to maintain her composure. "I'm innocent, of course."

The high priestess finally spoke, "Your boyfriend broke up with you, so you turned him into a cat. I'd hardly call that innocent."

That was *so* not how it happened. Crimson moved her other hand to her hip. "Did Jackson tell you that?"

"My information comes from his relative and was confirmed by the pack's alpha."

"Did they also tell you it was an accident? Because it was." Well, the actual turning him into a cat part was no accident. It had been part of a sex game they were playing: the wicked witch turns her familiar human and has her way with him. She turned Jax into a cat, easy peasy. The problem arose when she tried to change him into human form again.

Rosemary lifted one shoulder in a dismissive shrug. "Accident or no, you used your magic maliciously against another supe."

"I did no such thing."

Laila cleared her throat. "We've heard the accusations. Let's address them one at a time and give Crimson the opportunity to defend herself."

She crossed her arms. "Yes. Let's."

Rosemary clamped her mouth shut, nodding, and Laila continued, "Did you or did you not lie under oath about Jackson's disappearance?"

"I did not." Crimson lowered into the chair and crossed her legs. "The specific questions asked were whether or not I kidnapped Jackson or put a curse on his pack. I did neither of those things. Jackson stayed with me willingly for fear of ridicule if he returned to his pack in cat form. The so-called curse the questioning referred to involved the wolves being force-shifted at seemingly random times. I had no idea my attempts to change Jax back into his human form were affecting the other wolves, so no, I didn't lie about either of those things."

Laila nodded. "The Council has reviewed the questions and answers provided. I move to dismiss the charge of lying under oath. All those in favor?"

Everyone on the platform raised their hand, except Rosemary, of course, who made being in the coven feel like living inside the movie *Mean Girls*. Crimson suppressed a smile as she imagined dragging her chair up to the platform just so the priestess would say, "You can't sit with us."

"Moving on to charge number two: reckless and intentionally harmful use of magic." Laila scanned the paper on the table. "Did you or did you not turn the werewolf into a cat when he threatened to break up with you?"

"No." Crimson clenched her teeth. If she was going to get out of this with her magic intact, she'd have to throw Jax under the bus. Sure, he might be humiliated when the truth came out, but it was better than being turned human.

"So you *didn't* turn Jackson Altuve into a cat?"

"Oh, I did, but he agreed to it."

Fern's brows disappeared into her bangs, and Agatha's eyes widened.

Sorry, Jax. There's no way around it. Anyway, he said he'd call her, but he never did. Served him right. "It was a sex game."

Snickering sounded from the witches behind her, and Willow's cheeks turned pink. As Crimson explained what happened, the murmur in the audience grew louder. She twisted in her chair to stare daggers at the people making fun of her. "If you find it that amusing, I can't imagine how boring your sex lives must be."

Mouths fell open, and several people gasped. Crimson smirked and turned her attention back to Laila. "Intentionally harmful? Absolutely not. Reckless?" She cast her gaze to the ceiling for a moment and pursed her lips. "Not reckless, either. We planned it. The spell went wrong, that's all." It happened all the time. Crimson was bad at being a witch, but that was her lot in life, and she'd rather build on it than leave it empty.

Rosemary slapped her palm on the table. "And that was your third strike."

"I fixed it, so it doesn't count."

"It does."

"Let's move on to the final charge." Laila's soothing voice broke the tension. "Did you conspire with the werewolves to cover up your misdeed? A Sophie Burroughs to be specific?"

"Sophie wasn't a werewolf when I discussed the situation with her. She didn't become one until the entire ordeal ended." Thank the goddess they didn't ask about her boyfriend, Trace. He actually *was* a werewolf at the time. "In fact, Sophie was a witch with bound powers. If this coven were the welcoming place it used to be, we might have been able to help her."

The priestess narrowed her eyes. "You can skirt around the edges of these accusations all you want. It doesn't change the fact that you're an incompetent witch who's a danger to herself and others. You've already shrunk a politician's penis to the size of a Vienna sausage and made a priest speak all his thoughts aloud.

Now you've almost caused a war between the witches and the werewolves. We can't risk you having powers."

Laila came to her defense. "She did remedy the situation without the help of the council this time. I vote she gets one more chance."

The other witches nodded their agreement, and Rosemary's face pinched. "Without the help of the council, maybe, but not without the help of another witch. A dead one."

The whispering behind her grew into a murmur, and Crimson shot to her feet. "It's true. I needed to channel the magic of a fauna witch, so I convinced a necromancer to summon the spirit of a powerful one. With her assistance, I solved the problem without inconveniencing the coven in the slightest."

Rosemary stood, leaning her hands on the table and looming her authority over the coven. "We almost went to war for your incompetence."

"You'd love a war. You get off on all this power; everyone can see that. You're high priestess over a coven that cowers beneath your rule."

Straightening, Rosemary clasped her hands and nodded slowly. "Your inability to break the spell on your own is a symbol of your ineptitude. As high priestess of this coven, I demand your powers be bound at once." She cast her gaze to the witches on her right, then her left. "Does anyone oppose?"

Laila inhaled as if she were about to come to Crimson's defense, but much like Gretchen Weiners, the second-ranking Mean Girl in the clique, she kept her mouth shut to avoid being pounded by the bully.

Crimson's heart plopped into her stomach like a Mentos into a bottle of Diet Coke, and she swallowed the bitterness creeping up the back of her throat. "You can't be serious. No one opposes this?"

Every member of the council—aside from the Queen Bee,

of course—cast her gaze to the table or the ceiling, refusing to make eye contact.

"You don't belong here." Rosemary motioned toward an intern standing by the wall. "Bring the grimoire. The binding will happen immediately."

"This isn't a high school clique." Crimson's voice pitched in panic. "It's a coven, and I'm a witch—I belong."

A young woman laid a thick volume on the table, and Laila rested her hand on the wooden cover. "The binding spell in this book is permanent." She looked at Rosemary. "Are you sure you want to do this to her?"

The priestess sneered. "Absolutely positive. It's past time a threat like her was neutralized."

A threat? Seriously, what did this woman have against her? Rosemary had always been a snob, but the moment she was elected high priestess, she'd made it her mission to make Crimson's life miserable. Crimson could admit she wasn't the best at casting spells. On her deathbed, her mother had unbound all of her magic in a rush. Crimson was just a child, and something had gone wrong. It was the only explanation for her skewed magic, and it wasn't her fault.

The other witches took pity on Crimson, which annoyed the hell out of her, but Rosemary treated her like a mangy mutt who wouldn't get off her doorstep.

"Let's see. Where is that spell? Oh, here it is." The priestess tugged on a ribbon and opened the book to the exact page.

"You had it bookmarked?" Crimson gasped.

Rosemary knew. She *knew* she'd find a way to force the council to agree with her—to at least not oppose her. She always did. The coven trembled in fear with Rosemary as their leader, and her reign of terror needed to end.

Fisting her hands at her sides, Crimson stood and summoned her courage—or maybe her stupidity—the jury was still out on that one—and sent her words up in prayer. "In the name of the goddess Morrigan, I denounce your authority and hereby invoke the Supremacy Challenge Law."

Rosemary scoffed. "You can't do that. You're on trial."

Crimson lifted her chin defiantly and pressed her palms together. "Morrigan, goddess of battle and sovereignty, with your blessing, I call for the Supremacy Challenge to be granted."

The lights flickered, the energy in the room growing electric as a silence descended so deafening you could have heard a leprechaun scratch his ass. Crimson's arm hairs stood on end, and no one dared utter a breath as the goddess' decision charged the air.

In unison, every mouth in the room opened and said, "So mote it be." A collective gasp followed the proclamation, and Crimson's head spun like she was on a merry-go-round at top speed.

What had she done?

Rosemary stared blankly ahead, her eyes wide as hula hoops, no doubt in just as much shock as Crimson that the goddess granted her request. A Supremacy Challenge hadn't been issued in the past hundred years, and now Crimson of all people was to go up against the high priestess in a battle of magical skill?

What the hell was she thinking?

This pairing was like a chihuahua versus a pit bull. It didn't matter how much fight Crimson had in her, Rosemary would chew her up and spit her out like a stick of Fruit Stripe gum.

Laila took the grimoire and turned to a page in the back. "When the goddess grants a Supremacy Challenge request, the two witches will go head-to-head in a battle of magic. The winner will be high priestess of the coven, while the loser will have her powers bound for life and be exiled from the city, never to associate with another witch again. According to tradition, you have one month to prepare for the challenge." She looked at Crimson. "And you can't channel another witch's magic to win."

"I suggest you keep your head down for the next thirty

days." Rosemary stood. "Your witching days are over. This meeting is adjourned."

As the witches filed out of the great room, Crimson sank into her chair, chewing the inside of her cheek and stewing over her predicament. What in the goddess' name did she think would happen when she called for a challenge like that?

Well, for one, she didn't think the goddess would actually grant it. And channeling was her inborn gift. How was she to know she wouldn't be allowed to use the only magic that consistently worked for her? Not that it would matter. She'd need to channel the goddess herself to win this, which she *should* have been able to do if her magic hadn't glitched when her mother unbound it.

If this wasn't incentive to hit the books and study, she didn't know what was. Her spells worked sometimes. She'd just have to make sure those sometimes happened during the challenge.

Everyone in the coven agreed Rosemary was a ruthless bitch, and Crimson suspected that, secretly, they'd all love to see her removed from power. There had been peace among the supes of New Orleans for decades, yet she ruled like they were always on the verge of war. And the way she treated Crimson, singling her out the way she did, didn't make any sense at all.

A low-level witch whose spells went haywire more often than they worked wasn't a threat, yet the high priestess acted like she was. There had to be more to this vendetta than mean girl behavior.

Crimson rose to her feet and strutted toward the table. "Why do you hate me? Aside from my magic not working correctly, I've never done a damn thing to warrant this treatment from you."

Defensiveness flickered in Rosemary's eyes before she straightened her spine. "I don't want incompetence in my ranks. Nothing more. I only wanted to turn you human. Now that you've challenged me, I'm going to squash you like the dung beetle you are."

If I'm a dung beetle, then you're a piece of dung. Turning on her heel, Crimson strode out the door. She could smell bullshit a mile away, and the high priestess reeked of manure. There was a reason Rosemary wanted her without magical powers, and she planned to find out why.

But first, she had to devise a way to out-magic the most powerful witch in New Orleans.

CHAPTER TWO

M ike Cortez bit the inside of his cheek and forced himself to enter the meeting room at the Priscilla St. James Community Center. A registration table sat to the left, and he stopped to sign in, scribbling his name on a paper nametag and sticking it to his shirt—a ridiculous requirement, seeing as how he'd known everyone in the room for at least fifty years.

He passed the beverage station, inhaling the rich, earthy aroma of the world's worst coffee—seriously, it smelled divine, but that shit tasted like it came straight from the tarpits of hell —and dropped his food contribution, a box of mini angel food cakes from Sweet Destiny's Bakery, onto the snack table.

As soon as the package hit the surface, the other demons in the room swarmed it, shoving the pastries into their mouths and moaning as if they were better than sex with Aphrodite. For a full-blooded recovering demon, he supposed they were.

Sweet Destiny, the bakery next door to Mike's restaurant, was owned by an angel named Destiny Monroe. She baked a little extra magic into his weekly order for the Hellions Anonymous meetings, as it helped to curb his friends' demonic nature, at least for a little while.

"Thanks, Mike," Richard said, his mouth full of angelic cake. "If you weren't still Satan's bitch, I'd kiss you."

A famine demon back in the day, Richard used to appear as nothing more than skin stretched over a skeleton as he poisoned crops and spread drought throughout the lands. His work on the Irish potato famine had secured his release from the Devil's clutches, and he'd been a glutton ever since. Now, his potbelly hung over his belt so far Mike doubted the man had seen his own dick in decades.

"No worries," Mike grumbled. One perk of having a handshake from hell—no other recovering demon would touch him for fear of being sucked back into the underworld. Of course, they all knew his power didn't work that way, but no one wanted to take any chances.

Mike sank into a chair in the "Circle of Hope" and crossed his arms, tucking his fisted right hand beneath his pit. His palm itched, the first signal he was late on his payment to Satan. If he didn't make a deal on the Devil's behalf soon, his ass would be grass, and not the fun kind you could smoke.

"Good evening, everyone." Katrina crossed one long, slender leg over the other, lacing her fingers and resting them on her bare knee. That was all it took for the former succubus to command the room's attention. Her long brown hair cascaded over her shoulders in thick waves, and dark lashes fringed her striking lavender eyes.

A bit of drool rolled from the corner of Richard's mouth, and Sarah bit her bottom lip as she twirled a lock of blonde hair around her finger. Blood began to pool in Mike's groin, and he shifted uncomfortably in his chair. If the Hellions Anonymous leader didn't get her magic in check, this meeting would turn into an orgy faster than roux could scorch on an unattended stove.

He cleared his throat. "Katrina, your demon is showing."

Her eyes flashed red as she raked her gaze up and down his body. "You're not showing nearly enough."

Sarah rubbed a hand along her thigh, gripping her jeans as if to stop herself from rubbing another area. "Someone get this woman a piece of cake before we all end up naked."

Mike strode to the snack table but found the box empty. "Richard…" For fuck's sake, did the man have no control?

"Sorry," Richard said around a mouthful of cake. His plate held four more pieces, so he tossed one to Katrina.

She bit into the pastry, and an erotic moan emanated from her throat, electrifying the energy in the room. Mike held his breath as she finished the angelic cake, willing his dick to retreat. Succubi could get an entire crowd hot and horny with a snap of their fingers, and no one—not even Satan himself—was immune to their powers. It had been years since he'd seen Katrina without her glamour on, and the fact she'd dropped it tonight could only mean one thing: she'd gotten laid.

"My apologies." With a deep inhale, she activated her concealing magic, transforming her appearance from hottest stripper in New Orleans to Karen the soccer mom. "After seventeen years of celibacy, I had a moment of weakness last night. It seems I'm still not free from Satan's clutches."

"It's okay," Sarah said. "Your time will come."

Katrina grinned devilishly. "My date sure came. Again and again. I'm afraid I've ruined him for other women." She straightened her spine. "But I'm back on the wagon. No more sex until Satan releases me. I will abstain until he gives up on me."

"You know that's not how the Devil works." Mike rubbed his palm on his jeans, the mere thought of striking a deal making it burn. "No one is free from the bowels of hell unless they pay a price or win a bet."

She made a noncommittal sound and smirked at him before addressing the group. "Hi, my name is Katrina, and I'm a succubus."

"Hi, Katrina," the demons said in unison.

"I was banned from hell when Satan's flavor of the month found us in a compromising position in his chambers. After living topside for one hundred fifty years, I've grown fond of humans and refuse to use my sexuality as a tool to send their souls to the underworld. The devil *will* forget about me eventually, and my demonic desires will cease, at which time I'll be free to find love and live a normal life."

It'll never happen, Mike wanted to say, but he held his tongue. The Devil never forgot, but if she believed she had the stamina to give Satan a run for his money, more power to her.

They went around the circle, introducing themselves, telling their stories of how they won their freedom and mentioning any slip-ups they may have had between meetings. It was the same damn routine every week, but HA meetings were required—as part of the truce with the humans—of every recovering demon who called New Orleans home.

Most of the demons there had struck a deal with the Devil to earn their release. Sarah, a pestilence demon, bargained for her freedom and won release when she initiated the bubonic plague by sneezing on a bartender in London. Mark planted the seed that started World War II, and Denise was especially proud of herself for instigating the #metoo phenomenon that rocked Hollywood, knocking a slew of famous actors and directors off their pedestals. She outsmarted Satan on that one. Sure, it caused all the turmoil he was hoping for, but it also brought to light a persistent problem as women all over the country found solidarity in the movement.

The Devil wasn't happy about the good that came from Denise's "evil" deed, but the bargain had already been struck, and Satan never reneged on a deal.

Mike tapped his foot, fisting his hand until his nails dug into his palm. He should have been out there looking for a morally inept idiot to bargain with, not sitting in this boring room with its off-white walls and matching tile floor, the smell of coffee barely masking the stench of mildew growing on the window panes. He had a restaurant to run, a life to live, and he'd never been this late giving the Devil his due.

"Mike?" Sarah waved a hand in front of his face, pulling him out of his thoughts and into the meeting. "It's your turn."

"Right. I'm Mike, and I—"

"Hi, Mike," everyone said.

He ground his teeth. "I'm a Devil's advocate, and I won partial freedom in a poker game with Satan five years ago. As long as I make a deal for him once a month, I get to live topside, left to my own devices, but I'm two weeks late, so I've got to jet early." The burning sensation in his palm engulfed his entire hand.

"You should stay." Katrina folded her hands in her lap. "Show Satan he can't control you. Refuse to do his bidding."

"It doesn't work that way." He stood and stepped behind his chair. "A deal a month or I'm back in hell, never allowed to see the light of day again."

"You could hide," Richard said.

Mike shook his head. "Advocates can't hide. We make deals on behalf of Satan, so we're connected. I've explained all this before, and I don't have time to do it again. I've signed in and introduced myself, so I met the requirement. I'll see you next week."

He turned and strode out the door, stalking down the sidewalk toward Magazine Street. Though demons in hell were known for lying, cheating, stealing, and causing as much chaos as possible, those that lived topside strived to assimilate to the positive aspects of human nature. Mike wasn't lying when he said he had a connection to Satan. All advocates did, but while the Devil refused to sever the connection when Mike won the poker game, he did promise not to use it unless there was an emergency.

Now, as Mike passed the grand colonial homes of the Garden District, with their white columns and manicured lawns, a buzzing in his blood reminded him that connection was alive and well. Satan was calling, and Mike had no choice but to answer.

He slowed his pace as he passed a group of men congregating outside a bar. A tall brunet leaned against the blue wooden exterior, clutching his phone, while a short, stocky guy sipped his beer and shook his head. Eavesdropping on their conversation, Mike learned the tall one had recently been dumped and wasn't handling the breakup well.

Scorned lovers were easy targets, and Mike could have joined the conversation, steering it toward what the man would be willing to give up in exchange for another chance with his girl. But as he focused his magic, peering into their auras and breathing in their scents, not a single one of them reeked of malice; no evil danced in the energy around them.

He couldn't bring himself to curse an innocent. In the five years since he'd won his right to live among mortals, he'd made certain to target only wicked people when he made his monthly payments. He continued on his way.

"Voicemail again." The guy shoved his phone into his pocket. "Fuck that bitch. She'll be sorry she ever dumped me when I'm through."

Mike halted in his tracks, the malicious statement piquing his demonic interest. Perhaps he'd missed something in this guy's aura. He strolled toward the spurned human and placed a hand on his shoulder, activating his magic and willing the man to reveal his innermost desire. "What do you really want?"

The human's eyes blanked for a moment before filling with tears. "To talk to her."

"What would you be willing to trade?"

He tilted his head, giving Mike a curious look. "I'd give my left nut if she'd just pick up the phone."

Mike's palm turned red with the need to seal that deal. A man could function with only one testicle. Sure, the removal process wouldn't be pleasant, but that wasn't Mike's job. He just had to get a little bit of blood and a handshake, and he'd be good to go until the next payment was due.

A low growl rumbled in his chest as he remembered Satan's

last email. *No more testicles.* His collection already filled two chambers in his halls, and his current girlfriend insisted he not add another nut unless he had the dick to match.

"It's time to move on." He patted the guy's back and continued down the sidewalk.

The buzzing in his blood grew stronger as he stalked toward his restaurant. Situated in a nineteenth-century Victorian home with a blue and white façade and an expansive front porch, Honoré's served the best fried oyster po-boy in town. Their red beans and rice were a favorite among the locals, and it put them on the map as a popular stop for foodie tours in the area.

Wiping the scowl from his face, he nodded a hello to his manager before making his way through the dining area toward the kitchen. He caught bits and pieces of conversations as he passed the patrons, but no one sounded desperate enough to need the Devil's help. Pausing at the kitchen entrance, he turned and scanned the auras of his customers, not finding a single wicked soul in the building, aside from his own.

He shook his head and marched through the kitchen. Was it too much to ask to get a truly evil person to pass through his restaurant every now and then? Once a month would be nice, but he'd settle for a few times a year. It would make his life a helluva lot easier.

Stepping into his office, he slammed the door and leaned against the wall, not bothering to turn on the lights because demons could see just fine in the dark. Squeezing his eyes shut, he pinched the bridge of his nose as the humming in his blood grew stronger. What the hell was he going to do? "Satan's balls," he grumbled.

"They're hanging a little to the left today. Thanks for asking."

Shit. Mike opened his eyes as the high-backed leather office chair spun around, with the Devil himself perched on the seat like a James Bond villain. He wore a pinstriped suit in a shade of red so dark it was almost black, with a blood-red tie and matching handkerchief in his breast pocket. He had enough gel in his jet-black hair to hold it still in a hurricane. Thick brows peaked above eyes the color of molten lava, the liquid shades of red undulating like a storm in his irises. The only thing missing from the movie-like scene was a cat for him to stroke in his lap. Then again, Satan was more of a hellhound man.

Mike bit his tongue, holding in the urge to ask the Devil if he'd seen any good spy movies lately. Satan hated being compared to Hollywood stereotypes of wicked men. Pushing from the wall, Mike dipped his head in a bow. "To what do I owe the honor, oh Great Evil One?"

Satan chuckled. "You don't look the slightest bit surprised to see me, Michael."

Surprised? Not hardly. Disappointed, disgusted, and dismayed? All of the above. "I felt your impending approach."

The Devil propped an ankle on his knee and drummed his fingers together. "Ah, yes, that's right. We're still connected because *I own you.*"

"Thanks for the reminder." Cutting the pretense, he dropped into the vinyl chair across from the desk. "I know I'm late on my payment, but I'll have a deal made by the end of the day tomorrow." *Even if it kills me.*

Satan cocked his head. "Are you late? I hadn't noticed."

Mike's eyes widened. *Oh, shit.* "If you aren't here to collect…"

"Do you think I'd bother coming all the way topside for the simple issue of a late payment? I'd send one of my guards to collect." He leaned forward. "I have a job for you."

Mike lifted his hands, leaning back in the chair, away from Satan. "Oh, no. No more jobs. I won this sorry excuse for freedom fair and square. You can't default on your contracts."

"You used to be my favorite advocate." He swiveled the chair from side to side, examining his nails before rubbing them on his lapel. "Your half-human nature made you the perfect tool for securing souls and whatever else I've felt like collecting over the years."

He stopped swiveling and leaned his forearms on the desk. "I've moved on from testicles to dignity now. Did I tell you that? Extreme, life-altering humiliation in exchange for whatever frivolous thing the human thinks he needs. It's quite fun."

"Sounds like a blast."

"Anyway, I've run into a dilemma, and I need you to find a new witch to be my assistant. I'm afraid my girlfriend wasn't fond of my old one. My little pookykins is the jealous type—most banshees are. She was sentenced to eternal damnation for grinding her cheating husband's sausage to bits, and I just can't get enough of her."

Mike fought his eye roll. "You know I can't damn a witch, sir. There's a truce among the supes here. We all play nice and keep the balance, and everyone gets to live in peace."

Satan sucked in a breath through his teeth, grimacing like it pained him to make the request. "You know I've never cared for playing nice. Keeping the balance is important, but that's an angels and demons affair. Witches have nothing to do with it." He shrugged. "I need a witch, and you're going to get her for me. It's the last job I'll ask of you. I swear."

Mike held in a groan. "I mean no disrespect, sir, but my contract states that as long as I pay my monthly fee, I'm a free demon. I don't have to take on additional jobs." Why did he feel like he was negotiating with a mob boss rather than Satan?

"You make a good point, and I appreciate a demon who has the balls to stand up to me. Yours would make a nice addition to my collection. I wonder…" He shook his head. "I digress. What was I saying? Oh, yes. I want to make you a deal." Satan stood and paced around the desk.

"Let me guess. It'll be an offer I can't refuse?"

"I don't think you'll want to refuse this. You're two weeks late on payment. Since we never discussed a grace period, I assert that there isn't one. It's my right to take you back to hell with me immediately."

His stomach sank, attempting to take his entire body with it, but he held his spine rigid, refusing to cower before the leader of the underworld.

"I could make *you* my personal assistant. Now there's a thought." He crossed his arms and seemed to drift inward for a moment. "No, witches' powers make them much more efficient and valuable. My assistant has always been a witch, and I want a new one. Here's my offer."

Satan's molten eyes churned with his magic. "Get me a witch by month's end, a truly wicked one—they're much more fun—and I'll dissolve your contract. No more payments. No more direct line to the ruler of hell. You'll be free."

The Devil was right. He didn't want to refuse. There were plenty of wicked witches in the world. He'd find one who danced on the darker side of magic. Hell, he might be able to convince one to join Satan of her own free will. Personal Assistant to the Prince of the Underworld could be an enticing title to a powerful being with questionable morals.

But he'd be violating the truce. Sure, he may win his freedom, but upsetting the supernatural balance in the most magical city in the country would be detrimental. He'd be banished or vanquished. It might even start a war.

He closed his eyes for a long blink, his jaw ticking as he ground his teeth. "And if I don't?"

Satan lit a fireball in his palm, toying with it as a menacing chuckle rose from his chest. "You'll return to hell, and I'll burn your precious restaurant to the ground, with all your patrons inside it." He tossed the fire into a trash can, and with a wave of his hand, he opened a portal and stepped through it.

Mike groaned. "Fuck me."

The Devil's head appeared through the shrinking portal. "You should have made that offer *before* I met my pookykins." With a wink, he disappeared, and the portal closed completely.

CHAPTER THREE

"Are you sure you want to hang out here tonight?" Sophie touched Crimson's elbow, pausing outside The Tipsy Leprechaun. Her long blonde hair hung in loose waves over her shoulders, and her blue eyes held concern. "This is such a popular place for supes. There'll probably be some of your coven sisters here. Maybe we should go to a human bar."

Crimson glanced at the entrance. The black door blended in with the black wood slats in the wall, making it almost unnoticeable. From Frenchman Street, the space looked like it belonged to the jazz club next door. The windows were blacked out and the main door locked to discourage humans from coming in. Supes knew the entrance lay around the corner in the alley, and this was one of the few places they could hang out together and let their guards down.

Not that humans weren't allowed. They were, but there was usually so much magic mixing in the air inside, it would give the mundane a killer case of the heebie-jeebies, and they'd leave on their own.

"I've only got a month left of being a supe myself, so I better make the most of it." Crimson tugged on the hem of her royal blue sweater.

"Don't talk like that. You're going to win that challenge with so many flying colors they'll think you've turned into a unicorn."

"As long as I don't fart glitter and puke rainbows."

Sophie's mouth formed an O shape. "I have so much to learn about supes."

Crimson pressed her lips into a line, fighting a smile.

"Oh, you're joking." She stuck out her tongue. "Haha. Pick on the newbie. That never gets old."

Crimson laughed. "Actually, I've never seen a unicorn. Maybe they do fart glitter. Who knows?"

"Shall we?" Sophie gestured to the door.

"Yep. I hope some witches are here. They need to see I won't be intimidated by a bully who acts like she's queen bee of the high school lunchroom." Straightening her spine, she brushed her curls behind her shoulders and stepped through the door.

A bar lined the wall to the right, with colorful glass bottles holding every kind of libation imaginable filling the shelves. To the left, a stage behind the small dance floor held a five-piece band belting out Frank Sinatra covers, and tables dotted the rest of the room.

"There's an empty one over there." Sophie pointed to a spot near the dance floor.

As they made their way toward it, the hottest demon this side of hell approached, his dark brown eyes flashing red as a devilish smile curved his full lips. Crimson's stomach fluttered as she took in all six-feet-four inches of his solid, muscular frame. Even with her heels on, he was taller than her, and that tipped the sexiness scale in his favor. Not that he needed any help.

With dark, wavy hair, a light brown complexion, and strong, masculine features, Mike Cortez looked like sin on a stick. Exactly the type of man she needed to stay away from.

Holding a glass of whiskey in one hand, he stopped in front of them and took a sip, his eyes locking with hers. "A witch and a werewolf walk into a bar. There's a punchline in there somewhere."

"And they walk right past a demon." Crimson held his gaze —and her breath—as she stepped around him. The signals in her brain went haywire, part of her wanting to run as fast as she could, and the other part wanting to grab him by the shoulders and find out if sin tasted as good as it looked. *Damn him.* Oh, wait. He was a demon. He was already damned.

He chuckled and turned to Sophie. "How's canine life treating you? You left the old man at home tonight?"

"Hi, Mike. It's good to see you." Sophie gave him a quick hug while Crimson inched farther away from the temptation. "Trace is hunting with Jax tonight. I can't wait 'til he gets home, though. Being a werewolf has worked wonders for my sex drive. We fuck like rabbits." Her eyes widened, and she covered her mouth. "I did not mean to say that out loud."

"Well, tell him I said hello, and have fun tonight. I'll see you ladies later." He winked at Crimson and disappeared into the crowd.

"I have got to learn to watch my mouth." Sophie slid into a chair, and Crimson sat next to her. "You were acting weird. I'm no empath, but I think I detected some sexual tension between you two. Have you done it with a demon?"

Crimson laughed. "I wish." Well, part of her did anyway.

"With the way he looked at you, he seemed willing to grant. Do y'all have history?"

"I met him at a New Year's Eve party. All he had to do was look at me, and he set off enough fireworks to put the city's display to shame." Her lips tugged into a smile as she recalled the night. "We danced a bit and talked a lot. Then he asked me how I wanted to start out the new year, and I told him preferably bent over a table with him taking me from behind. I was mortified to say the least."

Sophie giggled. "But you *were* thinking it."

"Who wouldn't be? Anyway, I ducked out before midnight

to wallow in my humility and vowed to never drink enough to run my mouth like that again."

"Have you talked to him since?"

"I see him every now and then. I suppose you could call us casual acquaintances."

"Who have casual sex?" She wiggled her brows.

Crimson inhaled deeply as her gaze landed on Mike's backside while he leaned his elbows on the bar. How could someone so bad look so good? "Absolutely not. Don't get me wrong, the man is gorgeous."

Sophie nodded. "He's a panty-dropper for sure."

"But he's a *demon*. They're always up to no good."

"I don't know. Trace said he was a great guy and that he left hell for a reason. I assume that reason is because he's not actually evil." She shrugged. "I hear there's a support group for recovering demons, kinda like AA. I wonder if he goes."

"It doesn't matter if he does. My dad is an Earth-bound angel, and he always warned me to stay away from demons because, recovering or not, they're trouble. I'm in enough hot water as it is. I don't need to invite the devil into my bed, no matter how hot the sex might be."

Sophie gripped her forearm. "Wait. You're half angel? Why did I not know this?"

"My adoptive father is the angel. The biological one was human as far as I know."

"You never met him?"

She shook her head. "You know the saying 'What happens in Vegas stays in Vegas'?"

Sophie arched a brow. "Yeah."

"Well, for my mom, what happened in Vegas is now a twenty-six year old witch who's about to be turned human if she can't get her shit straight." She lifted a hand to flag down the waitress and ordered a vodka sour. "Make it a double, please."

"I'll have a glass of chardonnay," Sophie said. She waited for the waitress to walk away before placing her hand on top of

Crimson's. "If you need a volunteer to cast your challenge spells on, you know you can count on me."

"I couldn't ask you to do that."

"Why not? I did it for Jane. She glamoured and bit me in front of the entire vampire council. First time she'd ever drunk blood from the source. You can turn me into a cat for a few minutes or whatever else you need to do."

Crimson rubbed her forehead. "What if I can't change you back?"

"You've got my grandma's spell. I know you can do it."

"That spell required the help of a fauna witch, remember? I'm not allowed to channel another witch's magic."

"You've got a month. You'll figure it out." Something caught Sophie's gaze, and she narrowed her eyes. "Speaking of witches, are those friends of yours?" She nodded toward a table in the corner.

Crimson turned, and sure enough, Fern, Laila, and three other witches were chatting over drinks. She scanned the rest of the bar, but priestess Rosemary was nowhere around. "Do you mind if I go talk to them for a minute?"

The waitress delivered their drinks, and Sophie took a sip of wine. "Sure. I'll keep an eye on your demon for you."

"He's not my demon."

"He could be. Even if it's just for a couple of hours, he'd be a nice distraction."

"I'm sure he'd be a fantastic one." She was already in trouble up to her eyeballs. How much worse could it get? Crimson picked up her glass, sneaking one more glance at Mike's delicious backside—she might just consider Sophie's suggestion—before strutting toward the witches. "Hello, ladies."

The group quieted, their postures stiffening with unease as Crimson sank into an empty chair. She plastered on her most confident smile and looked each one of them in the eyes.

Laila, the only witch who didn't act like Crimson had the plague, smiled warmly. "How are you?"

She sucked down half her vodka sour in one gulp. "Aside from being granted a challenge I never expected to receive? Never better."

"Why did you make that request?" Laila asked. "And to call on the goddess in the form of Morrigan... What were you thinking?"

"I panicked. Morrigan was the first name I thought of to help, and..." She shrugged. "C'mon, you'd all love to see Rosemary dethroned. Admit it."

Fern shifted in her seat uncomfortably, and the others refused to make eye contact.

Crimson drummed her nails on the table. "I'm curious. Did y'all actually vote for Rosemary to be high priestess? I seem to remember her not being very well-liked in the coven before she was elected."

"She ran unopposed," Luna, a soft-spoken witch with short brown hair said, her eyes cast to the table.

"I wonder why that is." Crimson downed the rest of her drink, not expecting an answer.

Luna finally looked at her. "I heard she threatened to ruin anyone who ran against her."

Fern cleared her throat. "I heard that too."

Sounds like Rosemary. "Fern, I can't channel another witch's magic, but it doesn't say I can't have an assistant. Will you help me?"

Fern swallowed hard.

"I was thinking, since you're a fauna witch, maybe you could work with me? Stand with me during the challenge and give me some guidance if I start to do something wrong. I struggle with animal spells the most, I think."

"Uh..." Fern's eyes widened, and she cut her gaze between Laila and Crimson as she stuttered.

"Unfortunately, that won't fly," Laila said. "You can have assistance in your preparation, but the actual challenge is one witch against the other. No help allowed."

"Damn."

Fern's shoulders relaxed, and she sipped her daiquiri. "Sorry, Crim."

"Well, would you mind going over some spells with me ahead of time? Maybe you can help me figure out where I go wrong when I screw them up?"

"I would, but I really don't want to get on Rosemary's bad side."

"No one does," Laila said. "That's why she ran for high priestess unopposed."

"You would make an amazing high priestess, Laila," Luna said. "If Rosemary ever retires, you should run."

Laila shook her head "I'm meant to be an advisor, not high priestess. We have several members who are powerful enough to take Rosemary's place when she steps down."

Fern laughed. "That'll never happen. Someone will have to drop a house on that wicked witch before she'll give up power."

Now there was an idea... Crimson cast a glance toward Mike. Just how bad of a demon was he? She didn't have a clue what kind of magic he possessed, but he had to lack morals. All demons did. *Don't be ridiculous, Crim. You got yourself into this mess, and no amount of wishful heel-clicking is going to get you out.* It was a nice fantasy, though.

"Y'all talk like I don't have a chance of winning this."

No one responded.

"Well, if any of you can clue me in as to why our beloved high priestess has singled me out for her bitchery, I'm all ears." Still no one responded, so she set her glass on the table and stood. "No worries. I'll put her in her place after I beat her in the challenge."

"That'll take a miracle," Fern laughed.

Crimson turned on her heel and made a beeline for the restroom. *After I beat her in the challenge.* Now, that was funny. At least she'd sounded like she meant it. Confidence was key.

She brushed a dark curl from her forehead and stared at her

reflection in the mirror. It *would* take a miracle for her to make it through with her magic intact, and she had a direct connection with the miracle department. Well, it wasn't exactly direct. She'd have to go through her dad, but he was a reasonable man. His assignment of watching over her as a child may have ended, but he loved her as if she were his own flesh and blood. She'd call him first thing tomorrow.

The bathroom door swung open, and Laila hesitated in the threshold. Glancing around the small room, she stepped inside and peered under the stall door. "Are we alone?" she whispered.

Crimson peeked under the other stall. "Seems that way."

Laila nodded and waved a hand at the door, chanting a locking spell before turning to Crimson. "I'm not supposed to tell anyone this, but under the circumstances, I think it's only fair if you know."

"I'm listening."

"When a high priestess is sworn in, another high-ranking witch calls on the goddess for a prophecy. I was that witch."

Crimson straightened. The prophecy of a high priestess was held as the utmost of secrets, so Laila had her full attention.

"It was a lot of cryptic, convoluted language like most prophecies are, but one line stands out, and I think you should know." She hesitated, confliction dancing in her eyes. "The line said, 'Red will take you under.'"

Crimson blinked, stunned. "Red will... Seriously? That could mean so many things."

"All I did was channel the message. It's obvious how she's interpreting it." Laila lifted her hands. "Please don't let the others know I told you. I don't want to be next on Rosemary's chopping block."

"Of course. I'll take it to the grave."

"If you can actually beat Rosemary, the entire coven will thank you. And Crimson..." She touched her arm. "You've got the power. If only you could get past your block." She waved a hand in front of the door, removing her spell, and left Crimson alone in the restroom.

With a sigh, Crimson repeated the incantation to lock the door and tried the knob. It didn't move. "That spell worked at least."

Maybe if she practiced, she could pull this off. With her dad's help, the angels could grant her a miracle. Hell, maybe she could convince them the situation was dire enough for them to fix her magic so she could channel the goddess and puke those rainbows for Sophie. But would the coven accept her as their new high priestess? Could she even handle the job?

She waved her hand in front of the door to release the spell, but it wouldn't budge. She tugged on the knob, jiggling it and chanting a reversal incantation, but the lock held tight.

"Oh, for crying out loud." She jerked the knob, twisting it with all her might, and the damned thing came off in her hand. Still the door stayed sealed. "Well, that's friggin' fantastic."

She'd asked, and the universe had answered.

The spell would wear off eventually, but spending the rest of the night locked in a bathroom wasn't the least bit appealing. Setting the broken knob on the paper towel holder, she put one foot on the edge of the sink and hoisted herself up to the narrow window near the ceiling. Her heel slipped off the porcelain, leaving her dangling from the sill as she cursed her misfiring magic for the eighty-seventh time tonight.

All those yoga classes came in handy, and she managed to scramble up the wall and shimmy through the window before tumbling into the courtyard behind the bar. Her hip smacked the ground, but she caught herself with her hands before she could faceplant on the pavement.

"Goddess help me. Can anything else go wrong today?" She clambered to her feet and dusted off her pants. "Never mind. Please don't answer that."

She brushed her hair from her face, retrieved her dignity from the cobblestone, and strutted back inside the club.

CHAPTER FOUR

Mike leaned an elbow on the bar and sipped his whiskey, trying not to look too creepy as he watched Crimson interacting with her friends, which, since he was a demon, was a difficult task. Her curly black hair flowed just past her shoulders, and that clingy blue sweater dipped low on her chest, giving him a glimpse of dark brown flesh that made his mouth water for more. Heat flashed in his eyes, which meant they were glowing red, but he couldn't help himself. That woman lit a fire beneath every masculine urge in his body, making him boil over with desire.

"Hey, Mike." Asher nudged him with an elbow. "Your demon is showing."

Tightening his grip on his glass, Mike squeezed his eyes shut and forced himself to turn around. "Happens every time I see her."

"Why don't you do something about it?"

"Believe me, I've tried. She's like a glass of water in the seventh level of hell. Impossible to obtain."

"You thinking of sending her to Satan, then?"

"Oh, hell no. You'll freeze ice on the Devil's ass before I'll let that bastard get ahold of her. I want to date her, not damn her."

He'd come to The Tipsy Leprechaun to check out the witches, but no one here reeked of enough wickedness for him to make a deal with a clear conscience. He was about to call the night a waste—until Crimson walked through the door.

With those sexy high heels on, she stood about six feet even, which put her lips at the perfect height for kissing. It had been nearly a year since he met her, and he hadn't forgotten about the New Year's kiss he missed out on.

Asher pulled his phone from his pocket and groaned. "Satan's balls. I thought I was finally going to get some time off. I cleared my roster, and the bastard added five more names to it."

Mike glanced at the list on the screen. "At least the souls you take to the underworld are already dead. I'm sick of doing the Devil's dirty work."

Asher returned his phone to his pocket. "You get a month off in between."

"And you get to do your job guilt-free." Asher was a reaper. A descendent of Charon, he wasn't a demon, but he could travel in and out of hell at will. His sole job was to track down the spirits of the dead and escort them to whatever part of the underworld their behavior in life afforded them.

"You got me there, but man, I could use a vacation. I'd go somewhere quiet. Maybe a secluded beach in the Caribbean. It'd be nice to sit in the sand and watch the waves with a woman under my arm. If I could find a woman comfortable enough with death to date a reaper." He blinked and shook his head. "Damn you and your advocate magic. I'm not looking for a deal."

Mike chuckled. "I'm not offering one." Sure his palm tingled a bit, itching to seal a contract, but Satan was after a witch. A reaper had nothing to offer the Devil than what he was already required to give him.

"Have fun with your witch. I've got work to do." Asher gulped the rest of his beer and strode out of the club.

Have fun with his witch. Oh, Mike could think of all kinds of ways to have fun with a woman like her, if she'd give him the time of day. *Shit.* Raking a hand through his hair, he pushed from the bar and flagged down the waitress. He could sell swamp water to a Cajun. He could at least convince Crimson to give him a dance.

He ordered another round of drinks and sauntered toward the table where Crimson and Sophie sat. "Your glasses are empty, ladies. Allow me to remedy that for you." He set the wine in front of Sophie and offered the vodka sour to Crimson.

She hesitated to take it. "I don't accept drinks from strangers."

He grinned. "Good thing I'm not a stranger then."

"Oh, come on. It's Mike." Sophie swatted Crimson on the arm. "He's one of Trace's best friends." She took a giant gulp of her wine.

Crimson reached for the drink, and he pulled it away. "It's because I'm a demon, isn't it?" He hoped that was it and that he hadn't misread the heat in her gaze every time she looked at him.

"I…" She bit her lip.

"That's what I thought." He sucked down half the drink and set the glass on the table, cringing at the sweet and sour combination. No doubt she'd heard hellish stories about demons growing up. His defensiveness kicked in despite his best efforts to subdue it. "I'm half human, so I can't be all bad."

"Sometimes humans are worse."

Sophie nudged her again and gave her a look that said they'd already had a discussion about him. That was a good sign. Perhaps Crimson's desires from New Year's Eve were flaring to life again.

He suppressed a smile. "You make an excellent point, but you're generalizing. I take offense to that." He was about to launch into a negotiation, which was his specialty, after all, to convince her to give him a chance, but she shot to her feet, smirked at Sophie, and took his hand.

"Do you want to dance?" She tugged him to the center of the floor. "I need a distraction so my subconscious can work on my issues, and you seem like the perfect man to erase my worries for a while."

He blinked, missing a beat. He hadn't even laid on the charm yet, but she'd made an offer he couldn't refuse. Mike may have been in hot water with the Devil, but the Fates were smiling down on him tonight. "Nothing would make me happier."

"Can demons be happy?" She placed her hands on his shoulders as the band played "It Had to be You," and they swayed softly from side to side.

With his hands on her hips, he gazed into her dark brown eyes. "You don't know much about demons, do you?"

"Just what I've been told."

"Which is?"

Her gaze dipped to his lips for a moment before returning to his eyes. "That you're trouble and I should stay away."

"Hmm. That's sound advice." He narrowed his eyes, leaning back slightly to get a better look at her. "Who gave it to you?"

"My father. He's an Earth-bound angel."

He grimaced. "Ouch." No wonder she kept her distance. "I don't sense any angel in you, though."

"I was adopted when I was seven."

"I see. Well, as good-intentioned as I'm sure your father's advice was, I'm afraid he's misrepresented us. Some of us. Me, to be exact." Heat flashed in his eyes, and he inched a little closer, sliding his hands to the small of her back. She didn't pull away.

"What does it mean when your eyes glow red like that? Should I be afraid?" She linked her fingers behind his neck.

"That depends."

"On?"

"Demons have stronger emotions than humans. Well,

stronger within the range of emotions the particular demon is capable of experiencing."

"And what exactly is your range?"

"I'm half human. I experience them all. My eyes glow when I have strong feelings: anger, fear—though not much besides the Devil himself scares a demon—anticipation, happiness, *desire.*"

Her tongue slipped out to moisten her lips, and that little flash of pink sent the heat from his eyes down below his belt.

"Should I be scared of what you're feeling now?"

"Not unless you're afraid of being worshipped like a goddess, licked from head to toe, and experiencing so much pleasure you scream my name until you're breathless."

She laughed. "Wow. You cut right to the chase."

"This is the longest conversation I've had with you since the night we met. I don't want to waste any time."

"Good call. I could walk away at any moment."

"But you don't want to."

She searched his eyes, the look in hers dancing between desire and confliction. She wanted him, of that he was sure. But her preconceived notions about demons were keeping her from regarding him as an individual. From seeing him as a man.

He couldn't blame her. Most demons were downright dreadful. Very few ever developed the higher-level emotions that enabled them to experience things like empathy or guilt, which was why the HA meetings only had eight attendees. But Mike— being half human—was born with a full range of emotions intact. Aside from his abilities to light fire with his hands, get people to confess their deepest desires, and make deals on behalf of Satan, he'd always felt more human than demon.

Leave it to him to be attracted to a witch who was raised by an angel. Getting a date with Crimson might be the greatest challenge of his life, and Mike was always up for a challenge.

"What do you want, Crimson?" He pushed his magic toward her, urging her to open up.

"I want to climb you like a tree and find out if you're really as good as you claim to be." With a quick inhale, she unlinked her fingers and moved her hands to rest on his shoulders again.

"I can make that happen."

"I'm sure you could." She glanced at Sophie, who was busy chatting with a woman at the table next to her. "You don't smell as strongly of sulfur as other demons. If I couldn't see the magic in your aura, I might not even know what you are."

"A side-effect of being half human. I'm sure you could cast a spell to neutralize the scent completely if it bothers you."

"Oh, you wouldn't want me to do that. My spellcasting has me in shit so deep I'm drowning."

"Do you want to talk about it?"

She laughed. "Sure, let me unload my problems on a demon. That'll help." She chewed her bottom lip and stared at his chest, refusing to meet his gaze.

"Give me a chance. You might be surprised." He was tempted to push his magic on her again, but his desire for this woman made him want her to open up willingly this time.

"Unless you have wish-granting powers, I doubt it." She finally looked at him. "What kind of magic do you have, anyway?"

He shook his head. "Recovering demons never reveal their magic."

"Devious and mysterious. I find that oddly attractive."

"I was about to argue that I'm not devious at all, but if it works for you, I'll keep my mouth shut."

"It's working." She slid her hands behind his shoulders, moving toward him until their bodies touched. "I wasn't kidding about what I said earlier…about finding out if you're as good as you claim to be."

Holy hell, the feel of her soft curves pressed against him was enough to bring the Devil to his knees. He held her tighter, angling his face toward her hair and basking in the warm, spicy scent of her magic, like nutmeg and white pepper. He couldn't wait to show her just how good a demon could be.

She inhaled quickly and pulled back, her gaze following a group of witches as they exited the bar. Her jaw ticked, and her posture stiffened before she looked at him and forced a smile.

"Friends of yours?" he asked.

"I thought they were." She rolled her eyes, shaking her head. "That's not fair. Yes, they're my friends. I'm in some trouble with the coven, and no one can or will help me." She clamped her mouth shut.

"Why can't they help you?"

"I screwed up some spells. Big ones…royally screwed them up to the point that someone else had to fix them. The high priestess hates me because… Well, that doesn't matter, but I invoked the Supremacy Challenge. If I don't win the challenge, I'll lose my magic. I came here with Sophie to relax, but… I'm desperate. I should be studying."

Heat built in his eyes again, but it wasn't desire activating his demon magic this time. The burning in his right palm meant his inner demon had found a target. Desperate people were easy to convince.

"Maybe I can help you." His mouth formed the words against his will, and he ground his teeth. *Not Crimson. Anyone but her.*

"Do you have mind control powers? Maybe you can hypnotize the priestess so she can't remember how to work magic. Or wipe her memory completely. That would be nice."

"What do you really want?" He bit his tongue, cursing his demon side. Where was that angel food cake when he needed it? Maybe he could convince Destiny to make it pill form so he could carry it in his pocket.

"What do I want?" Her eyes glazed over for a moment before she blinked. "To win the challenge. To fix my broken magic, dethrone Rosemary, and make the coven a warm, welcoming place again."

Such a simple desire. So pure it wrapped around his heart

and squeezed. "Most people would wish death on their enemies."

"Oh, I'd never wish anyone death. If I had to wish something mean on her, I'd ask you to give her taste buds in her asshole. Let her experience the sensation of eating shit every day. That might slow her roll."

He laughed. "That is diabolical. I like it."

"Can you do it?"

"My magic doesn't work that way." But Satan's sure as hell did. The Devil could give her anything she wanted, so long as she paid the price.

"Well, it was worth a shot. I've still got a month to figure something out."

His spine tingled, his connection to hell sparking like a live wire. She was a witch—exactly what Satan was looking for. He pressed his lips together, but his demon side wanted to make this deal so badly he could taste the bile on his tongue. His jaw worked, the muscles involuntarily trying to pry his teeth apart.

Crimson stepped back. "Are you okay?"

He shook his head and tried to move away, but she grabbed his arm.

"Mike?" Concern filled her gaze.

"What are you willing to trade to get what you want?" The words tasted like day-old coffee grinds on his tongue. Bitter and gritty. "Tell me, and I can help you."

She tilted her head. "That's a good question. Maybe I'm going about this the wrong way. I need to do some more research."

He had to get away. If this conversation went any further, he'd be making a deal for Satan before Crimson realized what he was doing. Digging his phone from his pocket, he grimaced at the blank screen. "Oh, shit. That's my manager. There's an emergency at the restaurant. I have to go."

Her brow furrowed. "I hope everything's okay."

"Yeah. It was good seeing you." He spun around and marched out the door.

Damn that was close. Satan's order for a witch had the demon in him on high alert, but the man had to stay in control. He'd find a witch wicked enough to deserve the Devil's company, and it wasn't going to be Crimson.

He marched his ass straight home and opened the fridge, then dove into his secret stash of angel food cake to subdue his demon.

"Did you scare him off?" Sophie looked at Crimson quizzically as she sank into her chair.

"I don't know what happened." Crimson picked up what was left of the drink Mike bought her and took a sip. "We were talking and getting along fine. I'd decided to take your advice and let him distract me from my problems, but then he freaked. He said his manager from the restaurant texted with an emergency, but I saw his phone when he looked at it. The screen was blank."

"That's weird."

"I know. He'd just mentioned he thought he could help me with the challenge, and then he clammed up and ran away."

"He said he could help you?" Sophie's brows disappeared into her bangs. "Do you think he's some sort of a djinn? I hear those guys are dangerous. You think you're getting your wish granted, but it's never worth the cost."

"Nah. Djinns aren't demons, but it does make me wonder what kind of power he has. He wouldn't tell me." She'd be better off getting the help of an angel, no doubt, but if her dad couldn't get that miracle for her…

"I hear demons never tell. Did you talk about anything else that could have scared him off?"

Heat spread across her cheeks. "He said he wanted to lick

me from head to toe, and I told him I wanted to climb him like a tree."

Wine dribbled down Sophie's chin as she laughed. "Maybe you're more woman than he can handle." She held up a finger. "Or...I bet the Devil didn't just let him go. Maybe he had to trade his dick for his freedom."

"Unless he stuffed a zucchini in his pants, I don't think that's it." That was quite a package pressed into her hip when they were dancing close. She shrugged. "Whatever. It's probably for the better. My dad's wings would molt if he found out I was getting it on with a demon, and then I'd never get the miracle I'm about to ask him for."

CHAPTER FIVE

Crimson filled a paper cup with espresso and steamed milk and smiled as she handed it to the customer. "Thanks for visiting Evangeline's. See you next time."

The moment the woman stepped out the door, Crimson turned the key, locking it, and flipped the Open sign over so it read Closed. She'd planned to call her dad first thing this morning, but Tiffany called in sick, which left Crimson alone in the coffee shop all morning. She barely had a moment to breathe all day, and now it was closing time.

She rushed through her cleaning routine, took off her apron, and darted upstairs to her studio apartment. The moment she entered the loft, her nerves settled like they always did when she was near her paints and canvases. Dozens upon dozens of portraits, landscapes, and stylized views of New Orleans' famous landmarks stood on easels and leaned against the walls. It was time for another sidewalk art sale to make room for her to work.

Stopping in front of her latest creation, she chewed her bottom lip and stared at the image of the sexy demon. With his wavy, dark hair combed to the side, he wore a deep red suit and a wicked smile. A wall of fire reached up from behind him, licking at the top edge of the canvas, and he held his hand out as if offering it to shake.

She couldn't blame it on the alcohol—she'd only had two and a half drinks last night—but something had possessed her to paint a portrait of Mike the moment she'd gotten home. Sleep had eluded her until she finished it, and he'd been on her mind ever since.

With a shake of her head, she picked up the phone and dialed her father's cell. "Hey, Dad. How's it going?"

"Crimson, sweetheart, how are you?"

"I'm good. How's mom? Is her collarbone all healed?"

He chuckled. "Between you and me, I think she's better than she pretends to be. She's enjoying the extra attention."

"I can't say I blame her." She dropped onto the sofa and leaned her head back. "Listen, I was wondering if you could do me a favor."

"Anything for my favorite daughter."

"I'm your only daughter. Does that also make me your least favorite?"

"Let's hear the favor, and I'll let you know."

She explained her situation with the coven. Her dad was all too aware of her misfiring magic—it was why he'd been assigned to take care of her when her birth mother died. With a witch and an angel as her adoptive parents, her goddess-channeling magic should have been honed to a razor-sharp edge. Instead, it was jagged and crumbling like an eroding riverbank.

"Anyway, it's going to take a miracle for me to win the challenge, so I was hoping you could maybe put in a good word for me with the miracle department?"

He sighed. "Crimi, sweetheart, you know I'd do anything in the world for you, but angels can't get involved with Earthly magic."

Her heart thudded against her chest. Not him too. "I know that's not true. My magic was the reason you adopted me."

"I adopted you to protect you. Your mom did her best to

continue your training, but when your birth mother unlocked everything at once the way she did… You were too young for goddess-channeling, and something glitched, but it's not an issue for the angels to solve."

"Well, that glitch has gotten me into trouble. I'm going to lose my magic."

"If your life were on the line, then I could get involved. You can survive and even thrive without magic."

"Dad…"

"I suggest you pray to your goddess for help. I'm sure she wouldn't have granted the challenge if she didn't think you could win."

She tightened her grip on the phone. "Or maybe she's angry because I don't channel her magic like I'm supposed to, and this is her way of getting even." *I'm about as useful as a vampire who faints at the sight of blood.*

"You channel her spirit in your paintings. Maybe try connecting with her that way."

"Don't you think I've tried? I painted all night, but she didn't provide me with an answer. When it comes to my magic and the goddess, there's a block that no one, not even the most powerful healer I could find, can unlock."

"Perhaps the answer is there, and you just can't see it."

Unless the answer was a romp in the sack with a sexy-as-sin demon, that was highly unlikely. "I've tried everything. I've hired every necromancer in New Orleans, and not one of them was able to call my mother back from across the bridge to finish unlocking my magic. I don't know what else to do."

"Study. Try your best. I wish I could help you, but my hands are tied in matters of magic. I'm sorry."

She sighed and rose from the couch. "It's okay. It was worth a shot."

"Remember that confidence is key. You're perfect the way you are because what you lack in magical ability, you more than make up for in kindness, generosity, and a dozen other more important traits."

"Thanks, dad. Tell mom 'hi' for me." She hung up the phone and shoved it into her pocket. *Confidence is key, my ass.* His fake it 'til you make advice may have gotten her through adolescence and secured her spot in the coven, but now she was about to fake her way right out of witchcraft.

She plopped onto the couch again and held her head in her hands. Very few memories of her birth mom remained, but the one thing she remembered most was her mother telling her how powerful she'd grow up to be. Crimson wasn't a mere channeler. She was supposed to have the ability to channel the goddess herself. She should have been able to perform any type of witchcraft imaginable, cast any spell with ease.

Minor spells she could usually pull off. With a few successful incantations under her belt, her confidence would grow, and she'd cast harder spells. But it never failed, the moment she thought she'd broken the hex on her powers, she'd screw something up and be back to square one. Confidence level: zero.

When her adoptive mother ran the coffee shop downstairs, she offered healing potions and simple spells to other supes and humans in the know. Crimson could cast those spells without fail when she was channeling her mother's magic. The moment her parents retired and moved to Florida, the spells she'd been casting for years started getting mixed up. Things would shrink when they were supposed to grow. Love spells would affect the wrong people. They failed more than they helped until eventually Evangeline's Spells and Coffee became nothing more than a mundane café.

What if her dad was right? What if the answer was right in front of her, and she just couldn't see it? Dragging her hands down her face, she stared at the portrait of the seductive demon. She'd been ready to bring the man home with her last night, until he freaked out and bolted. He had mentioned he might be able to help her, and she felt the urge to paint his portrait so strongly last night, she couldn't have stopped if she'd tried.

Was she channeling the goddess in this creation? Was Mike the answer? She'd exhausted all her other options, so what did she have to lose?

She stopped by Casa del Burrito, her favorite Tex-Mex restaurant, for a couple of bean burritos while she waited until his restaurant closed, and then she marched her happy butt up the front steps of Honoré's. Yanking on the doorknob, she found it locked—*duh...the restaurant isn't open*—so she rapped her knuckles on the glass in the door.

"We're closed." Mike's deep, sultry voice drifted through the wood, making her shiver.

She leaned toward the jamb and caught a glimpse of him through the window. "Unless you're on the menu, I'm not here to eat." *Real smooth, Crim.* If he ran off last night because she'd turned on too much heat, that was not the best way to gain entrance. "I was hoping we could talk."

His eyes flashed red as he opened the door. "What if I *am* on the menu?"

"Then I'll have a feast." She fisted her hands. "God, why do I always blurt out this shit when I'm near you?"

He chuckled. "God has nothing to do with it."

"Obviously." She stepped into the restaurant, and he closed the door behind her.

"What did you want to talk about? Are you here to take me up on my offer of worship?" He grinned wickedly and slipped behind the bar to take a white pastry box from a mini fridge. When he bent over, she got a nice view of his backside, and as he grinned over his shoulder, her cheeks burned. "Like what you see?"

She should not have been this attracted to a demon, but everything about him—his muscular body, strong jaw, devilish eyes, and cocky personality—drew her in, making her want to say to hell with all her problems and just lose herself in his arms.

But she wasn't here to get down and dirty with a demon, no matter how hot a flame he lit in her core. "Let's get one thing straight: sex is not on the table."

"You're right. The bed would be more comfortable. I've got a rocking recliner upstairs that might be fun as well." He wiggled his brows and set the box on the bar.

She opened her mouth to speak, but an image of him naked in said recliner, her straddling his lap, flashed behind her eyes, and the words got stuck in her throat.

He nodded. "The recliner it is."

"No." She shook her head, trying to shake away the image. "We're not having sex."

"Well, that's no fun."

"You're a demon, Mike. I know you talk like this to all the women. It's your nature."

He opened the box and paused, his eyes narrowing. "I'm afraid you don't know anything about me if that's what you think of my nature."

"So you don't ignite a fire in every woman you touch, bringing all their carnal desires to the surface?" Because that's what he did to her every goddamn time he looked at her.

Picking up a white pastry, he placed a piece in his mouth, chewing slowly and swallowing before answering, "People do like to tell me things, yes. The Devil deals in desire, but…" He took another bite of cake and leaned toward her, resting his elbows on the counter.

"I don't create desire; it comes from within. So if what you're feeling is carnal, and I do hope it is, that is entirely your own emotion. I just get the luxury of hearing about it. If I'm lucky, maybe you'll show me too."

"You are full of yourself, aren't you?"

He shrugged. "You've told me what you want. I can't help it if it's me. Would you like some angel food cake? It's divine."

"A demon eating angel food cake. That's rich."

"It's light and fluffy, actually." He offered her a piece, but she shook her head, so he returned the box to the fridge. "If you didn't come to tell me how badly you want me to make you come, why are you here?"

"Last night, when I told you about the Supremacy Challenge, you said you might be able to help me. What did you mean? Do you have some kind of power that can fix my magic? What can you do?"

"Ah." He strode around the bar to stand in front of her. "I simply meant to be chivalrous. I'm always game to help a damsel in distress."

She stiffened, and the hairs on the back of her neck stood on end. "I don't need chivalry, and don't you dare call me that ever again. I may be in distress, but I'm a strong, confident woman, not a damsel." She should have known the goddess wouldn't guide her to a demon for help. What the hell was she thinking coming here? "I should go."

"Stay, please." He gently placed a hand on her arm. "I didn't mean to offend. How can I make it up to you? Aside from help with your challenge, what do you want?"

"I want to know you." The words tumbled from her lips before she could stop them. That was his magic talking. He somehow reached inside people and made them reveal their innermost desires, but there had to be more to it than that. "I want you to tell me about your magic. This getting people to tell you everything they want, does it have a purpose?"

"A recovering demon never reveals his magic."

"Not even to people you're close to?"

He tilted his head. "A few close friends know, but you'll never get it out of them. A lot of trust must be built before I can discuss it."

"So…" She opened her arms. "Let's build some trust."

"I'm intrigued." He ran his gaze down her body and back up to her eyes. "How do you suggest we do that?"

Her stomach bubbled, but she couldn't tell if it was in reaction to his heated gaze or the bean burritos she devoured on the way over. "By talking, and neither one of us runs out on the other if we say more than we mean to."

"It's a deal. Would you like to come upstairs for a drink? I promise to keep my hands to myself until you tell me otherwise."

Oh, lord. What was she doing? Upstairs, into his home, was the last place she needed to go. The man was trouble with a capital T, but she couldn't help herself. She did desire to know him. Maybe his magic wasn't the thing that would help her with the challenge, but she had been compelled to paint him. Any time she felt compelled to create art, it was always the goddess talking to her. Who was she to ignore a deity?

"Do you have whiskey?" She needed something stiff—other than his dick—if she was going to see this through.

"I certainly do." He took the pastry box from the fridge and motioned toward a staircase in the back.

"Whiskey and cake? Is that a good combo?" She followed him to the steps.

"I'm afraid I can't live without it."

Mike shoved another mini angel food cake into his mouth on the way up the stairs, and the tingling in his palm subsided. He gestured to the couch for Crimson to sit and placed the nearly empty box on an end table. Hopefully he'd ingested enough angel magic to keep his demon side at bay, but he'd polish off the rest if need be. Satan could rot in his own circle of hell. This witch would be Mike's.

Crimson sank onto a cushion and ran her hand over the plush chocolate fabric. "For some reason I expected your house to be decorated in red."

He offered her a whiskey and sat next to her. "That's the Devil's signature color, not mine. I prefer earthier tones."

"I see that." She sipped the drink and glanced around the

room. The blank screen of the television mounted to the wall cast a distorted reflection of them on the couch, and a potted succulent sat on a table near the window. "Everything looks so normal."

"Were you expecting fire and brimstone?"

"I suppose I was."

He tossed a spark toward the fireplace, setting the log ablaze. "Better?"

"Impressive." Heat flashed in her eyes as her gaze landed on the beige rocking recliner adjacent to the sofa, and she sipped her drink, glancing at him as if expecting him to make a racy comment.

He'd made a promise, though. She said sex was off the table, so he'd be a good boy…until she wanted him to be bad.

The painting on the wall behind him caught her gaze, and she gasped. "That's mine."

"Technically, I bought it, so it's mine."

"You bought one of my paintings?" Her eyes widened in awe.

He nodded. "At a sidewalk sale in front of your coffee shop. You're an amazing artist, by the way." He turned to take in the work of art, a rendering of the Mississippi River done in rich hues of green, gold, and blue. "Your work is divine."

"Well, I can't take all the credit. I channel the goddess when I paint. She speaks through me, expressing the beauty of nature and her love of New Orleans."

"Wow. *That's* impressive."

She shrugged as if it were no big deal. "Channeling is my inborn power. I'm supposed to be able to channel the goddess to cast spells too, but something went wrong when my mother unbound my magic. A glitch, so to speak, because of how young I was." She took another sip of her drink. "So the only goddess channeling I can do is through my painting."

He looked at the beautiful piece of art and then at the gorgeous woman sitting next to him, and his chest tightened.

"That makes me love my purchase even more. What was the last thing you painted?"

"Oh, I'm sure it was another landscape or something." She finished off the drink and set the glass on the coffee table. "What about you? Tell me something about Mike the demon. How did you come to live in New Orleans?"

"I bought this restaurant and moved into the apartment above." He set his glass next to hers, scooting closer until their knees bumped.

She glanced at the spot where they now touched. "And the Devil just let you go? Seems like Earth would be crawling with demons if it were that easy."

"I won my freedom in a poker game." He rested his arm on the back of the sofa.

"Seriously?"

"Five Card Draw. I called his bluff and won the game. Satan loves to gamble."

"I bet."

He chuckled. "The Devil did, and he lost. Now I get to live topside as long as..." Gazing into her dark eyes, he brushed a strand of hair from her forehead.

"As long as what?" She drifted closer to him, and the warm, spicy scent of her magic tickled his senses.

"As long as I keep my powers in check." He almost slipped and told her about the monthly payments he made in exchange for his freedom. Something about her made him want to open up and share everything about himself. Maybe this was what people felt like when they talked to him. The difference was, she wasn't using any type of hocus pocus to make him feel this way.

"When a demon wins his freedom, he keeps his magic? It seems like the Devil would strip you of your powers when he set you free."

"Satan prefers us to keep our demonic tendencies. He likes us to struggle. Being a recovering demon isn't easy."

"Which is why you go to AA meetings?"

"*HA*. We're hellions, not alcoholics. Well, most of us aren't alcoholics."

"We're friends now, right?" This time, she didn't just drift toward him. She lifted her butt off the couch and scooted until her hip pressed against his.

"I sure hope so." Holy Hades, the woman smelled heavenly, and the heat radiating from her skin sent all the blood from his head straight to his groin.

"Then you can tell me what other kind of magic you have." Her breath against his ear sent a shiver down his spine.

"That's a tricky subject, I'm afraid." He turned his face toward hers.

"How so?" She leaned toward him, her nose a scant two inches from his, and paused.

He nearly went cross-eyed trying to meet her gaze as he fought the urge to take her mouth with his. Damn him for making such an ill-conceived promise to keep his hands to himself. He had no willpower around her. "When you're a demon, people automatically judge you if they know your magic. I'm half human, yet no one can see past the demon side. I'd like you to get to know me before you judge me."

She rested a hand on his thigh. "I'd like to get to know you too."

Oh, damn it all to hell. He promised to keep his *hands* to himself, but he didn't say anything about his lips. He moved closer, tilting his head and gently brushing his lips to hers. When her breath hitched, he couldn't help himself, and he took her mouth with his.

Her lips were soft as velvet, and as she tightened her grip on his thigh, a shudder ran through his body. She tasted like whiskey, his favorite flavor, and her kiss was so hot, a ground fissure could have opened up with a blast of hellfire beneath him because he was about to go up in flames.

"Are you sure you don't have this effect on all women?" she whispered against his lips.

"The self-preservation instinct keeps most women away." He kissed her jaw before gliding his lips down to her neck.

She laughed. "I guess that's another part of me that's not working right, then." Cupping his cheek in her hand, she pulled his mouth to hers and kissed him again.

Devil have mercy, this woman was alluring. He slid a hand behind her neck, pulling her closer, the man in him completely in control. The angel cake had done its job subduing his demon. In fact, the urge to make a deal with this witch completely vanished from his mind.

A deep rumble sounded from her stomach, and she pulled away, clutching her abdomen. "Uh oh."

"Are you okay?"

Her eyes tightened, her gaze cutting between him and the exit. "I think…" Her stomach whined and groaned as if she'd swallowed a hell cat. "Can I use your restroom?"

"Sure. It's through the bedroom to the left." He pointed toward the door, and she shot to her feet, darting through and slamming it behind her.

Holy charro beans, that was a close one. Crimson barely made it to the bathroom before her protesting dinner reached its grand finale, and damn, did it end with a bang. And speaking of beans, what the hell did Casa del Burrito put in those things? Jet fuel? Hellfire? That shit burned. Literally.

She had tried to ignore the churning in her gut as she made out with Mike. His lips were soft and his body firm, and while her brain had attempted to tell her it was wrong to want a demon, every other fiber of her being had screamed at her to go for it. It had been hard to tell if the heat building in her lower abdomen was from desire or dinner, until it hit critical mass and she had to make a run for it. And not a moment too soon.

The second her butt hit the seat, the bomb dropped. She

turned on the water and faked a few coughs to cover up the sound, and thank the goddess the plumbing worked properly. But now, she stood at the sink in a cloud of funk that smelled worse than a Bourbon Street dumpster on Mardi Gras.

What the hell was she thinking eating Tex-Mex before going to see a hot guy?

She rummaged through the cabinet beneath the sink, but all she found were a few spare rolls of toilet paper. Leave it to a man to not keep a bottle of Poo-pourri, or any type of air freshener, on hand.

The linen closet only contained linens, and in the medicine cabinet sat a single jar of face cream. Demons needed to moisturize?

She opened the jar and sniffed. Unscented, of course. Not that she could have used a cream to neutralize the stench she'd created. What would she do? Smear it on the walls?

Think, Crim. Think. She could cast a spell. A simple incantation to freshen a room. Her mom used to do one every morning in the coffee shop to enhance the aroma of the brew. People loved the smell of coffee. Now, how did that spell go?

She ran the verse through her mind a few times to make certain she'd get it right. Then she straightened her spine—confidence was key—and recited the words: "Aroma rich, scent pure. Enhance the fragrance, increase it sure."

Her stomach burned—with magic rather than digesting food this time—and as the warmth spread, rolling down her arms, she cast it into the air.

Oh, shit.

That spell didn't cover up odor, it magnified it. Damn it, she knew that. She *knew* the spell intensified the scent of coffee, so why did she think it would have the opposite effect on this problem?

Because being near Mike short-circuited her brain. That's why.

She shook her hands and paced the small space. Pine. The

scent of pine or fir…any conifer…would help to cover this up. She took a deep breath, immediately regretting that action, and spoke another incantation. "Fragrant pine, cypress, fir, enhance this space with conifer."

The smell of Christmas trees filled the room, but it did nothing to mask the other odor tainting the air. *Crap.* Now it smelled like someone ripped a massive fart in the woods.

Mike tapped on the door. "Are you okay in there?"

"Fine." Aside from the fact she was choking on the stench. If she opened the door now, the smell would knock him over. It was probably seeping through the cracks already. *Oh, please, Mother Earth, open the ground and swallow me whole.* "Be out in a minute," she said in her most cheerful voice.

"Take your time."

As his footsteps receded, she yanked aside the shower curtain, desperately searching for something…anything to squelch the stench.

A window!

Thank the goddess. Stepping into the tub, she worked the pane open and fanned the air outward. But the night was stagnant, and with the door closed, no cross breeze encouraged the air in the bathroom to escape.

She peered through the window, down to the grassy courtyard below. It wouldn't be *that* far of a fall if she hung onto the ledge and lowered herself all the way before letting go.

Two bathroom window escapes in as many nights didn't say much for her dignity, but what choice did she have? She couldn't open the door and face Mike when his entire apartment would soon reek of Casa del Burrito discharge. She could never face him again.

This was what she got for trying to interpret a message from the goddess that wasn't there. She'd come here for her own selfish reasons, and this was her punishment.

So much for getting it on with the hottest demon in town. He was probably a beast in the sheets too.

The toxic fumes stung her eyes as she cast one last glance at the door, grabbed her purse, and climbed out the window. Luckily she'd worn flat shoes, so she didn't twist an ankle on the fall, but the impact jarred her joints, and she bit her tongue.

She swallowed the coppery taste from her mouth and trudged through the side yard to the street, leaving her dignity in the dirt where it belonged this time. It wouldn't be *that* hard to avoid Mike for the rest of her life, especially if she lost the challenge and had to move away. Even sadder…she needed to find a new favorite Tex-Mex restaurant.

CHAPTER SIX

Crimson leaned on the counter in the empty coffee shop, scouring the encyclopedia of magic her mom had overnighted to her four days ago. Ever since her walk of shame from Mike's house, she'd spent every spare second she had studying and practicing the myriad spells she could be called upon to cast for the challenge.

Avoiding him the past few days had been easy since she'd barely left the building, but she couldn't stop berating herself for screwing up a possible relationship before it even began. Despite her angelic upbringing, she was really starting to like him.

She couldn't get the man off her mind, and it was messing with her nightly painting ritual. Every time she picked up a brush and opened herself to channel the goddess' divinity, the only thing her hand would allow her to paint was portrait after portrait of the sexy demon. She'd memorized every cut and dip of his chiseled features, and she couldn't help but remember the way his lips felt pressed to hers as the brush glided across the canvas.

Focus, Crim. She'd blown it with Mike, and there was no coming back from that level of mortification.

A bell chimed, signaling the entrance of a customer, and she spoke with her gaze trained on the spell she was trying to memorize. "Welcome to Evangeline's. What can I get for you?"

"What are you offering?" The deep, velvety voice wrapped around her like a piece of silk sliding over her skin.

Her jaw clenched shut, and she lifted her gaze to find the object of both her desire and humiliation standing across the counter. Her throat thickened, her tongue feeling like it had turned into a giant cotton ball. Attempting speech was completely pointless, so she grabbed a menu and handed it to him.

He set it aside and slid onto a stool, folding his arms on the counter. "You disappeared the other night. I didn't know witches had teleportation powers."

Heat spread from the bridge of her nose across her cheeks, all the way to the tips of her ears. "We don't. I…uh…went out the window."

He nodded. "That's why it was open. I thought it was because of the smell."

Oh, sweet goddess, please send a wolf to devour me now. She knew she needed to speak, but what in the name of the triple goddess could she say? Clutching the countertop, she cast her gaze to the white marble.

"What happened in there?" he asked.

The heat from her face spread to her chest, and a bead of sweat dripped down the back of her neck. She slammed the encyclopedia shut and gripped the spine. "Were you going to order something?"

"Talk to me, Crimson." He put his hand on top of hers and caught her gaze. "Let's *clear the air.*" His lips twitched like he was trying really hard to suppress a smile.

The sentiment must have been contagious, because laughter bubbled from her chest before she could stop it.

"There she is." He squeezed her hand and let it go.

"Oh, god." She clutched the book to her chest. "I'm so sorry." Squeezing her eyes shut, she shook her head. "I had Tex-

Mex before I came over that night, and it didn't agree with me."

He chuckled. "That's an understatement."

"That wasn't." She sighed. "The smell was... I was embarrassed, so I tried to cast a spell to diminish the odor. Instead, I intensified it."

"And the pine scent?"

"After I magnified it, I tried to cover it up. I have a bad habit of screwing up spells, and I was mortified. We were just getting going, and then I stunk up the entire building. I should have just...well, I don't know what I should have done, but escaping through the window wasn't it." She rubbed her temple, cursing herself for making a bad situation worse. Did she honestly think she could avoid this man for the rest of her life? "I'm an idiot."

He drummed his fingers on the counter. "I'll tell you what. Let's start over. Have dinner with me tonight. I promise we'll go somewhere light on the stomach." He winked.

She looked into his eyes, and though they were filled with amusement, they also held sincerity. Second chances in life were few and far between, yet this demon was offering her just that. "Can we pretend the other night never happened?"

"We'll never speak of it again."

Her ears cooled, and though she'd never recover completely from the mortification, if he was willing to forget it happened, she'd give it a try. "Deal. Pick me up at seven?"

His eyes flashed red, and he squeezed his hands into fists before dropping them into his lap. "Seven works for me. What are you reading?"

She turned the book around to show him the cover. "I'm studying for the challenge. We each have to cast a series of spells, but we won't know which ones until the challenge begins. Not only do I have to cast them correctly, but I have to do it better and faster than Rosemary."

"You mentioned a glitch in your magic. Aren't you going to try to fix it first?"

"If there were a way to fix it, I would have found it by now. Believe me, I've tried everything. So, I'm going to win this the old-fashioned way. By hard work and determination."

"That's the honorable way to do it."

She set the book down and sighed. "Honorable, yes, but it's not likely to work. Honestly, I'm not even sure I want to be high priestess. I only challenged Rosemary because I panicked. I tend to act without thinking sometimes."

"No windows for you to climb out of?" He grinned.

She laughed. "Not at the time, no. She was about to bind my powers and make me human, so I spouted off the challenge. Now, if I lose, I'll become human *and* be exiled, never to speak to another witch again."

"That's harsh."

"I know. I should have just let her bind my powers. Now I'm going to lose everything: my home, my friends, this coffee shop that's been in my mom's family for generations."

She opened the book and sliced her finger on a page. The wound stung, and a drop of blood pooled on her skin. "Damn it. Papercut." She stuck her finger in her mouth to quell the bleeding.

"Do you need a bandage?"

She shook her head. "It's fine."

"Well, I think you'll make a fabulous high priestess when you win the challenge."

She let out a sardonic laugh. "Thanks. I sure don't want to lose everything. I swear though, sometimes I think I'd sell my soul to Satan if he could make this all go away. Can people really do that?"

Mike grimaced and set his fisted right hand on the counter. "Don't say things like that. You don't mean it."

"Does the Devil really make deals like that?"

"All the time."

She shook her head. "Hell, if he can make it so this challenge never has to happen, and things can go back to the way they were, he can have my body too."

His eyes flashed red, and he uncurled his fist, holding his hand toward her. "Satan accepts your offer."

"It's a deal." She laughed and placed her hand in his. "You're from hell. It can't be *that* bad a place."

His palm heated, and her papercut sizzled before the wound closed completely. She tugged her hand away and examined her finger. "You have healing powers?"

The color drained from Mike's face. "You were joking, right? You didn't really want to sell your soul to the Devil, did you?"

She waved a hand dismissively. "Of course not. My dad would molt if I did something that stupid."

"Good." He nodded and rose to his feet. "You really shouldn't joke like that, especially around a demon."

"Point taken. I'll be more careful with my words." She tilted her head. He was still pale. "Are you okay?" Had she screwed things up again by joking about selling her soul? That would be her luck. Or maybe healing her papercut had drained him.

"Yeah." He rubbed his palm on his jeans. "I've got some things to take care of, so I'm gonna go."

"Hey." She stepped around the counter and rested a hand on his bicep. Thankfully, he didn't pull away. "I'm sorry for kidding around about Satan. I haven't spent much time with demons, and I didn't mean to offend you."

He leaned toward her and pressed his lips to her cheek. "We're good."

His breath on her skin made her shiver. "See you at seven?"

"I'll be here." He stroked the backs of his fingers down her cheek before stepping out the door.

Holy hell. What the ever-loving fuck have I done? Mike stalked down the sidewalk and ducked into a secluded alley before waving his hand and opening a portal to his home. He landed in his living room and dropped onto the couch, raking his fingers through his hair and pulling it at the roots.

He made a deal. *Damn it!* He'd stuffed his face with half of a full-sized angel food cake before he went to see Crimson. He shouldn't have been capable of striking a bargain like that. With that much angel magic flowing through his system, he shouldn't have been able to send Satan a testicle, much less a body and soul.

It didn't happen. She was joking, so it couldn't be legit. He'd subdued his demon side with angel magic. Hell, he'd done everything but hog-tie the beast, and Crimson didn't mean it. But if it wasn't legit, then why the fuck did his spine tingle and his palm burn like hellfire when they shook? And that sizzle? That was blood. Sure, it was from a papercut and not a purposeful wound, but the Devil didn't care about details like that. She'd said the words, and Mike had accepted on Satan's behalf.

I'm a fucking idiot. He deserved to spend eternity in the tarpits for this. *Hell's bells and buckets of blood!* He had to fix this.

Taking the back staircase to avoid the restaurant, he marched his ass over to Sweet Destiny's and threw open the door. The soft floral scent of angelic magic folded around him, making his demon side squirm, but he forced himself across the threshold and rang the bell on the counter. A melodic *ding* filled the air, and his neighbor drifted from the kitchen into the storefront.

Her copper hair flowed down to her shoulders, and her fair skin held an ethereal glow. Peach lips curved into a comforting smile, and her voice reminded him of a cool stream running through a meadow. "Is it Thursday already? Let me box up your order."

"No, it's not. I need your help."

Her smile brightened. "I'm happy to assist. Tell me what

you need."

"Those cakes, the most recent batch, they had the usual dose of magic?"

"Of course. Just enough to subdue a demon without causing harm. Is there a problem?"

"And the full-sized one you made for me? It's the same?"

"Yes…"

"So if I ate half the full-sized cake…"

Her eyes widened. "I'd say you're lucky you're half human. That much angel magic in one sitting would render a full-blooded demon catatonic for hours."

"So it should have squelched my magic, right? I shouldn't have been able to seal a deal after eating that much cake."

Her brows scrunched. "Well, I don't know. Did it *feel* like the deal sealed?"

"Maybe. Fuck. Yeah, it did, but she didn't mean it. She was joking when she said it. Well, maybe only half-joking, but I know she didn't mean it. She's good. Pure. She doesn't belong in hell."

Destiny pressed her palms together and closed her eyes for a moment. When she opened them, they held sadness and compassion. "I'm afraid I can't help you. The only person who knows if the contract is good is Satan himself. You'll have to ask him."

"Satan…" he growled.

Destiny raised her hands. "Please don't call him here."

Mike nodded and stormed out the door. He focused on the tingle in his spine, activating his direct line to Satan—if the Devil could use it for emergencies, so could he—but the tingle turned to a buzz…a metaphysical busy signal.

"Figures." He stomped through the back door and darted up the stairs, glancing at the clock on the way in. Four p.m. He had exactly three hours to take a trip to hell, tell Satan he could shove that deal where the sun doesn't shine, shower, and pick Crimson up for their date at seven.

Plenty of time.

With a wave of his arm, he opened a portal to hell, but he hesitated to step through. He'd been topside for five years straight and had sworn to never set foot in the bowels of the underworld again. While his demon side exulted in the heat seeping through the opening, his human half wanted to puke.

But he'd be damned for all eternity before he'd let his sweet Crimson become a pawn in Satan's chess game of life and death.

Swallowing the bitter bile from his throat, he stepped through the portal, his heart missing a beat or twelve as the gate slammed shut behind him.

The demonic entrance to hell looked just as he remembered, with stone floors worn smooth from millennia of footsteps crossing over them and jagged, cavernous walls towering high above, looming in oppression. The screams of tortured souls echoed off the walls, and Mike froze, listening to the horrid sounds.

His lips tugged into a smile as he recognized the skip at the end of the loop before the cacophony started up again. Those screams weren't real. They were from the "Pits of Hell" soundtrack that came from a topside Halloween store back in the nineties. Satan piped it in through all the gates to get the demons riled up and to scare the shit out of the new souls entering the realm of the dead.

Mike flipped up the collar on his jacket and kept his head down as he made his way over the rocky terrain toward Satan's palace on the hill in the distance. This was to be a quick in and out mission. He didn't have time for run-ins with family and old "friends." His mother had disowned him when she'd heard the news of his plans to move topside, but not before she tried to chew his ear off—literally—over the ordeal. The other advocates never cared for his half-human nature, and now, with his demon subdued, he couldn't afford a challenge from one of his old associates.

A moat of molten lava surrounded the Devil's obsidian

castle, but even that was just for show. Demons were impervious to heat and flame, and the witch's magic used to seal off this section of hell from the dead was impenetrable.

He crossed the bridge and pressed his palm to the hot plate on the exterior wall. A human's skin would melt off the bone if they touched metal this hot, but Mike's demon side rendered him immune to heat like a full demon.

A loud *thunk* echoed from inside as the lock disengaged and the door swung open. Red glass spires soared six stories up to the rocky ceiling, and blood-colored velvet drapes hung from the windows, blocking the view of the cave surrounding the palace.

Making a sharp right, he paced down the expansive hallway toward the Devil's office and halted in front of the door. He lifted his fist and froze, unable to make his knuckles meet wood.

Don't be pathetic. His mother's words echoed in his mind. *You don't belong up there. You'll continue to damn the innocent, whether you want to or not.*

"Not this time, Mother Dearest." He pounded his fist against the door.

Heels clicking on the stone floor echoed from inside, and a moment later, the door swung open.

"Hello, I'm Esmerelda." A witch with short black hair, styled into a pixie cut, greeted him. Tall and slender, she wore a silk shirt and pencil skirt in the standard red Satan required of all his office employees. "How can I help you?"

He stepped into the waiting room, stopping in front of a red velvet couch. A massive fireplace took up the entire wall across from it, and flames licked all the way to the ceiling. This must be what Crimson imagined Mike's apartment would look like.

"I need to see Satan. It's an emergency."

Esmerelda shook her head. "I'm afraid that's not possible. He's on vacation."

Mike opened his mouth to respond, but as her words sank in, he paused. "Vacation? The Devil never takes a vacation."

She shrugged. "He does now. Would you like to leave a message for him?"

Satan, the Lord of the Underworld, had taken a vacation and left this witch in charge of his office? Hope filled his chest like a hot air balloon. Did this mean...? "Are you his new assistant?"

"Oh, no." She waved a hand dismissively. "I'm just filling in until his advocate finds a permanent replacement. I made my deal directly with the Devil before I died, and being his hand servant wasn't part of it."

"Damn."

"We all are." She laughed. "His new girlfriend thinks he works too hard, so she insisted he take her on a trip. They're on a transatlantic cruise and won't be back for three weeks."

Three weeks stuck in a tiny cabin on a cruise ship? "That sounds like pure hell."

"I'm sure it is. There's a rather foul drug lord on the same cruise. It's my understanding that Satan plans to spread a nasty stomach virus among his crew."

"Sounds diabolical."

"The man can't get away from work, can he?"

"Speaking of work, do you have access to his deal manifest? I need to check it for a name. There was a mix-up, and I'm not sure the last deal I made for him went through."

"Oh, you're an advocate? I should have known with your good looks." She strutted toward the assistant's desk and sank into a swiveling chair. "I'm afraid everything's been frozen and locked in his absence. New souls are being stored at the docks, and deals are hanging in limbo until he returns. You'll have to come by when he gets back."

"Thank you. I appreciate your help."

She smiled. "Anytime."

His hands curled into fists as he marched out of the palace and made his way to the demonic exit. Satan would be gone for three weeks, which meant Crimson's soul was safe for the time being, and Mike had twenty-one days to find an actual wicked witch who could take her place.

He tore open a portal and stepped back into his home before plopping in front of the computer and pulling up The Haunt Ads website. The Haunt Ads was like Craigslist, but for supes only. With a few clicks of the trackpad, he took out an advertisement.

Wanted: Personal Assistant to the Prince of the Underworld.
Requirements: Must be a witch with a heinous nature.
Willing to spend eternity in hell.

He deleted the *eternity in hell* part and changed it to *Willing to live in the underworld in Satan's palace.* That sounded much more appealing.

If the ad didn't work, his only other choice would be to coerce someone, but he hadn't used trickery to make a deal in decades. Could he even pull it off? He'd have to quit the angel food cake and avoid Destiny and the other angels at all costs. All the work he'd done to subdue his demon would have to be reversed. He'd become diabolical again. He'd have to if he wanted to save Crimson from his stupid mistake.

He swallowed the thickness from his throat. Would she even want him if he went back to his demonic ways? The woman was raised by an angel, after all. But he'd rather her hate him for the rest of her life topside than hate him from the hell he'd damned her to.

He rose to his feet, stripping out of his clothes on the way to the shower. Even he could smell the sulfur on his body after spending twenty minutes in hell. With the hot water blasting from the faucet, he scrubbed until his skin went raw.

The ad had to work. He'd find the Devil a new assistant, and he'd win the heart of the beautiful witch while he was at it.

CHAPTER SEVEN

"That was a fantastic play." Crimson slipped her hand into Mike's outside the Saenger Theater on the corner of Canal and Rampart, at the edge of the French Quarter. A streetcar rumbled by as they walked hand in hand, and they turned on the sidewalk, heading deeper into the Quarter.

"I'm glad you enjoyed it. The Greek's version of hell was actually the most accurate of all religions." Mike had taken her to see *Hadestown*, a musical account of Orpheus traveling to the underworld to save his fiancée, Eurydice, and while he could appreciate the story, sitting that close to Crimson, their knees touching, her hand resting in his, had been the highlight of his evening so far.

"Really? That's fascinating." She placed her free hand on his bicep.

Before the show, they had dinner at a small café on Rampart, where Crimson ordered a chicken salad sandwich with a side of fruit. She'd given him a pointed look both when she placed her order and when the food arrived, as if waiting for him to make a comment about the bathroom incident. Much like the Devil himself, however, an advocate always kept his word.

Now, as they shuffled down the sidewalk away from the crowd, the cool night air caressing his skin, his phone pinged with an incoming message. The first inquiry into his ad for the Devil's assistant made his heart jump into a little sprint. He shoved the device back in his pocket, the weight of his accidental deal with Crimson lightening. He could fix this. He *would* fix this. Tonight, he would simply enjoy her company.

"Such a sad ending, though. He should have trusted her." She faced him as they paused on the corner of Dauphine Street, her dark eyes glinting in the lamplight. She wore a deep emerald-green dress that showed off her curvy figure and mulberry lipstick he couldn't wait to be covered in. "They made it so far, but I bet she probably wouldn't have been allowed to leave whether Orpheus looked back or not."

"Satan enjoys the struggle, but he never goes back on a deal. A promise is a promise."

She inched closer, resting her hand on the lapel of his charcoal jacket. "But this was Hades, not Satan."

He placed his hand over hers. "He's had lots of names over the years, but he's always been the same guy."

"Really? Did you know him back then?"

"Nah. I'm not *that* old." They crossed the street. "I was going to ask if you wanted to grab a coffee, but seeing as how you're around it all day, I'm going to guess that's a no."

"Actually, I'd love to." She grinned, casting her gaze downward. "I know a place that serves the best latte in town. They're closed, but I think I can convince the owner to let us in."

She'd been acting shy since he picked her up this evening, and he could only imagine she was still embarrassed. This was the first sign they might be able to get back on track, and he wasn't about to waste the chance. Gliding his fingers along her jaw, he gently lifted her chin. "Are you asking if I want to go back to your place?"

"If I was, what would your answer be?"

He took her hand, lacing his fingers through hers. "It would be an adamant 'hell yes.'"

"Good, because that's exactly what I'm asking."

When they turned the corner, a couple stood in the middle of the sidewalk, blocking their path. The man glared at the woman, the hurt in his eyes battling with disbelief as he shook his head.

"So that's it?" the man asked. "You're going to pack your bags and move to Nashville with some dude you've known for a week?"

"We should go around." Crimson tugged Mike's hand, but he stopped, pulling her to his side.

"Hold on. I want to see how this plays out." The woman's true desire might as well have been painted on her face in bright red ink, but the guy was absolutely clueless.

The woman crossed her arms and shook her head, tossing her long blonde hair behind her shoulders. "He asked me to, so why not? It's not like there's a reason for me to stay here."

The hurt in the man's eyes was palpable, but it seemed the woman was just as blind as he was. "Well, if that's how you really feel, then go. Have a nice life."

"We really shouldn't be watching them fight," Crimson whispered.

"Seriously, Austin? You're supposed to be my best friend. The least you can do is be supportive of my decision."

Austin scoffed. "I'm not going to support you ruining your life over a man you hardly know, Anna. I hope he's worth it."

Austin turned to go, and Anna caught his hand. "Wait."

"Why?" He pulled from her grasp. "What do you want from me?"

"I want…" Tears collected on Anna's lower lids.

Mike rolled his eyes. Humans could be so dense sometimes. How could two people, who were supposedly best friends, be completely blind to each other's feelings? It wasn't like love was a difficult emotion to grasp.

He rested a hand on the woman's shoulder. "Tell him what you really want, Anna. What's your true desire?"

Her eyes widened as she looked at Mike, and when she turned her attention to Austin, her bottom lip trembled. "I want you to tell me to stay."

Austin's posture softened. "What? I thought you wanted to go to Nashville."

Anna shook her head as Mike gave her an extra push of magic to overcome the stubbornness. Finally, she spoke the truth, "I want you to love me like I love you." She dropped her arms to her sides and slumped, exhausted from the weight of carrying the secret for so long.

"Your turn, Austin." Mike clapped him on the shoulder. "Tell her what *you* want."

"All I've ever wanted is to be with you. I've been in love with you since eleventh grade."

Anna gasped. "Why didn't you ever say anything?"

"Because you made it clear you wanted me to stay in the friend zone."

"I don't want you in the friend zone. I love you, Austin." They hugged, and Crimson gaped as Mike tugged her away.

"That was...wow!" She bit her bottom lip and looked at him with wonder in her eyes. "I did not see that coming."

"I couldn't help myself. Humans act so stupid when it comes to their emotions, especially where relationships are concerned." He wrapped an arm around her shoulders. "If you want someone, you should tell them. It's simple."

"Is that so?" She slid her arm around his back. "What if you've done something so embarrassing, you're surprised you're even able to face the person you want?"

"Hmm..." He feigned deep thought. "That could throw a wrench into the situation. Good thing nothing like that has ever happened to us, right?" He winked, and she laughed.

"Are you sure you don't have any angel in you? That was a

very good deed you did back there. It's something my dad would have done."

He stopped walking and faced her. "Hasn't anyone ever told you not to compare a demon to an angel? Say that to the wrong person, and hellfire will shoot out his horns, setting his hair ablaze."

She paused, her mouth opening and closing a few times as she processed his words. "I'm sorry. Please don't catch fire."

He laughed. "I'm joking. Demons aren't flammable."

She narrowed her eyes, gazing at the top of his head.

"I don't have horns either. See?" He tilted his head down and ran his hand through his hair. "You weren't kidding when you said you didn't know much about demons."

"You're the first one I've gotten to know."

"Let me guess. You thought I was watching that couple argue because I enjoyed the conflict."

She flinched and shook her head. "No. I wasn't thinking that at all. I didn't know why you stopped. Maybe you were looking out for her safety because the guy looked pissed."

He chuckled. Demons were masterful liars, but it seemed witches were not. At least, this witch wasn't. But she was still here, by his side, strolling through the French Quarter with a demon, despite her angelic upbringing. He must have been doing something right. "Austin wasn't pissed; he was hurt. The woman he loves was about to leave him for a stranger."

"How did you know that? I thought you got people to *tell* you their deepest desires. With that couple, you already knew."

"You could see it on their faces." He pressed his lips together and continued walking. Even if he hadn't possibly damned Crimson to an eternity of servitude in the underworld, it still would have been too soon to share his magic with her. She was raised by a man whose mission was to save souls, and Mike's job for the past eighty years had been the exact opposite.

"Maybe *you* could see it." She shook her head. "It's usually men who are the clueless ones about emotions. You are full of surprises, aren't you?"

"I've got a few up my sleeve for when I get you alone, if that's what you mean." His eyes heated at the thought of all the devilish things he had planned for her, and he ran his hand down her back to give her butt a squeeze.

She laughed. "Now the demon is coming out. I'm not sure which side of you I like better."

"Lucky for you, I'm a package deal." He moved his hand to her hip, tugging her closer to his side. "You get both."

"Ooh, a man on the streets, a demon in the sheets? I can't wait."

"Neither can I."

Wow. Crimson couldn't wipe the stupid grin off her face as she walked, wrapped in Mike's arms, toward her home. Everything her dad had told her about demons was a lie. Well, not a lie—angels weren't capable of fibbing—but a gross over-generalization about a complex and diverse species of supe.

Mike was kind, sincere—*good,* even. Was it right to call a demon good? After the way he'd helped that couple get over their fears and admit their feelings for each other, she couldn't call him anything but.

"What are you grinning about?" He brushed his fingers down her cheek, sending a shiver up her spine. "You have a gorgeous smile, by the way. What's it for?"

He did say if a person wanted someone, they should say so. What did she have to lose? "It's for you, Mike. I like you."

"Of course you do. What's not to like?" He winked, and heat bloomed low in her belly.

Cocky. There was another word she could call him. He was drop-dead gorgeous; he had a way with people, and he knew it.

But he wasn't annoying about it, so maybe cocky wasn't the best word. Confident? *Confidence is key.*

Whatever it was, it lit a fire inside her, and she wanted to strip him bare and make him beg for mercy. The thought of a man like Mike trembling beneath her touch had her hotter than a love potion boiling in a cauldron on high heat. Forget coffee. She planned to head straight up to her apartment, and this sexy demon would be the main course.

They turned the corner onto Royal and found a woman leaning over a storm drain, wailing into the hole in the concrete. "Chopper! Come, Chopper. Come!" She reached an arm into the drain and pulled it back sobbing.

After the marathon of horror movies Crimson watched last week, she half-expected the woman to pull out a bloody stump, but thankfully, her arm remained intact. She rushed toward her and knelt by her side. "Are you okay?"

The woman sniffled. "It's Chopper. He fell down the drain."

Crimson peered into the darkness—though she didn't see anything—as Mike stopped next to her. "What's Chopper?" he asked.

"He's my dog."

"Your dog?" Crimson squinted and looked into the small rectangular hole. The name Chopper conjured images of a pit bull or German shepherd, but unless Chopper was a shifter, there was no way a dog that big would fit down the storm drain.

"He's a chihuahua, and he's my baby," the woman sobbed.

Mike patted her shoulder. "We'll get him out."

She nodded and looked into his eyes. "Can you also find a man to love me? I'm so lonely, and Chopper is all I've got. I haven't had a date in six months, and I just want someone to love me."

She clutched Mike's bicep, and he pried her off. *Poor guy.* "One thing at a time. How long has he been down there?"

"About ten minutes." She wrapped her arms around herself.

Crimson shined her phone's flashlight into the hole, and it

reflected off a tiny pair of eyes just out of arm's reach. "He's here. I see him." But there was no way in hell they could grab him.

Mike got on his hands and knees next to her and peered into the drain. "There are rats bigger than Chopper down there."

She suppressed a chuckle. "People unload their problems on you a lot, don't they?"

"Yep. It's all part of the magnificent package."

A package she couldn't wait to unwrap. But she couldn't leave with this poor little pooch trapped in the gutter. "So far, all your magic seems good. Got any that can save a rat-sized dog from the sewer monster?"

He looked at her. "Nothing I can do in public. Can you cast a levitation spell? Something to lift the little guy enough that we can grab him?"

Now, there was a thought. She'd just practiced an incantation to move objects yesterday, and it had worked...for the most part. She might have shattered a salt shaker the first time she tried, but the third time was the charm for that spell.

Then again, this was a living animal. What if she shattered Chopper?

"I don't know if that's a good idea."

Mike sat back on his heels, lowering his voice. "I could open a portal and travel through, then hand him to you from below. But, I'm not sure Chopper's momma could handle seeing that. If you levitate the dog, she won't be able to detect the magic from where she's standing."

Crimson shook her head. "I'm a bad witch. I screw up most of my spells."

"What happened to hard work and determination? Crimson, I know your greatest desire is to not be 'broken,' and I promise that you're not. You only *feel* broken."

"Mike..." She *was* broken. Always had been, always would be.

"Name one spell you've screwed up since the night we danced at the bar."

She snorted. "How about the one in your bathroom?

"Did you screw up the incantation, or did you simply cast the *wrong* spell?"

"I…" She clamped her mouth shut. When her mom used that spell, it was meant to intensify the aroma of the coffee shop. And when Crimson used it, the spell worked exactly right, *intensifying* her problem. Come to think of it, she'd managed to pull off all of the minor spells she'd been working on since she started training.

He rested a hand on her back. "You can do it. I have faith in you."

She nodded. Confidence was key, and if Mike thought she could do it…

"Please!" the distraught woman moaned.

"All right." Lying on her stomach, Crimson reached both arms into the drain and whispered the spell she'd practiced yesterday. Chopper whined and backed away, not allowing the magic to take hold.

"C'mon, little guy. Hold still for me." She whispered the spell again, willing the goddess' magic to flow through her, focusing all her power on the dog, and he squealed as she magically lifted him into the air. Her hands closed around the tiny, trembling body, and she passed the pooch to Mike before clambering to her feet and dusting off her knees.

She did it! She used her magic, and it didn't backfire. Sure, it was a simple spell, but it was important for the situation. Excitement bubbled in her chest. Maybe she could pull off this challenge after all.

"Oh, my sweet little puppykins. Mommy is so sorry you fell down the holey-woley. Are you okay?" The woman kissed the dog, and Chopper licked her in return, bathing her entire face in doggy slobber.

Man, she really does need to find a date.

With the woman and her dog reunited, Crimson took Mike's hand and led him toward her building. "Wow. Two good deeds in one night. Aren't you going to burst into flames now?"

"Nah, demons are impervious to flame, remember?"

"I'm sure Satan doesn't like it though. Does he give y'all hell when you do good deeds?" They paused in front of the entrance, and she took her keys from her purse.

"As long as I make my monthly payments on time, he leaves me alone." He clamped his mouth shut and swallowed hard as if he'd said more than he intended.

"Monthly payments? Is it like mafia protection or something?"

He glanced at the ground. "Something like that."

"That doesn't surprise me at all." She wanted to ask exactly how much he had to pay for his freedom each month, but she refrained. He'd open up when he was ready, and right now, she was ready to make him scream her name.

Bypassing the coffee shop entrance, she opened the door leading to the stairwell and dropped the keys back into her purse. "I'm on the third floor."

He lifted a brow. "No coffee, then?"

"Do you *want* coffee?"

"Not really." He grinned, moving toward her. "Do you?"

She rested her hands on his chest as her heart kicked into a sprint. "I think you know what I want."

He placed a hand on her hip. "Why don't you tell me?"

"I'd rather show you." Gripping the lapel of his jacket, she pulled him across the threshold and crushed her mouth to his.

A moan rumbled in his chest, and she kicked the door shut before pushing him against it, leaning into him as she tangled her fingers in his hair. He was right: no horns protruded from his scalp. The protrusion in his pants, however, pressed into her stomach like a horn of plenty.

"Showing is good. I like showing." He cupped her ass and held her close, grinding against her as he drank her in.

The nagging little voice in the back of her head whispered

this was wrong. Mike was a demon with access to people's innermost desires, and though she didn't know what devilish thing he could do with that knowledge, it could only lead to trouble. That's what demons were about.

But Mike was recovering. He went to HA meetings, and he'd been nothing but kind in her presence. As the pesky voice whispered again, she stomped it like a cockroach. She was done playing it safe.

"I'm sure my dress is filthy from saving the chihuahua," she whispered against his neck before grazing her teeth along his skin.

He shivered, his voice coming out more growl than words. "You should take it off then."

"Let's get out of the stairwell." She pulled from his embrace and immediately missed the warmth radiating from his skin.

"Good idea. With the things I want to do to you, we might scare your neighbors."

She laughed and guided him up the stairs. "Sophie is my only neighbor, and she spends most of her time with Trace. I doubt anything we could do would scare her."

"You don't know what I'm capable of."

A thrill shimmied up her spine at his words. The mystery surrounding him was part of the draw, and she couldn't wait to unravel him.

As they stopped outside her door, he stood behind her, his front pressed to her back, his hands roaming her hips while his lips caressed the bend between her neck and shoulder. Her skin turned to gooseflesh, and she dug in her purse, cursing under her breath when she couldn't find her keys.

"Problem?" His lips moved against her skin.

"I've got too much junk in here. I just had them earlier, but now I can't find my keys."

"Need some incentive?" He slid his hands up her stomach to cup her breasts, teasing her nipples through the fabric of her dress.

They tightened into pebbles, shooting a jolt of electricity straight to her core. "Oh, screw it." Reaching a hand toward the knob, she whispered an unlocking spell and threw open the door.

"Impressive." He followed her into the apartment. "The self-proclaimed bad witch has cast two spells in a row without a hitch. I'm starting to think you've been lying about your magic."

"Being near you seems to have a positive effect on me. Go figure."

"Hm." Something flashed in his eyes, an emotion she couldn't read alongside his signature demon red, before they widened and he turned to survey the room. "Color me mesmerized. Crimson, these are remarkable."

Her name rolled off his tongue like warm honey, and she gave him a moment to take it all in. Dozens upon dozens of her paintings lined the walls, the ones on the floor sitting in rows three or four deep.

"These are all channeling sessions with your goddess?" He walked along the wall, examining the paintings.

"Not all. Some come from my own mind, but they're mixed in." As she watched him admiring her work, her lips tugged into a smile. It felt nice to be around someone who appreciated her talents rather than pitied her inadequacies.

"I can't tell the difference. You're an incredible artist. Simply mesmerizing."

With his attention temporarily captivated, she might as well use the time to duck into the bathroom to make sure her stomach didn't have any surprises in store. "I'm going to freshen up while you recover from your mesmerization."

He caught her gaze, and his eyes smoldered. "Don't be too long."

Her stomach fluttered—in a good way this time—and she stepped into the restroom. Her dress was ruined, with black street-gunk smeared across the front, but her hair and makeup held up, though her lips were swollen from that amazing kiss.

With her confidence in her spell work at an all-time high, she whispered a quick spot-removing incantation. Her dress shimmered, and the street-gunk dissolved. *Damn.* Three in a row. Mike was as good for her magic as he was about to be for her libido.

She returned to the loft and found him studying the portraits she'd done of him. They were hidden behind a stack of landscapes, so he must have flipped through her entire collection to find them. Now, he had all three side by side, leaning against the wall.

The flutter in her stomach turned sour, and heat spread across her cheeks. "That's um… You weren't supposed to see those."

His smile brightened his entire face. "Why not? I'm honored you painted me. Though, this one…" He taped the first painting of him in a red suit, sitting on a throne. "I hope you weren't channeling the goddess on this, because I will never be the ruler of hell."

"I think it's metaphorical." She collected the paintings and laid them on a table, tossing a drop cloth over them. "That was after the night at the bar, when you walked out on me. My mind was racing."

His eyes tightened. "Right. Sorry about that."

"We seem to have a habit of running out on each other."

"Not anymore." He moved toward her, taking her in his arms. "You cleaned your dress. Another spell gone right?"

"Yep. It's a good thing I didn't really sell my soul to the Devil, huh? It seems I don't need his help after all."

His eyes darkened for a moment before he shook his head. "Let's not talk about that."

"Let's not talk at all." Linking her fingers behind his neck, she jumped and wrapped her legs around his waist. He caught her by the hips, his demon strength holding him steady as she crushed her mouth to his.

With one hand, he tugged down the zipper on the back of

her dress and popped open her bra with a twist of his fingers. His palm was hot against her bare skin, and as he brought it up to cup her neck, she let her feet slide to the floor.

Stepping back, she shimmied out of her clothes and stood before him in nothing but a pair of black satin panties and her heels. The red in his eyes turned liquid, his expression that of a predator who'd zoned in on his prey. *Absolutely thrilling.*

"Take off your clothes. Now," she ordered.

He blinked, then a sly grin curved his lips. "Yes, ma'am," he drawled as he shrugged out of his jacket and unbuttoned his shirt. "Would you like me to dance for you too?" He wiggled his hips as he tossed the garment aside and unbuckled his belt.

The man was solid muscle, hard and defined like he was carved from stone, yet she'd felt the tenderness in his touch. The passion in his kiss. She yearned for more.

"You've been holding out on me, Magic Mike. What else can you do?"

With inhuman speed, even faster than a vampire—and she'd had her way with a vamp or two, so she knew what they were capable of—he stripped off his clothes and pinned her to the wall. She gasped as his mouth closed around her nipple, and he gently sucked it, hardening it into a pearl while he roamed his hands over her body.

She returned the gesture, exploring the cuts and dips of his muscular frame. The sulfur on his skin was so faint she could barely smell the tell-tale demon scent, but the fragrance of his human side, warm and woodsy, permeated her senses, making her mouth water. She could never match him in strength, but she was determined to make his knees weak.

He glided his tongue up the side of her neck and nipped at her earlobe. "Is sex on the table tonight, love?"

She wrapped her hand around his dick and stroked him, reveling in the way his lids fluttered with her touch. "The table, the couch, the bed. Where do you want to have it?"

He groaned, the deep rumbling sound sending a shiver

down her spine. "Right here against the wall sounds good."

"Does it?" With Mike thoroughly distracted, she grabbed his shoulders and spun him around until he was the one pinned. She grabbed his dick again, and dropping to her knees, she circled her tongue around the head.

"Holy hellhounds." His voice came out as a raspy whisper, and he dropped his head back against the wall.

She took as much of him into her mouth as she could and slowly pulled back before taking him again. He exhaled a hiss, and his hands, which had been splayed against the wall, curled into fists.

She continued sucking him, enjoying the masculine grunts and moans emanating from his throat, until his knees began to give. Taking him in her hand again, she rose to her feet and gazed into his hooded red eyes.

"I need you, Crimson." So much raw emotion laced his words, she wondered if he was talking about sex or something more. He cupped her face in his hands as the red in his irises faded to a soulful, deep brown. "I want to worship you for…"

He blinked, the vulnerability in his expression slipping away, a devilish grin replacing it. Scooping her into his arms, he nodded toward a doorway. "Is that your bedroom?"

"It is."

"I believe I promised to lick you from head to toe." He carried her to the bed and laid her on the mattress. "Let's get started."

The man made good on his promise. Starting with her neck, he worked his way down her body, licking and nipping, raising goose bumps all over. He removed her panties, kissing down one leg and then up the other, all the while avoiding the one place she wanted him to lick most.

"You're teasing me." Her voice sounded breathless.

"I'm a demon. What did you expect?" His tongue bathed her sensitive nub, and she nearly screamed at the electric sensation shooting out to her limbs.

He chuckled, obviously pleased with her reaction, and then he went to town, licking and sucking until the orgasm coiled in her core and released in an explosion of fireworks to rival the Fourth of July. The man had to have a forked tongue with the oral acrobatics he'd just performed.

Wait… Did he have a forked tongue? He was a demon after all.

He rose to his knees and stroked his cock, his tongue slipping out to lick the moisture from his lips. No fork. He was just *really* good with his mouth. "Demons are incredibly fertile, but we don't spread disease. Well, my kind doesn't."

One corner of his mouth tugged into a crooked grin, and for a moment, the vulnerability she'd glimpsed in his gaze returned. "Are you…?"

"I'm on birth control."

He climbed on top of her, settling his hips between her legs, and held her gaze as he slowly pushed inside her. As he filled her completely, his eyes flashed red briefly before returning to their human brown, and they made love.

She'd expected the wickedness to spill over into sex. For him to be all about the physical pleasure, worshipping her body until they both climaxed in a frenzy. But the way he held her, his slow, deliberate movements, his breath against her skin… Everything about this felt like he was also worshipping her soul.

Her heart swelled with the intimacy, and she clung to his shoulders, another orgasm building in her core as his rhythm increased, his thrusts growing harder until he rose onto his hands and looked into her eyes.

Her entire world exploded with the next thrust of his hips. She cried out, her body shuddering as they came together, never breaking their gaze into each other's eyes. Her reality turned upside down and inside out as he relaxed on top of her, stroking her cheek with the backs of his fingers.

Holy hell. She was falling for a demon.

CHAPTER EIGHT

"Your application says you're a witch." Mike eyed the petite redhead from across the table and sipped his coffee. She wore a dark green tunic over light green leggings, and her eyes sparkled like emeralds.

"Oh, I am," she replied in a thick Irish accent, the wart above her lip bouncing with her words. "My great-great-grandmother was one hundred percent witch."

Mike rubbed his temple to ward off the impending headache and glanced over the application again. He'd conducted seven interviews in the past two weeks here, in the private dining area at the back of his restaurant, and so far, not a single applicant had been an actual witch.

They'd all been devious, vile, even downright evil, but not one of them met Satan's number one requirement. His personal assistant had always been a witch, and the chances of getting the ancient bastard to change his ways were slimmer than Frosty the Snowman surviving in hell.

But Mike wouldn't give up. In between interviews and running his restaurant, he'd also spent the last two weeks getting to know Crimson. Falling in love with her. He'd spent every spare second he had with her, watching her practice her magic, her confidence growing with every spell she cast correctly. And the nights spent between the sheets… She could give a succubus a run for her money.

He'd grown used to having her in his life, and he intended to spend forever with her, whether it was here in New Orleans, with Crimson as the high priestess of the coven, or somewhere else if she didn't win the challenge. It didn't matter where he lived, as long as it was topside with his magnificent witch in his arms every night.

He looked at the leprechaun in front of him, his gaze bouncing between her wart and her monobrow, and she glared back. She was ornery enough to spend eternity by Satan's side, that was for sure. "Tell me about your magic."

She disappeared from the chair and reappeared in the corner behind him. "Teleportation." She disappeared again, and the sound of thick heels on the wood floor echoed through the room before she swatted him on the back of the head. "Invisibility." Her form came back into view as she smiled smugly and plopped into the chair. "And demons don't intimidate me. You're not nearly as scary as everyone said you'd be."

"I'm not like other demons."

"I should hope not. I'm looking for murder, mischief, and mayhem. So, do I get the job?" She crossed her arms and arched a bushy brow.

He suppressed a smile. How he'd love to force this little elf on the Prince of the Underworld. If only Satan would accept her. "Can you cast spells?"

"Who needs spells when you can be invisible?" She disappeared and reappeared in a flash. "I also have a knack for finding gold."

"The Devil has no use for gold."

"But I bet you do…" She grinned, revealing rotting teeth nearly the same color as her shirt. What was it with leprechauns and green?

He sighed. Of course she couldn't cast spells. "Satan requires a witch with spellcasting powers. It was listed in the job description."

"You realize you're asking someone to give up their life to spend eternity serving the Devil, right? Witches can pretty much make anything they want to happen become reality. They solve their own problems, yeh know?"

"I realize that."

"Good luck finding one who'll be willing give up her freedom. Most of 'em are too nice for the Devil, anyway. Nature-loving hippies, the lot of 'em."

He knew that all too well, which was why, three weeks closer to his deadline, he hadn't found anyone worthy of damnation. "I'll be making a decision by the end of the week. Thanks for stopping by."

"The Devil'll be lucky to have me." She rose to her feet, though she wasn't any taller standing, and waddled toward the door as Crimson strutted through.

"Hey there, handsome." Her eyes locked with his, and his chest tightened. She didn't glance down to see the tiny woman moving toward her, and they collided, the leprechaun's head smacking into Crimson's hip with a *thunk*.

"Watch where yer goin', yeh hippie." She rubbed her head and glared up at Crimson.

"I'm so sorry. I didn't see you." Crimson reached toward the leprechaun to console her, but as the elf swatted away the gesture, she held up her hands and looked at Mike. "I didn't mean to interrupt. The hostess told me to come straight back."

He closed his laptop. "You're not interrupting. We're done."

The leprechaun narrowed her eyes at Crimson, raking her gaze up and down her form. "Are yeh a full-blooded witch?"

"Yes. I'm Crimson. Are you a leprechaun?"

"Aye. One-sixteenth witch, but apparently that's not enough for the Devil. His advocate won't even give me a chance." She jerked her thumb toward him, and he forgot to breathe.

His stomach dropped into his boots before ricocheting up to

his throat, lodging there and making him choke. He'd been outed by a leprechaun. *The little fuck.* He bit the inside of his cheek, fisting his hands in his lap to keep from strangling the horrid creature.

"Advocate?" Crimson stepped out of the leprechaun's way as the elf waddled out the door. "What's going on?" Wariness tightened her eyes, and she clutched her purse strap on her shoulder, staying near the exit.

With a heavy sigh, he flattened his palms on the table and gathered his thoughts. The truth had to come out sooner or later...though much, much later would have been his preference. *After* he'd completed his final job and could tell his witch, with one hundred percent honesty, that his evil-doing days were over.

Instead, he felt exposed. Naked in front of a crowd with stones clenched in their fists. Would Crimson be the first to throw?

He should have damned the little green elf when he had the chance.

"Why don't you join me?" He gestured to the seat next to him. "Are you hungry? I can order lunch."

"I'm fine." She sank into the chair. "Do you...?" She pressed her lips together, casting her gaze downward before locking eyes with him. "Do you collect souls for Satan? Are you the Devil's advocate?"

The disgusted look on her face tore him in two, but there was no turning back now. He refused to lie to the woman he loved any longer. "It's not always souls. It's..." He blew out a hard breath. That wouldn't matter to her. "I am."

She leaned back in her chair, away from him, her slow nod of understanding turning into a shake of disbelief. "And that leprechaun was bargaining with you? Were you planning to send her to hell before her time?"

"She wanted to go, but I wasn't going to send her. I swear."

"I had a feeling, but..." Her bottom lip trembled as her

mouth opened and closed. "I thought you were recovering. That you weren't working for Satan anymore. You said you won your freedom in a poker game, so why...? Why would you still send people to hell?"

He started to ask her for a minute so he could stuff his face with angel food cake before he explained things to her, but his demon side didn't need subduing. Come to think of it, he hadn't felt the need to ingest angel magic since he accidentally shook her hand more than two weeks ago. That was a bad sign.

"I only won partial freedom in that game." He picked at the edge of the laptop, casting his gaze downward. "I still have to make a deal for him once a month in exchange for staying topside."

Her lips parted on a quick inhale. "That's the payment you mentioned before? You don't pay him with money, you pay in souls?"

He reached for her hand, but she slipped from his grasp. "Souls or whatever the Devil happens to be collecting at the time. You'd be surprised how many men are willing to give up one of their testicles to get what they want." He smiled, hoping to break the tension, but she shook her head.

"I'm trying to stop. I swear I am. The Devil offered me a deal himself to get my full freedom. I had to do one more job for him, and he was going to let me go."

"'Had'? You said that in past tense. If you already made the deal, what were you doing with the leprechaun? What was the final job?"

Hell help him, he had to tell her. There was no way around the truth this time. "Satan needs a new personal assistant. I was supposed to find him one."

She pursed her lips, nodding. "There has to be more to this story."

"He's always had a witch as his assistant, so that was the deal. I find him a witch to be his servant for eternity, and in exchange, I get my freedom."

"I see."

"But here's the thing." He laid his palms on the table and straightened his spine. "For the past few decades, I've been trying to be good. I've purposely sought out those with wicked souls—people who were going to hell regardless—to make deals with. Since I won my freedom, I haven't damned a single undeserving person." *Until now.*

"My ability to see into people, to get them to tell me their desires...that's the advocate magic. I can get them what they want in exchange for a price. But I can also sense evil. I can spot a pure soul, and I only bargain with tarnished ones."

She clutched her purse in her lap, tensing as if ready to bolt. "So this witch assistant deal. If it's not part of your normal monthly expenses, couldn't you tell him no?"

"I was late on my payment. Very late. He used that as a bargaining chip and gave me a choice. Find a witch to damn, and I get my freedom. Fail, and he takes me back to hell. I'll never see sunlight again. Or you."

She swallowed hard and whispered, "Who did you damn?"

"I didn't mean to damn anyone yet. I was looking for a wicked witch."

Her voice grew louder. "Who did you damn, Mike?"

He hung his head. "I think I damned you."

Silence answered him. He flicked his gaze up to her face, and she sat frozen, expressionless. He waited, giving her ample time to tell him off, to slap him, to storm out. *Something.* But she didn't move. She just looked at him, giving him no clue what might be going on in her mind.

He didn't dare use his magic to pry into her current desires. She probably wanted to castrate him and wear his balls as earrings like Satan's former fling loved to do.

He waited as the seconds ticked into minutes, but she refused to speak. He'd rather spend an eternity with a crow pecking at his liver than endure another second of the silent treatment. "It happened in your café when you joked about selling your soul."

She crossed her arms. "Obviously."

"I tried to get you to stop. I told you not to talk about it, but you kept going. The call was too strong. I couldn't help myself, and I'm sorry." He lowered his head again, unable to meet her gaze.

"Oh, so it's my fault?" Her voice sounded incredulous.

"No, that's not what I meant."

"It better not be what you meant, mister, because I had no idea your power was making deals with the Devil. I never would have said something like that if I'd known."

"I'm sorry."

Her jaw ticked as she narrowed her eyes. "And whose fault is it that I didn't know?"

"Mine." He slumped farther in his seat, feeling like a scolded child. "I really didn't mean to. I care about you, Crimson, and I never wanted to hurt you."

"You didn't have to. You could just send me to your master and let him do the hurting." Her words stung, but he deserved every slice from her sharpened tongue. "So, that's it then? I'm damned to be Satan's servant for all eternity because of something I said in jest?"

His shoulders crept toward his ears. "You said it, and words are usually binding."

If she'd been part demon, her eyes would have flamed. "I was *joking*. I thought you understood that." She laughed, disbelieving. "Wait. Back up a minute. You said you *think* you damned me, and words are *usually* binding. Why don't you know for sure?"

"The Devil's on vacation."

"Vacation? I suppose he went down to Georgia? Is he searching for a soul to steal? Oh, wait. He has *you* for that."

Mike sighed. She might as well slice him open and disembowel him. He deserved worse. "He's on a three-week transatlantic cruise. I can't check the manifest until he gets back, so there's still a chance—since I confirmed you didn't mean it right after we shook hands—that it didn't take."

She tapped her foot. "And the leprechaun?"

"I put a listing in the Haunt Ads, and I've been interviewing potential candidates for two weeks. I was hoping to find someone who would take the job willingly, but no pure witches have applied."

"You're as bad as Orpheus."

"Orpheus?"

"He didn't trust Eurydice, and he damned her because of his stupidity. You should have trusted me. I know a lot of witches. I could have helped you."

He opened his mouth to reply, but the words wouldn't come. What could he say? He'd been so concerned about Crimson not liking him if she knew what he really was, he never considered asking her for help. "We keep our magic a secret for a reason. Aside from the other demons, only Trace and Destiny know what I am. I was afraid to tell you."

"Why? Do you think I can't see the goodness in you? Do you think I'm so dumb that I wouldn't be able to look past the job you were born into and see the man you've become?" She shot to her feet and paced in front of the table.

"I'm sorry, Crimson. I'm going to fix this. That leprechaun will make a perfect assistant to the Devil. I just have to convince him to give her a shot."

"And if this deal is sealed...if my joke has damned me, is there anything I can do to stop it from happening? What if I win the trial on my own, without the Devil's help? What if I refuse his assistance?"

He stood and stepped toward her. "Satan's deals are binding."

She continued pacing. "So there's absolutely nothing I can do?"

"I'm afraid not. The Devil never reneges on a deal, and he

won't let the other party back out either. All we can do is find a replacement, someone he'll like better."

She whirled to face him. "Maybe that's all *you* can do."

"We can do it together."

"Oh, no. It's too late for that. You've had weeks to tell me what was going on, and the only reason it came out now was because I nearly flattened a leprechaun. I've never cared for potato pancakes, and I don't like your bullshit either." She turned on her heel and marched to the door.

"I'm going to fix this," he called, but she didn't turn around.

"Go to hell," she shouted as the door swung shut behind her.

That was exactly where he needed to go, as soon as the Devil got home.

CHAPTER NINE

What in the goddess' name was Crimson supposed to do now? Roasting in the underworld for all eternity would be pure...well...hell. Not to mention what the heat and humidity would do to her hair.

She stormed into her apartment and slammed the door, the impact vibrating across the wall, sending a framed picture of her parents crashing to the floor. The glass shattered on the wood, but Crimson ignored the mess and made a beeline for her laptop.

Mike's hands may have been tied when it came to undoing a deal with the Devil, but Crimson was raised by an angel, for goddess' sake. Surely the whole gotta-keep-things-in-balance rule would apply here. Aside from lacking the genetics, she was practically an angel herself.

Double-clicking the video chat app, she called her dad and dropped into a chair. Her computer dinged as the call connected, and her father's image filled the screen.

"Good afternoon, sweetheart. How's the spell work going?" Her dad laughed as her mom stepped into view.

With her dark hair swept back into a tight twist, she wore

pink sweats, and her arm was cradled in a dark blue sling. "Did the encyclopedia of magic I sent you help at all?"

"Yes, it's been great. I'm getting better at the spells."

"Oh, that's wonderful news." Her mom sank onto the sofa next to her dad. "I wonder if you can convince the council to reevaluate the challenge? If your magic is getting better, maybe—"

"I've got a bigger problem." She rubbed her forehead, scrambling for a gentle way to tell them what she'd done, but she came up empty. She might as well shoot straight. No matter where she aimed, the arrow would come back to hit her in the ass. "I might have accidentally told a Devil's advocate that I'd give Satan my soul if he'd make this whole challenge mess go away."

She braced herself, expecting the slew of curses to flow from her mom's mouth, the feathers to drop from her father's wings. Instead, they sat quietly, their gazes slowly lowering before they looked at each other.

Tears collected on her mom's lower lids. "It didn't work."

Her father's jaw set, his face becoming a mask of stone. "Fate deemed it so. We did all we could."

"Am I missing something?" Crimson leaned her elbows on the desk. "What are y'all talking about? What did fate deem?"

"Your birth mother…" Her dad's voice was low and rumbly, as close to a growl as an angel could get.

"It's not her fault." Her mom put a hand on her dad's knee. "She was the messenger. Witches channel prophecies, but we don't create them ourselves."

"Did my birth mother receive a prophecy about me?" And they'd kept it from her all these years? Her mouth hung open as disbelief gnawed at her gut.

"We have to tell her." Her mom gave her dad a pointed look.

"I hoped it wouldn't come to this." Her dad's expression softened, and he looked at her with sadness in his eyes.

Her mom patted his leg and scooted closer to the computer. "When your birth mother found out about the cancer, she called on the goddess for a prophecy. She wanted to prepare you for whatever the future might hold, but what she learned was…" She shook her head.

"What, Mom? What did she learn? Did she know this was going to happen? Was it about my magic? My soul? Tell me!"

"In the first prophecy, she learned you were meant to channel the goddess in your magic and your art. That's why she unbound your powers all at once, so you'd have the best chance of fulfilling your destiny. But the ability to channel the goddess' magic isn't obtained overnight and never at such a young age. That part of your magic couldn't be unbound until you were older." She tilted her head, casting a look of sympathy. "Your mother didn't live long enough to complete the process."

Crimson's heart ached at the memory of her mother, but this wasn't new information. She'd been dealing with misfiring magic her entire life, and she knew it was because her mother didn't unlock everything. "What does that have to do with my current predicament?"

"As her disease progressed," her dad said, "and neither magic nor medicine could cure her, she begged the goddess for another prophecy." He slipped his hand into her mom's. "She wanted to know how things would turn out for you, and…she learned you'd sell your soul to Satan one day."

Crimson blinked, her face going slack with shock. "You *knew* this would happen, and you didn't think it might help to clue me in?"

"We were trying to protect you." Her mom's voice trembled.

"Wait…what did the prophecy actually say? You know those things are cryptic as hell."

"Crimson…" her dad admonished.

"Sorry."

He inhaled deeply, hesitating to tell her. "It said… 'The man from hell will finish her.'"

Her mom nodded. "It's why your father was assigned to adopt you. Your mother begged the archangel to interfere in your destiny. The powers that be thought if you were raised by a witch and an angel, you'd have the best chance of avoiding your fate."

"My fate." A sinking sensation threatened to drag her to the ground, so she clutched the sides of the chair. How could they let her live her entire life without this information? If her fate was predetermined, and they were trying to intervene, why would they keep it from her?

Her head spun, and she squeezed her eyes shut for a moment to still the dizzying sensation. When she opened them, both her parents stared at her with pity in their eyes. "Don't you think it might have been pertinent to share this with me sooner? If I'd known, I never would have…"

She clamped her mouth shut. They didn't need to know how close she'd gotten to Mike. They weren't the only ones who could play the secrets game.

"We tried our best, sweetheart," her dad said. "I thought if I instilled a fear of demons in you that you'd avoid them. How did this happen anyway?"

"Seriously? If anything, you made me more curious. All my life you taught me to see the good in people. To look past their vices and examine their souls. But not demons. You said even the ones in recovery were evil, but that's not true, is it? Demons can have goodness in their hearts."

He let out a heavy sigh. "Some of them can, yes."

She groaned. "So there's nothing else you can do to help me? Raising me to avoid demons was your best effort, and nothing you can say to your superiors will change their minds?"

"I'm afraid their hands are tied," her dad said.

Her mom nodded. "Fate's a tricky bitch."

Her dad cut a sideways glance at her mom. "When is the challenge?"

"In three days."

"Your mother and I will get on the first flight. We want to be there for you when—"

Crimson held up her hands. "It's not going to happen." Their hands were tied. Mike's hands were tied. Was she the only one left with the will to take on the Devil himself? She might have enjoyed a little bondage in the bedroom, but *no one* would tie her down in life.

Her dad leaned toward the computer. "Crimson, sweetheart, you can't stop fate."

"Watch me. I'll talk to you later." She slammed the computer shut, and as the anger boiled in her chest, she swiped the contents of her desk to the floor.

Pencils scattered across the room, and the laptop hit the wood with a crack, but it didn't matter. Those things would be of no use to her in hell.

A knock sounded on the door, followed by Sophie's muffled voice. "Everything okay in there?"

Crimson stomped to the door and threw it open. "Never better. I'm dating a demon who damned me to hell, and apparently my parents have known it was going to happen since they adopted me."

"What happened?" Sophie strode into the loft and plopped onto the couch. "Sit. Talk."

"I can't sit. I feel like I'm going to explode." She paced the length of the sofa and explained her ordeal. "Who knew joking with a demon would land me a life sentence in the underworld?"

Sophie blinked. "Wow. Okay, first, you need to settle down before you actually do explode. I'm not cleaning glittery witch goo out of the rug."

She dropped into a chair. "I knew dating him was a bad idea."

"Did you? Or is that your dad talking?" She shook her head. "Doesn't matter. Let's focus on the problem at hand. Does Mike know you were joking? If so, that should negate the contract, right?"

"He said it doesn't matter because I said the words aloud. And..." She picked at her nails. "If I'm honest, I have to admit I was only half-joking. At the time, living in hell sounded better than being human."

"Well, that's a problem."

"Tell me about it. I'm so furious at him. If he'd have just told me what was happening, what his magic was, I could have helped him. At the very least, I'd have known to keep my mouth shut instead of making jokes like that."

Sophie nodded, resting her elbow on the arm of the couch. "Sounds like he screwed up."

"Royally." She dropped her head back on the chair. Of all the men in all of New Orleans, why did she have to fall for the most dangerous one? Oh, right. Because it was her fate.

Sophie leaned her chin in her hand. "He said he didn't mean to make the deal with you, though?"

"He practically blamed me for it when we argued, reminding me he told me not to say things like that." Another spark of anger flared in her chest. *Damn him, and damn fate.*

"Did he tell you not to say it when the deal happened? Did he try to stop you?"

She shrugged. "Yeah."

Sophie nodded thoughtfully. "Did he apologize?"

"He did, but he should have trusted me, dammit."

"He should have. You're right about that." She leaned her elbows on her knees. "But does he have a way to fix it? Is he trying?"

"He mentioned a couple of ideas, but I really thought my connection to the angels would help. I stormed out before he could explain everything."

"Wow. Sucks to be him. Good thing we don't make mistakes, huh? It must be awful to screw up your magic, try to make it right, and then have the person you affected not forgive you." She leaned back on the sofa and pretended to pick lint from her pink blouse. "I can't imagine what that would feel like. Can you?"

Crimson narrowed her eyes. "Do you have a point?" But she already knew the answer. Jax still hadn't forgiven her for turning him into a cat, and that bothered her more than she cared to admit.

Sophie held up her hands. "I'm just saying this sounds like a classic pot and kettle scenario. Or maybe it's a glass house. Either way, you care about him, and he's your only chance at getting out of this with your soul intact."

Crimson closed her eyes for a long blink, letting her friend's words sink in. Sophie was right. She did care about Mike. She may have gone into the relationship simply looking for a distraction, but he'd grown on her. He'd proven demons could escape their nature and be good. If he could break from his destiny, why couldn't she?

She grabbed her phone and dialed Mike, but he didn't pick up. Swiping open the message app, she typed *Please call me* and sent the text. "I'm an idiot."

Sophie stood. "No, you're a badass witch who's going to make fate her bitch."

"You're right." Crimson rose to her feet and strode to the door. "But first, I have to find Mike."

CHAPTER TEN

"Damn Haunt Ads," Mike muttered to himself as he shuffled up the path to Sweet Destiny's. They'd pulled his ad from their site and canceled his account, citing a violation of their terms of service.

Apparently, Satan had struck a deal with the owners a few years back guaranteeing them a profitable business in exchange for not letting demons utilize their services in relation to their jobs. *Fucking Devil.*

He paused in front of the bakery, a two-story, nineteenth-century house painted pristine white with sky blue shutters that belonged on a cloud floating in heaven. Destiny kept the place immaculate, taking *cleanliness is next to Godliness* to a whole new level.

As he opened the waist-high wrought iron gate to enter the front porch of the angel's business, his demon side recoiled. His stomach clenched, and heat rolled through his body in response to the divine magic, but he forced himself inside.

After nearly overdosing on angel food cake when he first started dating Crimson, he'd laid off the magical delicacies lately in hopes that his demon side would be able to strike a deal for a new satanic assistant. But with the interviews complete and the ad no longer running, he'd run out of potential candidates.

He still held on to the sliver of hope that the deal didn't take, but it would be another few days before Satan returned to hell and opened the registry to find out.

Stepping into the seating area of the bakery, he found his reaper friend, Asher, sitting at a small pink table, scowling and stuffing a massive piece of cake into his mouth. Asher gestured to the chair across from him, and Mike forced a smile, sinking into it. He had two hours before he had to be at the Hellions Anonymous meeting, so he could spare a minute for his distressed friend.

"You okay, man?" Mike asked.

Asher closed his eyes, letting out a slow breath as he chewed and swallowed the chocolate cake. "Who'd have known the best devil's food cake would come from an angel's bakery?"

A bit of brown frosting marred his chin, and Mike wiggled a finger at his face. "You've got a little…"

"I was saving it for later." Asher swiped a napkin across his face and dropped it on the table. "Chocolate makes everything better."

If only. "Eating your emotions? I'd think with the Devil on vacation, you'd have a lighter workload."

"You didn't hear? That banshee he was dating nearly drove him insane. He left the cruise before the stomach virus hit its peak, and he's back in the underworld, ornerier than hell."

Mike's heart missed a beat or two before slamming against his chest. "He's back?"

"Yeah. And he slapped me with a priority delivery first thing. Someone promised their soul *and* body." He leaned back in his chair, shaking his head. "Souls are easy to wrangle to their fate. Bodies fight back."

Holy hell. His ears rang, the pressure in the room increasing until he thought he'd suffocate under the intensity.

"Here's your order, Mike." Destiny sashayed toward their

table with a white pastry box in her hands. "I put a couple extra in, free of charge, since Richard keeps eating them all." She set the box on the table and rested a hand on Mike's shoulder.

A cooling sensation spread to his chest, and he was able to breathe again. "Who's the priority? What's their name?"

Asher fished his phone from his pocket and swiped the screen. "Crimson Oliver." His brow furrowed. "Isn't she the witch you've been after? Did you make this deal?"

"Fuck." He raked his hands through his hair. "Satan's balls. Fuck. Fuck! Fuck me with a cattle prod. Shit!"

Destiny recoiled, and Asher slowly returned his phone to his pocket. "I'm gonna take that as a yes."

"You can't take her." He slammed his hand on the table. His deal-sealing, life-fucking hand. "It was an accident. She didn't mean it. *I* didn't mean it."

"Oh, Mike." Destiny laced her fingers together and tilted her head. "You've got a rather aggressive way of showing it, but you love her, don't you?"

"With all my heart." And the organ was currently being ripped from his chest and shredded into a thousand pieces. He looked at Asher. "You can't take her."

"Satan will have my balls on a platter if I don't."

"He's not collecting balls anymore."

"Then he'll have my head. C'mon, Mike, you know how this works. If I don't do my job, I might as well jump in the tarpits myself and save his minions the trouble."

Mike drummed his fingers on the table. This wasn't happening. He wouldn't allow it to happen. Crimson was the kindest, sweetest, gentlest soul he'd ever met. Satan would tire of her within a week, call her useless, and toss her aside like a charred appendix.

But Mike was the Devil's favorite advocate for a reason. Back in the day, there wasn't a deal he couldn't seal. It was time he brought out the big guns and showed Satan what a demon could do.

"I know you've got a job to do, but I guarantee she'll be off your list within an hour." He stood and grabbed the box of cakes. "I'm going to drop these off with Katrina, let her know what's happening, and then I'm going to pay the Devil a visit."

Asher nodded. "What are you going to do?"

Heat flashed in Mike's eyes. "I'm going to make him an offer he can't refuse."

Crimson looked everywhere for her demon. When she couldn't find him at work or at the bar he frequented, she snuck upstairs to his apartment, but it was empty. Her heart pounded in her throat as she made her way back to her building, but a sinking sensation threatened to pull the damn thing out through her ass if she didn't find him soon.

Something was wrong. Very, *very* wrong.

Inside her apartment, she set a blank canvas on an easel and squirted a blob of red paint on her palette. Brush in hand, she closed her eyes, willing the goddess to speak through her art and offer her a solution—or at least a hint—for this fiasco.

Her core tingled, the energy around her growing palpable as she waited for inspiration, but no images formed in her mind. The sound of someone clearing their throat made her jump, and as she opened her eyes to take in the form of a woman floating next to her, she squealed and fell backward onto her butt.

Sharp pain shot up her spine as her rear-end met wood, and the palette skidded across the floor. Crimson gasped at the ethereal beauty of the goddess, with her long dark hair flowing over her shoulders, almost floating as if she were underwater. She had sharp features, fair skin, and she wore a deep burgundy medieval-style gown.

Crimson opened her mouth, but the only words she could form were, "Holy shit."

The goddess suppressed a smile. "Is that any way to greet a deity?"

"I'm sorry." She scrambled to her feet and curtsied, squeezing her eyes shut and opening them again, not believing her vision. No one *saw* the goddess. *Jesus Christ on a bicycle.* "To what do I owe the honor of your presence?"

"You were trying to reach me, were you not?"

"Well, yeah, but we usually communicate through…" She held up the brush still clutched in her hand and shrugged.

The goddess smiled. "The man from hell has finished you. Your powers are fully unbound, and you can now use magic to your greatest potential."

"Yeah, about that…" She tossed the brush aside and clasped her hands together. "I didn't mean to sell my soul. I don't want to die."

"Who said anything about death?"

"How else will I meet Satan…the man from hell?"

The goddess tilted her head. "The Devil has nothing to do with your prophecy, child. The ability to channel my magic is rare and only granted to those who truly desire it, who truly desire to do good. Your demon has helped you realize your potential."

Crimson's mouth dropped open. Her demon? Mike was the man from hell? "I don't understand."

The goddess sighed. "You had accepted your incomplete magic. Your demon helped you realize you wanted more. When you truly believed, in your heart, that you deserved your full potential, the final piece of your power was unbound. You have access to my magic now."

"Oh, no." Crimson stumbled backward until the backs of her legs met the sofa, and she plopped onto the cushion.

"Do you not accept your full potential?" She lifted a hand. "I can take it away."

"I want it. I accept it." She looked into the goddess' emerald eyes. "But I accidentally sold my soul to the Devil."

The goddess nodded as if this wasn't new information. Crimson mentally smacked herself upside the head. Of course it wasn't. She was a goddess...all-knowing, duh.

"When you get there, find your line, and you will be saved."

Crimson scrunched her brow. "Find my line? What do you mean?"

The goddess pressed her palms together. "This is your first prophecy, child. Your demon is in peril, about to make a grave mistake. When you get to Satan's domain, find your line, and you will be saved."

"Do you have to be so cryptic? I mean, if I'm one of the few who can channel your magic and actually *see* you, maybe you can be a little more direct in your prediction delivery? What mistake? What line?"

With an amused grin, the goddess bowed her head and disappeared in a cloud of shimmering gold.

"Holy mother of glitter bombs." Crimson shot to her feet. What grave mistake was Mike about to make? Her stomach soured. She could think of several, and none of them boded well for his soul or their relationship.

She had to find *him* first, whatever the line was second. If she could keep him from making his grave mistake, maybe they could both be saved. When she tried his number, the call went straight to voicemail again, so she darted out the door and ran down the stairs.

Sharp pain sliced through Crimson's knuckles as she pounded on Sophie's door. As it swung open, her friend smiled. "Hey! Did you get it all worked out?"

"I can't find him." Her voice caught on the lump in her throat. "He's not answering his phone. He won't return my texts."

"He's probably licking his wounds. I'm sure he'll call you back. Wanna come in?" She opened the door wider, revealing her entire group of friends. Her fiancé, Trace, sat in the recliner, and her vampire friends Jane, Ethan, and Gaston occupied the sofa. "We were playing Cards Against Humanity. It's so much funnier when you're not actually human."

Crimson followed her into the living room. "Trace, you're friends with Mike. Will you text him and make sure he's okay?" If he was simply ignoring her calls, she might not be too late.

"Sure." Trace grabbed his phone and sent a text. The phone pinged, and he rubbed his beard, squinting at the screen. "It says the message was undeliverable."

Oh no. She sank onto the arm of the couch, the weight of her ominous feeling making it impossible to stand. "Oh, Mike. What did you do?"

"It's Thursday, isn't it?" Trace asked.

"What does that matter?" Crimson chewed her bottom lip. It could have been midnight on a leap year. It wouldn't have changed the fact that Mike was missing, and her gut was telling her he'd done something rash to save her soul. His grave mistake.

"He goes to his HA meetings on Thursday nights. I bet he turned his phone off."

Sophie rubbed her arm. "That's probably it, hon. Try not to worry."

"Hold up." Jane rose to her feet and parked her hands on her hips. "Sophie said something about you maybe accidentally selling your soul. Is that true?"

Crimson made a face at Sophie. She should have known the news would travel fast when she confided in her. Then again, she never asked her to keep it a secret. "Yes. He said he was going to fix it, and I'm afraid he might have done something stupid. I just spoke to the goddess, and she said he was going to make a 'grave mistake.' I have to find him."

"Fuck trying not to worry," Jane said. "If I were you, I'd march my ass down to that meeting and drag him out by his balls."

Trace shook his head. "They won't let you in. I picked him

up from a meeting once, and they had a guard posted at the end of the hall. I had to wait outside."

Finding him was more important than anything he could be doing at that meeting. Who knew what kind of power the other demons had? What if his mistake was enlisting the help of someone awful? Or worse, damning someone innocent? Crimson raised her eyebrows, glancing at each of her friends. "They can't stop all of us."

Gaston grinned, showing fang. "I do love smashing parties. Count me in."

Ethan stood. "It's *crashing* parties, and if Jane's in, so am I."

"You know I'm down." Jane took his hand and nodded at Crimson. "Let's go get your man and save your soul."

This right here was exactly why she'd half-joked about selling her soul in the first place. These people—her friends—meant everything to her, and if she had to leave New Orleans because she challenged the high priestess…

"Thanks, y'all. Let's go." She could worry about the what-ifs later. Right now, she needed to stop Mike before he did anything stupid.

When they arrived at the Priscilla St. James Community Center, only four cars occupied the parking lot. Most of the lights in the squat brown building were off, and the night air hung silent, except for the squawking of a crow sitting atop a light pole.

"Why is no one here?" Crimson's words created a fog in the chilly air.

Trace nodded toward a side entrance and led the way. "The place used to be packed at this time, but when the HA moved their meetings here, the other organizations slowly rescheduled theirs to different times. The humans may not understand or even believe in supes, but their instincts keep them as far away from the remnants of hell as they can get."

"And here I presumed they were all dumb as doorknockers," Gaston said.

"Watch it, buddy." Jane shook a finger at him. "I used to be human not too long ago."

"Hence my presumption." He arched a brow, and Jane stuck out her tongue.

They entered the building and made a left, but a human security guard blocked their way. Correction—the guy looked more like a mercenary than a rent-a-cop. He wore a black t-shirt with the sleeves ripped off to make room for his massive biceps, and two pistols were holstered at his sides, with a Bowie knife strapped to his thigh.

The soldier-for-hire crossed his arms and widened his stance. "You'll have to wait outside. This is a private meeting."

"It's an emergency." Crimson stepped toward him, but he didn't move. "I need to see Mike Cortez. Is he in there?"

"You'll have to wait outside," he growled.

"The hell we will." Crimson raised her hands and whispered a telekinesis incantation—since she could channel the goddess now and all—and the guy lifted from the ground, slamming back against the wall.

As Jane looked into his eyes and activated her vampire glamour, his face fell slack, his arms dropping to his sides, a bit of drool running from his mouth.

"What did you do to him?" Sophie gaped at the man.

"He'll be fine." Jane stepped back, eyeing the guy, and lifted his arm, letting it swing as she dropped it. "He might be limp all over for a while, but he can go a day or two without getting it up. Serves him right for trying to get in the way of love. Guys, why don't you stay here and babysit?"

Ethan chuckled. "Whatever you say, dear."

With hurried strides, Crimson burst through the door, and every head in the room swiveled to look at her. The demons sat in chairs arranged in a circle like it was some sort of group therapy session. She scanned the faces, but Mike wasn't among them.

"Can we help you?" A woman with dark hair swept into a

ponytail and a nametag that read "Katrina" stood and slinked toward them.

Crimson glimpsed the nametags of the other demons: Richard, Sarah, Mark. They all had the most common human names imaginable. Where were the Beelzebubs and Amdusiases?

"Why do they all look so normal?" Sophie whispered.

"Maybe because they're recovering?" Why Crimson expected horns and hellfire, she had no clue. Mike was nothing like the stereotypical demon, so why should these people be?

Katrina had the look of a soccer mom, but with her fluid, graceful steps, she moved like a dancer—either ballet or exotic. "A witch, a werewolf, and a vampire. Are you looking for a demon to make a complete set?"

"We're looking for Mike. Have you seen him?" Her hands trembled, and she was tempted to slap the smirk off the demon's face.

Katrina's eyes widened. "You wouldn't happen to be Crimson, would you?"

Her pulse thrummed. "Yes. Why?"

Katrina licked her lips, and though Crimson didn't swing that direction, something about the woman screamed sex appeal. "I can see why he did it. You are scrumptious, aren't you? Tell me…" The demon rubbed her neck and tilted her head, her lids fluttering as if she enjoyed her own touch. "Is Mike as virile as I imagine him to be? I haven't sampled him myself—I'm fasting."

Crimson narrowed her eyes, trying to ignore the growing desire to plant her fist in the woman's face. Mike was *her* man. "You're a succubus, aren't you?"

Katrina recoiled, peeling back her lips and hissing as her eyes turned molten red. Jane stepped forward, hissing back, curling her hands into claws. Between a succubus and a vampire, her money was on Jane, but as Sophie growled low in her throat, the other demons in the room stood. They didn't move toward them, but as their eyes took on a red glow, the energy in the room grew palpable.

Crimson gripped Sophie's and Jane's arms. "These aren't good odds, ladies. Cool it."

As her friends stood down, Katrina inclined her chin. "Mike's in hell. He's going to trade his soul for yours."

"What?" The room spun, and she clutched her head, the nagging bad feeling she'd had all afternoon coming true. "He can't do that. He said the deal might not have taken. He was going to find someone else. He…"

Katrina crossed her arms. "Oh, it took."

"No." Crimson grabbed her phone and dialed Mike's number again. She couldn't let him do this. She could help him find a willing witch—or her *line*, whatever the hell that was. They could do it together. "Pick up."

"There's no mundane cell reception in hell." Katrina turned and slinked back to the circle of chairs.

"Seriously?" Jane gaped. "Why not?"

Katrina shrugged. "It's hell. Duh."

"I have to save him." She looked at Katrina. "How do I get to the underworld?"

"Simple. Just open a portal and hop through. Oh, wait. You're a witch; you can't open portals to the underworld. I guess you'll have to wait until you die." She laughed, and the other demons joined in, creating a discord of ominous, out-of-tune music. The soundtrack to a horror movie.

"Can one of you take me?"

Silence descended over the cacophony, and fear filled the demons' eyes. "Not a chance," Katrina said. "We left hell for a reason, and we are not going back."

"We'll pay you," Jane said. "Name your price."

"There's not enough money in the world to make going back there worth it." Katrina sank into her chair and crossed her legs. "Good luck, ladies. Now, if you'll excuse us."

Crimson's heart sank, a suffocating sensation pressing on her chest as Sophie wrapped an arm around her shoulders and guided her out of the meeting room. This couldn't be the end. Mike didn't get to just take her place without consulting her. That wasn't how relationships worked.

"How did it go?" Concern filled Ethan's gaze.

As Jane moved toward him, she snapped her fingers in the mercenary's face, and the guy blinked, coming back to himself. "You'll have to wait outside." He crossed his thick arms over his chest.

"Yeah, yeah. We're going." Jane led the group out the door and into the parking lot. "We need to figure out a way to bust into hell."

"I beg your pardon?" Gaston looked at them like they were crazy.

"The recovering demons are too scared to take me there." Crimson chewed her bottom lip, an idea forming in her mind. "Maybe I can summon another demon. One who's not recovering." She'd have to delve into the world of black magic to do it, but if it meant saving Mike's soul, she'd do anything. "I'm sure I can find a spell online." But what would the goddess think of her using her newfound powers for evil?

"Hold on." Trace held up his hands. "What do you think you're going to do once you get there?"

"Kick ass and take names, of course." Jane crossed her arms.

"That's right." Sophie fisted her hands on her hips. "We're going to show them who's boss."

Trace chuckled. "The three of you are going to fight Satan?"

"The six of us," Sophie said. "You're going to help, right?"

Crimson shook her head. "We can't fight the Devil. You saw how scared those demons were at the mere mention of returning to hell."

"At least one of you is making sense." Trace took Sophie's hand. "Mike is one of my best friends, and I will do anything to help him. But busting into hell without a plan is going to land us all in hot water. Literally."

"Mike said Satan loves to gamble. We're going to have to figure out a way to outsmart him." Crimson wrapped her arms around herself. "And if we can't do that, I'll give myself up. I'm the one who offered my soul. Mike shouldn't have to suffer for my careless words."

Jane wiped a tear from her eye. "That's true love right there."

That's exactly what it was. She was in love with Mike, and there was no way—in hell or on Earth—she'd let the Devil have him. "I have to do it alone. I won't risk your souls too. Let me find a summoning spell." She opened the web browser on her phone.

"This is the worst idea I've heard since Miss Jane thought a vampire could sustain herself on rare steak," Gaston said. "Recovering demons are one thing, but you are talking about summoning a creature straight from hell. He'll devour you before he'll help you."

Crimson arched a brow. "Do you have a better idea?"

The vampire crossed his arms, inclining his chin. "Why don't you find a reaper? They cross between hell and Earth on a daily basis. Surely one of them could get you in."

"Can you summon a reaper?" Sophie asked. "How will we even find one?"

Trace let out a heavy sigh. "I know where to find one. Let's go."

CHAPTER ELEVEN

"Michael, my friend." Satan pushed back from his desk and propped his ankle on his knee, steepling his fingers. His iridescent red suit caught the light of the fire licking up toward the ceiling in his office, making it shimmer as if the garment itself were magical. Glittery flames adorned his black tie, and silver skull cufflinks glinted as he moved. "Have you come to deliver my witch yourself?"

Straightening his spine, Mike swallowed the bile from the back of his throat and approached the desk. "There's been a mistake. You can't have Crimson."

A slow smile curved his lips, and as he flicked his wrist, a scroll appeared in his hands. "The Devil doesn't make mistakes." He unrolled the parchment. "The contract is complete. I love her name, by the way. My favorite color."

"*I* made the mistake." His hands curled into fists, and he fought the urge to yank the contract from Satan's hands, tearing it to shreds.

"You're my advocate, an extension of myself. If I don't make mistakes, neither do you. Are you sure you want to give up that kind of perfection, by the way? I'm more than willing to let you stay on if you've decided freedom isn't all it's cracked up to be."

"She was joking. She didn't really want to sell her soul."

He scanned the contract. "It says right here she was only half-joking. Half-joking means half-serious, and that's good enough for me." He tossed the scroll onto his desk, and it disappeared in a puff of red smoke.

"Excuse me, sir?" Esmerelda, his temporary assistant, slipped through the door and stood against the wall. "Your ten o'clock is here."

"Thank you, dear. I'll just be a moment." Satan stood and strolled around the desk. "What do you say, Michael? Will you remain on the winning team, or do you want your measly freedom when my witch arrives?"

"I want more time. I want you to redact that contract and give me the remainder of my month to find you a suitable assistant. Crimson was raised by an angel. Believe me, she's not wicked enough to fulfill this role."

"She'll be plenty wicked by the time I'm done with her. No deal."

The door thudded behind Esmerelda as she scurried out of the room, and Mike's heart threatened to beat out of his chest. "Please, Satan. I can find someone better. I can—"

"I said, 'no deal!'" His voice boomed, echoing off the chamber walls.

"I love her!" He clamped his mouth shut. He didn't mean to say it out loud. The Devil didn't give a damn about love, but Mike's heart had been ripped from his chest, and Satan clutched it in his fist.

The Devil paused, and eerie quiet stuffed the room like cotton. Clasping his hands behind his back, he strolled in a circle around Mike, his gaze raking up and down his form before he stopped in front of him, face to face. "Well, why didn't you say so?"

Mike ground his teeth, cursing himself for letting his true feelings slip. "Does it make a difference?"

"In her fate? No. But it does make the entire ordeal much

more enjoyable for me. My favorite advocate won his freedom by damning the woman he loves. It simply can't get better than this."

No. He would not let this happen. Crimson was right; he should have trusted her from the beginning. If he'd have told her upfront what kind of magic he had, she could have decided for herself if she wanted to get involved with him. Instead, he'd resorted to his demonic ways—not truly tricking her, but withholding essential information she needed to make an informed decision about him.

Who was he kidding? He didn't belong topside. No demon did. "Take me instead. I'll be your assistant."

Satan laughed. "I've always had a witch."

"So? Times change, and so should you. I've got some ideas on how to liven this place up, and we can start with getting rid of that horrid nineties Halloween soundtrack."

The Devil crossed his arms. "I happen to like horrid."

"C'mon, Satan. You lost me in a *poker game.* Now's your chance to save face. Show everyone you can't be fooled. Set Crimson free, and take me instead."

The Devil's eyes narrowed, a look of confusion contorting his features. "You love this witch so much you'd give up your freedom for all eternity?"

"Yes, I do." He didn't even have to think about his answer. He'd do anything for her.

"I stand corrected. It can get better." A diabolical laugh vibrated in the devil's chest. "All right, Michael, but I don't want you as my assistant. You'll be my favorite advocate again, and your first job will be to find my new assistant. No more games. Crimson goes free; you stay. A soul for a soul. Do we have a deal?"

Mike's palm burned, and heat flashed in his eyes as he stretched his arm toward the Devil, shaking his hand and sealing his fate for eternity.

"You have to, Asher. It's the only way to save him." Crimson gripped the reaper's arm and pleaded with her gaze. Trace stood behind her, along with the rest of her friends, and Asher glared at the werewolf.

"He's going to kill me if I do. You realize that, right?"

Trace shrugged. "I thought reapers were immortal."

"He'll throw me in the tarpits. Or even worse, he'll have me reassigned to Alaska." He shuddered. "I can't stand snow."

"But you can do it, right?" Crimson begged. "You can get me into hell?"

With a heavy sigh, Asher tugged his phone from his pocket and swiped at the screen. "Crimson Oliver. Soul and body. High priority." He turned the device toward her, and she glimpsed her name along with several others. Hers was the only priority and the only one that required the body be delivered as well. "Mike asked me for an hour. It's only been fifty-five minutes."

"Good. Then I still have five minutes to stop him."

Sophie put a hand on her shoulder. "Are you sure you want to do this, hon?"

"I'd rather spend an eternity in hell than five minutes on Earth knowing Mike is suffering because of me. Besides…" She shrugged. "I'm channeling the goddess now. Between my magic, Mike's bargaining power, and finding my line, I'm sure we'll strike a deal that makes us all happy."

"Just so you know," Asher said, "I can get you into hell, but I've never tried bringing anyone back out. I'm not sure I can."

"Just get me in. I'll worry about getting out." *If I get the chance.*

"Crimson…" Jane stepped forward, pulling her into a bear hug. "You got this. I know you do."

"Thanks." She stood next to Asher and took his hand, her heart threatening to beat right out of her chest. "I'll see you on the flip side."

With a wave of his arm, Asher ripped a hole in reality and yanked Crimson through. They landed on a giant boulder inside a massive cave with red and black crystals coating the walls. A raging river, black as the midnight sky, cut through the rocks, blocking their access to the mainland in the distance.

"Don't tell me I have to swim for it." A nervous giggle escaped her throat as she peered at the steaming swirl of water below, and a tortured scream pierced through the sound of the rapids. She shuddered.

"All topside souls enter the Devil's domain here, but only those who've been invited can cross. If you fall in, you'll be boiled alive for eternity. The Greeks called this the River Styx."

She inched back, away from the ledge. "What's it called now?"

He grinned. "The River Styx."

Crimson nodded. "If it's not broke…" A small boat approached from the mainland, and Crimson squeezed her eyes shut, opening them again to find the same odd image. About the size and shape of a gondola, the boat cut across the river, slicing through the current, calming the waters around the vessel and making it look like it floated on a serene lake. "Is that our ride?"

"Hm?" Asher had been staring at his phone, but he glanced up at her question. "Yeah. This is weird."

"What's weird?"

"Your name is gone." He flashed the phone screen toward her. "You've been struck from the list."

"Because I'm here, right? You did your job and delivered my body and soul to hell."

"That's not how it usually works. You have to be processed first. How else would Satan know you've arrived?"

"He's not all-knowing?"

Asher shook his head.

"Maybe he's watching? I am supposed to be his personal assistant."

"Asher, what have you brought for us today?" The man piloting the gondola parked it alongside the rock, and it floated out of the water to their level. "You're a brave one promising your body too, young lady. Don't get on Satan's bad side; I hear torture of the flesh is almost as bad as that of the soul."

His brow furrowed, Asher shook his head and shoved his phone into his pocket. "This is Charon."

The man had messy, poofy brown hair—with his ghostly white skin and deep purple circles ringing his eyes, he most likely didn't give a damn about appearances—but the way it stuck up in the back and framed his face made it look like it belonged on a forty-five-year-old soccer mom with permanent resting bitch face.

Crimson bit her tongue, holding in a giggle. "Karen? As in 'I want to speak to the manager' Karen?"

"My name is Cha*ron*, child, and if you want to cross safely, you'd best hold your tongue."

"I'm sorry. You're right; that was rude of me." And insulting to the Karens of the world. "I'm a little nervous to be here."

"As you should be," Cha*ron* said.

"Lighten up. If you'd ever been topside, you'd know how funny that was." Asher dropped two silver coins in the man's hand and looked at Crimson. "Charon is my great-great-great-grandpa."

"You make me sound old when you say it like that." He placed the coins in the pocket of his long black robe.

"You're ancient." Asher gestured to the boat, and Crimson stepped inside. As soon as the reaper set foot in the craft, it lowered into the water, and Charon paddled them to the mainland. Though, saying he paddled was a stretch. The boat seemed to accelerate of its own accord while Charon moved the oar for show.

She started to ask what the man's purpose was if the ferry worked on its own, but spending eternity boiling alive in a raging river wasn't the slightest bit appealing. It was best not to piss off a man who could send her to a fate worse than death.

When the boat docked, Asher took her hand and helped her ashore. The tortured screams grew louder, followed by a pained howl and then a screech.

"Is Satan torturing a werewolf?" Her hands trembled, so she fisted them. She could not show weakness if she planned to bargain with the Devil himself.

Asher chuckled. "It's an audio track I bought as a gag gift back in the nineties. We had a white elephant party for Halloween, and Satan loved it. He plays it at all the entrances to intimidate people."

"At least he's got a sense of humor." She found a massive sign that read "To Processing" with a long line of people standing under it. Some were dressed in suits and formalwear, while others wore jeans, workout clothes, and even pajamas. They all stood stagnant, facing forward, not conversing and definitely not smiling.

"I guess that's the line I'm supposed to find." She moved toward it, though how it could save her, she had no clue. Maybe the goddess meant a metaphorical line?

Asher caught her hand. "That's the general processing line. You're a priority delivery, so I have to escort you straight to Satan's palace."

She looked at her hand nestled in Asher's and then at the stagnant line of people. It hadn't moved a single inch since she arrived. "Are there more lines in hell, because the goddess was specific. She said I have to find my line and I'll be saved."

"I don't know what goes on inside the palace, but I promise general processing is not where you want to be." He nodded at the mass of people. "See that guy with a black football jersey?"

"Yes." He stood in the sixth position from the end.

"I dropped him off last Tuesday."

She gasped. "The palace it is, then. Lead the way."

As she followed the reaper on the path to the palace, she

took in the jagged, rocky surroundings. From what she could see, hell appeared to be an enormous cave with soaring ceilings and ominous walls that seemed to loom over the inhabitants, threatening to crush them at any second.

And the atmosphere… If the intense smell of sulfur wasn't enough to choke her, the thickness of the air made August in the French Quarter feel like a windy winter day.

Sweat beaded on her forehead and dripped down her back, the heat and humidity winding her curls into tight spirals. "Is it always so hot here?"

"You get used to it." He paused twenty feet from a massive lava-filled moat and pressed his hand against some type of access device. A thick metal bridge slid across the channel, and Crimson peered upward at the colossal palace.

Made of obsidian, the castle towered into what would have been the sky if hell had one. Instead, its spires disappeared into the darkness of the vaulted cave, and the glass walls glinted in the firelight from the molten stream surrounding it. "Wow."

"Impressive, isn't it?"

"It looks like it should belong to a Disney villain. I could see Maleficent living here." She followed Asher across the bridge and stopped outside the front door.

"Don't compare the Devil to any kind of Hollywood bad guy, especially the ones from the James Bond series. He thinks he's original and that the movie villains are fashioned after him." He pressed a buzzer and stepped back. "Spend enough time around here, and you know it's the other way around. Ask him about the sharks with lasers on their foreheads. That's his favorite story to tell."

"Sharks with lasers?" This was going to be a quick in and out operation. She definitely did *not* want to ask the Devil about sharks. "You're coming in, right?"

Asher held up his hands. "I haven't been summoned, so this is as far as I'm allowed to go."

Icy panic flushed through her veins. "How will I know where to go? This place is massive."

"Just follow the signs to Satan's offices. Good luck!" He turned on his heel and disappeared. Literally disappeared, like into thin air.

"I'd love to learn that trick."

A speaker on the wall next to the door crackled, and a woman's voice said, "State your name and purpose, please."

She leaned toward the microphone. "Crimson Oliver. I believe I'm supposed to be Satan's new assistant."

A *thunk* sounded as the lock disengaged, and the ginormous glass door swung open. Crimson's heart leapt into her throat as she stepped through the threshold.

Her heels clicked on the black marble floor, and she stared in awe at the gleaming red spires jutting up from the floor to the soaring ceiling. The palace was enormous, with winding staircases leading up to who knew where and dozens of arches that opened into hallways darting out in all directions.

Any one of them could have been "the line" she was supposed to find, and she didn't have a clue where to go from here. She took two more steps into the grand foyer, and a row of flames shot up along the wall to her left, the heat blasting her like she stood too close to a pizza oven. Could that be the line she was looking for? *How the hell am I supposed to know?*

As she turned her face away from the fire, a sign illuminated above an archway. Then another sign lit up, and another, until every passage revealed the location it led to. She could go to the stalagmite gardens, the lava pools, the decontamination chamber…

She shivered. What on Earth would a person in hell need to decontaminate from? The widest archway held a sign that read "To Satan's Chambers." She moved toward it, but hesitated. *You're not seeing any lines here, Crim, so you might as well go straight to the top.*

Her footsteps echoed as she made her way down the dimly

lit hallway. Lanterns engulfed in blood-red glass provided the only light, and no side hallways jutted from the long, narrow, winding corridor she ventured down.

She walked for what felt like hours, or maybe it was only seconds. Time seemed to lose its meaning here, and as the hallway made a sharp bend to the right, it spilled out into a great chamber drenched in red.

Red velvet chairs lined one wall, and heavy red drapes hung from the darkened windows. A woman with a short, dark pixie cut sat at an onyx desk near a massive set of wooden double doors, and Crimson's breath caught at the sight of her. With dark skin, a soft jaw and delicate nose, the woman was the spitting image of Crimson's birth mother.

She couldn't stop her feet from carrying her forward, bursting into a run as she crossed the chamber. Skidding to a stop in front of the desk, she held her breath as the woman looked up from her computer and held her gaze.

"Mom?" Her voice sounded tiny in the massive room.

The woman blinked, a look of disbelief flashing in her eyes as she rose to her feet and strode around the desk. "Crimson? What are you doing here? You're saved. You shouldn't have come." She clutched her shoulders and then pulled her into a tight hug. "But I'm so happy to see you."

Pressure mounted in Crimson's eyes as she hugged her mother, the familiar scent of cloves mixing with the sulfurous aroma of hell. "Why are you here, Mom? Do you work for the Devil?"

She pulled back, cupping Crimson's face in her hands. "I'm filling in until he finds a new assistant."

"That's supposed to be me, but Mike's going to trade his soul for mine."

Her mom shook her head. "Oh, sweetheart, he already made the deal. You need to leave. Go back to Earth before Satan finds you here."

"What? No! No, he didn't. That's not how this is supposed

to work. The goddess told me to come here, to find my line, and I'll be saved. Mike is supposed to be free."

Her mom's eyes widened. "You...spoke to the goddess? Directly?"

"Yes, she came into my loft while I was trying to channel her. She told me I don't have to paint to channel her anymore, that Mike—bless his soul—and his demonic power to bring out my greatest desire finished unlocking the last of my magic. I can channel straight from the goddess herself now."

Her mouth fell open as she froze, stunned. "The man from hell will finish you..."

"The prophecy was talking about Mike. It didn't mean I would sell my soul—that was an accident. I'd been raised to accept myself for who I was—an incomplete witch. Mike made me realize what I really wanted...to be whole. I can't let Satan have him, Mom. I need to find my line."

"Your line?" Clutching the edge of the desk, she lowered herself down as if afraid her knees wouldn't hold her. "I believe your line is me."

CHAPTER TWELVE

"You are never to return to New Orleans again." Satan leaned back in his chair and laced his fingers behind his head, spreading his elbows wide. "I'm reassigning you to Los Angeles until you forget about your witch and rediscover your demonic nature."

That'll never happen. Mike bowed his head. "Are you sure you want to send someone with my experience to the Devil's playground? People beg to sell their souls there every day."

"That's exactly why I want you to go. You'll be making deals faster than a succubus can get laid. More often too."

A blast of hot air wafted in as the double doors swung open. Mike spun around to find Crimson standing at the entrance, her hands fisted on her hips, her head held high. She wore a tight black t-shirt and onyx leggings that not only showed off her curves but also made her look like she was ready to kick someone's ass. That or do yoga, but he was betting by the look on her face that ass-kicking was on the agenda. *Uh-oh.*

Her dark spiral curls flowed down to her shoulders, and she strode toward them with a confidence in her gait he'd never seen before. Gone was the broken witch afraid to use her powers for fear of screwing up. Crimson had gone from bad witch to badass, and he'd never loved her more.

Mike's mouth hung open, so he snapped it shut and scrambled for something to say. His new deal with Satan was binding. She was a free woman, yet she'd somehow managed to travel through hell, straight into the Devil's lair to find him.

"I demand you release him." Her voice was strong and confident, and as she stopped next to Mike, she rested a hand on his shoulder and kissed his cheek. "Hey, babe. Sorry I freaked out on you. I'm here to make things right."

"How did you...?" He couldn't finish the sentence. His brain hadn't caught up with the fact that the woman he loved was standing next to him...in hell.

"Your reaper friend brought me."

"Just who the hell do you think you are?" Satan clasped his hands on his desk. "And how did you get past my assistant?"

Crimson cocked her head. "Whoa. The Devil really does wear Prada. Did you start before or after the movie?"

Satan's eyes turned molten red, and a low growl rumbled in his chest. Mike wouldn't have been surprised if steam shot out of his ears too. "Before, naturally," the Devil replied coolly. "The humans mimic me; it's *never* the other way around." He pressed a button on his phone. "Esmerelda, remove this witch from my office immediately. Esmerelda?"

When she didn't respond, he mashed the buttons five more times and then swiped the phone from his desk, sending it crashing to the ground. Rising to his feet, he straightened his shoulders and strolled around the desk, his lips curving into a sneer. "Let me guess. You're the witch Michael gave up his freedom for. Crimson, isn't it?"

She swallowed hard and slipped her hand into Mike's. "I am, and I'm here to demand you release him. Your deal is with me. I'm your new assistant."

"Crimson, no." Surely she wasn't here to take his place. "I've already made a new deal. You're free. You shouldn't have come."

"But I *want* to be here." She looked at the Devil. "Let him go, and I'll fulfill my end of the deal. I'll be your assistant for the rest of eternity, or until you get tired of me. I hear there's quite a turnaround for this position."

Footsteps pounded on the floor behind them as John, one of Satan's grunts, stormed into the room. Standing nearly seven feet tall, the barrel-chested guard demon had skin the color of clay bricks. "I got your call, sir. How can I assist?"

The Devil pressed his lips together like he was fighting a smile. "This *witch* broke into my office, and I'm—"

Before he could finish his sentence, John lunged at Crimson. Mike started toward the demon, but Crimson threw up her hands and shouted, "Demon fat, you're now a cat."

John froze in mid-air, his eyes going wide a split second before he dropped to the floor and transformed into a fluffy white kitten.

He sat on his haunches, blinking at her and then at Satan. "Mew?" His meow sounded like a question, and Mike could only imagine what the poor fiend must have been thinking.

Crimson crossed her arms and turned to Satan. "I wouldn't advise siccing another dog on me. I doubt the Devil wants an army of kittens. Imagine what it would do to your reputation."

"Crimson…" Mike tried to lace his voice with warning, but truth be told, Crimson impressed the hell out of him. Satan could make the biggest, baddest demon cower with nothing more than a pointed look, and this witch, *his witch*, just threatened to turn his entire legion feline.

For the first time in the eighty-some-odd-years Mike had known the Devil, he looked dumbfounded. Maybe a little impressed too. Stooping to the floor, Satan scooped John into his arms and returned to his chair, stroking the cat's back… again like a James Bond villain, though Mike didn't dare mention the similarity.

"Your magic is impressive." Satan grinned when the cat purred. "What's stopping me from keeping both of you? Mike did make a deal with me, and you stormed into my office unsummoned. I believe I've landed a new assistant and gotten my best advocate back on the same day."

"You don't want to do that." Crimson sank into the chair across from the Devil's desk, and Mike stood behind her, still unable to believe this was the same woman he left topside. "If you keep us both, then we'll be together. As much as I hate the heat down here, if I get to be with Mike, I'll be happy. So will he, right, babe?"

He sat in the chair next to her. "She's right. That's why you should send her home and let me find you someone else. Someone I can't stand."

"No." Crimson shook her head. "You should release Mike, grant him full freedom and return him to Earth. I'll stay here and be miserable without him."

Mike took her hand. "Crimson, you can't do this. I'm a demon; I'm *supposed* to live in hell. You need to get back up there, beat Rosemary, and save your coven. I know you can do it."

"Oh, I can beat her. I'm channeling magic straight from the goddess now, thanks to you. But I don't need to if I'm Satan's assistant. You go home. You belong up there."

"Well, well." Satan laid the cat in his lap and steepled his fingers, chuckling. "This is getting more and more fun. What to do? What to do?"

"Keep me," they both said in unison.

He couldn't let her do this. With her kind heart, she'd never survive in the underworld. "It was *my* mistake. I shouldn't have shaken your hand. I shouldn't have offered the deal. I didn't mean to damn you, Crimson. I love you. Please let this be the last thing I do to prove my love. Let me allow you to live."

Tears collected on her lower lids, and her bottom lip trembled. "Oh, Mike. That's the sweetest thing anyone has ever done for me. I love you too, and that's why *you* have to go. I said the words aloud. I agreed to the deal, so it's on me." She turned to the Devil. "Satan, what do you say? Send him topside, with one hundred percent freedom, and you can have me, a witch who can channel the magic of the goddess herself."

The Devil tapped a finger against his lips. "The goddess in what form?"

"All of them, though she visited me as Morrigan."

As Satan shot to his feet, the kitten tumbled to the floor with a *thunk*. It appeared that only those born feline always landed on their feet. "You have a deal." He jutted his hand toward Crimson, and before Mike could stop her, she shook, sealing the bargain.

His spine tingled, and then it snapped, the twenty-four-seven connection to the Devil dissolving like an all-night diner going out of business. He was free, and she... "Crimson, what have you done?"

"I granted you your freedom." She smiled proudly. "Your greatest desire."

"My greatest desire is to spend the rest of my life with you. Now that will never happen."

"Don't be so sure." She winked and turned toward the entrance, where Esmerelda strutted in.

The temporary assistant stopped next to Crimson, who stood, grinning like she hadn't just promised Satan an eternity of servitude. The Devil rose and cut his gaze between the two women, his eyes calculating, and Mike stood because...well, everyone else was standing, so it seemed like the right thing to do.

"It's time for you to hold up your end of the bargain, Satan." Esmerelda rested a hand on Crimson's shoulder, and the Devil let out a long, slow, overly controlled breath, which meant he was pissed.

"This is cheating. You tricked me." Satan scooped the cat from the floor and ran his hand over its back. *Poor John. His buddies will never let him live this down.*

"It's not cheating at all," Crimson said. "You made a deal with me, but the deal you made with her is still binding."

"Would someone mind explaining what's going on?" Mike asked.

"Crimson is my daughter," Esmerelda glanced at Mike before casting a loving gaze at Crimson.

"She received a prophecy from the goddess that she *thought* meant I was going to sell my soul one day. So, on her death bed, she made her own deal with the Devil. She'd serve as a magic instructor for his demon/witch hybrids in exchange for a get-out-of-hell-free card for me whenever I needed it." Crimson wrapped an arm around her mom's shoulders. "And here we are, come full circle."

"Wait." Mike squeezed his eyes shut, trying to make his brain catch up with the events unfolding before him. "Even though I damned you, you would have been released because of the deal your mother made when you were a kid?"

"Yep. We had nothing to worry about."

He glanced between the two women. "Would have been nice if you'd told me that a couple of weeks ago."

"I just found out today." Crimson's smile was warmer than the flames licking the walls behind them. "I had no idea my mom was here."

Esmerelda nodded. "And you never told me what name you were looking for on the manifest when you were here before."

Mike shook his head. "I have got to get better at communicating."

They all looked at Satan, his molten eyes undulating as he observed their exchange. "I must say, I have respect for anyone who can pull one over on the Devil himself. Good show, all of you." He flicked his wrist dismissively. "You're both free. Esmerelda, you'll return to your teaching duties as soon as a permanent assistant is found."

"Mom, can't you come with us? Can we make another deal?"

"No more deals, sweetheart." She took her daughter's hands. "It's not a bad afterlife here, and Satan's not as bad as he pretends to be either." Esmerelda winked at the Devil, and unless Mike's eyes deceived him, he could have sworn he saw a blush spread across the Prince of the Underworld's cheeks.

The Devil sighed and cast a longing gaze toward Crimson. "I was looking forward to your magic. I don't know how I'll find an assistant as powerful as you. Are you sure you don't want to stay here with your mom?"

"Don't even think about it, Crimson," Esmerelda scolded. "You belong topside with that demon of yours. The prophecy stated it, so mote it be."

"I'm going to miss you, Mom." Crimson hugged Esmerelda, and then she stepped toward Mike, taking his hand. "Let's go home."

He pulled her to his chest, wrapping her in his arms and memorizing the way she felt against him. This amazing woman had traveled all the way to hell to save him. To be with him. *That* was true love.

"Oh!" She lifted her head from his shoulder. "Satan, I may know of someone who'd make a diabolical assistant. She's powerful too."

He dropped the cat on his desk. "I'm listening."

"Meet us topside day after tomorrow at three."

He tapped on his smart watch. "I'll be there with bells on."

"Hell's bells?"

He grinned. "Of course."

"Are you going to fix John?" Mike nodded toward the kitten swatting at a pen lying on the desk. "He's been humiliated long enough."

Crimson opened her mouth to speak, but Satan moved in front of the cat, blocking her spell. "Don't touch him. I rather like him this way."

CHAPTER THIRTEEN

The sun shone brightly in the cloudless afternoon sky as Crimson walked hand in hand with Mike toward the coven house. Sophie and Trace followed behind, and as they turned the corner, the house coming into view, a sense of pride washed over Crimson, lighting in her heart.

Massive ferns overflowing their pots hung from the eaves, and the deep blue paint on the exterior gave the witches' headquarters a welcoming façade.

Welcoming. That was something the coven *hadn't* been since Rosemary became high priestess six years ago. Things were about to change.

"I don't understand," Sophie said as they stopped on the sidewalk outside. "If the challenge starts at two, why did you tell Satan to come at three? Wouldn't it have been easier to let him talk to Rosemary beforehand so you don't even have to *do* the contest?"

"It would be easier." Crimson glanced through the great room window where the crowd was gathering. "But I've spent my entire life as a broken witch. They were nice to me because they felt sorry for me, and when a spell went wrong, no one was surprised. I need to prove—to them and to myself—that I don't need their sympathy anymore. That I deserve to be high priestess because the goddess deemed it so."

"Gotcha." Sophie nodded. "You need to kick some witch ass and show them who's boss. Jane would have loved to see this."

Crimson smiled. "We can tell her all about it over drinks tonight."

Mike chuckled. "Are the boys invited?"

"You know it. I wouldn't have the confidence to win this challenge if it weren't for you." She kissed his cheek, and he swept her into his arms, spinning in a circle before lowering her feet to the ground and planting one on her lips.

Her body warmed as his strong arms held her, and when his tongue brushed hers, she detected a faint hint of angel food cake. Though he was no longer required to make deals for the Devil, recovering demons—even ones with one hundred percent freedom—still had demonic urges from time to time.

The cake helped to subdue his demon side, and that was fine, as long as it didn't tame his beast in the sheets. She was looking forward to some more of that action.

Trace cleared his throat. "Incoming."

Crimson reluctantly released Mike's lips and turned to find Asher striding toward them. Her stomach bubbled, the thought that Satan may have changed his mind turning it sour. "I hope you're not here to take one of us this time."

Asher laughed. "Nope. I'm here for the show. Anyone who knows Rosemary wants to see her get her ass kicked. I'm not late, am I?"

"You're right on time." Crimson led the way into the coven house. The murmur of voices grew louder as they paced down the hall toward the great room, the plush green runner on the floor masking the sounds of their footsteps.

She rested her hand on the knob and turned to her friends. "Nothing like a grand entrance, right?" Twisting the knob, she flung open the door and strutted inside like she owned the place —because in an hour, this coven would be hers.

A hush fell across the crowd as Crimson paced to the center of the challenge arena, and her friends found seats among the other witches.

Rosemary stomped forward, her permanent scowl even more defined as she glared at Crimson before gesturing to her friends. "Who are they?"

"Witnesses." Crimson inclined her chin. "You may have every witch in the coven under your thumb, but you can't fool my friends. They're here to make sure you play fair."

"And to watch you get your ass kicked," Asher called from the second row.

Rosemary grunted. "You brought a reaper to scare me? I know he can't do anything to me unless I'm called to the underworld. He's nothing but a slave to Satan."

Crimson fought a smile. "I have no need to intimidate you, Rosemary. I'm going to win this challenge fairly…and easily."

She snorted. "Riiight. Laila, let's get this over with. I don't want to miss *Dancing with the Stars* tonight."

Laila stepped into the arena wearing a long, burgundy robe trimmed in gold braided rope—the judgment robe—and lifted her hands in the air. "I call on the goddess to begin this rite and select our high priestess with justness and honor."

Her fingers sparkled with golden magic, and a fledgling witch in the back gasped and slumped into her mother's side. *Amateur.* As the air wavered around Laila's hands, the sparkles formed into words. The name of the first test. *Rejuvenation.*

Two witches wearing mauve robes shuffled in, each one carrying a dying miniature potted rose bush in her hands. They set the flowers on the tables, and Crimson and Rosemary approached their first test.

Crimson eyed her flower. To say it was dying was a stretch. This thing looked like a vegetarian vampire had sucked it dry and left it to wither on the asphalt in July. She touched a bud, and every damn leaf and dried-up petal—save for one—rained to the dirt. *Good job, Crim. Way to make things harder.*

Rosemary snickered, and when no one else laughed, she glared at the witches closest to her. When two of them forced out fake giggles, Rosemary smiled smugly. Crimson half-expected her to stick out her tongue too. It would've been fitting since the priestess was acting like a grade school bully.

"You must bring the flowers back to life," Laila said. "Your time starts now."

Crimson took a deep breath, shuffling through the spells in her mind. She settled on a twist of an incantation her mom used when she'd forgotten to water the ivy in the coffee shop. From the corner of her eye, she glimpsed the priestess' flower growing, the life returning to its petals before she'd even cast her spell.

She could do this. She had goddess magic now. "Delicate flower, it's time to show. In the name of the goddess, I ask you to grow."

As she aimed her magic toward the flower, she opened up, allowing the goddess to flow through her. The rose stem straightened, and then a new bud and leaves formed. Rosemary laughed and crossed her arms, her tiny rose completely revived.

Crimson opened her channel further, giving one more push of magic, and the flower bloomed. Then another bud popped up and bloomed. Then another. The small plant grew into a bush, and as the roots became more than the pot could hold, it shattered, spilling dirt over the table and eliciting startled squeals from the audience.

"That's my girl," Mike hollered from his seat in the back row, and Crimson's heart warmed. She smiled at him, and he mouthed the words *they all want you to win*.

Her lips parted on a quick inhale, and he nodded, pressing a hand to his chest to indicate he could feel their desire. The coven *wanted* her to win. They wanted to be rid of Rosemary as badly as she did.

"Looks like I win that round." Rosemary raised her hand, drawing the attention back to herself. "I got mine up faster."

"Maybe, but mine's bigger, and no matter what people say, size *does* matter." She winked at her demon. "I should know."

"Hell yeah!" Sophie shouted. When the other witches turned to look at her, she clamped her mouth shut and muttered, "Sorry."

"The goddess will determine the winner at the end of the challenge." Laila raised her hands again, and the next spell appeared in the air.

They went through the series of tests, each spell becoming harder and more complex. Rosemary completed them all with ease, but Crimson hesitated on the first few. Her hands, slick with sweat, trembled as she mixed the potions. The priestess was faster at first, but as her confidence grew, Crimson caught up. The challenge was close, with no clear winner yet.

"The final test." Laila lifted her arms one last time, and the final spell illuminated the room. *Shapeshifting of Another Being.* Beneath the name of the spell came the words *Form of a cat and back to human.*

"Oh, you've got to be kidding me. This has to be rigged." Crimson parked her hands on her hips, cutting her gaze between Laila and Rosemary. The spell that landed her in hot water to begin with—the one incantation she hadn't practiced— was the final spell in the competition?

Rosemary laughed. "I hope you've got someplace to stay, because your banishment starts the moment this is done."

"Don't be so sure of yourself." Like Crimson could talk. She was the one lacking confidence at the moment.

Laila shook her head as if disappointed in their attempts at trash talk. "Who volunteers to be Rosemary's subject?" After a slight hesitation and some hard, audible swallows, several hands lifted in the audience.

"Amarillo, I choose you." The priestess smirked at Crimson. "What happens when she can't get a volunteer?"

"If no one is willing to be her subject, the test is forfeited, and the opponent will be declared winner of that spell." Laila closed her eyes, swaying slightly as if receiving a message from the great beyond. "Who volunteers to be Crimson's subject? It cannot be anyone with shapeshifting abilities."

Sophie, who had started to stand, sank into her chair. All the witches in the audience cast their gazes downward, which Crimson expected. Even if they trusted her to be able to change them back—and Crimson didn't even trust herself—going up against Rosemary would be suicide if she won.

"I volunteer as tribute." Mike stood and strode into the arena.

"Can you shapeshift?" Laila asked.

He stood next to Crimson. "Nope. That's not how my magic works."

"Demons are liars." Rosemary gave him a once-over with her gaze. "Unless he's willing to reveal his magic to the entire coven, he can't be trusted."

"No, Mike. You don't have to do that." Crimson scanned the crowd, but none of the witches would look at her. "Asher? Could you?"

"I'd love to, but reapers can shapeshift. Sometimes turning into a giant skeleton and wielding a scythe is the only way to convince people they're dead."

Crimson shook her head. "Let me call someone else. Demons never reveal their magic."

"The challenge is a timed trial," Laila said. "I'm afraid we only have ten minutes left."

"It's okay." Mike took her hand and flashed a reassuring smile. "If my magic scares people away, so be it. I've got you, and that's all that matters." He looked at the crowd. "I'm a recovering Devil's advocate. I used to make deals for Satan, but thanks to this amazing woman…" He wrapped an arm around Crimson's shoulders. "I'm free. I don't damn people anymore."

Rosemary's mouth dropped open. "You worked directly for Satan? Where were you a month ago when I… Never mind."

Laila's eyes turned glassy as she channeled the goddess'

decree. "He is telling the truth, and he may be used as her subject."

"Don't expect anyone in the coven to help you change him back when he gets stuck." Rosemary swept her gaze across the audience, driving the order home.

Crimson swallowed hard. Turning him into a cat would be easy peasy. She transformed that three-hundred-pound demon into a little fluffball like a pro, but she'd never gotten the chance to try undoing that spell. "Mike, I'm not—"

"Shh…" He took both her hands in his. "Don't even say it. I *know* you can do this. Confidence is key."

She nodded. "Confidence is key." Real confidence. Not the fake it 'til you make it kind she'd fabricated in the past. She *could* do this. She had to.

"Your time starts now."

"I love you, Mike," she whispered as she slipped from his grasp.

"I love you too." He straightened his spine and winked. "I'm ready."

With a deep inhale, she opened her channel to the goddess, whispered the incantation, and turned Mike into a sleek black cat. He sat on his haunches, his red eyes trained on her as Rosemary transformed Amarillo into a brown tabby. Crimson had performed the spell faster, but could she change Mike back?

Her stomach churned like she'd eaten a dozen bean burritos and washed them down with expired milk. She swallowed the dryness from her mouth, opened her channel to the goddess full blast, and with as much confidence in her voice as she could muster, she chanted the undoing spell she'd never gotten right before.

The air around Mike's fur shimmered, and he let out garbled meow as his shape wavered. Crimson blinked, holding her breath as his form elongated. *Please work. Please work.* The sparkling magic around him dissipated, and she looked into the deep brown eyes of her demon.

"That was fun." Red flashed in his irises as he grinned. "I knew you could do it."

She flung her arms around his neck and squeezed him tight. "Oh, thank the goddess, thank the Devil, thank *you*."

His chest rumbled with his laugh. "This gives me an idea for a little role-playing game tonight."

"Oh, no." She shook her head adamantly. "No spells in the bedroom."

"Okay." He brushed a curl from her forehead. "We'll be making plenty of magic on our own anyway."

"That we will."

"Who won?" Rosemary shooed Amarillo back to her seat. "She was faster on that one, but I beat her on everything else. I know I did."

Laila closed her eyes, lifting her arms as magic sparkled on her fingertips. "The name of the high priestess of the New Orleans Coven of Witches." The air above her shimmered, and a name appeared in golden glitter. *Crimson.*

Her head spun, and as she swayed, Mike held her close to his body, steadying her.

"What?" Rosemary gasped. "That can't be right. She's incompetent. She's a fool. She's—"

"Crimson has won the challenge," Laila said.

Every witch in attendance looked at Crimson and said, "So mote it be." A few gasps sounded from the audience, and Sophie let out a "Woot!"

"No. No! This isn't right." Rosemary held up her hands, backing away from Crimson. "She's in cahoots with a demon. She had help from the Devil himself. You don't want her as your leader. You want me. Me!"

A witch in a mauve robe handed Laila the massive volume of coven law, and she opened it, nodding solemnly. "The new high priestess will now bind the magic of the loser before the exile begins."

"Actually…" Crimson checked the time. Exactly three

o'clock. "Someone has an offer for you that might be a better deal."

A hole ripped in the air next to Crimson, and she and Mike moved back as Satan stepped through the portal. He wore a deep red Prada suit with an onyx tie and polished red shoes. A collective gasp sounded from the audience, and Rosemary's eyes widened when the Devil strolled toward her, a devious grin curving his lips.

"Is this the one you told me about?" he asked over his shoulder.

"She's the one," Crimson replied.

"What's your name?" Satan raked his gaze up and down her squat form.

"Rosemary Duncan." She straightened to her full height, which wasn't much, and inclined her chin. "You've got some nerve showing up here after my repeated requests for help. Some Devil you are."

Satan laughed. "A sharp tongue and she shows no fear. Rosemary Duncan. Oh, yes. I remember seeing your name on my list. Your request came in while I was on vacation with a banshee. My own personal hell, if you're inclined to ask. The woman wouldn't stop screaming. I won't be doing that again."

"You could have sent an advocate," she retorted. "What happened to *no rest for the wicked?*"

The Devil glanced at Mike. "My best advocate was busy exploring another witch, I'm afraid. All requests were frozen as I attended to the whims of a woman who would never understand me. I'm afraid my slip in judgment has caused a world of trouble for all of you, and for that, I am deeply…amused. This ordeal has been sincerely entertaining, but I must get back to work. I'm down one advocate, and I have a slew of souls to process, which is why I'm going to make you an offer."

He walked a slow circle around Rosemary, nodding. "Yes, she'll do fine." He stopped in front of her. "I need a new personal assistant. You'll help me process souls and assign them to the appropriate levels of the underworld."

"You want me to live in hell and be your assistant?" Rosemary's expression was incredulous.

"You'll get to help me torture wicked souls. It'll be so much fun." He held out his hands, palms up. "Or you can accept your punishment from the coven and live the rest of your measly life as a human. What do you say? Personal Assistant to the Prince of the Underworld is quite a title."

"*Red* will take me under," Rosemary whispered. "Not Crimson." She swallowed hard and stuck out her hand. "You have a deal."

Satan glanced over his shoulder. "Michael, would you like to seal this one, for old time's sake?"

Mike shoved his hands into his pockets. "I'm good."

The Devil sighed. "Very well." He shook Rosemary's hand, opening a portal with his other and dragging her through.

As the gateway snapped shut, stunned silence filled the room. The Devil had made an appearance in the coven house. Rosemary was gone. Crimson had won the challenge, and that was probably the most surprising of all.

She looked at Laila, expecting her to speak, but her friend's reassuring smile reminded her that *she* was now the high priestess, and she needed to address her coven. "So, that was wild, wasn't it?"

A nervous giggle escaped her lips, and the energy in the room lightened. She cleared her throat. "This is Mike, my boyfriend, and it's true that he's a recovering Devil's advocate. I do know Satan, but only because I had to travel to hell to get Mike back. Oh, and my mom was there too. Anyway, I know the goddess proclaimed me high priestess, but I don't want to force myself on you the way someone *else* did."

Some of the witches whispered to each other, but Crimson couldn't make out their words. She stepped forward, filling her voice with confidence. "I'd like to call a vote. My magic works properly now, which I believe I've just proven, but if you don't want me as your leader, I will step down and allow you to elect the priestess of your choice." She looked at Laila. "We can do it blindly. Have everyone write down their decision."

Laila smiled. "I don't think we need to."

"Anyone willing to take on Rosemary will be a fantastic leader." Fern rose and stepped onto the floor. "I move we keep Crimson as high priestess."

Willow stood. "The goddess deemed it be, and that's good enough for me."

"And me," Agatha said.

One by one, every witch in the coven stood, nodding her agreement to keep Crimson on as high priestess, and her heart swelled with joy and gratitude.

"I know my vote doesn't count," Sophie said, "but y'all are lucky to have Crimson. She's the best witch I've ever met."

Crimson smiled. "Well, then, I promise to be the best high priestess I can be until I'm too old to lead you."

Mike cleared his throat. "About that… Anyone who makes it to hell and back with their body intact is granted immortality. It's a clause in all Satan's contracts that he doesn't tell anyone about."

"Then I guess I'll be the best high priestess I can be until y'all get tired of me or I retire, whichever comes first." She slinked toward Mike, linking her fingers behind his neck. "But you, sir, are stuck with me for all eternity."

As he grinned, his eyes flashed red. "*That's* my greatest desire."

READ A PREVIEW OF SANTA GOT RUN OVER BY A VAMPIRE

"You killed Santa." Gaston's mouth fell open as he stared at the strange man lying in the dirt.

"No." Jane shook her head and slammed the car door shut before creeping toward the body. City Park was eerily quiet, not a soul in sight to witness the whoopsie she'd just committed— yet another benefit of existing under the cover of night. Who said vampires were damned?

"I killed *someone*, yeah. But Santa isn't real." She toed the man's shoulder with her boot, but he didn't move.

Sure, he had white hair and a beard; he was a big guy, and hell, he looked like he might have been a jolly dude, but Santa? C'mon. It was a week before Christmas. What the hell would Santa Claus be doing in New Orleans?

Anyway, Santa was nothing more than a ploy made up by parents to finally get their kids to behave for at least a month out of the year. Jane knew this because it was the only thing that worked on her when she was little. Tell a six-year-old Santa wouldn't bring her a pony, and she'd eat her damn broccoli. Brussels sprouts too.

Gaston gently shut the passenger door of Genevieve, his beloved Maserati Quattroporte, and ran his hand over the dent in the hood. "I forget just how young you are, *ma chère*. Santa Claus is most definitely real. I've known him since I was a wee tot."

Jane scoffed. This had to be the tallest of tall tales she'd ever heard from the ancient vampire. It was just like Gaston to blow off a possible manslaughter charge with a joke. "Right. You know Santa, and I'm the Easter Bunny."

"The Easter Bunny is a fae who chooses to take the form of a rabbit to honor Eostre, the goddess of spring. Santa assumes a human form."

She gaped at Gaston, trying to decide if he was yanking her chain, but he looked as serious as could be. He wore his dark hair pulled back in a band at the nape of his neck, and his ice blue eyes were calculating, cutting between the dead man and Jane. The muscles in his jaw were tense, which meant he was grinding his teeth, which meant, for like the third time since she'd met the man, he was actually concerned about a situation.

In fact, he hadn't said a word about the damage she'd done to Genevieve, and he loved that car more than he loved Cuervo-tainted O-negative.

Well, shit. "You're not kidding, are you?"

"I never kid about the fae."

She looked at the dead guy, tilting her head as the reality sank in. "Oh. My. Goat cheese pizza. I killed Santa." *And holy crap! Santa is real!*

Well, Santa *was* real…until she ran him over.

ALSO BY CARRIE PULKINEN

New Orleans Nocturnes Series

License to Bite

Shift Happens

Life's a Witch

Santa Got Run Over by a Vampire

Finders Reapers

Swipe Right to Bite

Batshift Crazy

Collection One: Books 1-3

Crescent City Wolf Pack Series

Werewolves Only

Beneath a Blue Moon

Bound by Blood

A Deal with Death

A Song to Remember

Shifting Fate

Collection One: Books 1-3

Collection Two: Books 4-6

Haunted Ever After Series

Love at First Haunt

Second Chance Spirit

Third Time's a Ghost

Love and Ghosts

Love and Omens

Love and Curses

Collection One: Books 1 - 3

Collection Two: Books 4 - 6

Stand Alone Books

Flipping the Bird

Sign Steal Deliver

Azrael

Lilith

The Rest of Forever

Soul Catchers

Bewitching the Vampire

ABOUT THE AUTHOR

Carrie Pulkinen is a paranormal romance author who has always been fascinated with things that go bump in the night. Of course, when you grow up next door to a cemetery, the dead (and the undead) are hard to ignore. Pair that with her passion for writing and her love of a good happily-ever-after, and becoming a paranormal romance author seems like the only logical career choice.

Before she decided to turn her love of the written word into a career, Carrie spent the first part of her professional life as a high school journalism and yearbook teacher. She loves good chocolate and bad puns, and in her free time, she likes to read, drink wine, and travel with her family.

Connect with Carrie online:
www.CarriePulkinen.com